Then the arms released their cruel hold, one hand stroking the silken softness of the holoku, *slipping down the slender back, while the other hand slid beneath the plunging neckline of the silk gown and caressed the even silkier swell of flesh beneath. A trembling excitement began inside of Lani at the touch of Keith's hand against her breast, so that it was almost painful to twist away, murmuring against his mouth, "No, don't . . ."*

But the hand did not stop its practiced seduction until the satin peak was teased to tautness, and Keith laughed softly, triumphantly at Lani's startled gasp of pleasure. "This is what you want, isn't it? Why pretend? This is what you've wanted all along. . . ."

MISTRESS OF PARADISE

Marcella Thum

FAWCETT GOLD MEDAL • NEW YORK

To my friends in Hawaii, with much *Aloha*.

Chapter 1

With her feet bare, and stepping as lightly as possible, Lani Tucker closed her bedroom door softly behind her and hurried down the wide, koa wood staircase. Unfortunately, she remembered, a second too late, that the third from the bottom stair tread always protested loudly when trod upon. The sharp sound, like a twig breaking beneath her foot, seemed to fill the darkness of the stairwell around her. Lani felt her breath catch in her throat and her hand tightened on the handrail, the dark red wood polished over the years to a glossy smoothness.

It was not the servants discovering her departure from the Tucker home at an hour when she should be sound asleep in her bed that concerned her. The Japanese housemaids had long since learned to giggle, embarrassed, behind their hands and ignore the outrageous behavior of their young mistress. As for plump, easy-going Loki, who had been Lani's nursemaid since the girl's birth fourteen years before, she had the Hawaiian's habit of indulging children, petting and cajoling and rushing to sooth Lani's temper tantrums when she was a child, and turning a blind eye no matter how wild and willful her charge's behavior became as she grew older.

No, it wasn't the servants appearing and ordering her back to bed that worried Lani. Her glance flew to the entry hall and the half-open door to the right of the staircase. A square of light fell from the room out into the hall, and she could hear the sound of male voices, the slap of playing cards on a table, and the tinkle of glasses. If her Uncle Daniel should discover her sneaking out of the house at night . . .

Lani cautiously descended one more step, cocking her head and listening intently. She could hear a man's rasping, angry voice, arguing loudly. "And I say the Hawaiian League should have thrown out the king two years ago, the same time we got rid of his charlatan prime minister, Gibson, and forced Kalakaua to accept our new constitution. The United States will never seriously consider annexing these islands with a corrupt buffoon like Kalakaua as the king."

A deep male voice answered, thoughtfully. "You must admit, though, that the monarchy is popular with the people." The voice took on an amused note. "Especially, I hear, with Robert Wilcox and the members of his Kamehameha Rifle Association. I've even heard rumors that they're plotting to overthrow the Reform constitution."

"Wilcox? That *hapa haole* strutting around town like a rooster in his red Garibaldi uniform, thinking that a couple of years in Italy makes him a military genius! Who takes Wilcox seriously?" the first voice scoffed. "As for the people, it's not the *kanakas* who pay the taxes. It's planters and merchants and businessmen like us who keep the government treasury full, allowing the king to throw money around like a drunken sailor on a new palace and that ridiculous coronation of his. It's not King Kalakaua who has brought wealth to these islands, it's King Sugar."

A second voice added gravely, "Putting the power of the ballot in the hands of the native would be as much a mistake as placing a sharp knife in the hands of an infant. White men set up the government and we can destroy it when we choose to. You've been away from these islands too long, Stewart. You'll see. The monarchy is rotten and will fall."

"Thurston's right, Adam." It was her Uncle Daniel speaking now. Lani recognized the familiar, slurred sound in her uncle's voice that meant he had had a few drinks. "Mind you, I'm fond of David Kalakaua. I've never met a man who could hold his liquor so well or throw a finer party. But annexation's the only answer for Hawaii. How else are we going to make sure America keeps letting our sugar in duty free?"

Lani had crept the rest of the way down the stairs. She would have to pass the open study door in order to leave the house. But with her Uncle Daniel and his friends arguing, as usual, over politics, she was confident that she could slip by without being seen, especially since all the guests in the room had their backs to the door. She stepped into the square of yellow light that fell across the darkened entrance hall. Then suddenly she froze in her tracks, as one of the men half turned toward the open door, reaching for his glass on the table beside him.

She did not recognize the man, but then she knew very few of her uncle's *haole* business friends. Still, there was something vaguely familiar about this man. He was broader in the shoulders and taller than any of the other men present, and younger. There was no gray in the thick reddish-brown hair, almost the same shade as the koa wood beneath her hand, and the spray of lines around the eyes, she suspected, was from weather, not age. But it was the air of command about the man, the way he stood arrow straight, the thrust of the strong chin, that made him stand out even in a room filled with some of the wealthiest men in Hawaii, men who were accustomed to giving orders and having them instantly obeyed.

Just for a second Lani was sure that the man saw her in the hallway, then that oddly penetrating gaze swung by her as the man turned back to the other guests. Lani realized that she had been holding her breath and let it go with a soft sigh. Without looking back, she scurried across the hall, pulled open the front door, and stepped out onto the broad veranda which completely surrounded the first floor of the Tucker home.

The instant she set foot into the sultry July night, rich, damp fragrances from the garden assaulted her. The heady scent of plumeria, star jasmine, and ginger blossoms, that trembled in the moonlight like exotic white moths, overpowered the delicate scent of English roses, Michaelmas daisies, and begonias. It was a never-ending task, Lani knew, requiring a score of gardeners, to keep the luxuriant tropical garden pruned to the stiffly formal landscape her uncle preferred.

Lani stood a moment on the veranda, happily taking deep breaths of the scented night air and listening to a mourning dove cooing in a nearby tree. Yet despite her pleasure in the evening and her sense of triumph at having successfully made her escape from the house, she was aware of an inexplicable ache just behind her breastbone. It was the same ache she sometimes felt lying awake at night with the moonlight falling across her bed, her limbs oddly heavy beneath the bedcover, her body filled with a vague, restless yearning, for what she didn't know.

The girl shrugged. Oh, well, it probably had something to do with the unwelcome visitor she now had each month, which meant, Loki had assured her, smiling happily, that Lani was no longer a *keike*, but a *wahine*.

At least she was free of the unwanted intrusion this evening, she thought, as she walked over a path carpeted with fallen scarlet poinciana blossoms to the front gate. At the gate she paused, glancing regretfully back to the stable at the rear of the large grounds, but Mikala, the elderly Hawaiian who guarded the stable, was a light sleeper. He was sure to raise the alarm if she tried to take a horse. Anyway, she reminded herself, Tom had promised to bring a horse when they had made their arrangements to meet earlier that day.

She had no sooner closed the gate with its squeaky hinges behind her than a voice almost at her elbow said teasingly, "Aloha, Lani. You're late. I thought perhaps you weren't coming."

She bristled indignantly. "I said I'd come, didn't I?" she said, conveniently forgetting how close she *had* come earlier in the evening to changing her mind. After all, it was one thing slipping away from school during the day to go to the beach, and quite another to go sea bathing alone with a young .man at night.

As if sensing her uncertainty, Tom said, "You're not afraid you'll get into *pilikia* with your uncle sneaking out like this, are you?"

"How will he find out? We'll be back before he knows I'm gone." Lani gave her companion a shrewd glance. "Maybe you're the one that's afraid of getting into trouble with your brothers."

Like her, Tom Stewart was an orphan; Lani lived with her bachelor uncle, Tom with his two older half brothers. That was what had drawn the two together in the beginning at the small private school they attended, that and the fact they both had a similar distaste for rules and regulations.

"I'm not afraid of my brothers," Tom protested, then, reaching down and drawing Lani onto his horse behind him, added sheepishly, "Anyway neither Adam or Keith are home."

He jerked his chin behind him. "They're both at your house."
He glanced over his shoulder at Lani, who had hitched her
skirt up to her knees and was riding astride behind him.
"Hold on to me so you don't fall off."

Lani scowled at Tom's back. As if she would fall off a
horse! She had been riding since she was five years old,
when her father had put her on a small horse with a saddle
that Pili, the head *luna* at Palekaiko Ranch, had handmade for
her. Unhappily her Uncle Daniel had no affection or feeling
for horseflesh, except, of course, for wagering on the race-
horses that ran at Kapiolani Park. When Lani, at her father's
death four years before, had left the ranch on Maui and
moved to Honolulu to live with her father's younger brother,
she had been dismayed at the horses she found in her uncle's
stable. They had less spirit, she thought, disgusted, than the
horses that pulled the horsecars that ran through Honolulu.

But her irritation was forgotten in the feel of a fine horse
beneath her, bringing back memories of Palekaiko and early
morning horseback rides with her father, a tall, whip thin,
handsome man that she had adored. Matthew Tucker had
named the Tucker family ranch Palekaiko—Paradise—and to
the widowed Matthew and his daughter the ranch was, indeed, their paradise. Although Lani's father had run the ranch
and everyone on it with an iron hand, as if it were his own
private kingdom, he had also worked harder and longer than
any of his *paniolos*. Lani's earliest memories of her father
were of the way he always smelled deliciously of horses,
tobacco, and whiskey; the sound of his laughter booming
through the house; and the happiness she had felt, when she
was only a child, riding on horseback in front of him, sheltered within his arms, as he inspected his beloved domain.

Suddenly the horse beneath her shied at a shadow, and she
managed to keep her seat by tightening her knees around the
mare. She carefully did not grab hold of Tom, feeling ill at
ease at the thought of putting her arms around the young man.
In such close proximity, she was sure he couldn't help but be
aware of her breasts pressing against his back. The inconvenient swellings beneath her shirtwaist had been embarrassing
enough this last year. No matter how tightly she bound her
breasts, she couldn't hide them from sight.

They had left Beretania Street now. Tom began to take small side roads—*makai*—to avoid being seen by any late-roving citizens or patrolling police. The houses became more scattered, set back behind spacious, fenced gardens. The new electric arc streetlights disappeared and the road became a narrow, marshy path. Lani could see small rice paddies and taro patches, shanties built on high poles between groves of coconut and kiawe trees, and finally glimpses of the ocean, the line of surf a misty white in the moonlight.

At a strip of secluded beach, Tom stopped and slid off the horse, tying the mare to a coconut tree so ravaged by wind that the palm fronds were in tatters. Lani did not wait to be helped but slipped from the horse to the ground.

A rising wind whipped the spray from the low curling surf and pulled at Lani's hair, wrapping it in black silken ribbons across her face. Tom gazed, frowning, at the dark blue skirt and full-sleeved middy blouse. "You can't swim in that get-up."

"Don't be silly," Lani said. "I have a bathing dress beneath. I'll just be a minute."

In the shelter of the palm trees, she quickly slipped out of her skirt and shirtwaist. The skirt of the striped blue and white bathing costume that she wore underneath hung to her knees, and the sleeves reached to her elbow, so that she was almost as covered up as she had been in her skirt and middy blouse. Lani yanked irritably at the heavy material, trying to make it fit more comfortably.

When she returned to the beach, Tom had already undressed and was standing at the water's edge, his shirt and trousers thrown on a blanket on the sand. Disdaining to wear a *haole* bathing costume, he had only a *malo* wrapped around his slim hips. Two years older than Lani, the boy was tall for his age, but his body was long and angular, his hands and feet too large, as if the rest of his body had not yet caught up with them. There was a softness of immaturity about his face, the boyishly fine, pale brown hair that fell across a high forehead, but there was strength, too, in the straight, dark brows above golden sherry-brown eyes and the chin that was well cut and firm.

Walking toward him, Lani all at once felt awkward and

unsure of herself, the same way she had felt when she had ridden pillion on the horse behind Tom, as if he were all at once a stranger. But that was foolish, she thought, annoyed. It certainly wasn't the first time she had been swimming with Tom. Well, not at night, of course, or alone, but it was still the same familiar Tom she had known for almost four years now. Nothing had changed.

Tom gestured toward the reef where men were fishing for squid, their kukui nut torches flickering like candle flames on the surface of the water. "I'll race you to the reef and back."

"I think I'll stay here," Lani demurred. She was a strong swimmer, but she knew that her bathing costume, when wet, would cling to her like a deadweight, making any real swimming on her part impossible.

But before she could settle down on the blanket, a grinning Tom had picked her up and carried her, kicking wildly in his arms, out into the surf, dumping her unceremoniously into the ocean.

The water closing over her felt as warm as the night, as Lani splashed to the surface, choking and gasping for breath.

Tom was waiting for her. "I never thought you'd turn into one of those *haole* tourists, afraid of getting your bathing suit wet," he taunted her.

"I'm not afraid!" Lani said indignantly, diving into the phosphorescent, gilded water and with swift, sure strokes, headed for the reef. As she expected, her waterlogged suit soon began to weigh her down. Although she managed to reach the reef before Tom, he easily overtook her as they raced back, and was waiting on the beach when, exhausted, she finally splashed ashore again.

"That wasn't a fair race," Lani protested. She looked down in disgust at her bathing costume. "How can anyone swim in this thing?"

Tom frowned. "Why do you wear such a stupid costume, then? Why don't you wear a *pa'u* like the Hawaiian women do when they swim? Then maybe you'd swim like a real Hawaiian instead of a *hemahema haole*."

"I'm not clumsy," Lani shot back angrily, as furious at his insulting her as she was at losing the race. She flung herself at him, pummeling his chest with her fists. Tom tried to hold her away from him, but his foot snagged in the blanket, and he tripped and fell. Catching Lani's ankle, he pulled her down on top of him. They tumbled like puppies on the blanket, with Tom trying to gain a hold, and Lani, slippery as an eel, sliding away from him. Finally Tom began to laugh and held up his hands in mock surrender. *"Pau! Pau!"*

Lani rolled away from him and sat up in one graceful motion, tossing her head so that her hair swung in a wide arc, casting off drops of water that sparkled like diamonds in the moonlight. Despite glistening, raven-black hair, a sensuously curved mouth, and deep, sculptured eyelids that betrayed Lani's part-Hawaiian heritage, her eyes were a surprising blue-lavender shade and her skin was of such a pale creamy texture, like the luminous petals of a gardenia, that Tom was tempted to run his finger over its softness.

"How pretty you are, Lani," he said huskily. "Will you miss me when I'm gone?"

The frown that had started to touch her face at his words turned to surprise. "Where are you going?"

"My brother Adam is sending me to the United States to finish my schooling," he said, his voice forlorn. "I'm almost sorry that Adam gave up being a captain on a whaler."

"Why did he?" Lani asked curiously.

"Adam hurt his hip in an accident aboard ship last year. He decided to give up whaling and return to Hawaii to live."

Lani knew of the dangers of whaling, which had once been the islands' most profitable industry. Her own grandfather, Morgan Tucker, had been a whaling captain, but he had given up the dangerous whaling trade when the ships had had to go farther and farther afield to find the great sperm whales.

"Can't you talk your brother into changing his mind?"

"You don't know Adam," Tom said glumly. "Once he's made up his mind, nothing can change it. Keith never cared what I did, but Adam watches me like a hawk." He jerked to his feet, staring broodingly out into the ocean. "I'll end up like my father if he has his way."

Lani got more slowly to her feet. "What's wrong with that?" she asked, puzzled. The Stewart family was not only one of the wealthiest, but one of the most respected *haole* families in Honolulu. Tom's father, Silas Stewart, was the son of one of the first missionary families to come to Hawaii in the early 1800s, and Tom's own mother, his father's second wife, had been the granddaughter of missionaries.

Tom kept his back to Lani, as if he were ashamed to face her. "Do you know how my father got the land for our sugar plantation at Ewa?" he asked. "He gave the Hawaiian families who owned the land a small token payment and some bottles of *okolehao*. They didn't even know they were signing a bill of sale. I asked my father once if he thought it was right, what he had done, and you know what he said? He said the Bible commanded the white man to subdue the earth and have dominion over it, that the Hawaiian people refused to labor and toil long hours on their land, as the white men did, so they weren't entitled to own it."

Tom turned to face Lani, anger bringing a rush of color beneath the boy's deeply tanned skin. "And now the *haoles* are talking about how wonderful it would be to have Hawaii turned over to America. Well, if America is so wonderful, why don't they go back there to live? I went to hear Robert Wilcox speak the other night, with the Lane brothers, and he said Hawaii should be for Hawaiians."

"But you're white, a *haole*, too," Lani pointed out practically. "The Tucker and Stewart families have lived in Hawaii for generations. Doesn't that make them Hawaiians? And my father was white, even if my mother was Hawaiian. Because I'm *hapa haole*, does that mean I'm not entitled to live here in the islands?"

"Of course not," Tom said, annoyed at her female illogic. "The Lane brothers are half-Irish, half-Hawaiian, and they'd fight to the death for Hawaii."

Having met the Lane brothers, a brood of six sons with handsome Hawaiian features and quick Irish tempers, Lani suspected the young men would happily fight to the death for almost any cause. And then she thought absently, studying her companion beneath half-lowered eyelashes, how handsome Tom looked when he was angry. She was surprised at herself for thinking such a thing, and even more surprised when she reached out and shyly touched her friend's hand, somehow vaguely wanting to comfort him.

At Lani's touch, the anger drained from Tom's face. He

stared hungrily down at the girl. Before she could step away, his arms were around her, pulling her clumsily against him. Startled, she felt Tom's warm mouth covering hers, his lips hard and crushing, frightening her, so that she tried to pull away, but the arms held her too tightly.

Tom was dimly aware of the girl's struggling against him, but despite his sixteen years, his experience with young women was surprisingly and embarrassingly limited. There had been a few exploratory kisses, and one humiliating experience with a young, knowledgeable miss who had laughed at his lack of expertise, but nothing more.

Tom had never felt about any of those other young women the way he did about Lani. Everything about her pleased and excited him, from her enormous blue-violet eyes to the faintly Polynesian cast to her slender, small-boned face. Something leaped painfully in his chest when she smiled at him, and an even more disturbing sensation took place lower in his body, especially when Lani walked away from him, her hips swinging provocatively. When she had accepted his invitation for a moonlight swim this evening, something which no prim and proper *haole* girl would have ever done, he had hopefully persuaded himself that she felt the same way about him.

In any case, there was no way he could back down now. Lani's supple body twisting in his arms, the mouth that he was forcing open intoxicatingly beneath his own, the feel of her soft flesh beneath his hands, was an agony that was both pleasure and pain, building up inside of him, demanding release.

He was fumbling awkwardly with the bodice of her bathing costume, attempting to reach a small, hard breast, when a familiar voice behind him said, amused, "Throw her back, little brother. She's too small a fish to keep."

Chapter 2

At the sound of that voice, Lani felt Tom's arms fall away. As he stepped to one side of her, she was able to see the man who had come quietly up on the beach behind them. Even in the pale moonlight that washed the sand, she recognized him at once; the man she had seen at her uncle's house as she had crept down the stairway. He was an inch or two taller than Tom and heavier, nor was there any softness in a face that was all angles from the jutting nose to a long, uncompromising mouth. Yet she could see the resemblance to Tom in the straight slash of eyebrows and the stubborn set to the strong chin, so that she would have known who the man was even before Tom, stammering slightly, said, "Adam! what . . . what are you doing here?"

Adam Stewart glanced from his brother to the girl beside him, his appraising gaze traveling slowly over Lani in a way that made her stomach knot with embarrassment.

The intense gaze swung back to Tom, Adam's voice roughening with anger. "Do you know what sort of *pilikia* you'd find yourself in, robbing the cradle with that child?" He picked up the shirt and trousers from the blanket and threw them at Tom. "Get out of here," he ordered tersely, "before I give you the thrashing you deserve."

For a moment, clutching his clothes, Tom stood uncertain, then blurted unhappily, "It wasn't Lani's fault. . . ." Seeing the wrath settling like a black cloud over his brother's features, the icy glitter in the gray eyes, his courage deserted him. He turned abruptly and, stumbling in the sand, made for his horse.

"Where are your clothes, Miss Tucker?"

Lani turned her gaze back to Tom's brother, the barely hidden contempt in his voice making her face flame, red hot.

When she didn't move, he ordered brusquely, "Get dressed. I'll take you home."

No one had ever used that tone of voice with Lani Tucker before. She stared with loathing at the man. How dare he order her around like a coolie! Did he think he could treat her the way he did his brother? "I'm not going anywhere with you!" she replied, her voice childishly shrill.

Adam surveyed the girl dourly. What a skinny little creature she was, with her straight, wet hair hanging like black tails over her shoulders, reaching but not covering her small, half-formed breasts. To his mind, she looked like nothing so much as a hissing, half-drowned kitten, and a blasted nuisance in the bargain, as children usually were in his limited experience. He was tempted to turn and walk away, except that Daniel Tucker, despite their difference in age, was a close friend. He could hardly leave Daniel's niece stranded here on a deserted beach in the middle of the night.

"I don't recall asking you to come with me," he said, his voice holding an ominous softness. "You have a choice. You can ride across my saddle or on it. Either way I'm taking you home."

Sensing an inexorable force that she had not met before in her young life, Lani took a cautious step backward, then spun away and sprinted across the sand toward a clump of palm trees. She had not gone a half-dozen steps in the soft sand when the man overtook her, cursing softly beneath his breath as he caught her shoulders and jerked her around to face him. It was fear that Lani felt then, not anger, as she saw the man's eyes. Her hands lifted instinctively, her fingers curled to claw at the man's face.

She only managed to reach one cheek—and draw a thin scarlet line of blood—before her arms were pinned to her side and she was lifted and hauled over the beach, dangling under the man's arm like a sack of potatoes. When they reached Adam's horse, she was dropped unceremoniously onto the sand.

The man jerked his chin toward the animal. "Take your choice," he snapped. "Over the saddle or on it."

Lani struggled to her feet, glaring at him with impotent fury. He was no longer holding her, and she cast a quick nervous glance over her shoulder. If she could make the water, perhaps she could escape this mad man by swimming. . . .

"I wouldn't," her captor said quietly.

For a moment their eyes clashed, the girl's bright with fiercely held back tears, the man's no longer angry, but with a coldness in their depths that was somehow even more frightening.

Lani stiffened her shoulders, her chin lifting haughtily. "I was just going for my clothes."

Adam studied the girl's face for a moment. The delicately drawn features were still immature, unmolded, waiting for time to shape them. But there was breeding there, he saw, and courage in the girl's ability to accept defeat with grace and dignity—a rare enough quality, Adam well knew, and one that many grown men never possessed.

He nodded and stepped back. Lani went off into the trees, returning in a few minutes, tucking her shirt into the waistband of her skirt. Without a word, she followed Adam Stewart to his horse, noticing that the man limped a little. He swung onto his horse without any difficulty, though, then reached down and pulled her up behind him.

Once again riding pillion, Lani held her body stiffly erect and away from the man, her amethyst eyes bright as daggers probing at his back. What a detestable, underhanded person he was, she raged helplessly to herself. He must have seen her leaving her uncle's home earlier that evening and had deliberately followed Tom and her to the beach. And no doubt would take pleasure in telling her uncle about her moonlight swim, she realized with a start of dismay.

Then she shrugged mentally. Oh, well, even if her uncle did hear about her escapade, she knew he wouldn't remain upset with her for very long. He was too fond of her to scold her, much less raise his hand against her.

Or was he simply indifferent? The thought caused a hollow feeling within Lani. Ever since she had come to Honolulu to live with her handsome bachelor uncle, she had sensed, without ever putting it into words, that he took only a bemused, half-hearted interest in his guardianship over his dead brother's daughter. As little attention as he paid to actively running the ranch on Maui, in which he held a half interest, or supervising the Tucker sugar plantation near Waianae. When trouble with either his niece or the business interests of the Tucker estate arose, he retreated into his study and drank, or disappeared for days on end with his cronies, until the trouble blew over. Sometimes, irrationally, Lani almost wished her uncle would punish her for her misdeeds. At least then she would know he felt something, some emotion toward her, even if it were only anger.

Pushing away such disturbing thoughts, Lani glanced around her, noticing that Mr. Stewart was not taking the winding, dark back roads on their return trip, but had turned onto Richards Street, a more direct route which led past Iolani Palace. The controversial new palace had been completed by King Kalakaua in 1882, only seven years before. Although Lani had never been inside, she had heard her uncle's friends complaining about the king's extravagance in building his new home, buying crystal chandeliers and ebony and gold furniture for his throne room, and lighting the palace grounds with the new, expensive electric arc lights.

Curious, she squirmed around in the saddle to try to get a better look at the palace, but was disappointed. The eight-foot-high stone walls that had only recently been built around Iolani for the king's protection made it impossible to see anything except the tall square towers of the palace and the king's guards, lounging sleepily at their posts at the entrance gates.

"Sit still," Adam Stewart ordered irritably, turning around in the saddle and scowling at her. They had turned onto Beretania Street, passing Washington Place, the home of Princess Liliuokalani and her husband, John Dominis.

"I put a *kahuna* on you," Lani muttered beneath her breath. It was a childhood curse that she had almost forgotten.

"What did you say?"

There was a glint in the narrowed eyes, from amusement or anger Lani wasn't sure, but she wisely decided to duck her head and keep silent. The anger still churned inside of her, but she could wait, she thought coldly. Oh, she would get even with Adam Stewart, but not here, not now. She would pick the time and place, and like the ancient Hawaiian *kahunas*, she would get her revenge.

Neither Lani nor Adam Stewart spoke again. The only sounds around them were the night noises, a bird calling drowsily, the rustle of a *kona* wind through the leaves of a breadfruit tree, and the clop of a horse's hooves against the hard-packed dirt road.

Through the lush gardens that surrounded the solidly built Dominis house, the woman standing at the open window staring out into the night could hear the horse's hooves on the street. For a moment, the Princess Liliuokalani wondered if she was going to have another late-night guest. As if, she thought, sighing to herself, she wasn't having enough trouble deciding how to cope with the uninvited visitor she already had waiting to see her.

Postponing the moment of having to deal with the man waiting for her in the small receiving room, the princess stood a few seconds longer at the window, taking deep breaths of the heavily scented air. Her mother-in-law's rose garden lay under the window. No, not Mary Dominis's rose garden anymore, she mentally corrected herself. With her mother-in-law's death three months before, the garden now belonged to her. Liliuokalani was finally mistress of Washington Place, which for so many years had been dominated by her small, overbearing *haole* mother-in-law in the same way Mrs. Dominis had completely dominated her son John's life, even after his marriage.

Despite the fact that her son had married High Chieftess Lydia Paki—who years later was renamed Princess Liliuokalani by her brother, King Kalakaua, and made heir apparent to the throne of Hawaii—it was still a *kanaka* marriage as far as Mary Dominis was concerned. When the newly married couple arrived at Washington Place, where they were to live with John's mother, it was soon made very clear the inferior role Lydia was to occupy in the household. Nor could she expect any support from her new husband, who hated scenes and would either side with his mother or refuse to become involved in any quarrel between his mother and his bride.

The scent of the roses all at once painfully reminded Liliuokalani of the first moment when she had realized how alone she would be in her new home. Loving flowers, she had gone out into the garden and cut a bouquet of rosebuds for the house. Her mother-in-law had descended upon her, furious as a hornet. Didn't Lydia know better? How dare she cut Mrs. Dominis's roses without her permission, and the best buds, too, not full-blown roses. Didn't Lydia know that only roses in their prime were to be cut, the dead to make way for the living.

Bewildered, her quick *alii* temper aroused at being treated in such a humiliating fashion, Lydia had turned to her husband for help. What had she done that was so terrible? To a Hawaiian, all flowers were to be enjoyed. But John had already turned away, either insensitive to the friction in the room or deliberately ignoring it. It was the first of many times that Lydia was to look to her husband for moral support in vain.

And the first of many times in the next years that she had had to guard her temper in dealing with her prickly, narrow-minded mother-in-law. Immediately Liliuokalani felt a familiar pang of guilt at such un-Christian-like thoughts about a woman now dead. Such self-inflicted guilt feelings were not unfamiliar to the princess. They had been instilled in her years before at the missionary-run High Chiefs' School she had attended as a young girl. Always, Lydia had felt an unworthy outsider at the school, the same way she always felt here in this house.

Liliuokalani straightened her back and moved away from the window, her naturally optimistic nature returning. Well, that part of her life was over with now, and in the end she had kept faithful, loving watch at her mother-in-law's deathbed. As for John, Lydia was no longer a romantic young bride expecting more of love and passion, or even faithfulness, from her marriage than her husband was able to provide.

As she walked into the receiving room with the fluid grace of a young *wahine* for all that she was heavyset and middle-aged, a man in an Italian military uniform came quickly to his feet. Liliuokalani immediately signaled for her attendant standing by the door to leave. Whatever Robert Wilcox had to tell her, it would be better, she suspected, if she was alone to hear his words.

She sat down with regal dignity and smiled at the young

man. Her rather plain face with its strong, resolute features and large, beautiful dark eyes was transformed and softened by the smile. When she spoke, her voice had a clear, musical quality. "Forgive my keeping you waiting, Robert. I wasn't expecting such a late night visit."

"You know why I've come," he blurted. "The revolution is ready. In the morning, we march on the palace. I have the new constitution with me. Once the king signs it, the authority that is rightfully his by inheritance will be restored."

Liliuokalani frowned. Could it be that simple? She had been attending Queen Victoria's golden jubilee in London when the Hawaiian League had forced their bayonet constitution upon the king. When she heard the news, she remembered she had been incensed that her brother had signed away his high powers so easily, without even trying to put up a fight.

"What part is the king playing in all this?" she asked bluntly.

The young man standing at attention before her flushed uncomfortably. "He knows nothing about what will happen tomorrow," he said quickly. "We thought it best to wait till we secure the palace, and then he can sign the constitution."

That was the problem, Liliuokalani thought, her frown deepening. She loved her brother, but she had no illusions about David. The Merry Monarch, wasn't that what the newspapers called him? He was intelligent and genial, popular with the people, but she was also aware of his heavy drinking and gambling, and that he had no stomach for fighting. That was why he hadn't been able to stand up to white men like Lorrin Thurston and Volney Ashford. And that was why he had meekly signed the lease, granting the United States exclusive use of Pearl Harbor as a naval station, the first step, his sister was sure, in an attempt to annex the Hawaiian Islands to the United States.

Still, David was her brother and the king; before others, she would never speak against him. "Suppose," she pointed out mildly, her frown softening, "the king refuses to sign your constitution. What then?"

"He will sign," Wilcox said with a sidelong glance at the

princess. "If he doesn't, then I've heard that you, as the heir apparent, have been approached to take over the throne."

The frown quickly returned to Liliuokalani's face as she stared coldly at her companion. It was true enough that she had been approached, not only by native Hawaiians but by a member of the Reform Legislature, asking that she take the throne from her brother. She suspected that that was why David's manner toward her had changed of late, as if he believed she might be *kipio*, a traitor to him. Her *alii* temper flared at the thought. "And as you well know, always I refused! How could you believe I'm so lacking in loyalty that I'd push my own brother aside? I'll have nothing to do with the matter, nothing."

She rose imperiously to her feet, the look of royal displeasure on her face, making Robert Wilcox apologize hastily. "No one is questioning your loyalty. But neither can my courage be doubted. I'll gladly lay down my life for the king," he said with a dramatic flourish.

"You might just have to," the princess said grimly. Then, studying Robert, who looked so young and handsome in his Italian military uniform, his dark Hawaiian features showing little of his *haole* blood, her frown faded into a look of affection.

For all his age and his years spent at an Italian military school, Robert reminded her of her adored adopted son, Kaipo—the same curly black hair, engaging, infectious smile, and irresponsible ways. In some ways, she couldn't help feeling that Robert was as much of a child as Kaipo. Perhaps that was why she had lent the young man a home to live in when he had returned to Hawaii, penniless and with a pregnant wife to support. His aristocratic wife had divorced Robert and returned to her noble family in Italy when her husband could find no work for his military or engineering knowledge in Hawaii.

Liliuokalani mentally debated waking John and telling him of Wilcox's revolutionary plans, but now she decided not to disturb her husband's sleep. With his rheumatism, John slept very badly as it was these days, and it was impossible for her to take seriously the idea that Robert would actually lead an attack on the palace.

She smiled at the young man, and her lovely, lilting voice was softly maternal as she said, "I'm sure you are very brave, Robert, but now, if you'll excuse me, it's late and I am tired."

She walked to the door and rang for her attendant to show her visitor out, turning at the last moment to say warningly, "But if you'll take my advice, Robert, you'll speak to the king before you proceed any further with your plans."

Chapter 3

"Lani-san, wake up! Mr. Daniel wants to see you, wikiwiki."

Lani opened her eyes slowly, still half-asleep. A flustered Mitsu leaned over her bed. Her Japanese maid seldom lost her serenity, but now the woman's doll-smooth face was flushed. She hurried Lani out of bed and helped her dress, then brushed the girl's long hair until it shone, finally plaiting it into a thick braid down her back.

"What's wrong, Mitsu?" Lani asked uneasily, memories of the night before returning in a guilty rush. Of course! Mr. Stewart must have told her uncle about finding Tom and her together at the beach. Not just together, she thought, watching her own face grow pink in the mirror, remembering the kiss, the startling and not completely unpleasant sensation of Tom's lips pressed against hers. She had hoped that when Mr. Stewart had dropped her unceremoniously at the front gate last night, then rode away without a word, that the man had decided not to tell her uncle after all.

Mitsu shrewdly studied the girl's face in the mirror, then shook her head sadly. "Lani-san, Lani-san, why you always make shame for Mr. Daniel?"

Lani jerked to her feet, her violet eyes staring coldly at the woman. "Don't you dare scold me! You're only a servant."

Mitsu stepped back, tucking her hands into the folds of her kimono sleeves, and gazed calmly at the girl without speaking.

Suddenly ashamed, Lani remembered the times when she had been ill and Mitsu had sat beside her bed all night, her voice as gently soothing as the cool cloths she had put on Lani's head. "I'm sorry, Mitsu," she mumbled, rushing from the room.

She was in no hurry, though, to face her uncle, and she descended the koa staircase slowly. Family portraits in carved gold frames lined the wall of the staircase, and Lani lingered before the one of her grandmother and grandfather. Her grandmother, Jasmine Tucker,* was dressed in a red silk gown with a rope of pearls around her throat, and her husband, Morgan, stood behind her, his one hand resting lightly, but possessively, on his wife's shoulder. Lani had always been in loving awe of her beautiful grandmother who had died when Lani was five. Her grandfather had died when Lani was just a baby, and she didn't remember him at all.

She looked up into Morgan Tucker's stern face, the broad shoulders beneath the dark blue jacket of a whaling captain, the long, hard mouth, and suddenly she knew why Adam Stewart had seemed vaguely familiar. There was the same hard, uncompromising look on her grandfather's face that she had seen on Mr. Stewart's last night at the beach. How had her grandmother ever loved such a man? Lani wondered.

Her Uncle Daniel appeared at the foot of the stairs, his voice impatient. "Why are you dawdling, Lani? Didn't Mitsu tell you I wanted to see you? Come along."

Reluctantly Lani followed her uncle into his study. The windows were open, but the room still held the faint, stale smell of liquor and cigar smoke from one of her uncle's all-night poker games. Bookshelves lined one wall of the room, and glass-covered gun racks covered another wall. Her uncle took a seat behind his desk, which was placed in such a way that he could look out into the garden of the house. Then he cleared his throat loudly, a habit he displayed before approaching any distasteful subject, Lani knew, and she prepared herself. Tears immediately quivered behind her eyelashes, her mouth turning down at the corners with practiced ease as she murmured, "I'm sorry, Uncle Daniel. Truly I am."

*See Marcella Thum, *Jasmine* (New York: Fawcett Crest, 1984).

Her uncle was a slender, elegantly dressed man with a neatly trimmed mustache and beard, pale skin that never tanned but always burned, and soft brown hair that was beginning to thin at the top so Lani could see the pink scalp beneath. His long, thin hands trembled, Lani noticed, as he reached for the cut-glass decanter on a desk cluttered with files and papers. Now he stopped and stared at his niece, surprised.

"Why should you be sorry?" he asked. "It's certainly not your fault that that mad man, Wilcox, decided to attack the palace this morning."

Lani ducked her head to hide her relief. So Adam Stewart hadn't told her uncle after all. Vaguely now she became aware of noises she hadn't noticed before, sounds amazingly like gunshots in the distance, the footsteps and excited voices of people milling up and down on the road in front of the house.

"What is it? What's happened?" She flew to the window to take a better look.

Her uncle got to his feet and pulled her away from the window. "It's none of your concern," he said firmly. "Early this morning, a man by the name of Robert Wilcox, along with some of his friends, attempted to overthrow the government by taking over the palace, that is, the palace grounds. Fortunately, they never gained entrance into the palace itself."

"They shot the king's guards?" Lani asked, wide-eyed.

"No, no," her uncle said quickly, taking his seat again behind the desk. "As a matter of fact, the takeover was quite peaceful. The king's guards simply retreated inside the palace. Wilcox and his men stayed out on the grounds and sent a message to the king, evidently expecting him to join them." Daniel Tucker's mouth twisted in an ironic smile. "Apparently, Kalakaua has very wisely refused to involve himself. I have no doubt he suspects it is really his sister, Liliuokalani, Wilcox wants to put on the throne. In any case, the king has holed up safely in his boat house at the harbor."

"But the gunshots . . ."

Her uncle sighed. "Yes, well, the government has placed sharpshooters in the windows and on the roof of the Opera House and Kawaiahao Church overlooking the palace grounds.

They could just as easily have starved Wilcox and his men out, but instead they fired down at the rebels. Wilcox's men returned the fire, using a small loaded cannon that they found on the grounds. Unfortunately, now, it seems a small battle has developed.''

Then, realizing that he might be frightening his niece, he smiled reassuringly. ''There's no reason for you to be afraid. Some of the *haole* residents have sent their wives and daughters to the American consulate for safety, but I see no real cause for alarm. Wilcox and his men will be running out of ammunition, and it should all be over with soon. However,'' he added sternly, ''I sent for you to tell you that under no circumstances are you to leave the house and grounds today. Is that understood?''

Lani nodded demurely, her lowered eyelids hiding the excitement dancing in her eyes. ''Yes, Uncle Daniel,'' she murmured.

Her uncle got to his feet, gazing uneasily at his niece. As if his brother's marriage to a native girl wasn't unfortunate enough, why, he wondered irritably, had his mother insisted upon the child being named Lani? Certainly it would have been much more sensible to forget completely that scandalous branch of the family tree.

Still he supposed it was his own fault that he felt helpless around the child, always wondering what was going on behind those striking violet eyes so oddly at variance with the girl's Polynesian heritage. Even when his niece stared at him directly, as she had a disconcerting habit of doing, he was never really sure what she was thinking or feeling. His mother, he thought suddenly, had been like that. Although he never doubted Jasmine's love for him, there was always a part of his mother that was somehow private and remote that as a small boy he could not reach.

He came around the desk and hugged Lani clumsily. ''I don't want you to worry. Everything will be fine. Now run along and have your breakfast before it gets cold and Ah Sing threatens to quit again.''

When Lani left the study, her uncle had already returned to his desk, poured himself another drink, and was leafing unhappily through the pile of papers on his desk, mostly unpaid bills.

In the dining room, the disgruntled Chinese cook hovered in the doorway, muttering to himself about the laziness of young people who didn't get up early enough to have breakfast at the proper time. Ignoring him, Lani quickly ate her breakfast, then headed for the French doors that led out onto the veranda.

"Where young missy go?" Ah Sing demanded suspiciously.

Lani gave him an innocent smile. "Into the garden." And for several minutes she did stay in the garden, until she was sure that Ah Sing and the rest of the servants were occupied elsewhere, then she slipped quickly out the front gate. After all, she told herself, her uncle couldn't really expect her to stay cooped up in the grounds. Not with all the excitement going on just a few blocks away from the Tucker home.

There was no difficulty in mingling with the crowds of people rushing to the palace to see for themselves the pitched battle taking place there, while troops of the government— dubbed the Honolulu Rifles—marched up and down, trying to maintain the crowd in some semblance of order. The majority of the onlookers were Hawaiians and Chinese, with most of the white residents staying prudently off the streets.

The *mauka ewa* corner of the palace wall seemed to be the center of activity, and as Lani pushed her way down Richards Street the sharp sound of rifle fire was intermingled with louder, more thunderous explosions, making the air around her tremble and her ears ring.

"Dynamite," a young Hawaiian man near Lani said knowledgeably. "All *make* soon."

Then through the crowd she saw the tall figure of Tom Stewart, towering over the Chinese who were standing near him. "What's happening?" she asked breathlessly after she had finally been able to wiggle her way to his side.

"You shouldn't be here," Tom said, gazing at her, annoyed. "It's no place for a girl."

Lani ignored his bad humor, suspecting it had more to do with the embarrassing ending to their swim last night than with her presence here today. "What are they doing?" she asked, standing on tiptoe so that she could glimpse the men creeping along the top of the palace wall.

Tom stared at the wall, his eyes bright with anger. "Wilcox and what's left of his men have taken refuge in the king's bungalow on the palace grounds. They refuse to give up, so now the *haoles* are throwing dynamite bombs at the roof of the house, trying to force them out."

All at once, Lani found herself imagining much too vividly the scene within the bungalow, the beleaguered men, with the bombs blowing the building to pieces around them, the helpless despair they must be feeling. An explosion made the ground rock beneath her feet, and she clutched, frightened, at Tom's arm. How could anyone survive such an attack? "They'll have to surrender now, won't they?"

Tom thrust her away, his young voice harsh. "I wouldn't! I would never surrender to the damn *haoles*!"

He stalked away through the men who were pushing closer to the wall to see better. Lani perforce found herself being carried along by the crowd.

Near her, a white man cried out, "Get the caged rebels!" But Lani noticed that most of the Hawaiians watching were quiet. Some of the dark faces were bewildered; others held a sullen bitterness. A few Hawaiian women were crying softly.

Then one of the men on the wall called out triumphantly, "He's surrendered! Wilcox is waving a white cloth!"

Immediately, a squad of the Honolulu Rifles rushed the gate into the palace grounds. The crowd streamed forward to see the last act of the drama. Lani, struggling to fight free of the mass of people, was elbowed violently to one side. She felt her legs give way and, stumbling, would have fallen except for an arm that circled her waist and lifted her bodily, holding her tightly as the crowd parted and surged around her.

"Are you all right?"

There was a startling familiarity to that voice. Lani, twisting in the man's arms so that she could look up into his face, half expected to see Adam Stewart frowning coldly down at her. But the man, holding her so tightly she could feel his hard, muscular body pressed against the length of hers, was smiling, and his only resemblance to Adam Stewart was the prominent nose and straight brows in a broad, tanned face.

With the sun in her eyes, Lani blinked against the dazzling whiteness of that smile; the man's eyes were of such a pure, crystalline blue they seemed to catch and hold the sunlight in their depths.

The smile dimmed a little as the man gave her shoulders a gentle shake. "You're not hurt, are you?"

Lani took a deep, trembling breath. Her knees felt oddly weak, and her heart was pounding in her chest. She stared, dazed, up at the man. Then, realizing he was still waiting for her answer, she shook her head quickly. "No . . . no, I'm fine."

"Good." He released her and stepped back. "Then perhaps you'll allow me to escort you away from here. Now that the sideshow seems to be over."

Lani turned and saw that the Rifles were leading a group of men, under guard, from the grounds of the palace. The tall, huskily built man in the forefront of the group was wearing a scarlet uniform and glanced haughtily around him as he was led away.

"What will they do with them?" she asked her companion.

He shrugged indifferently. "Try them for treason, I suppose. But since natives have to be tried by a jury of their peers, I doubt if any jury of *kanakas* will convict them."

Then once more he turned that disarming, dazzling smile upon Lani. "And now where can I take you, Miss . . . ?"

"Tucker, Lani Tucker," she said, flustered.

He gave her a quick, surprised glance, then doffed his hat with a gracious bow. "Keith Stewart, Miss Tucker. I believe I've heard my brother, Tom, speak of you. And, of course, your uncle and I are good friends."

So this was Tom's other brother, Lani thought, casting a curious glance at the man as they walked back to Beretania Street. How different he was than his older brother, Adam. Even the way he dressed, all in white from his well-tailored suit fit snugly over his broad shoulders to the white Panama hat circled with a white jasmine lei. He slowed his pace to Lani's, an ivory-headed malacca walking stick held nonchalantly in one hand, his sparkling blue eyes fastened with a flattering, unwavering attention upon her face.

He wanted to know everything about her, how long she had

been staying with her uncle, was she enjoying Honolulu, did she miss the ranch on Maui? Then he listened closely to her answers as if she were the only one who existed for him, completely ignoring the women passing by, their appreciative glances turning to follow his tall, lithe figure.

They reached the Tucker home much too soon, as far as Lani was concerned. She wished desperately that there were some way she could prolong the meeting. Her companion held the gate open for her, a mischievous glint in the blue eyes. "I'd escort you inside, but I have a feeling your uncle wouldn't be too pleased if he found out where you've been."

His warm, teasing smile brought a flush to Lani's face, and once again she felt that odd, weak-in-the-knees sensation. Annoyed, she heard herself stammering like a silly schoolchild, "Thank . . . thank you, Mr. Stewart."

"My pleasure, Miss Tucker," he assured her, his smile broadening as he gave her a conspiratorial wink, then turned and strode away.

Lani stared after him for a long moment, then walked slowly into the house, not even minding when Loki descended upon her like a duck on a june bug, demanding, "Where you been? Everybody worried crazy sick about you. Wassa matter you no listen to your uncle? Now he's mad. Never seen him so *huhu*."

The Hawaiian woman fell silent, surprised by Lani's strangely quiet manner. It wasn't like the girl not to flare up when scolded. As a matter of fact, there was a look in the lavender eyes that made Loki feel uneasy. Having raised the girl since she was little more than a baby, she was sure she knew everything there was to know about Lani. Yet she could have sworn she had never seen that particular expression on the girl's face before.

"Who was that *kane* at the gate with you?" she asked suspiciously.

Lani started slowly up the steps without answering, then stopped and turned, her hand trailing on the stair rail, a smile of pure bliss on her face. "That was Mr. Keith Stewart," she said dreamily, "the man I'm going to marry."

Chapter 4

Within three minutes of leaving the Tucker home, Keith Stewart had forgotten all about Lani Tucker. He made his way quickly through the crowded streets, where brown-skinned Hawaiian women in flowing, colorful *holokus*, and Chinese women in black, shing trousers, mingled with fashionably dressed *haole* women whose figures were squeezed into hourglass shapes by their whale bone girdles. White men walked briskly next to dignified Chinese merchants in black alpaca suits. Portuguese, Chinese, Japanese, British, and German accents all added to the babble of tongues that could be heard on the streets of Honolulu, giving the town—for all its small size—an international flavor.

Some men were still gathered in clusters, discussing the uprising at the palace. Many, however, the day's excitement over, were drifting homeward or toward their places of employment as Keith walked down Fort Street toward the wharves. As he walked past the dingy brick offices that lined Fort and Merchant streets, he remembered the conversation at Daniel Tucker's home last night and thought to himself, glancing shrewdly around him, that it wasn't sugar or King Kalakaua who wielded the power in the Hawaiian islands. It was the men in these buildings, the bankers and merchants and, most important of all, the factors, the men who arranged loans, handled the business interests, and negotiated the sale of the sugar for the plantations.

These were the men who had turned Hawaii from a simple, backward kingdom into a thriving, bustling country. Although a sprinkling of these businessmen were recent arrivals in the islands, and a few were British or German, the majority were sons or grandsons of American missionaries, like Keith himself. His grandfather, Seth Stewart, had come to the Sandwich Islands from New England and dedicated his life to bringing Christianity to the native Hawaiians. Seth Stewart had died almost penniless, but his son, Silas, who had been educated in the ministry, soon left the church to start a sugar plantation, then formed his own profitable mercantile and shipping company. Only a score of such men, and their descendants, controlled the economy of Hawaii. And they were all white men.

When Keith turned into a narrow, two-story brick building with Silas Stewart and Sons written in discreet gold letters on the door, his office clerk was nervously waiting for him.

"Mr. Adam Stewart is in your office, sir, waiting to see you." At the anger he saw leap into his employer's face, the clerk bleated unhappily, "I couldn't stop him, Mr. Stewart. He . . . your brother . . . was very insistent, and he had a key to the door."

Keith pushed by the small, frightened man and strode into the inner office, a large, modestly furnished, dark-paneled room, dominated by a portrait of Silas Stewart frowning down at his two sons. In the background of the portrait could be seen the spire of Kawaiahao Church, which Silas's father had helped found. In his hand, Silas held a Bible.

Keith waited for Adam to get up and give him the seat behind the desk that had been Keith's for the last five years. When his brother remained seated, Keith took a chair across from the desk, concealing his rage behind a disarming smile as he said, "You should have told me you wanted to visit the office, Adam. I would have made the necessary arrangements."

His brother lifted a quizzical eyebrow. "Since when do I need to make arrangements to visit the office? I seem to recall father left the firm equally to all his sons."

For a moment a petulant anger broke through Keith's sunny smile. "Tom should never have received one-third of the estate. It was our mother who brought money into the marriage so that Silas could buy the sugar plantation. Tom's mother brought nothing." Then he saw the open account books spread out on the desk before his brother, account books that he always kept carefully locked in the wall safe behind the desk. "I see you've managed to break into the safe," he said caustically.

"There was no need. Silas gave me a duplicate set of keys to the office and the safe the year before he died." Adam studied his brother's face thoughtfully. "Even as ill as he was, I think he suspected there was something wrong."

Keith stiffened indignantly. "Are you saying that Silas didn't trust me? I've more than doubled the profits since I took over the management of the firm. As for the sugar plantation . . ."

"I know exactly how you increased your profits on the plantation," Adam interrupted curtly. "I spent several days at Ewa last week, looking around the plantation, talking to the *lunas* and the Japanese workers you've been importing recently."

If his brother was surprised to hear about the visit, he gave no sign, but his expression was all at once wary. "There was nothing we could do but bring in the Japanese. The Hawaiians are too lazy to work cane, and as soon as the Chinese coolies finish their work contracts they head for the city, setting up their shops, working for next to nothing, and driving out the native tradesmen. Not that the Japanese aren't hard workers. I'll give them that, but all they do is complain about the labor contracts they signed and their living quarters. And they stick together like ticks."

He gave his brother an amused glance. "Or maybe you don't approve of the labor contract system? I don't remember that Silas ever objected to it. He was one of the first to import coolies from China under the master-servant law."

"It's more like a slave labor system from what I've seen of it," Adam said dryly, "but if a man is fool enough to sign a labor contract, that's his decision. As for the living conditions on the plantation, I've seen worse sleeping arrangements in the fo'c'sle of a whaler." His voice hardened. "But I doubt that even Silas ever approved of the use of a blacksnake whip on his plantation workers by the *lunas*."

Keith shrugged indifferently. "How else can they get an honest day's work out of the men? When one worker sees the whip liberally applied to his friend who ran away and was dragged back by the police, he'll think twice before making the same mistake."

"And paying the workers nine dollars a month when their contracts call for twelve?" Adam asked.

Keith frowned. "It's a perfectly common practice. The worker's pay is docked when he's sick or breaks rules or is caught malingering on the job."

"I've been through the plantation account books," Adam said. "I find it strange that every man's pay has been docked on the plantation, every month."

"You forget," Keith pointed out quickly, "the Japanese imperial government requires that each plantation owner deposit twenty-five percent of a Japanese national's wages in a government postal bank each month."

"I didn't forget," Adam replied. "But I did some checking. No money from the Japanese workers on our plantation has ever been deposited to any government bank account." The gray eyes narrowed, studying his brother. "How did you manage that, Keith? You couldn't have done it without help. Did you bribe someone from the Japanese Immigrants Bureau to keep quiet about the nonpayment? Is that how you managed to show a profit for the plantation when the books show that cane production has been down for the last two years?"

Across the desk from each other, the faces of the two brothers might have been two sides of the same coin: the same slanted bone structure, jutting noses and strong chins, the same thick reddish-brown hair. But while Keith's eyes were a sparkling, guileless blue, Adam's were a chill gray. Keith's mouth was soft and full with a sensuous curve to the lower lip. Adam's mouth pulled to a straight, hard line as he asked, "Or has the money gone into your own pocket, to pay your gambling debts?"

Keith's handsome face turned a dull brick red. His hands tightened on the clawed arms of the chair as he half-rose to his feet. "I'm the president of Stewart and Sons. What right do you have to come in here and accuse me. . . ."

"Sit down, Keith." Adam's voice was quiet, but there was no mistaking the lash of command in that calm voice.

Keith sat down again, slowly, a sullen look spoiling the smooth handsomeness of his face.

Adam gestured toward the books on the desk. "Did you really imagine I wouldn't find out how you've been running the company into the ground, not only pocketing money that belongs to the Japanese workers, but keeping a double set of company books to hide your losses? It's no wonder Stewart and Sons is almost bankrupt. For years now, you've been siphoning off money to yourself from the plantation, the profits from the voyages of the *Miranda*, the Stewart real-estate holdings, money that should have been reinvested to build up the company.'' A wry smile twisted the hard mouth. "Not to mention money that you've gulled from Tom and me as partners in the firm.''

"You'll get your money, of course," Keith said with a patronizing wave of his hand. "All I need is a little time. You don't understand business, Adam. All you know is the deck of a ship and handling common seamen.''

"You forget I spent several years working in this office," Adam reminded his brother. "Until it was decided I should ship out on the *Miranda*, and father brought you into the business.''

"You've always resented me for that, haven't you?" Keith said accusingly. "As the older brother, you thought you should have taken over the company." He smiled, a lazy smile that did not completely hide the malice in the clear blue eyes. "I suppose you would have taken over, too, if father hadn't learned about your *kanaka* mistress and illegitimate child. Father was only too glad to have you leave Honolulu then.''

Adam's eyes narrowed speculatively as he gazed at his brother. He had always wondered who told his father about the *hapa haole* child in the convent orphanage, the child who had too much of the look of a Stewart about her to be denied her parentage. Now he wondered, not for the first time, if Keith hadn't been the informer, as well as the father of the child. He knew his brother had been seeing Rebecca Kalia, a dancer in Kalakaua's court. However, Rebecca had suddenly left the islands and there was no way to prove that the child was hers, or who the father was.

Oh, he supposed he could have protested his innocence. But Adam had sown too many wild oats for his father to trust him. Silas still held to the principles of his stern, moralistic missionary forebearers. Pulling a sharp deal in business, taking advantage of the native's ignorance and gullibility to gain a valuable piece of land, was simply shrewd New England hardheadedness, but fathering an illegitimate child with a native woman was a sin not to be forgiven.

In any case, Adam thought ruefully, at the time he had been glad to snatch at any excuse to stop clerking in the office of Stewart and Sons, work which he found dull and tedious, especially when there was a whole exciting world waiting to be explored outside of the islands. He had been young and naive enough to believe that he would discover the adventure he craved on a whaling ship like the *Miranda.* Instead, he had found hard, backbreaking labor aboard what was little more than a floating slaughterhouse, with poor food and poorer living conditions. There were weeks of boredom and monotony broken only occasionally, as the whaling ships pressed far up into the frigid Alaskan waters, by the sighting of a white whale.

Silas Stewart had made sure that even though Adam was the son of the owner of the *Miranda*, he would receive no special treatment aboard the ship. If anything, Adam had had to prove himself to the crew over and over again, with his fists on shore, and by working harder than any other man on board at sea. In time, he had moved from being a foremast hand to a harpooner, then first mate. At last, at the age of twenty-eight, he had become master of the *Miranda*, staying on as skipper for two years until the accident that had almost taken his life.

Adam shifted in the chair, the sharp, thrusting pain in his hip which never completely left him, a constant reminder of that last voyage. Now he frowned, puzzled, at his brother. "Why, Keith? Why did you need money so desperately that you had to rob the company blind? How much money have you lost at your poker games with the king and his cronies?"

His brother cocked an amused eyebrow. "How sanctimonious you sound, Adam. I suppose you've never lost money in a poker game? Your friend, Daniel Tucker, has almost gone through the family fortune, making bad wagers and losing at cards. And I could name a dozen others, not to forget the king himself, who has lost several fortunes and half of the crown lands playing poker. I admit I've had a streak of bad luck, but my luck will turn, you'll see.''

"I don't give a damn about your playing poker," Adam said harshly. "What I mind is you're playing and losing with the company's money.''

"And just what do you plan to do about it?" Keith asked lightly, jeeringly. "Take me to court? Can't you just imagine the scandal? You'd be sullying the good name of one of the first families here in Hawaii. Grandfather and father would be twirling in their graves. The Stewarts might even be voted out of the Cousins' Society." He shrugged, smiling. "Not that I would care. I've always found the meetings of the descendants of the missionaries exceedingly dull.''

"There'll be no scandal," Adam said quietly. "I'm buying you out of the company. Twenty-five-thousand dollars should be more than sufficient, considering how much you've already bilked from the firm.''

"And where will you get twenty-five-thousand dollars?" Keith asked, curious now, leaning forward in his chair.

"I'm selling the *Miranda*.''

"You can't do that!" Keith objected, startled. "Tom and I are equal partners in the ship with you. The *Miranda* can't be sold without a majority vote.''

"I own the majority vote," Adam said. "I bought out Tom's shares a week ago. I've already started converting the *Miranda* from sails to steam. Then I plan to sell her.''

Keith gazed at his brother, an uneasiness forming behind the clear blue gaze. "And what do you plan to do with yourself without a ship to command?''

"I plan to run the family business," Adam said, and then added dryly, "That is, what you've left of it.''

Keith jerked to his feet, his voice half strangled with fury. "You won't get away with it. I won't be forced out of the company without a fight!''

"I think you will," Adam said, his face hardening. "Unless you want to face a prison sentence. I've been studying the logs of our intercoastal ship and talking to the crewmen. It was interesting how often the ship dropped anchor off Maui at Kahoolawe Island." Anger turned his voice raspy. "How long have you been using the *Seabird* to smuggle opium into the islands, Keith?''

His brother's face for a moment went blank, then he threw back his head and laughed. "Careful, Adam. You're beginning to sound as self-righteous as father.''

Adam struggled to hold onto his temper. "Silas would never have sunk to making money from smuggling opium into the islands.''

Keith smiled sardonically. "No, but father was quite willing to make a huge profit from owning buildings in Chinatown, renting out filthy, rat-infested rooms no bigger than holes in the wall with cesspools beneath the floors, the stink enough to knock you out when you climbed the stairs to collect the rent.'' He lifted a protesting hand. "I'm not complaining about the exorbitant rents we get from those buildings, you understand. As a matter of fact, I always admired the way Silas managed to ignore the mote in his own eye, preaching the gospel with one hand, taking from the natives with the other, all for their own good, of course!''

Adam scowled. He had felt uncomfortable himself when he had visited the Stewart holdings in Chinatown, where two and three families were crammed together in one tiny room. He had seen how quickly disease could spread aboard a crowded ship. He couldn't help wondering how many would die if the same disaster should strike Chinatown.

Keith sensed the discomfiture his brother was feeling, and smiled tauntingly. "But then you never would admit what a bastard father was, would you, Adam? After all, you were always his favorite.''

Adam stared, surprised, at his brother. It was Keith who had always been their father's favorite. It was Keith who even as a young boy when he got into trouble had always managed to smile winningly and shift the blame to one of his brothers. It was Keith whose good grades at school made his father beam with pride and never suspect that it was Keith's cleverness at cheating and charming his teachers that brought him those grades. It was Keith who had beaten a young Hawaiian boy almost to death for some fancied insult, then convinced his father that the *kanaka* had attacked him. And it was an older Keith who could charm his way into any woman's bed, and if caught contrived to conciliate the cuckolded husband or outraged father. Adam remembered the look of betrayed anguish on his dying father's face the day he had turned the keys of the office over to him. Silas had fought almost to the end against his suspicions, trying to deny to himself that his beloved, golden son could be a liar and thief.

The disarming smile slipped back across Keith's face, his eyes triumphant as he sat down again and murmured, "You wouldn't really turn me in for smuggling, now would you, Adam? Your own brother?"

Steeling himself against that charm, Adam thought wearily, no, he probably wouldn't. However, he had run a bluff too often in a poker game not to know it wasn't always the cards you held, but how you played them, that mattered.

He pushed a document across the desk to Keith. "You can't be sure, can you?" he asked, his eyes an opaque slate-gray so that it was impossible to read any expression in them. "It's your choice. Sign the bill of sale and pocket the twenty-five-thousand dollars, or take your chances that I won't turn you over to the authorities." He smiled coldly. "I've seen the inside of Oahu Prison. I doubt if you'd find it to your liking."

For a moment longer the triumphant sparkle burned in the lucent blue eyes, then slowly it died away beneath that steady, unblinking gray gaze. Uttering a low oath, Keith reached for a pen and signed the document, pushing it away from him savagely as he lunged to his feet.

At the door to the office, though, he stopped and looked back at his brother. The anger was no longer visible. A beguiling smile once more lit up Keith's face as he said cheerfully, "No hard feelings, brother. Forgive and forget?"

Adam nodded. "No hard feelings."

But what Adam saw behind his brother's sunny smile was the small boy who had never felt a moment's regret for any mischief he got into, and who always found a way to get even with anyone who crossed him.

Chapter 5

"How do I look, Mitsu?" **Lani** *twisted and turned before the* mirror that sat in one corner of her bedroom. "Do I look all right?"

"Very pretty, Lani-san," Mitsu said, studying the girl uneasily. Mitsu had little knowledge of western clothing, but she sensed that the red silk ball gown with its low-cut neckline was inappropriate for a girl Lani's age. And the girl's dark hair, piled in a rather haphazard fashion on top of her head, with a fringe of bangs that Lani had cut herself, made the girl's face look even thinner and somehow more childlike.

Mitsu wished fervently that Loki, instead of being sick in bed, were here to supervise Lani's dressing. She sighed to herself. Not that even Loki could change her young mistress's mind about the gown, if Lani was determined to wear it.

Curious, she touched the shimmering silk. "Where you find, such a beautiful gown?" she asked.

"Packed away in the attic." Lani winced as the top of the bone stays in the waistline jabbed painfully into her tiny breasts. "It must have belonged to my grandmother Jasmine. It's the gown she's wearing in her portrait." She stared regretfully and a little nervously at the expanse of pale flesh above the tucked bodice, wishing she had the rope of pearls that her grandmother was also wearing in the portrait. She remembered Uncle Daniel telling her that her grandmother's jewels were in a bank vault, and she would have to wait until she came of age to wear them.

She twisted around to get a better view of the back of the gown, the scarlet flounced skirt gleaming in the lamplight as the folds fell gracefully to the floor from her tiny waist. It was a beautiful gown, she thought happily. She could hardly wait to see how proud her Uncle Daniel would look when she joined him and his guests in the front parlor. It was the very first time her uncle had allowed her to be present at an adult dinner party. Always before when her uncle entertained, she had been banished to eat in the kitchen with Ah Sing and Loki. But tonight, oh, tonight, she thought eagerly, her heart pounding with excitement, everything would be different.

And she knew, with a nervous tightness in the pit of her stomach, that it wasn't her uncle she wanted to impress with her suddenly grown-up beauty this evening. It was Keith Stewart. As soon as she had heard that Mr. Stewart was to be one of the guests at her uncle's dinner party, she had pestered and begged and pleaded with her uncle until he had finally given her his reluctant permission to attend the dinner.

Almost a month had passed since her meeting with Keith Stewart, but not a day had gone by that Lani had not thought about the man, not a night that she hadn't fallen asleep with the memory of those sky-blue eyes fastening with a flattering intensity upon her face, a delicious warmth stealing through her body as she remembered how she had felt when his arms had held her, as if she had never wanted him to let her go. She had been disappointed when Mr. Stewart had made no attempt to see her again, but then she realized it was simply due to the fact that Tom's brother had undoubtedly mistaken her for a child.

She took a last pleased look into the mirror. Well, she certainly didn't look like a child tonight, she decided. In her mind's eye she could see Mr. Stewart's handsome face fill with puzzled surprise, then admiration, when he saw her. Perhaps he might not recognize her at all, and she would tease him for not remembering her, she thought, shivering a little with pleasure at the idea as she left her bedroom.

Walking very carefully, so as not to trip over the hem of her gown, and trying to ignore the painful discomfort of the too small red silk slippers that she had found with the gown, she reached the staircase landing. As she descended the stairs, she could hear the low murmur of masculine voices from the front parlor, and caught the odor of cigars and whiskey mingling with the almost overpowering fragrance of jasmine drifting through the open windows.

At the arched entranceway into the parlor that was filled

with a half-dozen men in evening attire, Lani hesitated. Almost as if pulled by one string, all eyes in the room turned toward the girl in the vivid scarlet gown at the doorway. The murmuring voices died away abruptly.

It was her Uncle Daniel who broke the startled silence. "What are you doing in Mother's gown, Lani?" he asked, shocked. "You look ridiculous. Go and change at once."

Lani had the odd feeling that her flesh was both freezing and on fire at the same time. Dimly she was aware of faces through a thin haze of smoke, her uncle's flushed with embarrassment, Adam Stewart trying to smother a smile, Keith Stewart's eyes bright with laughter. Fighting back a sob, Lani turned and fled from that laughter, tearing the fragile silk hem of the gown as she stumbled up the stairs and ran down the hall to her room.

Mitsu took one look at Lani's white face, the wide, staring, tear-filled eyes, then gathered the girl into her arms. Lani pushed her aside. "Get away," she choked. "I hate you . . . I hate everyone! Let me alone!"

She tore off the red gown and flung herself across the bed. "I wish Uncle Daniel were dead! I wish they all were dead!" Then she was too racked with sobs to continue, her body shaking convulsively. The maid sat on the edge of the bed and, murmuring softly in Japanese, caressed the dark hair that had fallen in a wild tangle around the girl's shoulders. Finally, the tears subsided and the trembling stopped as the girl fell into an exhausted sleep. Mitsu drew a coverlet over the girl, picked up the discarded clothing, and quietly left the room.

It was several hours later when Lani awoke to the sound of gravel being thrown at her bedroom window. Still half-groggy, she went to the window and saw Tom standing in the garden beneath her window. "Come on down," he whispered loudly. "I want to talk to you."

She remembered then, a wave of humiliation washing over her, that Tom's had been one of those faces in the parlor. "Go away!"

"Please, Lani," he pleaded huskily. "I'm leaving the islands tomorrow for school. This is our last chance to see each other."

She hesitated. Tom's face, she remembered, had looked sympathetic back there during those humiliating moments in the parlor. And they were friends. The least she could do was say good-bye to him.

She dressed quickly, then took the back stairs down to the kitchen. Ah Sing was, as usual, sitting, reading his Chinese newspaper at the kitchen table. He gave her a quick, sideways glance, but made no protest as she walked by him without a word. No doubt Ah Sing knew what had happened, she thought bitterly. By now, probably all the servants knew what a fool she'd made of herself before her uncle and his friends.

Tom was waiting for her by an old cane bench beneath a silver-trunked kukui tree draped with staghorn ferns. "Why aren't you with them?" she asked, shrugging her shoulder back toward the house.

"Oh, Adam sent me away, just as the poker game was getting interesting. He said I was too young to stay." In the pale, watery moonlight, Tom's young face was indignant. Then, glancing down into Lani's face and seeing the tear-stains there, the hurt still visible in the amethyst-shaded eyes, he said in a rush, "I thought you looked beautiful in that red gown."

"I looked foolish," Lani said stiffly, refusing to be comforted. She was sure if she lived to be a hundred she would never forget those faces smiling and laughing at her, particularly Keith Stewart's face.

"No, you didn't," Tom protested. "Why, I heard my brother Keith tell your uncle that you were going to be a tearing beauty one of these days."

Lani glanced at him, startled. "He said that, your brother?"

Tom nodded and Lani let the words sink in, like a soothing balm on her wounded pride. Perhaps this evening hadn't been a complete disaster after all. A hope she thought extinguished stirred tremulously to life. She remembered how tall and handsome Keith Stewart had looked in his dark evening clothes; something in the easy, arrogant way he stood had reminded her of pictures she had seen of the early Hawaiian *alii*, the powerful, haughty chiefs who had once ruled Hawaii absolutely.

"Will you write me, Lani?"

With a start she realized that Tom had been talking to her and she hadn't been listening. "Of course I will," she replied automatically. "I'll miss you, too."

"Will you?" Tom asked eagerly. He grasped her hands in his, pulling her awkwardly toward him. She was surprised to discover his palms were damp, the skin on his forehead beaded with perspiration. This time she was not quite as startled when he kissed her, nor did she find the kiss as frightening as she had the first time on the beach. Still, when the mouth on hers clumsily forced her lips apart and tried to insert an unfamiliar tongue, she pushed him away, furious.

"What do you think you're doing, Tom Stewart?" she demanded, glaring at him, hands on her hips.

Tom felt as if he were in the midst of running a race, breathing hard, air thrusting painfully into his lungs, his heart jerking wildly. The feel of Lani's soft, young body pressed against his had caused an instant swollen reaction, so that his trousers felt suddenly too tight. He wondered, embarrassed, if Lani had noticed. How did other males manage it, he thought in despair. He had, of course, heard his *kanaka* friends bragging about their sexual conquests. Tom himself had even hinted, lying through his teeth, about his own. The Hawaiians always made it sound so simple, as if all you had to do was kiss a girl and the rest happened without any fuss. Why was it so difficult for him? Was it because he was a *haole*? Or was there something wrong with him?

He stared at Lani helplessly. How pretty she was, even with her amethyst eyes still pink and swollen from crying, her sensuous mouth turning up softly at the corners, her small, taut breasts pushing against the soft material of her white blouse. He was stronger than Lani, he thought, his mouth dry. He could force her to submit to him, except, of course, no gentleman would do that. But he was going away for two years. Loving her as he did, how could he bear to wait?

"Please, Lani," he mumbled. "I promise I'll marry you."

Almost involuntarily, as if he could not be close to her and not touch her, he reached out clumsily for her again. But this time Lani was ready for him. She pushed him away so abruptly that he staggered against the cane bench. The bench tumbled over and, off balance, he almost fell too. "Marry you!" Lani said hotly. "Don't be ridiculous, Tom Stewart!"

Then, with a last furious glance, Lani turned and stalked away into the house.

A few minutes later, Tom found himself walking along King Street without even knowing how he had gotten there. Damn Lani! Damn them all, he brooded, tasting anger like bile choking in his throat. Damn Adam for sending him away from the poker game as if he were a baby. He was sick and tired of being treated like a *keiki*. He would show them he was a man, full grown. He would show them all.

He had reached the narrow alleyway leading from King Street into Chinatown, and he paused a moment. He had never been in Chinatown at night before, but, angry as he was, he had enough sense to stop and take the money from his pocket and place it inside his shoe. As he walked down the dark, foul-smelling alley, he wasn't even sure he could find the house he was looking for, the one he'd heard his friends whispering and laughing about, bragging how they'd bedded women old enough to be their mothers at Wo Tai's.

All the two-story wooden hovels lining the streets looked much the same, almost every other building bisected by a narrow, twisting alley, with second-story balconies running the length of the street. The balconies were draped with clothes of the slum dwellers, and beneath the balconies hung signs announcing wares for sale within the buildings. Tom had walked by Wo Tai's sign before he realized he had passed it, and he backtracked quickly. The sign pointed down one of the dank, smelly alleys only large enough for one person to walk along at a time. Once within the alley, Tom gazed around him uneasily. He was closed in on both sides by the dirty, whitewashed boards of buildings rising on either side of him. Then he noticed an opening in the wall, little more than a hole made by missing boards, and, stepping through, found himself in a courtyard.

Here there were more clothes, recently washed, but still smelling sour, as they hung from clotheslines and over railings, filling the courtyard, almost hiding from view a door into the ground floor of the building. Two sailors came lurching out of the door, almost running into Tom, who stepped aside quickly. For a moment, stepping closer to the open door, he glimpsed the well-lit, surprisingly clean interior of the building, caught the sounds of low, female laughter, the fragrance of heavy musk-scented perfume, and another odor he could not identify, but which made his stomach clench into a knot.

Then, before he could turn away, a woman's arm reached out, and he was pulled into the room, a voice giggling in his ear, "Where you go, pretty boy? You'll like it here, you'll see. Lots of pretty girls here."

The brothel keeper, a plump Chinese man, hurried into the room and, smiling broadly, bowed low before Tom as he asked, "What kind of woman will the young master require?" He gestured toward the women seated around the room in various stages of disattire and from at least a dozen different countries.

Tom swallowed hard. What he was about to embark upon was terrifying enough, but if he couldn't even speak the woman's language . . . "Do they speak English?" he asked. To his dismay, his voice broke halfway through the sentence.

The Chinese man shrugged. "A few. It is not necessary, you understand. But Marie, there," he pointed toward a blond-haired woman, "she's from California. Laia speaks pretty good English, and Kimiko . . ." He looked around him, annoyed. "Where is Kimiko?"

Several girls stepped aside, and Tom saw a young Japanese woman standing by herself. Her eyes were cast down, her hands hidden in the sleeves of her white kimono.

The brothel keeper had already sized up Tom and said shrewdly, "I think, you'd like Marie. She's more . . . experienced."

Marie was the one who had dragged Tom into the room, and he had already decided he didn't like her pointed, foxlike face. As a matter of fact, now that it was coming down to the wire, he was wishing frantically, a churning feeling in his gut, that he had never come to Wo Tai's at all. Suppose whichever woman he picked laughed at his clumsy efforts to possess her. Or even worse, suppose he weren't able to perform at all! Only because the Japanese woman seemed as shy as he felt, he blurted, "I'll take Kimiko."

The woman did not say a word as she led him down a dark hallway into a narrow room that was not much larger than a closet. The room was more dimly lit than the reception hall, a kerosene lamp illuminating the few pieces of furniture—a bed and a table where a bowl and pitcher of water stood. The girl had turned away to light the lamp, and when she turned back to face Tom he realized, startled, that she was his age, certainly not more than a year older.

He also saw, with a stab of pleasure, that she was as fragile and beautiful as a Dresden statuette his mother had once treasured. Her black hair hung in a braid down her back, and the features in her pale golden face were delicately molded from the faintly slanted, almond-shaped eyes to the softly arched cheekbones.

Then, casually, she shrugged the cotton kimono off her shoulders so that it fell to the floor. He saw, shocked, that she wore nothing beneath the kimono. And that her small-boned body with the firm, high breasts was as exquisitely formed as her face. She smiled shyly at him. "Okay?"

When he made no move toward her, staring at her as if he were struck dumb, a faintly puzzled look passed over her face. She stepped hesitantly forward, and, unbuttoning his shirt, her hands slipped inside, her fingers brushing lightly as feathers teasingly over his chest. When the hands moved downward, unclasped the trousers, and caressed the hard, flat abdomen, Tom needed no further incentive. He tore off his clothes and pulled the girl to the bed.

If his companion realized it was his first experience with a woman—and he suspected she did by the way she instructed him, without appearing to, where to place his lips and hands on her body to bring him the greatest pleasure—she did not laugh once at his clumsiness. He had the odd but not unpleasant sensation that he was falling, and, unable to put off his desire a moment longer, he pulled the Japanese girl beneath him, entered her roughly with a groan of pleasure, and found his relief almost immediately.

For a few moments afterward he lay as if poleaxed, unable to move. He had never felt so exhausted in his life, and he had never felt so alive. Then he realized the girl was lying crushed beneath him, and he lifted himself on his elbows, gazing down at her guiltily. "Are you all right? Did I hurt you?"

Her smile this time was not shy but impish. She laughed softly. "Is better, not so *wikiwiki.*"

She´ was right, Tom happily discovered. It was more pleasureable when he took his time. And the third and fourth times when they made love were even better, as if there were no end to the delights, the diversions to be found in Kimiko's arms. Her slender body, which had seemed so fragile, was as eager and indefatigable as his own.

He had no idea how long he had been in the small room when Kimiko finally wiggled out from under him and, going to the pitcher, poured water into the bowl. She wrung a cloth out in the cool water and, returning to the bed, began to bathe the perspiration away from his body with the damp, faintly scented cloth. At first, Tom felt uncomfortable at a female's bathing him, but the girl was so matter of fact that he soon got over his embarrassment.

When she had finished with him, she stood before the table and bathed herself. All the movements of her small, slender body were so graceful, so uninhibited, that Tom watched, entranced. Then he noticed her wrists, the raw red marks there, and asked, worried, "Did I do that?"

She shook her head quickly.

"Then how did you hurt yourself?"

She shrugged. "I try run away. Wo Tai caught me. He tie me up, make sure I no run away again."

Tom scowled. "He can't do that. It's against the law!"

She turned toward him, surprised. "Wo Tai owns me. He can do what he wills with me."

Tom almost protested again, but then he remembered the Japanese contract workers on the sugar plantations. If they ran away and were caught, they were punished. It was one of the reasons why he hated working on the family plantation, the way the workers were treated. It was the same sense of outrage he always felt when he saw anyone being oppressed, the strong taking advantage of the weak. But at least the cane workers were men. The thought of a young girl like Kimiko being deliberately hurt made him feel sick inside, so that his voice shook as he asked, "How did it happen? How did Wo Tai come to own you?"

She told him the story haltingly, her English failing her at times, of her peasent father, without enough food to feed his starving family, selling his daughter to a foreigner who came to their village in the prefecture of Hiroshima. The man had told her father there were Japanese men in a country named Hawaii who needed Japanese wives and were willing to pay for them, especially young, pretty women like his daughter Kimiko. It wasn't until several days after Kimiko's ship sailed from Yokohama that she realized the foreigner had lied to her father. As the stinking, filthy cargo ship wallowed from one Pacific port to another, she quickly learned that the women of a dozen different nationalities crowded into the hold of the ship weren't being delivered as wives, but were being sold to brothels in Hong Kong, Macao, Shanghai.

Kimiko was among the last of the women to be disposed of in Honolulu. Wo Tai, an enterprising entrepreneur, had noticed the growing number of Japanese men without wives in Honolulu. Since the plantation owners discouraged married men from signing work contracts, a Japanese man would eagerly spend a month's wages to spend one night with a woman of his own race. Wo Tai had ordered several Japanese women for his house. The second girl, however, recruited in Yamaguchi, had slashed her wrists aboard the ship when she had discovered her true destination. Kimiko had been tempted to follow her example, to accept death rather than dishonor. Always, though, some hard core of survival inside of her would not let her take the honorable path, a desperate hope that often flickered but never died during the six months she had spent at Wo Tai's: Somehow she would manage to escape.

"How is it you speak English so well?" Tom asked curiously.

"A seaman aboard the ship, he teach me a little. And Marie, I listen to her," Kimiko said. She added proudly, "I have a book in English." She did not say that while the other girls slept in the late mornings when business was slow, she would study the book, committing to memory the meanings of the odd-sounding, difficult words. She had long ago accepted the fact that, dishonored as she now was, she could never return to Japan. And she was clever enough to know she must learn the language if she was to make her way in this new, strange land.

Now she slipped into her kimono, her eyes taking pleasure in the young man in the bed. How young he was and handsome, she thought. And gentle for all his strength.

She smiled, her shyness suddenly returning. "Have I pleased you, *Donna-san*?" she asked.

"What does it mean, *Donna-san*?"

"Master," the girl replied, after searching her limited English vocabulary for the proper word.

"I'm not your master," Tom objected, then grinned, "but you certainly have pleased me!"

"You come back?" Kimiko asked hopefully.

"I can't," Tom replied unhappily. "I'm leaving the islands."

"Oh." Kimiko cast her eyes down quickly so that he could not see the disappointment she was sure was reflected there.

"Listen, Kimiko, I'm going to talk to Wo Tai," Tom said eagerly. "You won't have to stay here." The thought of leaving the girl behind, trapped in this brothel, pawed by any brutish lout who paid a few dollars for her time, was not to be borne.

Tom always thought it was the money he took from his boot, all the spending money that was supposed to last him for a year at school, that bought Kimiko's freedom from Wo Tai. He couldn't know that the Chinese brothel keeper had seen at once Tom's resemblance to his brother, Keith Stewart, a *haole* with many powerful friends and interests in Chinatown, including partial ownership of several houses like Wo Tai's. And a man, it was rumored, that no sensible businessman would cross.

In any case, Wo Tai had thought philosophically as he pocketed Tom's money, the Japanese girl was no great loss to his establishment. For all the girl's beauty, too many of her customers had complained of the lack of fervor in Kimiko's performance in bed.

It was only later, walking through the gray, early morning streets of Chinatown, with Kimiko, all her possessions wrapped in a kerchief, trailing behind him, that Tom belatedly wondered what he was to do with the girl.

*   *   *

In her bedroom, Lani came awake with a start. She was not sure what the sound was that had awakened her, but as she sprang from her bed she was aware of a sense of black terror choking her, a fear that propelled her from her room and down the stairs.

She reached her Uncle Daniel's study just as Adam Stewart stepped through the door of the room into the hallway. She stared at the man, bewildered, wondering what he was doing visiting her uncle so early in the morning. Then something in Adam Stewart's face when he saw her—a shocked horror, or was it pity?—made her try to push by him into the study.

"Don't!" Adam's arms wrapped around her, holding her back, trying to hide with his broad shoulders her view into the study. Trying but not completely succeeding.

For a split second, Lani saw her uncle sprawled on the floor of his study, a gun in one outstretched hand, his face looking strangely peaceful in spite of the blood that flowed from a gaping wound in his chest, staining the flowered rug a vivid scarlet.

Chapter 6

"You wanted to see me?"

Lani hesitated in the archway of the front parlor, gazing with open hostility at Adam Stewart, who stood before the fireplace, one arm resting comfortably on the carved wooden mantelpiece. As if he had a right to be there, she thought, furious both at the man and at herself. For just a moment, when Loki had told her Mr. Stewart wanted to see her in the front parlor, she had felt a quick thrust of joy, thinking that it might be Keith Stewart. And then was immediately ashamed that she would feel anything except grief, with Uncle Daniel dead only a few weeks.

Adam studied the girl standing stiffly in the doorway. He

had purposely decided to hold this meeting, which God knows
was going to be difficult enough, in the parlor rather than the
study, because he didn't want to remind Lani of the terrible
morning of her uncle's death. He would never forget that morning, the stunned look on the girl's face, the amethyst-shaded
eyes glazing with horror as she stared at her uncle's body.

"It's my fault!" she had whispered. "I wished him dead!"

Alarmed at her words, and as helpless then as he felt now,
he had clutched at her shoulders. The bones had felt fragile as
bird wings beneath his hands. "Of course, it wasn't your fault,"
he had said sharply, giving her a shake. "It was an accident.
Daniel must have been cleaning his gun and it went off."

At least, Adam had thought grimly, that was the story he
was going to make sure Daniel's niece and all Honolulu
believed: that Daniel Tucker had met his death accidentally
discharging his pistol while cleaning it. Why should his friend's
name be whispered and gossiped about in the parlors and
back alleys of Honolulu now that he was dead? But Adam
knew he himself would always wonder. Had Daniel's death
been an accident or suicide? Had his friend taken his own life
in despair, after the disastrous card game of the night before
when he had drunkenly gambled and lost the last of the
Tucker holdings to Adam?

Well, it was his guilt and he alone would have to learn to
live with it, Adam thought now, frowning, as he eyed the girl
in the archway and gestured toward a chair. She paused a
moment longer, then advanced with an insolent swagger into
the room and dropped ungracefully into a chair.

"Has Mr. Andrews, your uncle's attorney, spoken to you?"
Adam asked abruptly.

She nodded, surprised at the question. "He came to the
house . . . after the . . . after the funeral." Her throat burned,
but her eyes were dry. She had cried so much these last
weeks that she felt empty inside, as if she had no more tears
to shed. "Mr. Andrews told me that when I came of age, I
would inherit my uncle's estate."

And precious little there was left for the girl to inherit,
Adam thought wryly. Not that there was any reason for Lani
to know the true state of her uncle's financial affairs. What he
was going to tell her would upset her enough, he suspected.

He had told Mr. Andrews that he wanted to tell the girl himself, that it would be better coming directly from him, but now, sensing the girl's obvious antagonism toward him, he was no longer sure. Perhaps it would have been easier if he had let Mr. Andrews tell her.

"What is it?" Lani asked, wondering why the man was staring at her with that penetrating gaze. "Is something wrong?"

The awkwardness of the situation made Adam's voice unconsciously brusque, although he chose his words with care. "Since you are underage, and have no immediate family, you will need a guardian. Your uncle left a letter with Mr. Andrews, requesting that I be appointed your legal guardian until you come of age or marry."

He saw shock flood the girl's slender face, the violet eyes flaring wide with dismay. Well, she wasn't any more shocked than he had been when Mr. Andrews had shown him the letter, Adam reminded himself. "What do I know about raising a child?" he had protested. "I'm a bachelor." A confirmed bachelor, he might have added dourly.

"The letter is not legally binding," Mr. Andrews pointed out. "You can refuse the guardianship if you wish."

Adam's first instinct had been to refuse. He had enough problems of his own, rebuilding Stewart and Sons, without taking on Daniel's spoiled, willful niece. He still wasn't sure why he had accepted Daniel's request. Perhaps it was the guilt he felt about the card game, or the thought that if he had arrived at the Tucker home a few moments earlier . . . or perhaps it was simply that Daniel had been his friend.

"I don't need a guardian," Lani said resentfully. "I can take care of myself."

Adam's gaze roamed over the girl, noticing the tear in the hem of her skirt, the unpleasant sulky look on her face, the way she slumped ungracefully in the chair. Suddenly he found himself remembering Lani's appearance at the dinner party in the outlandish scarlet gown, like a child dressed up in her mother's clothes. There had been something touchingly vulnerable about the stricken look on her face before she had turned and fled from the room, so that he had been immediately ashamed of his laughter.

Who looked after the girl anyway? he wondered angrily. It

was no wonder she was growing up wild and feckless as a colt with no woman to take her in hand and teach her civilized manners and proper dress.

Lani had half risen to her feet when Adam said, "Sit down, Lani. I haven't finished."

His voice was quiet, but once again, as she had that night on the beach, Lani sensed a force to be reckoned with. Reluctantly she sat down, her gaze resting disdainfully at a point just beyond the man's shoulder.

"Look at me when I'm speaking to you," Adam growled, annoyed.

Slowly, warily, she turned her gaze toward him. He could see the anger burning in the pale face and felt his own temper rising. He took hold of himself with an effort. Damn it, what was there about this impossible, prickly girl that set him off, as if they could not both be in the same room together without sparks flying between them.

Lani saw the stormy anger gathering in the face that was so much like his brother's and yet so different. She couldn't imagine Adam Stewart's slate-gray eyes sparkling with laughter, or that hard mouth softened into a warm, dazzling smile. Even the way the man stood, braced, as he swung around to face her, instantly reminded her of the bruising strength of those powerful arms, the frightening hardness of that body when he'd held her on the beach. How different when Keith Stewart had held her, the gentle strength in his arms, the sweetness of his smile making her feel as if she were somehow special and infinitely precious.

She glared back at the scowling man. Well, she wouldn't let Adam Stewart browbeat her, the way he treated Tom. And from conversations she had overheard among her uncle's friends, the same way he had run roughshod over his brother, Keith, forcing him out of the family business, a turn of affairs that had set the Honolulu community buzzing.

Her mouth tightened stubbornly, and her voice was sullen. "Loki and Kimiko and the rest of the servants can look after the house, the way they always have. We don't need you."

"You won't be living here." Adam Stewart corrected her curtly. "You'll be living at the ranch. I've made arrangements for you to leave for Maui tomorrow morning. This house will be closed."

"You can't!" Lani said, shocked. "You can't send me away." Ordinarily, she would have been overjoyed to return to Palekaiko, to the easygoing camaraderie of the *paniolos*, who allowed her to ride with them as if she were one of them. But if she left Honolulu, she realized unhappily, she might never see Keith Stewart again.

"I can't?" One eyebrow lifted dauntingly as the man stared coldly at her. "As your legal guardian, I assure you where and how you will live is my decision, not yours."

"I'll have to leave school," Lani protested, grasping at straws.

"I don't imagine you'll find that a great loss," Adam said dryly. "I've talked to your teachers. You've not only shown a remarkable lack of interest in attending classes, but you're close to failing in every subject. If you're too stupid to learn, then there's no point in wasting money on schooling."

"I'm not stupid!" Lani sprang indignantly to her feet.

Adam shrugged, "We'll see. I've hired a tutor who'll live on the ranch with you. She'll not only teach you your lessons, but you will be completely in her charge. Is that understood?" There was a flicker of amusement in the narrowed eyes as he surveyed the rebellious girl before him. "Frankly, I don't envy her her job. Now I suggest you start packing. The inter-island steamer for Maui leaves very early in the morning."

Lani dug in her feet, her voice mulish. "I won't go! You can't make me."

Adam had half turned toward the door, but he swung back abruptly. The look on his face made Lani step back, suddenly wary. But he made no move toward her, and his voice was mild. "You can walk aboard the steamer tomorrow, or you can be carried, kicking and screaming. I'd suggest walking. It will be less embarrassing for you."

Then, as if the matter were settled, he turned once more toward the door. Swallowing around the hard knot of anger in her throat, Lani blurted, "Wait!"

He turned back again without speaking.

"What about the servants?" she asked. "What will happen to them if you close the house?"

If Adam was surprised that she was concerned for the

welfare of the servants, his face showed nothing of what he was thinking. "A few will be kept on to maintain the house. I'll see that the rest find other positions."

"I want Loki and Kimiko to come with me to the ranch," Lani said.

Her guardian frowned. "I thought I met all the staff. I don't remember a servant named Kimiko."

"She's new," Lani said quickly. "She took my maid Mitsu's place when Mitsu had to return to Japan to be with her ill mother." She smiled wistfully, a few crystal tears suddenly trembling on the long dark lashes that fringed the lilac eyes. "It's so lonely with Uncle Daniel gone. I don't know how I'll bear it if Loki and Kimiko leave me, too."

Adam pushed down a swift feeling of discomfort at the sight of those tears. The child wasn't going to go all weepy on him, was she? Just when he had been congratulating himself on how well the interview had gone. All the girl needed was a firm hand at the helm. Anyway, what harm could there be in sending a few of her servants with her to Maui?

"Take whomever you want," he said, heading hastily for the door. "Only be at the wharf on time tomorrow morning."

Perhaps if he had looked back he might have been surprised to see how quickly the tears had disappeared from Lani's face, replaced by a look of self-satisfaction. How silly of her to worry about the obnoxious guardian her uncle had chosen for her, Lani thought complacently. Given time, she was sure she could twist Adam Stewart around her finger as easily as she had managed her Uncle Daniel.

Lani, Kimiko, and Loki were among the last passengers to board the *Carolina* the next morning, scrambling aboard as the steamer was getting ready to pull anchor. Despite the early hour there was a crowd of people on the dock, waving a loud and jovial farewell to the passengers, draping flower leis around the necks of friends, relatives, strangers, it didn't matter. Boat Day, even when it only meant the leave-taking of a small inter-island steamer like the *Carolina*, was always a noisy, joyous occasion.

Standing at the railing, Lani was caught up in the excitement. Several of the servants had come to bid farewell to their young mistress, and as she waved to them she saw

Adam Stewart standing off by himself on the dock. No doubt making sure that she was aboard the boat, she thought. Deliberately she turned her glance away from the man, her gaze searching in vain for another figure. But then, of course, Keith Stewart couldn't know she was leaving Honolulu, she reminded herself. Otherwise, in spite of the debacle of her appearance at her uncle's dinner party, she was sure he would have been present at the wharf to see her off.

It wasn't until the *Carolina* pulled away in the pearllike morning light, passing a gray-hulled ship by itself at the end of the wharf, that she became aware of a long, drawn out, dreadful wailing coming from the dock.

Kimiko, who had joined her at the railing, gave a start of fear, while Loki's usually good-natured face grew grave. "*Auwe*," she said unhappily, "it is the government steamer, taking those poor souls with *maipake* to Molokai. Their family and friends know they will never see their loved ones again."

Maipake. That was what the Hawaiians called leprosy, wasn't it? Lani thought with a shudder. The loathsome disease had been brought into Hawaii years before by coolie laborers and had spread like wildfire through the islands. There had been so many sufferers of the disease, many hiding out in the hills for fear of their terrible secret being discovered, that the government had been forced to hunt them down, finally requiring by law that all lepers be removed to the remote, primitive settlement of Kalaupapa on the island of Molokai. Horror tightened Lani's throat as she wondered how it would feel to be a passenger aboard that ship, to know you were being sent to a living death, from which you would never return.

For a moment, Lani felt as if she might be physically ill; the knuckles of her hand, clutching the rail, turned white. Then she felt a hand gently cover her own hand. "Come," Kimiko said softly. She led the girl to Lani's cabin where breakfast was prepared and waiting: hot tea, rolls and butter, and slices of papaya.

At first, Lani didn't think she could eat with the sound of those grief-stricken wails still in her ears, but there had been no time for breakfast in their rush to reach the ship before it

sailed, and her usually hearty appetite soon returned. As she
ate, Kimiko moved quietly around the small cabin, unpacking
the clothes Lani would need for the two-day trip to Maui.

Lani gestured to the food spread out on a neat white cloth.
"You must have some breakfast, too, Kimiko."

The young woman shook her head, and Lani knew it was
useless to insist. She had already discovered that her new
maid had very definite ideas about the proper behavior of a
mistress toward a servant. Kimiko would eat later, alone.

Lani stared curiously at Kimiko, wondering, as she had so
often before, where Tom Stewart had found the young woman.
Certainly the note he had sent with the girl had explained very
little, only that the Japanese girl needed a job desperately,
and Tom would be forever in Lani's debt if she would help
her. A hastily scribbled postscript added that Tom would be
even more grateful if Lani didn't mention the matter to his
brothers.

When she had asked Kimiko where she had met Tom, the
girl was equally secretive, which had only served to pique
Lani's curiosity. Yet she knew it was more than mere curiosity that had made her decide to hire the girl as her personal
maid. Perhaps it was the girl's doll-like beauty, or the shy,
pleasant smile that belied the soft determination in her voice
as she lifted her gaze to Lani that first day and said, "I work
very hard. I damn good maid, you see."

Lani's shocked laugh had disconcerted Kimiko, and her
voice, all at once uncertain, asked, "It is wrong, what I
say?"

Lani realized that it was the first time she had laughed
since her uncle's death. She studied the girl more closely. As
much as she missed Mitsu, she wondered if it might not be
fun to have someone in the household closer to her own age.
For all of Kimiko's air of dignity, she suspected the girl was
only a few years older than she was.

She also suspected within the next few weeks that Kimiko
had never been a maid before, but the girl learned quickly,
moving deftly about each task, whether it was mending Lani's
gowns, brushing her hair, or helping her mistress dress—her
hands always warmed within her kimono sleeves before she
touched Lani. One night, several weeks after her uncle's

funeral, Lani had awakened, sobbing, in the middle of the night, both grief and guilt stricken, remembering how she had wished her uncle dead the night before he died. All at once she had heard a soft, rustling sound and smelled the faint citrus and tea scent that was Kimiko's. The maid's arms had closed around her, as she crooned softly in Japanese, words Lani did not understand, but whose comfort was like gentle hands soothing away her nighttime terrors and heartbreak.

After that night, although Kimiko still maintained an air of dignified reserve around her mistress, Lani sensed that a barrier had been breeched between them. Kimiko was more than a maid. She was her friend.

After finishing breakfast, Lani went up on deck again. Loki, a huge lauhala hat covering her head, had already found a Hawaiian friend and was sharing her damp bag of poi. Then, like the other Hawaiian and Chinese crowded aboard, who could not afford cabins, and in any case preferred the fresh air to stuffy rooms, she spread her mat on the deck and curled up and went to sleep. However, Loki was happy enough to retreat to Lani's cabin when the small ship, packed to its gunwales and sluggish in the water, ran into the high seas and rain squalls.

Lani was a good sailor, but both Loki and Kimiko suffered from seasickness. Loki groaned loudly; Kimiko's small face turned pale, but she did not make a sound. Lani spent the remainder of the trip nursing both of them. By the time the ship reached Maui, however, the squalls had passed, and a gentle trade wind pushed the ship toward Kahului Harbor.

Lani hastened to the rail near the bow of the ship to catch her first glimpse of Maui's spectacular coastline, mountains plunging to the sea, cleft by deep green valleys with narrow ridges lifted above dark gorges, like the folds of a fan half opened. Silver streams rushed in narrow falls from almost every valley, the water glittering with fragments of rainbows in the sunlight.

How she had missed Maui and the ranch, Lani thought, gazing happily at the wild, untamed coastline. What fun it would be to ride again on a decent horse, to chase down cattle with the *paniolos*, to be free of school and all its rules and regulations. Fleetingly she thought of the tutor Adam Stewart had mentioned he had hired for her, but her father had had tutors for her before on the ranch. None of them had lasted very long before hurriedly returning to Honolulu. Lani had seen to that.

When the passengers for the Tucker ranch debarked at Makena, brought ashore by long, white whaling boats, Lani recognized several *paniolos* from the ranch waiting by a stone corral. Years before Mexican vaqueros had been brought to the islands to teach the Hawaiians how to handle horses and cattle. The ranch hands still wore the Mexican costume, complete with jingling spurs, knives stuck in their slashed leggings, brilliantly colored kerchiefs, and floppy sombreros with broad brims. The only Hawaiian accents were the flowered leis the men wore around their necks and the gardenias stuck in their hat brims.

As soon as she had been tossed from the whaleboat into the waiting arms of the men on shore, Lani raced to the *paniolos*. "Johnny, Likeke, did you bring Jubal?"

The taller of the two men grinned widely and gestured to a small, powerfully built brown horse with a perfect Arab head, small ears, and dark eyes, who was pawing the ground nervously.

"Oh, Jubal, how I've missed you!" Lani flung her arms around the neck of the horse that she had raised from a colt as her very own.

It was only when she lifted her head that Lani saw the young woman standing, waiting beside the saddled horses. She was wearing a *haole wahine*'s black riding habit, but with her dusky skin, her lustrous black hair and dark, luminous eyes, there was no doubt that the woman was pure Hawaiian.

Moving with a lithe, proud grace, the woman left the horses and crossed to Lani, a faint, cool smile on her face as she placed a lei of rosebuds around the girl's shoulders. "Welcome home, Lani," she said, her voice low, melodious. "I'm Rebecca Kalia, your new tutor."

Chapter 7

Lani awoke before dawn the first morning of her return to the ranch. For a few minutes she lay quietly, listening to the familiar sounds of early morning that she always associated with Palekaiko. Through her open bedroom window she could hear the tolling of the bell, summoning the *paniolos* to breakfast, and from the kitchen the cook banging pots and pans noisily as he prepared the early morning meal for the ranch hands.

Too excited to wait for Kimiko to come and help her dress, Lani climbed quickly out of her four-poster bed. At the bedroom window her gaze roamed eagerly over the dawn-shrouded garden and beyond, above the trees, to an unobstructed view of the sleeping volcano, Haleakala, the House of the Sun. The indigo-colored slopes of the majestic volcano dominated the eastern horizon, its summit soaring into the sky. The fifty-thousand acres of the ranch, from black lava scarred ground—which had once run red-hot and molten to the sea—to rolling hills, rich pastures, and eucalyptus groves, sprawled across the back of the volcano.

Lani had been born in the shadow of the ten-thousand-foot-high volcano, where, ancient Hawaiian legend recorded, the god Maui had snared the sun to make it travel more slowly. She knew the volcano's every mood as she knew her own. Now she watched, hardly daring to breathe, as the first rays of the sun were caught and held in the bowl of the summit for a split second, then, overflowing, flooded the flanks of Haleakala like a lava flow of molten gold.

Lani let her breath go with a sigh. More often than not the Cloud Warriors, trade-wind driven clouds from the north and south, battled for possession of the peak of the volcano. But this morning there was a clear sapphire-blue space above the

summit, a space the Hawaiians called *Alanui O Lani*—the
Highway to Heaven. It was a good omen, Lani thought
happily, as if the volcano were welcoming her home after her
long absence.

Then she heard the bell-spurred boots of the ranch hands
stamping into the kitchen. Hurriedly she pulled on an old pair
of faded blue dungarees and a *palaka*, a blue-and-white-
checked work shirt, gave her sleep-tangled hair a lick and a
promise with her hairbrush, and ran down the stairs. Passing
through a long, comfortably furnished living room with an
enormous stone fireplace, she paused at the kitchen door,
savoring the delicious smells of freshly ground coffee, salt
pork, baking bread, and the tantalizing, elusive scent of
ginger.

The plump half-Hawaiian, half-Chinese ranch cook, named
Kealoha but called Charlie, turned away from a stove that
almost covered one wall of the kitchen and greeted her with
an enthusiastic "Aloha, Lani." Then, frowning, he shook his
head as he studied the thin, leggy girl. "No good. Too
skinny. All bones." He filled her plate quickly with fat pieces
of pork, sweet potatoes, and poi, and stood over her sternly.
"You eat Charlie's cooking. Soon fatten you up."

Lani hardly had time to eat, as she took her plate out onto
the lawn where the *paniolos* were already having their breakfasts, their plates piled high, great steaming cups of coffee by
their sides. Lani had known most of the men almost all her
life. Now they gathered around her, laughing and teasing,
calling her Paakiki, the pet name they had chosen for her
when she had first learned to ride and time after time had
stubbornly climbed back onto the horse after she had fallen
off.

For her part, Lani wanted to hear all the latest news about
the ranch—which mares had foaled, had any of the ranch
horses brought trophies home from the races at Kahului,
would there be a roundup of cattle soon for shipment to
market. Such a shipment, she knew, meant driving wild cattle
down from the slopes of Haleakala to Makena, then roping
and swimming the beeves out into the sea to be tied to whale
boats, and finally hauling them aboard a steamer that took the
cattle to market in Honolulu.

Pili, the head *luna* and Lani's closest friend since childhood, shook his head, the merriment slipping from his dark, lined face. "No, Paakiki. I shame-my-eye, but Palekaiko steers not make good glue," he said, his voice disgusted.

"Father always had the best bloodstock on Maui," Lani protested.

Although the ranch belonged to the Tucker estate, it was her father who had built Palekaiko into one of the largest and finest ranches on Maui, she thought proudly. Matthew Tucker had spent a fortune importing pure, registered cattle from America, constantly experimenting with new, improved pasture grasses, and building more and more paddocks and breeding pens for Palekaiko cattle that roamed freely over the upper slopes of Haleakala.

Pili gazed sadly into the distance. "Matthew, yes, when he was alive, no cattle better than ours. Now, water almost *pau*, grass, no good, beeves skinny like rails." He turned his gaze to the girl beside him, his voice softening. "We all feel sad, your uncle *make*. Mr. Daniel, fine fellow, but no damn good rancher."

That was true enough, Lani thought as she finished her breakfast and walked slowly toward the stable. She had always known that her uncle had little interest in Palekaiko, although he was half owner of the ranch. And now she was sole owner of the ranch, Lani all at once realized, her face glowing with excitement at the thought. As the owner, she could make sure that new pedigreed stock was bought, the worn out grasslands replanted. . . . She frowned, suddenly remembering. She wouldn't really own the ranch until she came of age. Until then Adam Stewart, as her guardian, controlled the Tucker estate and its properties. And she didn't suppose a sea captain was any more knowledgeable or interested in the ranch than her uncle had been. Nor, remembering gloomily her last encounter with that gentleman, did she imagine Mr. Stewart would listen to anything she had to say.

Lani's chin set stubbornly. Somehow, she would find a way to convince Mr. Stewart that money must be spent on the ranch. After all, although her uncle had naturally never discussed finances with her, she had always known that her family was wealthy. Why shouldn't she spend her own money as she pleased?

As she walked into the stable, she had made up her mind to ride with the *paniolos* that morning as they went about their chores and see for herself the condition of the ranch. Jubal lifted his head as she headed for his stall, his small ears pricking up, as if he recognized his mistress.

Lani petted the horse's glossy neck and hugged the velvety muzzle. When she turned to Keoka, though, who had been in charge of the stables for as long as she could remember, and asked for her saddle and bridle, his old wrinkled face seemed to crumble. "No can do," he said, sadly shaking his head. It seemed that Keoka had been given strict orders that Lani was not allowed to take a mount from the stable without her new tutor's permission.

Lani could feel the anger exploding inside of her as she stalked from the stable. There were a half-dozen cottages set back among the trees between the house and the stable. When her father had been alive, the cottages had constantly been kept full with visitors—sugar planters, cattle ranchers, visiting celebrities, even royal personages—who had gathered at the ranch for parties, or wild boar and pheasant hunting. She had noticed when they arrived at the ranch yesterday that Rebecca had retired to one of these cottages, instead of staying at the Big House with Lani.

Now she stormed up to the cottage and, without waiting to see if her new tutor was awake, pushed open the door and walked inside. Rebecca was awake. She was seated in the tiny living room, eating breakfast. She wore a pale yellow *holoku* with an illima blossom tucked behind her ear, her black hair curling damply as if she had just left her bath.

"What do you mean, telling Keoka I couldn't have a horse without your permission?" Lani demanded, her voice shaking with rage.

Rebecca set down her coffee cup, staring calmly at Lani. "Hasn't anyone taught you that it's rude to enter a room without knocking?" she asked. Her gaze swept over Lani, from her dirty boots to her worn shirt. "Or that a young lady doesn't wear a ranch hand's clothing?"

All at once, Lani had the unnerving feeling that she was a

child again and, having been caught in some act of mischief, had been hauled before her grandmother Jasmine. Her grandmother was the one person in her young life who could quell Lani's rebellion with just one regal look of disapproval, a look that somehow hurt Lani more than any of her father's spankings did. Her new tutor had that same expression of icy disapproval on her face.

But she's not my grandmother, Lani reminded herself, struggling to regain the fine edge of her temper. "You can't stop me from riding," she protested arrogantly. "This is my ranch."

"I already have stopped you," Rebecca pointed out. She got to her feet with a slow, sinuous grace, as if each movement of her body flowed effortlessly into the next. "If your class work is satisfactory, we'll discuss your riding again. In the future, I'll expect you to report to this cottage each morning promptly at eight o'clock, properly dressed, and you will knock before entering."

"Why?" Lani blurted, wanting to shame this woman the way she felt humiliated. "Why should I listen to you? You're not a real tutor."

"You mean because I'm Hawaiian, not *haole*?" Rebecca asked.

"All my other tutors were white women," Lani said, flushing. "And all the teachers at my school were *haole*."

Rebecca gazed curiously at her pupil. "You're part Hawaiian, Lani. Do you think that makes you less intelligent than a white girl?"

"Of course not," Lani answered, outraged. "What good are lessons anyway?"

Her teacher smiled, and once again Lani was aware of the woman's rich Polynesian beauty, from the gracefully arched brows over the black, lucent eyes to the soft bloom that touched the smooth skin of Rebecca's face. "I can think of one perfectly good reason why you should study. One day you'll marry. Do you suppose a man of any intelligence wants an ignorant wife, a woman who can't conduct herself properly with his friends and in society?"

Keith Stewart's handsome face instantly flashed into Lani's mind, the warmth that leaped into the clear blue eyes when he smiled at her, touching something deep inside of her so that she had felt herself opening, blossoming beneath that smile like a plant uncoiling in the first spring sunlight. She had never changed her mind about the decision she had made that day in Honolulu, that she would one day marry Keith Stewart. Now, she sensed that Rebecca was right. A man like Keith Stewart, who could undoubtedly have any woman he wanted, wouldn't choose an ignoramus for a wife. He would pick a beautiful, well-educated woman to grace his home and raise his children, a wife of whom he could be proud.

Well, she would be that woman, Lani decided without a second thought. There was nothing she wouldn't do to win Keith, even if it meant learning by heart every dull book her tutor inflicted upon her!

If Rebecca was surprised at the change in her pupil's attitude, the willingness with which Lani showed up at the cottage each morning, the fervor with which she threw herself into her lessons, she made no comment. And Lani, to her own surprise, discovered that with Rebecca as her teacher learning was not at all the drudgery it had been at the school in Honolulu. Her tutor seemed able to transfer her enthusiasm, her own enjoyment in the subjects she taught, to her pupil.

Even history, which Lani had always found particularly dull, came alive when Rebecca talked about the history of Hawaii, the early Polynesians who, in only frail canoes, had crossed thousands of miles of ocean to reach the islands of Hawaii.

"But that's not really true, is it?" Lani asked when Rebecca had finished. "The teachers at school said that the Hawaiians like to tell of such trips, but of course it's only a myth, that without compasses and stronger boats it would have been impossible for the early Hawaiians to make such a voyage."

For the first time since she had met her tutor, she saw a flash of anger in the dark eyes beneath the sculptured eyelids. But when Rebecca spoke, her voice was composed, as always. "The Polynesians didn't need compasses, any more than Hawaiians do today. They used the sun and the stars, the winds and the flights of seabirds to guide their way."

"But how could the Hawaiians know what happened centuries ago?" Lani persisted. "They didn't have a written language or books, before the missionaries came and taught them."

"There was always a man in each village whose duty it was to memorize the stories of the great deeds of his ancestors and pass them on to his son, and his son to his son," Rebecca explained. "It has always been so. In the village in which I grew up, there was a *kahu* who could recite the history of our village back beyond the time when the first Hawaiian sailed from Tahiti."

A shadow crossed Rebecca's face. "Today, of course, such old ways are fast disappearing. The Hawaiian culture will soon be gone, replaced by western customs, the same way more than half of the Hawaiian people have been killed off by the diseases the *haoles* brought with them to our islands."

Listening to her tutor, Lani realized that Rebecca sounded a great deal like Tom when he used to talk to her about the native Hawaiian people. Not that she had paid that much attention to what Tom said. After all, the plight of the Hawaiian people had nothing to do with her. Or did it? She wondered uneasily, all at once remembering that she was part Hawaiian.

She was saved from such uncomfortable thoughts by Kimiko coming into the cottage, bringing a tray of cookies and a pitcher of cold fruit juice. After the maid had poured the fruit juice and served the cookies, Rebecca noticed that the girl lingered in the doorway, gazing wistfully at the books and papers piled on an improvised desk.

"Would you like to join our class, Kimiko?" she asked, smiling at the girl.

Kimiko ducked her head, murmuring, "My poor woman's brain would bring dishonor to your class."

Rebecca laughed. "I've never noticed that a female brain is any poorer than a male's, quite the contrary. When a woman applies herself, she can be just as smart or smarter than a man."

Lani gazed at her teacher, astonished at such a heretical thought. At her school in Honolulu, it was always the boy pupils who had been pushed forward, while the girls had been encouraged to take the easier, less demanding subjects. In any case, she thought, giving her maid a worried glance, how could Kimiko possibly keep up with the lessons? Kimiko often had a hard time speaking English.

She was therefore chagrined when, several months later, it was very apparent that Kimiko was not only holding her own in her studies, but in her quiet, unobtrusive way, was surging ahead of Lani. For as much as Lani enjoyed the classes with Rebecca, her first love was still to be outdoors, riding with the *paniolos*, making the rounds of the home pastures. She would sit in the small cottage in the morning and through the open windows watch the ranch hands, their spurs jingling, jogging away to their chores. She longed with an almost physical ache to be with them.

One morning when she reluctantly returned her gaze to the classroom, she saw Rebecca watching her, a look of amused sympathy on her face. "Keoka tells me that Jubal needs exercising, Lani. Since he's your horse, it would seem your responsibility."

When Lani started eagerly to her feet, Rebecca lifted a hand, laughing. "Not this moment. This afternoon. After classes."

As soon as Rebecca dismissed her students that morning, Lani changed her clothes and rushed to the stable, where Keoka already had Jubal saddled and waiting for her. At first she walked Jubal around the stable pasture, then held the horse to a canter. Finally, Lani's slender body gathering itself, as eager as the horse beneath her, she allowed the horse to break into a gallop. The wind pulled her hair loose, snatching off her hat as she sailed over the pasture fence and headed for the open range, the taste of freedom in her mouth.

She did not see her tutor standing at the pasture gate with Keoka, watching the girl streak away on the powerful horse.

Rebecca turned, worried, to the stable manager. "She will be all right, won't she?"

"No need worry. She damn fine rider. Good as any *paniolo*," Keoka said, grinning. "Young miss just have to letta-go-blouse, sometime."

Rebecca frowned as she studied the fast-retreating figure of the girl on horseback. That's what worried her. As fond as she had become of Lani this last year, she was not blind to her pupil's passionate, undisciplined nature, perhaps because she remembered herself too well at Lani's age. Unhappily, she also knew the problems such an impetuous, headstrong temperament could bring. The difficulty was in walking the fine line, guiding the girl to maturity without crushing that ardent spirit in the process.

After that day, as soon as morning lessons were over Lani would rush back to the house, change into her dungarees, old shirt, and boots, and race out to the stable where Jubal was always waiting for her, whinnying impatiently for his afternoon gallop. And after that day, Lani's feelings toward her teacher gradually changed from at first open hostility, to a wary liking, and at last to a fast friendship.

Not that Rebecca was anything like the other Hawaiian women Lani knew. Most were like Loki, good-natured and gregarious, quick to laughter and tears. Rebecca, however, despite the closeness that had grown between Lani and her teacher, never lost her air of cool reserve. She said little about herself, only once mentioning that she had received her teacher's education at Mills College in California. If she had family, she never spoke of them. She took her meals by herself at her cottage, and although she often joined Lani at the Big House in the evenings, she always returned to her cottage at night.

And each afternoon, while Lani rode with the *paniolos* around the ranch, her tutor always mysteriously disappeared from the ranch for several hours.

"Where do you suppose she goes?" Lani asked Pili one afternoon as they rode together, a plover whistling overhead in the cloudless blue sky, the dust rising in little puffs beneath the hooves of the horses, while somewhere nearby in a tree-filled hollow a steer lowed to a calf.

The *luna* turned to look at her, surprised. "You don't know?"

Lani shook her head, and then, curious, asked, "Does she have a lover in the village?" A beautiful woman like Rebecca, surely there must be many men eager to court her.

Pili frowned, as if her words displeased him. "I know nothing of lovers. Your teacher has a small school in the village. In the afternoons she teaches all, young and old, and charges nothing. No more than she charges for nursing those who are sick and cannot afford a *haole* doctor. Your teacher is a true *kokua*."

Lani knew that to be called a *kokua* among Hawaiians was an honor not taken lightly. She felt a sudden stab of jealousy at the respect she heard in Pili's voice when he spoke of Rebecca, and was even more curious about her tutor. "Where does she come from? Is she from Maui?"

Pili shrugged. "I think Oahu. What does it matter? She teaches the *keike* to be proud to be Hawaiian, to learn what they can from the *haoles* but not to be ashamed of their own people."

Was there a note of gentle reproof in the head *luna's* voice? Lani wondered. Had Pili guessed that, with Lani's pale skin and lilac eyes, it had often been easy for her to overlook her own mixed ancestry? Even sometimes, she remembered guiltily, to pretend her mother hadn't been Hawaiian at all?

While living at the ranch, her Hawaiian mother hadn't mattered. At the school in Honolulu, though, she had quickly discovered that there were those white students who looked down their noses at the boys and girls who were half-Hawaiian. There had even been that time at school when she had overheard two girls whispering and giggling about an old scandal involving some of Lani's Hawaiian relatives, a half sister of her grandmother Jasmine who had followed the ancient Hawaiian custom and married her brother. After she had bloodied both their noses, Lani was grimly sure the two girls would not be repeating that lie again! But when later she had questioned her Uncle Daniel, he had not immediately denied the story, only shrugging with annoyance and scolding her for listening to gossip.

She glanced at the Hawaiian riding beside herself, who in some ways had been more of a father to her than her own father. "Do you hate the *haoles*, Pili?"

"It is foolishness to hate," the older man said quietly.

"Rebecca said that soon the Hawaiians will have no land of their own, that the *haoles* will own it all. They are even trying to take the Crown Lands that belong to the king."

Pili's broad, brown face broke into a perplexed frown. "I do not understand the ways of the foreigners. How is it possible that a piece of paper takes land from one man and gives it to another?" He gazed around him at the land that rushed down from Haleakala in a green torrent to the sea.

"To the Hawaiians, the land belongs to all. They know men are mortal, but land lives on forever, a mother that never dies."

Lani and the *luna* jogged along in a companionable silence, until Lani asked suddenly, "What was she like, my mother?" Her father had never spoken of her mother, as if it were too painful to relive memories of his young bride who had died, only a year after their marriage, while giving birth to Lani.

"*Auwe*," Pili said softly. "Nakeli was very beautiful. Her father was a *haole* seaman, with blond hair and eyes much like yours. Her mother was the granddaughter of a great warrior who fought at the battle of Wailuku, when the Maui chiefs fought to the death against Kamehameha's army and the river ran red with their blood." He glanced sideways at Lani. "You are much like your mother." He smiled teasingly, wrinkles gathering in the corners of his eyes. "But not so gentle, I think."

"I wish I had known her," Lani said wistfully.

"Look in your mirror, Paakiki," the *luna* advised, his voice tender. "You will see her in your eyes. She will always be a part of you." Then, as if to wipe away the sadness he saw on Lani's face, he said, "Tomorrow we bring down beeves for market. Why don't you ride with us?"

"Could I?" Lani asked eagerly. Then, her face downcast, she added, "I can't. My guardian is arriving from Honolulu today."

"Bring boss man along," Pili said cheerfully. "Maybe talk him into buying new stock."

She could try, Lani thought, not too hopefully. She suspected that Adam Stewart was coming to Maui to check up on her, not to inspect the ranch. Each month Rebecca had required Lani to write a letter to her guardian in Honolulu. Lani had used the letters to ask for additional money to rebuild the ranch. And each month the brief letter she had received in reply from her guardian—dictated she was sure to his office clerk by the formal tone of the letters—ignored all her requests and repeated his advice that she work hard at her studies and not cause her teacher any trouble.

Well, at least face to face Adam Stewart couldn't ignore her, Lani thought now determinedly. Somehow she would

convince the man how desperate the ranch's need was for
more funds. Then, noticing the way the sun was slanting on
the flanks of Haleakala, the blue shadows caught in the
deep gulches in the steep hills, she turned Jubal hastily back
toward the stable. The horse stretched out into a gallop, and
Lani bent low over the rhythmically moving withers as he
raced across the grassy stretches, sailing over fallen logs. It
had rained the night before, and clods of muddy earth flew up
beneath Jubal's pounding hooves. By the time they reached
the stable, Jubal's coat was as mud stained as Lani's face and
clothes.

As she left the stable, after currying Jubal, she debated the
strategy she would use with Mr. Stewart to make him realize
how badly the ranch needed additional money. She would be
very poised, very grown-up, she decided. And she wouldn't
lose her temper, no matter how the man might provoke her.

The air was heavy with the fragrance of crushed grass as
she hurried across the pasture and opened the gate into the
garden. Then she hesitated when she saw the two figures
standing alone in the garden by a hedge of oleanders, her
tutor and Adam Stewart, deep in conversation. There was an
air of intimacy about the man and the woman, standing so
close together, although their bodies were not touching. The
two sprang apart, almost guiltily, as Lani slowly approached,
and it seemed to Lani that her tutor's dark eyes were unusually brilliant, as if with unshed tears.

What had Mr. Stewart said to upset Rebecca, Lani wondered indignantly, turning an accusing gaze upon her guardian.

Only to discover that Adam was staring at her, aghast.
"Good God, child, what have you been doing? Making mud
pies?" He turned, amused, to her tutor. "This is the grown-up
young lady you were telling me about?"

Remembering her decision not to lose her temper, Lani
swallowed the angry retort that sprang to her lips. "I was
riding with Pili," she said, taking off her kerchief and scrub-
bing ineffectually at the mud dabs on her face.

Adam frowned. "And who is Pili?"

"The head *luna*," Rebecca explained, resting her hand
lightly on Lani's shoulder as she smiled at the girl. "Pili's

been running the ranch since the last manager left. You'll meet him tomorrow.''

"I'll be leaving tomorrow," Adam said. "I have business in Lahaina, then I'm returning to Honolulu."

"But you can't go!" Lani protested. "Pili wants to take you on a roundup in the morning and show you the ranch."

"I know all about the ranch," Adam said. "It hasn't shown a profit since '73. It should have been sold years ago."

Sell Palekaiko! Lani felt as if a hand had closed around her heart. It would be like selling a part of herself. She glared at Adam Stewart. Was that all the ranch meant to the man, dollars and cents? Her father had spent his life building up the ranch; her mother was buried in the small cemetery near the house. More than a dozen *paniolos*, not to mention the other servants, depended for their livelihood on the jobs provided by the ranch.

Before she could speak, she felt Rebecca's hand tighten warningly on her shoulder. Her tutor smiled at Mr. Stewart. "Surely you can stay one extra day, can't you, Adam?"

Lani noticed, surprised, that her tutor had called Mr. Stewart by his first name, and that the harshness in the man's voice softened as he turned to Rebecca and said, "Well, I suppose one day won't matter. It might be interesting to take a look at the ranch." But when he turned his gaze back to Lani, his voice was once more crisply disapproving. "Now I suggest, young lady, you wash your hands and face and make yourself presentable for dinner."

Lani stalked back to the house, fuming. The gall of the man. She was sixteen years old. How dare he talk to her as if she were still a child who had to be reminded to wash before dinner. Her hands clasped into helpless fists at her side. If only there was some way she could get back at her guardian, make him pay for that overbearing, condescending manner.

Then, suddenly, an imp of mischief leaped into the violet eyes, a smile of anticipation tugging at the corners of Lani's mouth. For all at once she knew exactly how she could get even with Mr. Stewart. Just wait till tomorrow, she gloated to herself as she hurried to her room. Adam Stewart would be the sorriest man on Maui.

Chapter 8

Darkness was still pressing against her bedroom windows the next morning when Lani hurried down to the kitchen to find Adam Stewart already having his breakfast. She noticed, annoyed, that Charlie was laughing and chatting with Mr. Stewart as if they were old friends. Ignoring the both of them, she poured herself a cup of coffee and stood by the stove, shivering despite the heavy sweater she wore, as if the cold wind that swept down the slopes of Haleakala penetrated even the warm and steamy kitchen. Pili and the other ranch hands had already had their breakfasts and gone ahead to start rounding up the cattle high on the upper slopes of the mountain. It had been arranged that Lani and Mr. Stewart would meet the cattle drive halfway up the mountainside.

As Lani drank her coffee, she gave Mr. Stewart a quick, sidelong glance. Someone must have lent him a ranch hand's clothes. Despite the fact that the shirt fit too snugly over the broad shoulders, the outfit seemed to suit the man, as if he'd been wearing such clothes all his life. Well, dressing like a *paniolo* didn't make Adam Stewart ride like one, Lani thought. She swallowed the rest of her coffee hastily, then announced, "I'll just go ahead and see to our horses." At the door, she swung back to face her companion. "By the way, Mr. Stewart, are you a good horseman?"

Her guardian gave her an appraising glance. "Good enough."

At the stable, Lani slipped the bridle over Jubal's head, while she instructed Keoka to saddle Blackbird for Mr. Stewart.

The stableman stopped short. "Blackbird? This Stewart, red hot rider? Blackbird's spooky, scared of his own shadow."

"Oh, Mr. Stewart can manage him," Lani assured the stable man, smiling to herself. It would be sweet revenge to watch her stuffy, overbearing guardian trying to ride Blackbird, who had thrown some of the best riders on the ranch. The black horse appeared docile enough, though, as she rode Jubal and led the stallion back to the house. Only the nervous, quickly moving little ears gave any hint of the horse's skittish disposition.

Mr. Stewart was waiting for her in a circle of lamplight by the hitching post. He ran his gaze thoughtfully over the stallion, the great sloping shoulders and powerful quarters, the rippling muscles under the polished black coat.

"If Blackbird's too much horse for you, I can get another mount from the stable," Lani offered, smiling sweetly. "There's Coquette. She's easy as a rocking chair to ride."

Without answering, Adam swung slowly onto Blackbird's back and settled himself in the saddle. Blackbird tossed his small, beautiful head, but made no objection to the stranger on his back. Watching, Lani had to admit grudgingly to herself that the man sat the horse well enough as they cantered away from the house. Still, what was so dangerous about Blackbird, she knew, was that when the horse seemed perfectly under control, the slightest unexpected noise, a shadow, or even the wind moving through a tree could set him bucking. Even a skilled, strong rider could take a header before he knew what was happening.

For a moment, Lani felt a twinge of guilt at what she had done, then quickly shrugged the feeling aside. She remembered the first night she had met Adam Stewart, and how she had sworn she would make the man pay for humiliating her. Anyway, she had offered to get another mount for Mr. Stewart, hadn't she?

Then she forgot about her companion as the two horses headed up the mountain slopes toward the high grasslands, and she watched the ghost dawn spreading its pale luminescence across the sky. Behind the ghostly white veil, the stars still blazed brilliantly. *Wanaao.* Lani remembered that that was what the Hawaiians called this first eerie dawn. As she watched, the whiteness dimmed, the stars gradually faded. For a few seconds, the darkness intensified before the second dawn flooded the sky with a pure golden light.

How lovely it was! Lani let her breath go with a sigh. If only, she thought achingly, it was Keith Stewart, instead of

his brother, riding beside her, enjoying the beauty of the
dawn with her, as if such moments were meant to be shared
with the one you loved.

"Miss Kalia tells me you're doing very well with your
studies." Adam Stewart's voice held a note of wry amusement. "I must admit I'm surprised."

Lani tore her thoughts away from Keith Stewart and gazed
coldly at his brother. Was she supposed to be pleased that he
had discovered his ward wasn't stupid after all? A bitter retort
sprang to her lips, but curiosity got the better of her, and she
asked instead, "Have you known Rebecca long?"

She was sure she didn't imagine the slight hesitation before
Mr. Stewart replied, "We met, briefly, some years ago." He
turned in the saddle to look at Lani. "Are you interested in
going on to college? Rebecca speaks very highly of Mills in
California."

Lani shook her head. "I'm not going to college. I'm going
to stay here and run Palekaiko, the way my father did."

Adam cast a startled glance at the young girl riding beside
him. Was she serious? Did she really think she could run a
ranch the size of this one? Not even her ranch, he thought
dourly, although there seemed no reason to inform the girl of
that fateful poker game, when Daniel had signed over his half
ownership in Palekaiko to Adam to cover his losses. Especially as he had every intention of giving the ranch back to
Daniel's niece when she came of age, or married a man with
the good sense to run the ranch properly.

At her guardian's silence, Lani continued eagerly. "All the
ranch needs is enough money to build up a new herd of
purebred cattle, repair the fencing, and replant the grasslands.
If you'd read the letters I sent you . . ."

"I read your letters. I also know you would have to pour a
small fortune into this ranch before it would begin to show a
profit."

"It's my money!" Lani exploded angrily. "You have no
right to keep it from me."

"I have every right to stop you from throwing good money
after bad," Adam said calmly. "And as your guardian, I
intend to do just that."

Then, the discussion finished as far as he was concerned,

he urged Blackbird forward toward the line of cattle Lani could see being moved down the mountainside. Riders flanked the running herd, turning back those wayward steers determined to make a last dash toward the mountain slopes they had left. The air was suddenly filled with the furious bellowing of the cattle, the shouts and curses of the *paniolos*, running hoofs striking against the hard, lava-covered ground.

The frightening, unexpected noise of the cattle was all that Blackbird needed to set him off. He abruptly went into explosive spasms of bucking and sent his rider flying over his head to the ground. It was what Lani had been expecting, but now that it had happened she had a queasy feeling in the pit of her stomach. Particularly when Mr. Stewart lay so terribly still where he had fallen. She galloped her horse to within a yard of where the man lay, pulled Jubal to his haunches, and vaulted off.

Panic-stricken thoughts raced through her mind. Dear God, was he dead? Had she killed him? She hadn't meant to hurt him, only embarrass him. Kneeling down beside the man, she fumbled for his wrist, trying to find his pulse. Adam Stewart's eyes were shut, his face filled with an awful stillness.

"Mr. Stewart, please . . . please . . . don't be dead," she moaned softly.

With a swiftness that caught her off guard, it was her own wrists that were suddenly imprisoned. She was flung on her back to the ground. Mr. Stewart was astride her, his grasp tightening painfully on her wrists as he held her pinioned to the ground. His narrowed eyes were as hard and cold as his voice as he snapped, "Are we even now, Miss Tucker? Isn't that what this school-girl's game was all about, getting even?"

He pulled her to her feet so roughly that she stumbled and fell against him. He shoved her contemptuously away as Pili came riding up. The foreman gazed puzzled from Lani to Blackbird, who was now grazing quietly nearby. Then understanding flooded his face, the dark eyes both sad and angry as he turned accusingly to Lani. "What kind big crazy you make? You know that horse *pupule*."

The look on Pili's face hurt Lani worse than the pain throbbing in her wrists. She swallowed hard, then turned to her guardian, lifting her chin proudly. "I'm sorry, Mr. Stew-

art. It was childish of me not to warn you about Blackbird."
She held out Jubal's reins to the man. "Take my horse. I
trained Jubal myself. He won't cause you any trouble."

Adam's hat had fallen to the ground in his spill. He picked
it up slowly, slapping the dust from the hat against his legs as
he studied Lani, the girl's hand unconsciously, lovingly caressing the silken mane of the horse that was nuzzling at her
shoulder. He turned to Pili. "Do you have another horse I can
ride?"

"No problem." The *luna* called out to a cowboy who
brought up a big gray gelding, quickly transferring the saddle
from his own horse to the gelding. Pili watched closely as
Adam adjusted the length of the stirrup leathers for his longer
legs, then swung into the saddle. Apparently satisfied that
Adam knew what he was doing, the *luna* nodded and said,
"Stay uphill above the beeves. If they start stampeding,
you'll have a better chance of getting out of their way."

The two men rode off together, without a backward glance
to Lani, who glumly mounted Jubal, pulled her hat down over
her hair, and followed them. She regretted now that she had
asked Adam Stewart to join in the roundup. She should have
known she couldn't persuade a man as cold and unsentimental
as her guardian to share her feelings about Palekaiko. All she
had done was make a fool of herself and spoil what should
have been a wonderful day.

She could see the cattle pouring down the mountainside
like a surging sea. The *paniolos* rode after them at a full
gallop, and she raced to join them. Soon she forgot her own
unhappiness as she joined the ranch hands in happily and
noisily chasing down the occasional steer who decided to
make a mad dash back up the mountain. Usually the steer
could be cut off and headed back to the rest of the herd. At
times, though, a lasso was needed to be swung by an eager
paniolo, who then flung his horse to its haunches and braced
back, while the steer, reaching the end of the rope, crashed to
the ground, the wind knocked out of him.

Adam found himself riding stirrup to stirrup with Pili,
racing after the cattle in their headlong plunge down the
mountainside. Far below he could see the strip of narrow land
joining the two halves of the island. The West Maui moun-

tains, with their sharp ridges and deep valleys, and the white fringed ocean glittered like crystal in the sunlight. The hoofs beating on the hard lava rock around him, sending up clouds of dust, might have been the crashing of the surf. The earth shook with the vibrations, sending a startled plover whistling into the sky.

Pili pointed in the distance to the lead fence that ended in sturdy holding corrals for the cattle, then he shouted above the sound of the pounding hooves. "Having fun, Mr. Stewart?"

"Great fun," Adam said, gritting his teeth against the pain in his hip that the wild ride was only making worse. Almost as much fun as riding out a northeaster aboard a whaler, he decided.

Pili threw an approving grin in his direction. "You ride okay for a *haole*. After you learn to swing a lasso, you'll make damn fine *paniolo*."

The herd was slowing a little now as the ground leveled off, and the cowboys, flanking the cattle, steered them toward the corrals. Then one of the big roan steers made a sudden last bid for freedom, veering off from the herd. Adam watched as a young, slim *paniolo* wheeled his horse and started off in pursuit. The steer with its wide-spreading, needle-sharp horns, sensed the horse close upon it and suddenly swung around, charging his pursuer. At the last moment, the rider pulled his mount so that the horse was flung to its haunches, and the steer's horns missed the rider by inches.

Adam watched admiringly as the *paniolo* wheeled and threw his lasso, almost in one motion. Then he tensed in his saddle as he recognized the rider and whipped his own horse forward at a gallop. He reached the rider just as the lassoed steer fell, crashing head-over-heels to the ground.

Adam scowled blackly at Lani, pushing his own horse forward between her mount and the fallen steer. "What are you trying to do, kill yourself?" he demanded angrily, surprised at the gut wrenching fear that had gripped him when he had realized the rider lassoing the steer was his ward.

Lani took off her hat and shook loose her black hair. Her face was flushed, her eyes dancing with excitement. Before she could answer, Pili rode up. "No *pilikia*, Mr. Stewart. I taught Paakiki to ride and rope. She threw her first steer when she was ten."

"I've never seen better riding myself," a voice drawled. "I'm only sorry I missed all the fun."

At the sound of that familiar voice, Adam swung immediately away from Lani, or he would have seen the girl's eyes widen, a melting softness in their depths. Pili noticed and cast a searching glance at the stranger. There was something about the man's smoothly handsome face that disturbed the *luna*. This was a *kane* who no doubt threw a wide lasso around women, but there was something disturbing about that charming, quicksilver smile, a blankness behind those eyes that were a sparkling, transparent blue. A man who'd lost his *mana*, his spiritual self, Pili decided, turning his troubled gaze away from the stranger. Such men could not be trusted.

Adam frowned at his brother. "What are you doing here?"

Keith grinned, enjoying his brother's displeasure. "Business . . ." He glanced back toward the ranch. "And pleasure."

So Keith had discovered that Rebecca was at Palekaiko, Adam thought grimly. As for business, the island of Kahoolawe just off the coast of Maui was known as a haven for opium smugglers, and Adam had heard that his brother had bought a small, fast coastal vessel, ideal for such illegal traffic.

Keith moved his horse closer to Lani's, his glance moving approvingly over the girl's long limbs, the graceful way she sat the horse like a young Valkyrie. "I've already intruded upon your hospitality, Miss Tucker, borrowing a horse from your stable, but if I could trespass further and beg a room for the night. . . ." He let his voice trail off, as he gave the girl a charming smile.

"There are hotels in Lahaina," Adam said curtly.

Lani gave her guardian a reproachful glance. Open handed hospitality was part of the Hawaiian way of life. When her father was alive, visitors were never turned away from Palekaiko, staying anywhere from overnight to months in the small guest cottages.

"You're more than welcome to stay, Mr. Stewart," she said, pleased that her voice was steady despite the nervousness, fluttering like butterfly wings, in her stomach. She clutched at the pommel of her saddle, her gaze clinging with childlike happiness to Keith Stewart's face, afraid that if she blinked he might disappear as miraculously as he had appeared.

Adam cleared his throat, his voice dry. "Am I included in that invitation, Miss Tucker?"

She tore her gaze away from Keith. "Of course," she said, unable to resist adding, "but I thought you were in a hurry to return to Honolulu."

"My business can wait," Adam said, deciding that his presence at dinner might, at least, help Rebecca through what was sure to be an awkward evening for her. After all, it was because of him that Rebecca was at the ranch, and Keith had been able to find her.

Lani felt awkward, too, as she dressed for dinner that evening, but for a different reason. Suppose she made a fool of herself before Keith again, the way she had the last time at her uncle's home in Honolulu? Remembering the disastrous scarlet gown, the look of shocked amusement on the faces of her uncle's guests that night, she could feel her hands grow cold and clammy. She let her hair brush drop to her lap and stared helplessly at her pale face in the dressing-table mirror.

Loki, who was helping Lani dress while Kimiko supervised the decorating and setting of the dinner table, gave the girl a shrewd glance. "I got big happy in my heart," she said cheerfully. "Everything okay. Charlie make one fine dinner."

Lani got to her feet, smoothing her gown over her hips. She had agonized over which dress to wear for the dinner. All her gowns had seemed suddenly too ruffly and schoolgirlish. Finally she had settled on a *holoku* that Rebecca had given her for Christmas. Of pale creamy silk, the deceptively simple fitted Hawaiian gown embraced the curves of Lani's slim body, the skirt descending in a graceful train to the floor. Around her neck she wore a lei of white pikake blossoms that filled the bedroom with their fragrance. A five-pointed, heavily scented plumeria was pinned into her black hair that had been brushed until it shone then pulled to one side so that it fell in a soft, lustrous coil over her shoulder.

Now, gazing nervously at her appearance in the mirror, she wondered if she had made a mistake, choosing to wear the *holoku*. At the school in Honolulu, the students had been forbidden to wear Hawaiian-style clothes, much less speak the language. Even her Uncle Daniel had frowned upon her speaking Hawaiian in his presence or wearing anything but western-style dresses. Had her uncle been secretly ashamed that his brother had married a Hawaiian woman? Lani wondered suddenly.

The thought brought a flood of color to her face. What if Keith Stewart should be embarrassed when he saw her in the *holoku*? She turned anxiously to Loki. "Are you sure I look all right?"

Loki's dark eyes welled with tears as she gazed proudly at Lani. How beautiful her *keiki* was. No, no longer a child, she thought, noticing the way the silk *holoku* clung to the slim, willowy figure, the full, high breasts and gentle swell of hips. Lani's face might still hold a childlike, untouched innocence with its softly curved mouth and the look of uncertainty in the wide amethyst eyes, but the seductive body was already that of a full-grown *wahine*.

"Never in my lifes I see anyone so pretty," Loki said, wiping unself-consciously at her eyes with the fold of her own voluminous *holoku*. She smiled suddenly, mischievously, through her tears. "Bet you my eyes, big surprise when *haoles* waiting in parlor see you."

A small, icy knot of apprehension remained with Lani as she left her bedroom and walked down the steps, the long train of her *holoku* held over her arm. She passed the dining room. One quick glance told her that Kimiko had outdone herself as she saw the glittering crystal and the white damask tablecloth. The centerpiece of scarlet, ruffled hibiscus had been artfully arranged so that the blossoms quivered at the ends of their stems like butterflies in the faint evening breeze. Leis of red carnations intertwined with fern leaves were hung over the backs of two of the ladderback chairs.

Taking the leis from the chairs, Lani continued on to the front parlor, pausing a moment in the archway of the room. Rebecca in a sea-green *holoku* with her dark hair piled on top of her head sat in a chair at a distance from the two men. Her face was cool and still as always, but there was an unusual tightness at the corners of the full, sensuous lips and an oddly ungraceful stiffness in the way she held her head.

It was the two men, seated by the great stone fireplace,

though, that caught and held Lani's gaze. There were almost identical looks of stunned surprise on the faces of Adam and Keith Stewart, turned toward her.

The two men sprang to their feet as Lani crossed the room with a proud, unconscious grace. Smiling gravely, she placed a carnation lei around the neck of each man in turn, murmuring, "Aloha. Welcome to my home. Welcome to Palekaiko."

Chapter 9

Staring into the almost comical looks of shocked disbelief in the faces of Adam and Keith Stewart, Lani experienced a moment of pure panic. Had wearing the *holoku* been a mistake after all? Had she made a fool of herself again?

Breaking the awkward silence, Keith stepped forward and took both her hands in his. "I knew you'd turn into a raving beauty," he said, smiling down at her.

It was not his words alone, though, that sent a thrill of pleasure through Lani. It was the way he looked at her, an expression she had never seen in a man's eyes before. Oh, Tom had gazed at her with a cow-eyed, besotted look, but it was nothing compared to this, like comparing a spring breeze to a kona wind. She felt her heart pounding in her throat. There was something frightening and yet exciting about having Keith look at her in that way, as if she was a beautiful, desirable woman.

Rebecca, alarmed, saw the bemused look on Lani's face, the melting softness in the amethyst eyes gazing at Keith Stewart. She rose quickly to her feet. "Perhaps your guests would like to take their drinks to the table, Lani," she said pointedly. "You know how upset Charlie becomes when meals are late."

Lani tore her gaze away from Keith to glance, surprised, at her tutor. Rebecca sounded as if she was expecting Lani to

act as hostess at the dinner party. The social graces were part
of the lessons she had been taught, but the few times they had
had guests at the ranch, Rebecca had always taken on the
duties of hostess.

Keith held out his arm. "May I take you in to dinner, Miss
Tucker?" he asked gravely.

She gave him a grateful smile and hoped she wasn't clutching his arm too tightly as he escorted her into the dining
room. Rebecca followed on Adam Stewart's arm. After Lani
was seated at the head of the table and the rest of her guests
had taken their places, she rang the silver bell that sat beside
her plate. And was delighted when she discovered that Kimiko
must have talked Charlie into letting her serve the meal.
Charlie often liked to serve his own meals, and had a habit of
slamming plates on the table.

Although Kimiko glided unobtrusively around the table,
Lani noticed that Adam was watching the girl closely. After
Kimiko had left the room, however, it was Keith who said,
"Strange, but I could swear I've seen your servant some-
where before. Where did you find her?"

Lani remembered just in time Tom's asking her not to tell
his brothers that he knew Kimiko, and she lied airily, "Oh,
my former maid, Mitsu, found her."

Glancing across the table, she saw that Adam's rain-gray
eyes were studying her face, one eyebrow lifted quizzically.
As if he knew she was lying, she thought, annoyed at how
that penetrating stare seemed to look straight through her.
Deliberately she turned her gaze away from the man. She
would like to have ignored him completely, but she knew that
a good hostess included everyone in the table in the conversation. Dutifully she gave her attention to both men. To her
surprise, Rebecca did not attempt to enter into the conversation and scarcely touched her food. It wasn't until Keith
began relating amusing tales of the royal court that Rebecca
even seemed to be listening to what was being said.

"Things should be quiet at the palace for a while now that
the king has left for California, supposedly for reasons of
health." Keith grinned broadly. "Although the rumors are flying
through Honolulu that he's really on his way to Washington,
to annex the islands to America at a nice profit for himself."

"He wouldn't do that, would he?" Lani asked, shocked. Of course, as long as she could remember there had been talk of Hawaii being annexed by the United States. Even before she had been born, other countries had cast covetous eyes at the chain of islands lying across one of the world's most valuable trade routes. For a short while, Russia, France, and even England had used force to temporarily overpower the small island kingdom. Always, though, the Hawaiian people had managed to regain their independence.

Keith shrugged. "I don't suppose he would. Anyway, the constitution of '87 took away most of the royal powers. But Kalakaua is head over heels in debt, and there are many people in Hawaii who would like to see these islands become an American possession."

For the first time since they had sat down to dinner, Rebecca looked directly across the table at Keith, her dark eyes brilliant with anger. "What people?" she asked, indignantly. "Foreigners who have grown rich in this country but have never taken out Hawaiian citizenship, Americans who were born here but whose first loyalty is still to the United States? The Princess Liliuokalani, the Hawaiian people themselves, will never allow their country to be meekly handed over to America."

Keith smiled indulgently. "I agree that the princess would be furious to lose her chance to become queen." The smile deepened as the blue eyes probed as if with secret amusement at the cool beauty of Rebecca's face. "As for the Hawaiian people, I've always found that they were much better at making love than fighting battles."

A faint pink stained Rebecca's face, but before she could reply Adam asked dryly, "Haven't you forgotten Kamehameha the First? His battles to forge these islands into one country were among the best fought in military history."

Keith turned his amused gaze to his brother. "And just where do you stand on annexation, Adam? Now that the Louisiana and Colorado sugar barons have dealt a death blow to Hawaiian planters like yourself with the McKinley Tariff Bill, annexation to the United States could be your salvation."

"I haven't time for politics," Adam replied curtly.

"Oh?" Keith leaned back in his chair, his voice lightly

vindictive. "I heard that you had been asked to run for the
legislature by the Missionary party. They've been pushing for
annexation for years."

"No doubt you also heard that I turned down the offer,"
Adam said, and then added irritably, "And there is no such
thing as a Missionary party. There's the Reform party, and
there are more merchants and planters in it than missionaries."

Lani glanced nervously from Adam Stewart's scowling
face to the hostility she glimpsed behind Keith's mocking
smile, sensing that the antagonism between the two men went
much deeper than politics. Tactfully, she tried to change the
subject by turning to Keith and asking, "Is this your first visit
to Palekaiko, Mr. Stewart?"

"Keith," he corrected her, smiling. "If you'll allow me to
call you Lani. No, I've been to the ranch before, while your
father was alive, a weekend boar hunting party." He shook
his head, laughing in memory. "I don't remember shooting
any boar, but I do remember your father showed us a fine
time. The party ended up lasting several weeks."

The rest of the dinner Adam remained quiet, sorry that he
had allowed Keith to goad him into irritation. But then, he
thought wryly, it had always been that way, even when they
had been children. Keith had always known exactly how to
place and turn the knife in his victim, while smiling disarmingly all the while.

In any case, the uncomfortable truth was that it wasn't only
his brother that had set him on edge this evening. It was the
shock he had felt, like being hit in the ribs with a belaying
pin, when his ward had walked into the front parlor earlier.
How could it happen so suddenly? he marveled, studying the
young woman seated, poised and lovely, across the table
from him. How was it possible that a female could change
almost overnight from a muddy urchin into the alarmingly
beautiful creature Lani had become?

Not just beautiful, he decided. There was wit and intelligence in the lilac eyes that looked at you with a disconcerting
New England directness. And what Lani had inherited from
her Polynesian mother was even more disturbing than beauty.
There was an incandescent quality about the girl. Everything
about her glowed from the faintly moist, inviting sensuality of

the softly curved lips, the creamy skin that seemed brushed with sunlight, to the burnished black hair. And the fact that Adam had experienced an unexpected tightness in his loins when he had seen how invitingly the young, lissome body moved beneath the silk *holoku* didn't help matters any.

Well, he had wanted Rebecca to turn his ward into a young lady, he thought ruefully. He just hadn't realized how well she had succeeded! Now, instead of putting up with Lani's willfulness, her childish peccadilloes, he supposed he would have to start keeping a close eye on the young men who would doubtlessly be pursuing his lovely ward, hopefully with matrimony and not some other, nefarious purpose in mind. Adam suddenly realized that the thought of Lani's being carried off into marriage by some young, lustful lad, thus removing from his hands the onerous burden of being responsible for Daniel's niece, didn't fill him with joy, but rather with a vague resentment.

After Kimiko poured the brandy for the men, Keith lifted his glass to Lani with a smile. "As I recall, Palekaiko means paradise in Hawaiian. I raise my glass to our charming hostess, the beautiful mistress of paradise."

Then he swung his gaze to Rebecca, and with that secret look of amusement once again in his eyes he added, "And, of course, her lovely companion."

As Adam rose to his feet and joined with his brother in lifting his glass to the women, Lani was once again struck by how similar and yet how different the two brothers were. Thick, reddish-brown hair and carefully clipped sideburns outlined the slanted bones and deeply tanned features of both men, but while a good-natured smile seldom left Keith's expressive face, the smile that occasionally softened Adam's hard, uncompromising mouth had a sardonic edge to it. Keith's blue eyes were open, sunlit; her guardian's gray eyes were more often than not narrowed, impossible to read.

Beneath the necessary surface politeness, Lani could sense the hostility that she had felt at the dinner table between the two brothers, invisible but as savagely real as the never-ending battle between the trade-wind-driven Cloud Warriors, Naulu and Ukiukiu, to possess the summit of Haleakala.

She was so caught up in the image of the two Stewarts as

Cloud Warriors that she hadn't been listening to the conversation around her, until she heard Tom's name mentioned. Guiltily she realized she hadn't written or heard from Tom in months.

"How is Tom?" she asked Adam eagerly. "It's been ages since I heard from him."

"The lad's not a great letter writer, except when he needs money," Adam said dryly. "I'll never understand how he managed to arrive at school without a cent to his name. At least he's kept up his grades, although I gather he's not the most popular student with the dean, not after he led a hunger strike against the food in the dining hall."

"He asks about you in every letter," Keith assured Lani, his eyes warm on her face. She seemed to feel that warmth piercing her skin, as if she'd been out in the sun too long, making her feel oddly light-headed. He added, teasingly, "Shall I tell my baby brother that you're pining away for him, Lani, or have you found another beau to take his place?"

"Tom was never my beau," Lani protested quickly, and saw a look of amusement flicker across Adam's face. She knew he was thinking of that evening on the beach when he had found Tom and her together, and color rushed beneath her skin, even as she said, with as much dignity as she could muster, "We were good friends."

"Ah," Keith said softly, smiling at her over the rim of his glass, "then when Kalakaua returns from his trip, perhaps you'll allow me to escort you to a court ball. There's sure to be a gala ball in honor of the king's return, and it's time a beauty such as yours was presented at court."

Lani spun around to Rebecca, her eyes shining with anticipation. "Oh, could I, Rebecca? Wouldn't it be fun? I've never been to a ball."

She was too excited to notice that her tutor did not seem to join in her pleasure. Rebecca's face had a stony stillness about it; her voice was harsh. "Don't be ridiculous, Lani. You're much too young to attend a court ball. When you are old enough, you will, of course, be presented properly at court by a woman friend of your family." She rose to her feet, picked up her shawl from the chair, and said, "Now if you'll excuse me, it's late. . . ."

Lani stared at her teacher, bewildered, tears of embarrassment stinging behind her eyes. Rebecca had never spoken to her in that cold tone of voice before.

Keith put down his drink. "You must allow me to see you to your cottage, Miss Kalia," he said politely.

Adam shot his brother a warning glance. "That won't be necessary. I'll escort Miss Kalia."

To Adam's surprise, Rebecca smiled tightly and shook her head. "Thank you, Adam, but why don't you stay with Lani? I'm sure you two have a lot to talk about."

She preceded Keith quickly out the door. At the last minute, Keith strode, grinning, back to Lani, standing so close to her that only she could hear him whisper, "Don't worry, little one. I'll see that you get to the court ball, just as long as I have your promise that you'll save me the first dance on your program."

Then he followed Rebecca out into the garden, catching up with the slim, erect figure when she was halfway to her cottage. He caught Rebecca's arm, turning her around to face him, his voice softly mocking as he drawled, "It's flattering that you're in such a rush to get to your bed, my sweet. You were planning to invite me in to share it, weren't you?"

She shrugged off his hand and stepped away from him. "Stay away from Lani, Keith. I warn you. . . ."

He lifted an amused eyebrow. "You were always a jealous little creature. I remember the time you almost scratched my eyes out because . . ."

Rebecca broke in violently, her voice trembling. "She's only a child. I won't have you hurt her."

"Hardly a child," he said thoughtfully, taking her arm again and holding it tightly so she couldn't pull free, forcing her body to brush intimately against his as they continued walking side by side. "You weren't much older when I first met you. It was at a palace ball, as I recall, and the king couldn't keep his eyes off you. I'm sure he would have coaxed you into his bed faster than I did into mine except for your position in the Princess Liliuokalani's household. I suppose poor Kalakaua was terrified of his sister's wrath if she found out he had seduced one of her retainers." Malice crept into the softly mocking voice. "Or do you suppose it's jealousy the princess feels because she can't even keep that cold codfish of a husband of hers in her own bed."

"The princess isn't like that at all!" Rebecca protested, annoyed. "She's good and kind. I don't know how I would have managed afterward, if . . ." She broke off abruptly.

Curious, Keith looked down at her. "So it was Liliuokalani who paid your way to that college in California. I wondered, when you mysteriously disappeared after you had the baby." Then, almost casually, "I looked for you, you know, for quite a while. Oh, I found where the child was, of course. .. . ."

He could feel the slender body within the pale green *holoku* stiffen with fear, and he shook his head, amused. "Don't worry, my pet. You can't imagine I have any interest in the child? I was looking for you."

They had reached the small cottage where Rebecca lived, a monkeypod tree throwing its spreading branches over the roof. Near the cottage a row of pink-and-white oleanders spilled their spicy sweetness into the night. There had been oleander bushes near the beach cottage where she and Keith had first made love, Rebecca remembered suddenly.

She turned toward her companion. Although a dappled moonlight lay across the garden, her face was almost hidden in the shadows cast by the monkeypod tree. "Why?" she asked bitterly. "Why did you look for me? You made it very clear that you no longer wanted me."

Keith sighed. "Oh, I wanted you. I just didn't want to marry you. There's a difference." Why couldn't women understand that? he thought. Resentment clouded the clear blue eyes.

As disturbingly beautiful and passionate in bed as Rebecca was, he had never had any intention of saddling himself with a wife whose dark skin might be acceptable in certain sections of Hawaii's society but would make her completely unacceptable within social circles in America. And it was in America that Keith hoped one day to live, after he had shaken the dust of this backward island kingdom from his boots.

Not that he found the color of Rebecca's skin unattractive, he thought, smiling to himself. He remembered only too vividly the endless pleasure he had found in that dark, warm body moving with such insatiable abandonment beneath him. Smooth brown skin and feather soft, full breasts with dark rosy nipples had always excited him more than skin like milk curd and pristine breasts like inverted porcelain tea cups.

He smiled teasingly at Rebecca and circling her neck with his hands, caressed with his thumbs the long, delicious line of her throat, his eyes never leaving her face. "Remember how we made love all night in the beach cottage, then swam out into the ocean and . . ."

Rebecca thrust him away from her, her voice cold. "It's over, Keith. What was between us was finished long ago."

He laughed softly. "Is it? Are you sure? I've always wanted you more than any other woman I've ever known." A hardness crept into the softly teasing voice. "You belong to me. And what belongs to me I never let go."

His brother, Adam, who had robbed him of his inheritance, would find that out to his sorrow, he thought savagely. Now he studied, annoyed, the dark, cool beauty of Rebecca's face, and, remembering the haughty airs she had put on during dinner, he decided it was time she was taught that lesson, too. Did she think he had forgotten that only a few years before he had only to snap his fingers and she would come running?

He let his hands drop away from her, his voice almost indifferent as he said, "Of course, if you insist on sending me away, I suppose I'll be forced to find my pleasure elsewhere." He cast a suggestive glance over his shoulder toward the large house. "I have a feeling Miss Tucker won't find my presence so repulsive."

Rebecca took a deep, ragged breath. "You would, wouldn't you? You'd use Lani to get back at me."

Keith looked shocked. "What an ogre you make me out to be, my pet. I mean no harm to the girl. In fact, I suspect Miss Tucker would find it all most enjoyable." He laughed lightly. "You did, didn't you? Don't tell me you've forgotten. Or maybe you need reminding. . . ."

This time his hand slipped beneath the bodice of the *holoku*, to capture a thrusting, tantalizing peak in his fingertips, pulling gently at the velvet, rose-red nipple until it hardened beneath his hand. Rebecca stood quietly, her eyes like dark, fathomless pools; only a muscle that jerked, then was still, beside her mouth, betrayed any emotion at all.

Her voice was curiously flat, her body rigid. "Damn you," she whispered. "Damn . . ."

Then his mouth covered hers bruisingly. His body forced her back against the wall of the cottage where he held her, as his hands roamed slowly, lazily, over the familiar curves and hollows of her body. At last, with a faint sigh, her lips parted beneath his, allowing his probing tongue entry, and the stiffness drained from her body beneath those seeking, knowing hands.

It wasn't until he felt her soft and pliant in his arms, leaning against him, clinging to him, that he swept her up in his arms, kicked open the door of the cottage, and carried her inside.

Chapter 10

"*May I pour you another brandy?*"

Lani turned politely to Adam Stewart, feeling ill at ease at being left alone with her guardian. And although it was gallant of Keith to offer to walk Rebecca back to her cottage, she couldn't help feeling an almost childish sense of disappointment at his abrupt leave-taking.

"Don't bother. I'll serve myself," Adam said.

As he walked over to the small side table where Kimiko had left the decanter of brandy, Lani noticed that the slight limp was more pronounced than usual. "I'm sorry," she blurted, guilt stricken. "I hope Blackbird's throwing you didn't hurt your injured leg."

"I'm not a cripple," Adam said irritably. "My leg's fine."

With a sudden flash of perception, Lani thought: Why, he hates admitting that he has a bad leg. She felt an unexpected surge of sympathy for the man. Somehow it had never occurred to her that her overbearing guardian might have weaknesses, feelings, and emotions like any other man. She wondered how he had hurt his leg—hadn't Tom said something about an accident aboard his brother's ship?—but deciding that this wasn't the moment to ask she said instead, "Now that you've had a chance to inspect the ranch, what do you think of Palekaiko?"

"Chasing steers down a mountainside is hardly my idea of an inspection," Adam said dourly. He waited for Lani to be seated before he chose a chair across from her, stretching out his long legs to the small fire that Charlie had prepared against the late evening chill. "I did have a talk with Pili about what would have to be done to turn the ranch into a paying proposition."

Lani eagerly leaned forward. "Then you'll give me the money to rebuild Palekaiko, the way it was when my father was alive."

"No."

Anger ripped through Lani. She could feel her temples pounding, as they always did just before she exploded in rage. But that was the reaction he expected from her, she thought suddenly, gazing into her guardian's impassive face. What was it that Rebecca had taught her? When you lose your temper, you lose the argument. If she allowed her anger to control her, the advantage would be Adam Stewart's, his cool self-control to her childish temper tantrum.

Lani's hands closed into fists, her fingernails digging sharply into her soft palms as she fought to control the fury racing through her. When she spoke, she looked directly at the man sitting across from her, her voice low but steady. "Why? I think I'm entitled to know. If you agree the ranch can show a profit, why won't you let me have the money from my uncle's estate?"

She thought, for a moment, that he might ignore the question, the way he had ignored her letters. Instead she was uncomfortably aware of the gray eyes narrowing, studying her intently, as if she were being sized up in his mind against some invisible measuring stick. She wanted to look away from that hard, appraising stare, but instead she forced herself to return the gaze calmly, her hands clasped tightly in her lap.

Finally, flatly, Adam said, "There isn't enough money in the Tucker estate to rebuild Palekaiko."

Lani's eyes widened. "That's not possible! I always thought

. . . that is . . ." she stammered. "My father and my uncle inherited a fortune from their father, Morgan Tucker, didn't they?"

Shirtsleeves to shirtsleeves in three generations, Adam thought wryly. Wasn't that how the saying went? Louisa Tucker, Captain Tucker's mother, had shrewdly built a successful commercial empire in New England. Her son, Morgan, had made his own fortune as a whaling captain and added to that fortune in the years he had lived in Hawaii. And the third generation, Morgan's two sons, Matthew and Daniel, had managed to run through that fortune in a matter of years: Lani's father by living like a king and entertaining just as lavishly on this ranch into which he had poured his inheritance, and Daniel Tucker by living equally well, while having an almost snobbish disinterest in anything to do with business and a compulsive obsession with gambling.

A helpless rage at having to be the one to tell Lani the brutal truth about her inheritance set Adam's face into grim, forbidding lines. But there didn't seem to be any easy way to go about it. He spoke slowly. "Your uncle made some bad business investments, and with the depression of the Hawaiian sugar market, he had to sell the Tucker sugar plantation. The money that was left when he died was used to settle debts outstanding against the estate, pay the expenses of keeping this ranch going—as well as your expenses—and maintain the house in Honolulu."

"The house?" Lani asked. "Can't it be sold?"

"Under ordinary circumstances, yes, but aside from being mortgaged to the hilt, there is no money in Honolulu at this time for buying a large, expensive home." Adam stared broodingly into the fireplace. "My brother was right about one thing. The passage of the McKinley Tariff Bill will be a disaster for the Hawaiian sugar industry. Several plantations, like your uncle's, have already gone under. Others are sure to follow." He turned to Lani, smiling tightly. "And whether Hawaiians like it or not, the prosperity of these islands is built on sugar. Without the profits from sugar, all Hawaiians suffer."

He tried to read Lani's face as he spoke, but her head was half turned away from him. All he could see was the fall of black, shining hair, the proud, slender line of her throat, the graceful curve of cheek and brow. He noticed that the hands held quietly now in her lap were tapered, as delicately molded as a court dancer. He stared at those motionless hands and wondered what the girl was thinking. It had to be a shock, to discover she was not the wealthy heiress she had always thought herself to be. At least she hadn't burst into tears at the news, he thought, relieved. His gaze roamed over the girl seated in the large wing chair. She looked so young and vulnerable that he felt a sudden, ridiculous notion to pull her to her feet and cradle her protectively in his arms.

Instead he said gruffly, "You're not poverty stricken, you know. You should make enough from the sale of this ranch to provide you with a sufficient income for life."

"I won't sell Palekaiko."

When Lani rose to her feet and faced him, he saw that the lavender-shaded eyes shimmered in the firelight but held no trace of tears. And the softly curved mouth was set with a disconcerting firmness as she asked, "How much longer can I keep the ranch going on the funds that are left in the estate?"

"Four, five years at the most." Exasperation boomed in Adam's voice. "You don't think I'll let you throw away your last cent on a ranch that even in your father's time never turned a good profit!"

"You can't force me to sell the ranch." He saw the flash of anger in the violet eyes, staring at him defiantly. "Perhaps I should talk to a lawyer. I must have some rights under the law."

Adam winced mentally. It wasn't the idea of her going to court that bothered him, or even the field day the newspapers would be sure to have with such a case. Any sensible judge would agree with him that the girl was too young to know what she was doing. What did alarm him was the thought that if the case went to court, Lani was bound to discover that legally he was half owner of her beloved Palekaiko. And she would learn all the rest, too, the real truth about her uncle, how he had gambled away her inheritance. Perhaps even the unvarnished facts about Daniel's death would come out. And no matter how much he would like to shake some sense into the girl, he couldn't let that happen.

Sensing that she had her guardian on the defensive, Lani

smiled mockingly. "Or I could marry. Then you wouldn't be my guardian any longer, would you?"

Adam rose swiftly to his feet and in two strides was standing before the girl, his hands gripping her shoulders. He could feel the warmth of that young, vibrant body through the silk of her *holoku*, see the proud, upthrust breasts rising and falling rapidly in her rage. And suddenly, unaccountably, he knew he didn't want to shake the girl. What he wanted to do was take that taut, hostile body into his arms and caress those smoothly passionate lips with his own until that rage changed into an equally heated, trembling passion. Swiftly, angrily he thrust the thought aside. What was the matter with him? He wasn't some lovesick, unshaven boy, unable to master his desire for every passing female. And for all of Lani Tucker's grown-up airs, the girl wasn't many years out of the cradle.

It was anger, more at himself than at Lani, that darkened his face. "Do what you damn well please, Miss Tucker." The gray eyes traveled rakingly over the silken *holoku* clinging so seductively to the girl's body. "Only remember," he warned coldly, "if you're going to play at behaving like a full-grown woman, you'd better expect to be treated like one."

After the front door had slammed behind Adam Stewart, Lani discovered she was trembling. She wasn't sure whether it was from fear because she suspected that Adam Stewart was not a man accustomed to accepting defeat, or a reaction to the vague, undefinable emotion that had surged through her when those hands had bit into the flesh of her shoulders, and those hard gray eyes had mercilessly raked her body. She hugged her arms tightly to her chest. Still, she thought, triumphantly, she had won. Palekaiko would not be sold away from her.

As she undressed for bed, though, her sense of discomfort, the knowledge that she had made an enemy of Adam Stewart, a man she sensed would not forgive or forget easily, returned and remained with her until she restlessly went to stand at the window that looked out upon Haleakala. As always, the view of the mountain, moonlight spilling down its lava studded slopes, the scent of the rich night fragrance from the garden, the faint, distant sound of the ocean, of birds closer at hand, cooing sleepily, filled her with a peace and contentment almost too great to be borne. She would never sell Palekaiko, she thought fiercely.

Her naturally youthful confidence buoyed her. After all, she had four or five years to think of some way to raise the money to keep the ranch going. Why, in five years anything was possible! And although she had mentioned marriage to her guardian only to annoy him, it was a possibility. A smile teased at the corners of Lani's sweetly curved lips as Keith Stewart's face slipped easily into her mind.

Moment by moment she happily relived the evening, remembering how Keith hadn't been able to keep his eyes off her at the dinner table, the warmth of his smile in the front parlor when he had raised his glass to her and called her the beautiful mistress of Palekaiko, his flattering insistence upon introducing her to the court of Kalakaua. For a second Lani's smile faded, remembering Rebecca's swift rejection of that offer, but she quickly shrugged aside her tutor's odd behavior. She was sure she could change Rebecca's mind, and hadn't Keith practically promised her that he would be her escort at her first court ball?

When she finally fell asleep, it was to dream of herself at Iolani Palace, a guest at the royal ball in honor of the king's return to Hawaii. She was wearing a silver ball gown, and she was dancing, floating, in the arms of Keith Stewart, who was gazing down at her with an adoring smile on his darkly handsome face.

Honolulu was in the midst of preparing a lavish homecoming celebration for King Kalakaua when Liliuokalani rode in the royal barouche along Fort Street. It was early in the morning, but workers were already busy festooning garlands of evergreens over the arches that had been constructed at the wharf area. Banners and pictures of the king could be seen everywhere. At first sight of the *Charleston* rounding Diamond Head with the king aboard, fire bells would ring, the other ships in the harbor would fire their guns, and the royal salute would be given from the battery at Punchbowl Hill. And Liliuokalani's days acting as princess-regent in her brother's absence would once again end.

*   *   *

As the princess gazed, almost absently, at the crowds of people already thronging the streets in anticipation of her brother's arrival, she knew it wasn't giving up her role as regent that filled her with foreboding. It was the whispers that she had heard among her servants at Washington Place, that "the red fish had come up from the sea." The red fish were the traditional sign of the death of royalty. If only, Liliuokalani thought now, the cable between California and Hawaii had been laid she would at least have some news of her brother.

Then she sat up straighter in the carriage, pushing aside her uneasiness as she smiled and nodded at the Hawaiians who recognized the handsome woman in the carriage. She was being foolishly superstitious, Liliuokalani told herself sternly. Still the disturbing thought lingered. The red fish had appeared, hadn't they?

After completing several official calls, the royal carriage arrived back at Iolani Palace, driving down a short *allee* between rows of young royal palms. On the left, amid a grove of trees, Liliuokalani could see a low frame building with latticed verandas, the king's bungalow, reconstructed after Wilcox's ill-fated uprising. To the right stood the octagonal pavilion built for Kalakaua's coronation, where court concerts were now held. As the carriage stopped before the rococo palace, tier upon tier, still sparkling new and gleaming like an iced wedding cake, native footmen ran down the grand staircase to open the carriage door for the princess.

Walking up the stairs and into the long, narrow reception hall, Liliuokalani caught a glimpse of herself in one of the ornate gold-framed mirrors that lined the wall. It was fortunate, she thought, smiling to herself, that the Hawaiian people preferred large women. Even when she had been young and slender, she had never been a beauty like her sister, Bernice, or her niece, Princess Kaiulani, but she had never lacked for dance partners or suitors, she remembered proudly. And despite her fifty-two years, her black hair now streaked with gray, she still carried herself with a youthful grace, her dark eyes reflected in the mirror, large and sparkling with a zest for living.

Then she saw the royal chamberlain hurrying across the hall to her. At the look of sorrow on his face, the premonition she had felt earlier returned full force so that she knew at once what had happened before the man told her. The *Charleston* had been sighted sailing around Diamond Head with her yards cockbilled and her American and Hawaiian flags at half-mast.

Her brother was dead, Liliuokalani thought, her throat aching with grief. Instead of being greeted with a joyous celebration, the *Charleston* was bringing David Kalakaua's body home. Then from the top of the split staircase that vaulted gracefully to the second floor of the palace, she heard a woman's terrible scream, sending shivers down her spine. She cast a helpless glance at the chamberlain. "The queen knows?"

He nodded.

"I must go to her," Liliuokalani said quickly.

Before she could move, he said quietly, "Your ministers are waiting for you in the Blue Room, Your Majesty."

She stared at him, dazed, at first not understanding. Her ministers? Then pulling upon a strength that had always been the bedrock of her character, she faced the fact that her womanly concern for her sister-in-law would have to wait. She wasn't simply a woman anymore. She was the queen. From now on, affairs of state must always come first.

That same afternoon, as soon as the *Charleston* docked and Admiral Brown relayed the sad news to the palace that his royal passenger, King Kalakaua, had, indeed, died in San Francisco after a lingering illness, Liliuokalani was informed that a meeting of the Supreme Court and the cabinet had decided she must take the oath of office immediately.

"Can't it wait?" she asked, shocked. Her brother's body hadn't yet reached the palace.

Then she saw her husband walk slowly into the room, his face gray with pain, and she hurried to him. John was so feeble with his rheumatism that he seldom left his room these days.

"Thank you for coming, my dear," she said, reaching out her arms to him, but remembering just in time how he hated public displays of affection she let her arms drop to her side. She glanced toward the ministers, gathered to witness her taking the oath of office, and said unhappily to John, "Can't this wait until after David's funeral?"

Irritation disrupted the gray pallor of her husband's face as he retorted, "Of course it can't wait. It's the law. You must be sworn in immediately."

Reluctantly she turned back to the gathering. It wasn't being rushed into taking the oath that upset her, she realized, as Chief Justice Judd read the oath of office aloud and she lifted her hand over the Bible. It was being hurried into swearing to uphold the bayonet constitution, a constitution that every man in this room must know she hated with all her being. The new constitution had made her brother into little more than a figurehead, and deprived her people of their rights as surely as they had deprived the king of his royal powers.

No doubt they expected her to accept their constitution with as little protest as her brother had, she thought, struggling to hold her temper in check at the reception held in the Blue Room immediately after the swearing-in ceremony. It was difficult to maintain her composure, though, especially when Chief Justice Judd came up to her at the reception and advised, "Should any of the members of your cabinet propose anything to you, say yes!"

When she stared at him, puzzled by this sweeping statement, the minister of foreign affairs informed her arrogantly, as if he were lecturing a not too bright student, "The cabinet naturally intends to remain as it is. No changes can, of course, be made without the consent of the legislature."

That wasn't true, Liliuokalani realized, gazing coldly at the man. Surely at her brother's death she would have the right to appoint her own cabinet. But this wasn't the time or place for a quarrel, not with her brother's body due to arrive at the palace at any moment, and still facing her, the long, exhausting ritual of a royal funeral.

"I shall defer all political matters until after my brother's funeral," she said in her soft, musical voice. There was something about the resolute set of her chin, the way she held her head with the arrogance of an early Kamehameha accustomed to absolute obedience, that made the ministers present gaze at one another, dismayed. Queen Liliuokalani dismissed them with a curt nod of her head and swept regally from the room.

Chapter 11

The news of King Kalakaua's death spread rapidly through Honolulu. Festive decorations to greet the returning monarch were hastily torn down from streets and buildings and replaced with black bunting. Throughout the gloomy, cloudy day, grieving crowds of natives gathered outside the palace grounds. Forgotten now were the king's faults, the whispered debaucheries at the parties at his boat house, his spendthrift habits. What was remembered was his merry, generous nature, and the great love he had for his people.

David Kalakaua's body lay in state in the Red Chamber of the palace, his casket placed on a cloth of scarlet and yellow feathers. Only those guards who could claim ancestry from ancient Hawaiian chiefs bore aloft the royal plumed feather standards, the *kahilis*, at the bier. The Hawaiian death wail and mourners chanting traditional *meles* intermingled with the singing of Christian hymns, requested by the new queen.

After the state funeral service, the casket was carried in a long, colorful procession through the Nuuanu Valley to the Royal Mausoleum. When the family was finally left alone in the tomb, Queen Kapiolani, sobbing hysterically, flung herself on the coffin of her husband. Liliuokalani stiffened her back, aching from the injury she had received years before when she was flung from a runaway carriage, and refused to give way to her grief even as the dank cold of the tomb seemed to sink into her bones. Her gaze moved broodingly around the interior of the dimly-lit tomb, the crypts of former kings, queens, and high chiefs, lit by flickering candles.

The bones of Kamehameha I were not to be found here, she knew. Following the ancient custom of his time, his body had been hidden away on the island of Hawaii, so that his bones could never be found and defiled. Before he had died, though, Kamehameha had seen the Hawaiian islands joined in one strong, peaceful kingdom, so that on his deathbed he could proudly tell his people, "Endless is the good that I leave for you to enjoy."

What would Kamehameha think if he could see his kingdom today, Liliuokalani wondered, his people decimated by foreign diseases, *haoles* owning the life of the land, the Hawaiian people themselves becoming aliens, outcasts in their own country. The foreign newspapers were even predicting that in a few short years the Hawaiian people and their way of life would disappear completely. Well, she would not let it happen, she thought, her heavy-featured face, the dark, intelligent eyes, taking on a stubborn, ebony hardness. She was the queen now, *moi wahine*, the mother of her people. She would protect them as a mother does her children. And although she could speak faultless English, as well as French and German, Liliuokalani realized that she was no longer thinking in English, but in Hawaiian, her native language.

On the outer islands, in the deep valleys where the natives still lived in simple huts in the old Hawaiian fashion, taking only what they needed from the soil, pounding taro root into poi, growing fish in mud-walled ponds as their ancestors had done, the grief at a king's death was not so restrained. For days and nights on end, their wails of sorrow echoed and reechoed, floating up and down the valley.

In the big house at Palekaiko, sitting in the front parlor with Rebecca, Lani could hear the faint ghostly sound drifting in through the open windows.

"I wish they'd stop!" she said, shivering. "It sounds so . . ." She fell silent, looking sideways, embarrassed, at her companion.

"Pagan?" Rebecca asked mildly, looking up from her sewing. "At least it's better than the days when mourners would file their teeth to points and shave off their hair to show their respect for a dead chief."

Lani shuddered. "I had a tutor once who told me that the Hawaiians were no better than savages, worshipping heathen idols, until the missionaries came to these islands."

Rebecca nodded thoughtfully. "The early chiefs and their

kapus were savage and cruel. But not much earlier, in Spain, men, women, and children were tortured and burned at the stake for being heretics; in America, black people were being sold into slavery; and in England, children were forced to work from dawn to dark in factories. And these were acts by supposedly civilized people."

Rebecca's voice grew brisk. "But your tutor was wrong about one thing. It wasn't the missionaries who rid these islands of the worship of idols. It was a remarkable queen-regent, Kaahumanu, who in 1819 had the courage and wisdom to overthrow the *kapu* system and order the idols to be burned."

A proud smile suddenly illuminated Rebecca's face. "You know I believe the *haoles* in the government will find that our new Queen Liliuokalani has much the same spirit and intelligence as Kaahumanu."

It occurred to Lani that it was the first time in two weeks that she had seen her tutor smile. It was also the first time since the night of the dinner party that she and Rebecca had talked together as they did now, without an odd feeling of constraint between them. Remembering the dinner party suddenly reminded Lani that, with the court in mourning, there would be no ball to which Keith Stewart could escort her.

Putting down her sewing, she got restlessly to her feet. "I don't suppose I'll ever be presented at court now," she said wistfully.

Watching the girl's unhappy face, Rebecca sighed to herself. She had watched her young charge mope around the house these last weeks and was sure it wasn't not being presented at court that was making Lani so miserable. The girl was wondering if she would ever see Keith Stewart again. Rebecca had recognized only too well the bewitched expression on the girl's face when Keith had smiled at her. It was the same look Rebecca had seen on the faces of other women mesmerized by the man's charm. Undoubtedly it was the same look that had been on her own face when she had first met Keith.

Even now, when she was well aware how worthless any promises the man might make were, how luckless a woman was to be trapped in the web of that amoral charm, Keith

Stewart had only to walk through the door and she knew blindly, inexorably, she would go to him. She had told herself it was to protect Lani against the man that she had allowed him into her cottage, and into her bed, but she knew that was only partly true. The moment Keith had placed his hands on her, she had felt in her body the treacherous response to his touch, the terrible hunger that possessed her to have him hold her even closer.

It was like an illness, she decided hopelessly, a fever in her blood, and no matter how she fought against it, she would never be free. Desperation pulled at her nerves as she saw the misery shadowing Lani's young face. It was as if she were watching someone she loved racing toward a fatal abyss, and was forced to stand by, helpless, unable to save her. For she knew by now her pupil's headstrong nature. If she forbade the girl to see Keith, it would only make the man more tempting in Lani's eyes, make her more determined than ever to see him again.

Picking up her sewing, she said quietly, "Mr. Keith Stewart is very attractive, isn't he?"

And watched, trying to hide her distress, as Lani's eyes were suddenly radiant, her young face incandescent as she said eagerly, "Oh, yes, he is, isn't he?"

Rebecca pretended to be engrossed in her sewing. "I'm sure Miss Nellie Samuels considers herself a very fortunate young lady."

Lani knew Nellie from school, a not too attractive young lady who was very proud of the fact that her banker father was one of the wealthiest men in Hawaii. "Nellie?" She stared at Rebecca, bewildered. She couldn't imagine a girl like Nellie even knowing a man like Keith Stewart.

"I believe they've been keeping company for several months now," Rebecca said.

"How . . . how do you know?"

Because he told me. Rebecca swallowed the words as she had swallowed her pride and rage when, her body still warm from their lovemaking, Keith had told her about the girl in Honolulu he was planning to marry. "Nellie's plain as a mud fence," he said, propping himself on an elbow and smiling lazily down at Rebecca. "Fortunately William Samuels is wealthy enough to make up for any lack of beauty in his daughter.''

Rebecca looked down to see a drop of blood on her hand and realized, startled, that she had jabbed her needle into her finger and hadn't felt the pain.

"I don't believe it!" Lani protested, her voice childishly shrill. "It's not true."

Rebecca turned her attention back to Lani, to the girl's forlorn face. "I'm afraid it is true," she said quietly. "Mr. Stewart told me himself. The engagement hasn't been announced as yet. I suppose they're waiting until the court comes out of mourning."

She pretended not to see the pain that filled the amethyst eyes as she rolled up her sewing and rose in one swift, graceful movement to her feet. "I understand that once the mourning period for the king has finished, the new queen plans to tour the islands, to meet with as many of her subjects as possible. There are sure to be parties given in her honor wherever she goes. Why don't you invite Liliuokalani to Palekaiko?"

For a moment, Lani forgot her own unhappiness as she blurted, shocked, "The queen . . . here?"

Rebecca shrugged, smiling. "Why not? I've been told Kalakaua, as well as many other famous people, visited the ranch when your father was alive." Her glance moved approvingly around the spacious front parlor, the comfortable blend of Oriental and Hawaiian furnishings, the look of luxury now a little threadbare around the edges but still beautiful to the eye. "We can hold a luau in the garden and invite all the people from the neighboring ranches and plantations."

Lani found herself caught up in Rebecca's plans. She remembered the luaus that had been held at Palekaiko when she had been a child, the women guests like exotic flowers in their colorful gowns, the delicious smells when the pig was taken from the heated, porous stones of the *imu,* the sound of the dancing and the music of drums and guitars. Her father had always looked so young and handsome in his white flannels and cummerbund when he came to her bedroom and fetched her so that she could watch the festivities for a little while before carrying her off again to bed.

"Do you really think Queen Liliuokalani will accept?"

Her tutor answered by grinning mischievously. "Didn't I tell you? I have friends at court."

The reply to Lani's carefully written invitation to the royal chamberlain came with flattering swiftness. The queen and her entourage would be delighted during her state visit to Maui to be the guests of honor at a luau at the Tucker ranch. In a postscript, the queen sent her aloha to Rebecca.

"You didn't tell me you knew Liliuokalani," Lani said accusingly.

Rebecca looked up from the lists she was already starting to make, preparing for the royal party. "I was a member of the Princess Liliuokalani's household, many years ago. It was the princess who gave me the money to attend Mills College in California. The princess was always generous to the lowliest servant as well as high *alii* who had become paupers with no understanding or skills for existing in the new *haole*'s world. Her husband would scold her for giving away her money so freely, but the princess could never turn away anyone in need."

"Some of the newspapers are saying that the queen is autocratic with an ungovernable temper," Lani said.

Rebecca straightened, her own eyes snapping with anger. "Only because she insisted upon a cabinet of her own choice, and the Supreme Court agreed with her. As for the stories Wilcox and Bush are writing in their newspaper about the queen—that because she is a woman, she is too weak to rule—I don't blame her for threatening to have their press smashed to pieces. I would, too, although, of course, the queen would never permit such an act to take place. She knows Bush and Wilcox are *huhu* because they didn't receive political posts in her government."

Lani remembered that morning . . . how long ago it seemed now . . . when she had watched Robert Wilcox, after his failed attack upon the palace, being led away, a prisoner. That was the same morning, she also remembered, when she had first met Keith. Thinking of Keith Stewart marrying another woman, she felt a swift, almost unendurable thrust of pain.

Glancing at the girl, seeing the unhappiness in her face,

Rebecca said briskly, "We'll have a great deal to do before the luau. First, we should decide upon the guest list. . . ."

The next weeks Lani was kept so busy, what with making plans for the royal visit, along with the usual heavy ranch work that took place every spring, that she fell into bed, exhausted, each night. Fleetingly, she wondered if that hadn't been Rebecca's reasoning behind the luau, to keep her pupil too occupied to have the time or energy to think of Keith Stewart. When Lani wasn't working with the *paniolos* at the paddocks, separating bawling calves from their mothers so they could be branded, ears notched, and inoculated against blackleg, she was working with Rebecca, deciding upon the guest list, decorations, and menu for the luau.

Instead of serving the food at the luau in the traditional way, on mats on the ground, Rebecca had decided that low wooden tables would be built by the ranch carpenter and placed beneath the trees in the garden. The Japanese gardeners worked night and day, raking the lawn and cleaning the lily ponds, pruning the shrubs and flower beds, making sure that not one browned leaf or wilted blossom could be found. Then, the day before the luau, earthen pits for the *imus* were dug, and every worker who could be spared went into the forests with pack horses to gather fragrant maile vines for leis and *palapalai* ferns to cover the tables.

The morning of the royal luau Lani was up before dawn spilled over the summit of Haleakala. Although the royal party wasn't expected until afternoon, guests began arriving at the ranch late in the morning and had to be greeted. In her reply accepting the invitation, the queen had asked that not only the owners and managers of the sugar plantations and ranches be asked to the luau, but the workers, too, as well as the Hawaiians who lived in the neighboring small villages. The garden soon filled with *haole* women in fashionable gowns and men in white flannel suits, along with young, screaming Hawaiian children, their legs flashing in the sunlight, plump *wahines* proudly displaying their Sunday best *holokus*, elderly men with feather leis around their hats and *tutus* with happy, wrinkled faces sunning themselves along the garden paths.

Rebecca seemed to be everywhere at once, moving calmly

through the confusion, checking the myriad of details, while Kimiko hovered over the fern-covered tables, arranging and rearranging the flowers, and Loki oversaw the twining of maile leis around the trunks of trees. The delicate scent of the maile soon mingled with the fragrance of roses, oleanders, Chinese star jasmine, and wild ginger, perfuming the air.

On a small platform, *paniolo* musicians practiced their songs while happily sipping from bottles of *okolehao,* and in the kitchen a red-faced Charlie was shouting orders to everybody.

At the last minute, waiting on the front lanai for the queen to arrive, Lani, in a clinging, pale pink *holoku* and wearing an open lei of entwined maile and pink rosebuds, turned nervously to Rebecca. "Show me again how to curtsy. I'll fall flat on my face. I know I will."

But it was too late for further instructions. The *paniolos,* who had gone to escort the queen's party up the steep, winding road to the ranch, rode proudly up to the house on either side of a procession of flower-decorated carriages.

The guests pressed forward, the better to see the queen as she stepped out of the lead carriage. As Rebecca dipped into a graceful curtsy, Liliuokalani smiled and reaching out her hand, pulling the young woman into a warm embrace. "It's been too long, my child."

She turned the warm smile upon Lani as Rebecca made introductions. "I remember seeing your grandmother once, years ago, at a court ball." The queen's dark eyes sparkled in memory. "I was too young to attend, of course, but several of us at the Royal School played hooky to watch the ball from the palace garden. I remember seeing your Grandmother Jasmine arrive. She wore a gold brocade gown and was quite the most beautiful woman I'd ever seen. You look much like her."

Dumbstruck, Lani looked into the round face, the dark, expressive eyes of the woman standing before her and was all at once reminded of a picture she had seen of Queen Victoria. Liliuokalani bore herself with the same proud grace of one born to royalty.

At the last second, flustered, she remembered to bow, and arising from her curtsy saw Adam Stewart standing beside one of the carriages, watching her, amusement dancing in the dark gray eyes.

"You both must sit at my table," Liliuokalani murmured to Lani and Rebecca before turning to greet the other guests.

Lani edged closer to her guardian. "What are you doing here?" she demanded, annoyed.

"I was invited, of course. And the queen very kindly allowed me to accompany her entourage."

His name hadn't been on the invitation list that she had seen, Lani thought, casting an irritated glance at Rebecca, who discreetly hurried away.

She looked hopefully beyond Adam to the empty carriages, and his brows drew together into a scowl as Adam said curtly, "My brother's not with me, if that's who you're looking for."

Lani felt her face grow warm, infuriated that he could read her thoughts so easily. Was she so obvious then, her feelings about Keith so apparent? "Considering your support of the Missionary party," she said tartly, "I'm surprised to see you in the queen's company."

Adam gazed after Liliuokalani, who was moving among the guests, smiling and gracious. "Oh, I have nothing against the queen. I'm sure she'll be a much better ruler than her brother, that is, if she's wise enough to agree to a constitutional rather than an autocratic monarchy."

"You mean a monarchy run by the *haoles* and the Missionary party, don't you?"

The flash of amusement returned to the gray eyes. "I had no idea you had turned into such a rabid royalist."

"Why shouldn't I be loyal to the queen?" Lani demanded hotly. Contempt laced her voice. "Unlike some people who were born in these islands, my loyalty is to Hawaii, not to America." She swept the train of her *holoku* over her arm. "Now if you'll excuse me," she said coldly. "I have guests to look after."

The rest of the afternoon she deliberately stayed away from Adam Stewart, which wasn't difficult with the crush of people at the luau needing her attention. Lani worried that they would run out of food, but somehow Charlie miraculously managed to keep the tables groaning with succulent roast pork, calabashes of pink poi, chicken stewed in coconut milk, dried shrimp, butter-yellow *opihis*, and salmon mixed

with plump tomatoes and onions. For dessert, there were two
kinds of pudding—rich, dark *kulolo* resembling an English
plum pudding, and semitransparent slices of *haupia,* tasting
deliciously of coconut—along with polished wooden bowls
heaped high with mangoes, pineapples, bananas, and ruby-
colored mountain apples.

When the tables became too crowded, the guests took their
food and casually sat under the trees, eating and gossiping
and listening to the *paniolos* playing loud, rollicking tunes on
their guitars and ukuleles. Lani stopped a moment to listen to
the fragments of music and laughter. Her eyes half-closed,
she could almost imagine she was a child again at one of her
father's parties, during the long, sun-filled, happy days she
had spent here at Palekaiko that she had never thought would
end.

Then someone clapped his hands for silence and the queen
rose to her feet and made a short speech, first in Hawaiian,
then in perfect English. She spoke of the need to renew the
Hawaiian nation. "Foreigners have prophesied the extinction
of our people, of our land. Shall we sit by and see the
structure erected by our fathers fall to pieces? If the house is
dilapidated, let us repair it; let us renovate and educate our-
selves to the end that the nation may grow again with new life
and vigor."

Every guest at the luau knew that the first official visit
Liliuokalani had made as queen was to Molokai, making her
the only monarch to visit the tragic lepers isolated there. It
was as if by her visit Liliuokalani had proclaimed that she was
queen of all Hawaiians, the poor and the helpless as well
as the rich and the powerful. As the queen spoke, Lani could
see in the faces of the Hawaiians present the pride and love
they felt for their queen, an almost visible outpouring of
aloha.

"You look exhausted." Lani turned to discover her guardian standing beside her. Adam frowned, studying Lani's face.
"Have you eaten at all?"

Lani realized with a start that she had forgotten to eat. No
wonder she felt so light-headed, she thought, but when she
started toward the tables, Adam's hand on her shoulder gently
pressed her to the ground. "Wait here," he said.

In a few moments he returned with a plate filled with food, then stretched comfortably out on the grass beside Lani. My *holoku* will be ruined with grass stains, Lani thought, but she was much too hungry to care. She was even too tired to mind that when she finished eating Adam showed no inclination to leave. At least he didn't try and make conversation, she thought, relieved, closing her eyes and leaning her head back against the trunk of a kukui tree, breathing in the faint, woody scent of anise from her maile lei, now beginning to wilt.

When she opened her eyes again, she was dismayed to see that it was dusk. The Chinese lanterns hanging between the trees had been lit, and kukui torches burned like golden flowers in the garden. She was even more dismayed when she realized that Adam Stewart must have watched her sleeping, making her feel somehow vulnerable, as if her privacy had been invaded.

With his irritating habit of guessing what she was thinking, Adam murmured, amused, "Don't worry. You look very nice asleep."

Lani glared at the man—as if she cared what he thought! —and started to scramble to her feet. Adam's hand on her shoulder prevented her from rising. He nodded toward the sound of drums coming from the trees around them. "The dancing's about to begin."

To the slow, deliberate beat of the hidden drums was now added the cadenced chanting of men and women seated in a semicircle on the grass, their grave faces caught and then hidden in the flickering torch lights. Adam's hand still on her shoulder, Lani sank back to the ground. The drums and chanting built slowly toward a crescendo, the night filled with the sounds, the air reverberating around her like surf crashing against the shore.

From an opening in the trees near where Lani and Adam sat, a dancer appeared, then several more. All the young women had their dark hair unbound, garlands of flowers around their heads, necks, wrists, and ankles as they swayed in unison to the beat of the drums, their ti-leaf skirts making soft, whispering sounds. Gracefully gesturing hands and arms invoked pictures of warm rain falling, wind blowing, the moon rising, and flowers blooming. All the glories and wonders of nature were animated by the movements of the supple, swaying dancers.

The drums picked up their beat, the chanters' voices growing shriller, the dancers making sharp, staccato answers but never missing a beat, never a foot or gesture awkward or out of place. Lani had seen hula dancers before—Loki had even taught her a few basic steps—but she had never seen dancing like this. These women, she suspected, were dancers carefully trained at Kalakaua's court. His detractors said the dancers had been taught for the king's own personal gratification, for entertainment at the parties he gave at his boathouse; others insisted it was an effort by the king to revive and preserve the ancient, traditional hulas, telling Hawaii's history through *meles* and dance.

Then the dancers, like waves, parted, and another woman came from behind the trees to join them, stepping so close to Lani that she could have reached out and touched Rebecca. Rebecca! Lani straightened, her eyes widening, startled. Her tutor hadn't changed from her *holoku,* and to Lani's mind the lithe, undulating body moving beneath the silken sheath was much more sensuous than the swishing ti-leaf skirts. The chanting and the drums were softer now; Rebecca's answering call, a high, mournful wail, sent shivers down Lani's spine. One graceful movement of the hula glided effortlessly into the next, telling the story of a mortal woman attracted into a forbidden love affair with a handsome young god.

As the drums grew louder, the chanting more insistent, the sensual movements of the dancer's hips faster, Lani could picture the passionate possession of the young woman by her god-lover in a furious, rhapsodic lovemaking. All at once she was acutely aware of Adam's hand still resting on her shoulder. The heat from that hand, from the man's body, seemed to pass through her flesh and radiate a delicious warmth through her own body. She knew if she were to turn her head she would see those dark gray eyes fastened upon her. If she were to turn and look into those eyes . . .

The soft mournful cries coming from Rebecca's lips all at once escalated into a heartrending wail, as the dancer discovered her lover was gone and she was alone. The dancer's movements were slower now, almost painful, accepting her loss, her face growing blank and empty with despair, until, as she disappeared once more behind the bamboo thicket, it was as if she hadn't left but had faded away into nothingness.

There had been complete silence in the audience as Rebecca danced, but now suddenly there was a rustling, an appreciative murmur as the chanting and drums abruptly ceased. Lani, as if shaking away a spell, pulled herself free from that hand resting lightly, possessively, on her shoulder and stumbled to her feet.

She turned and saw Rebecca moving, wraithlike, between the trees, past the burning kukui torches. Lani started toward her, almost at the same moment that she saw a sudden breeze tease a golden flame from a torch toward the sleeve of Rebecca's pale green *holoku*. Horrified, Lani watched as the gauzy material of the gown caught fire. She did not even realize as she ran toward the woman that she was the one screaming in terror—not Rebecca.

Chapter 12

As quickly as Lani moved, Adam was at Rebecca's side before her. He flung the woman to the ground, beating at the flaming sleeve with his own hands, tearing away the flimsy material so that the flames could spread no further. As fast as he had acted, Lani could see the skin on Rebecca's arm already turning an angry, mottled red where the fire had touched.

Rebecca was staring at her arm, her dark eyes beneath glistening eyelids wide with shock, as if she still did not comprehend what had happened.

Lani helped Rebecca to her feet, her own voice shaken. "Are you all right? Is the pain very bad?"

"No." Rebecca turned a dazed gaze toward Adam. For

a moment, panic twisted her face. "No, it's not bad at all."

"I'll send for a doctor," Lani said.

"No!" Then, more quietly, Rebecca shook her head and said, "There's no need to make a fuss. I have some ointment at the cottage that will take care of the burns. You stay with your guests."

Before Lani could protest further, Adam intervened. "Rebecca's right. The queen will be leaving soon. As the hostess, you should be here to bid her farewell." At Lani's concerned look, he added, "Don't worry. I'll take Rebecca to her cottage and make sure her arm's looked after."

Reluctantly, Lani returned to her guests. Only a few had seen the near tragedy, and Lani assured them that fortunately Rebecca had come to no great harm. The queen had another party she was to go to that evening, and was preparing to leave as Lani joined her.

"You're sure Rebecca is all right?" Liliuokalani asked Lani, having been informed of what had happened by one of her ladies attending her. "You will give her my warmest wishes for her swift recovery?"

"Yes, Your Majesty," Lani said.

A sadness touched the dark, expressive eyes. "You are very fortunate, child, to have a good friend like Rebecca, someone you can trust implicitly. Such friends are difficult to find." As if shrugging away unhappy thoughts, she quickly smiled and said, "When you visit Honolulu, you must attend a party at the palace so that I can return your delightful hospitality today."

Even after the guest of honor had left, the other guests at the luau lingered, the music growing less sedate as the hour grew later, the hula dancers more risqué. It was almost three o'clock before the last guests had left, carrying sleeping children in their arms, and an exhausted Lani made her way to Rebecca's cottage. The small cottage was dark. Probably Rebecca was getting some much-needed sleep, Lani decided, standing a moment at the door then turning slowly away.

The next morning, as soon as she awakened, she hurried back to the cottage. To her surprise, the door stood open. She knocked, and when she received no answer stepped inside.

Almost before she saw the envelope with her name on it on the hall table, she sensed that Rebecca was gone. The cottage had an empty, forsaken look about it. A feeling of foreboding gripped her as she opened the envelope, pulled out the sheet of paper, and read.

My dearest Lani,

Please forgive my abrupt leave-taking, but I've always hated lengthy good-byes. By the time you read this, I will have already gone to my new teaching position. I was so very proud of you tonight at the luau, and knew, as I've already suspected for many weeks now, that my pupil was no longer in need of my services. You have learned all that I can teach you, and as is the lot of all teachers, I must let you go to make your own way in life. I know that I will be proud of you in whatever you undertake, and in my heart I will always carry for you my deepest aloha.

When Lani burst into the Big House a few seconds later, she was startled to find Adam Stewart sitting at the big koa table in the dining room, having coffee. She had supposed that her guardian had left with the other guests the night before. "She's gone!" she blurted. "Rebecca's gone."

"Oh?" Adam calmly put down his coffee cup and reached for the letter Lani was waving in his face. After reading it, he said, "Rather sudden decision, wasn't it?"

Lani studied the man's face, but except for a look of strain about the eyes she could read nothing in his carefully guarded expression. Yet somehow she was sure that her guardian was not surprised at her news. "You knew, didn't you?" she demanded accusingly. "Rebecca told you she was leaving, didn't she? Why didn't you stop her?"

"Miss Kalia was my employee. I didn't own her," Adam said. "She's free to come and go as she wishes." He shrugged. "Apparently she decided it was time she moved on."

"Well, she can't go, not like this, not without saying good-bye," Lani protested. She whirled toward the door. "She can't have gone far. I'll saddle Jubal and . . ."

Adam thrust back his chair so violently getting to his feet

that it fell over onto the floor with a crash. "You'll stay where you are!" he commanded sharply.

Lani turned, startled at the rage in the man's voice, the fury in his face, No, not fury, she thought, surprised. If she hadn't known better, she would have sworn it was fear she saw in her guardian's face. Adam threw his napkin on the table and stalked around the fallen chair to stand before Lani. When he spoke, each word was clipped. "You will make no attempt to find Miss Kalia. She has made her decision, and you will respect her wishes. Is that clear?"

He jerked his chin toward the door. "What you will do is go to your room and pack your clothes. You'll be returning with me to Honolulu on the next steamer."

"And what if I choose to remain here at Palekaiko?" Lani asked, her voice frosty. "In case you haven't noticed, Mr. Stewart, I'm no longer a child that you can order about as you please."

"Oh, I've noticed," Adam said grimly, his glance sweeping over the slender figure standing defiantly before him. Lani was wearing her riding outfit, and the faded dungarees hugged the slim hips and long legs, the cotton palaka shirt outlining the provocative breasts. "Which is exactly why I have no intention of letting you remain here at the ranch without a proper chaperone."

Beneath that familiar, and yet oddly impersonal, glance, Lani found herself remembering the evening before at the luau, the disturbing pulsation of the drums and chanters, the erotic swaying of the dancers' hips, and Adam Stewart's hand resting lightly, possessively, on her shoulder, so that for a moment she had felt curiously breathless, feeling the man's warmth flow through her body. If only it had been Keith Stewart instead of his brother, she thought, wistfully. If only . . .

Of course! Elation surged through her. If she was living in Honolulu, she would have the perfect excuse to see Keith again. Honolulu's society was not that large. She was almost certain to run into him at parties and social gatherings. She could even give parties herself at her uncle's spacious home, beautifully organized balls, so that Keith could see that she would be the perfect wife and hostess for him. In time, she was confident she could make him forget all about Nellie Samuels.

Then she frowned, realizing that giving lavish balls, moving in wealthy social circles, possessing the new modish wardrobe she would need to make the proper impression on Keith, all that would take money. And she had none, except for the small allowance her guardian provided her.

She lowered her eyelids demurely. "If I should agree to go to Honolulu, Mr. Stewart, I would stay at my uncle's home, wouldn't I?"

"Why not? It's your home now."

His quick acceptance emboldened her so that she lifted her gaze and stared directly into his face. "And, of course, I'd need a staff to run the house, and a larger allowance so that I can entertain my friends properly." She made a face as she glanced down at her dungarees. "And naturally I'll need a new wardrobe."

The gray eyes narrowed, but not before she thought she saw again that flash of fear in their depths, just for a moment, before once more they were like slate, revealing nothing of what the man was thinking. "The house will be staffed," he said curtly. "As for the larger allowance, the clothes, and the entertaining, we can discuss that later."

And with that, reluctantly, Lani had to be satisfied. As she said her good-byes to Pili and the other ranch hands gathered to see her off, she had to keep reminding herself it wasn't as if she were leaving the ranch forever. And when she did return to Palekaiko, she would be a married woman, she thought proudly, with a husband to help her run the ranch, a husband who loved Palekaiko as much as she did.

It had been decided that Loki and Kimiko would return to Honolulu with her, but at the last moment Loki tearfully announced that she was staying at Palekaiko. "Too much hustle-bustle in Honolulu," she said when Lani tried to dissuade her. "I no like all that *pilikia*. Much better for me here on Maui with my friends."

Tears were caught in Lani's eyelashes as she stood at the rail of the steamer, watching the shining peak of Haleakala, the green, folded hills of Maui, fall away. How long would it be before she saw Palekaiko, again, and Rebecca? The memory of Rebecca's abrupt leave-taking was still raw and painful, leaving her with the same desolate feeling that had possessed her when her father had died suddenly of a heart attack, and her young, secure world had collapsed around her. And then, just as unexpectedly, her Uncle Daniel had died. Flinching, she shut from her mind the picture of her uncle, crumpled on the floor of his study, his blood making a scarlet blossom on the flowered rug.

"Is your cabin comfortable, Miss Tucker?"

She hadn't heard Adam Stewart come up beside her at the rail. The day had already grown warm, and he had removed his jacket. His shirt was open at the neck and his tall, muscular body was braced against the roll of the ship in the heavy seas. He looked as much at home on the deck of the ship, Lani thought absently, as she did riding Jubal.

"Yes, thank you." She glanced around the crowded deck where Hawaiians, Japanese, and Chinese families were already unrolling their sleeping mats, spreading out their food—moist bags of poi and string containers of rosy mangoes. From the forward deck, she could hear protesting, restless steers being shipped for sale to Honolulu, and smell the crates of pigs and chickens and bags of brown sugar packed away in the ship's hold.

"The ship's so crowded, I'm surprised you were able to get cabins at the last minute," she said, feeling a little uncomfortable beneath the man's intense scrutiny.

For a moment longer, his glance lingered on her face, then he turned away and said, "It helps if you own a partial interest in the Inter-Island Steamship Company." He studied ruefully the crowded, noisy deck of the squat, clumsy ship that had been obviously built as a workhorse, not for beauty or speed. "It isn't exactly a China clipper, is it?"

Lani wondered suddenly if her guardian missed being at sea, striding a quarterdeck instead of an office. "I've always wished I could have sailed aboard a three master, the way my grandmother Jasmine did," she said, turning her gaze back to the billowing sea. "She used to tell me wonderful stories about the days when she sailed aboard a whaler with my grandfather. There was one time when the ship was attacked by cannibals off the Gilberts."

"We never had any trouble with cannibals, chasing whales in Arctic waters," Adam said, smiling dourly. "Nothing more exciting than hunting whales twenty-four hours a day during the summer season when the sun hardly set, hoping you'd fill your hold and manage to head for home before the September freeze-up, before your ship, trapped in the ice, was crushed like an egg shell."

"Did that ever happen to you?"

"Once, but I wasn't a captain then. I was a second mate aboard the *Mariana*, whaling two hundred miles north of the Arctic Circle, off Point Lay. Unfortunately, the captain was greedy and waited too long. When the *Mariana* headed south, the sea was already frozen solid in one passageway, and in the other there were enough ice floes to smash a dozen ships. It was the first and last time I ever walked back from a whaling voyage."

"You walked alone across Alaska in the winter?" Lani asked incredulously.

"It was either go for help or sit around and hope a rescue expedition would reach us before we all starved to death or died of scurvy." The indentations on either side of Adam's mouth deepened into a grim smile. "I've never liked sitting around and waiting for anything. And I wasn't alone. I had two Eskimos with me and a dog sled that I fitted out like a sloop, with a mast and sail. It took us five months, but we finally reached civilization, a whaling station on Kodiak Island, over a thousand miles south of Port Lay. From there we were able to outfit a rescue expedition and go overland to the stranded whalers."

Adam turned his body so that his shoulders shielded Lani from the worst of the sun's rays as he continued his tale. "Before we reached Kodiak, we had to kill two of the dogs for food."

Lani listened, absorbed in the story of the trek of the three men across frozen, barren wastes, enduring blizzards that froze eyelids shut and struggling across the towering Alaska mountain range, as well as half-frozen water barriers where the treacherous ice cracked into floes beneath their sled. Although her companion made the undertaking sound almost lighthearted, like the audacious adventures of a foolhardy young man, she could imagine the terrible toll the trek must have taken on the three men.

She eyed her companion thoughtfully. She suspected that same foolhardy young man, who had refused to give up to the Arctic, had turned into the man who now stood beside her, just as determined to have his way in whatever he undertook.

"What happened to the Eskimos?" she asked when he had finished his story.

"Oh, I took them with me to Portland. They took one look at civilization and very sensibly decided they preferred their native village," Adam said, his mouth twisting into an ironic smile.

Then with a knowledgeable eye he observed the roiling sea and scudding, suddenly darkening clouds overhead. "The wind's rising. We'll be hitting rough water soon. You'll be more comfortable in your cabin."

Lani thought of the stuffy cabin and shook her head, her violet eyes sparkling as she gazed out at the white caps racing alongside the ship. "I like storms." She gave her guardian a mischievous, challenging smile. "Of course, if you'd prefer to go below . . ."

Adam didn't answer, but simply positioned his body closer to Lani's and braced himself more firmly as the ungainly ship caught the full force of the wind and the roughening seas. Lani's hands tightened on the railing. She felt the deck of the ship lift and fall beneath her and was possessed of the same excitement she always felt when riding an unbroken horse. She could taste the salt spray against her lips, stinging her eyes. Her hair, loosely tied away from her face, pulled free of its ribbon and whipped around her face.

In spite of her hands clutching the rail, a sudden lurching of the ship in the turbulent seas almost threw her off balance. She felt Adam's arm slip around her waist, pulling her tightly against him so that she could feel the hardness of his thigh pressed against her. Now it was as if they were riding the sea together, her body braced within the protection of his arms, her face lifted eagerly into the wind as the ship pitched and rolled beneath them. Adam Stewart didn't speak, but she sensed that he was feeling the same sense of exhilaration that she was, something within him answering the wind and spray and sea with the same reckless, joyous abandon that she felt.

She wasn't aware that her clothes and hair were soaked from the sea spray until the storm ended, as suddenly as it had begun. Looking down at her, Adam ordered brusquely, "Get out of those wet clothes before you catch a chill."

"Yes, sir. Right away, sir." Lani smiled meekly at her guardian, but her eyes were brightly teasing.

As if all at once aware that he still had his arm around her waist, Adam abruptly stepped back, smiling sheepishly. "I suppose I do have a tendency to bark orders."

"Yes, you do," Lani replied gently. "But you're right. I should change my clothes."

He escorted her to her cabin, stopping at the door to say, "I'll send the steward to your cabin with some hot tea." That intense, searching gaze was back in the dark gray eyes fastened upon her face. "You'll be all right?"

"Of course," Lani assured him, wondering if she looked as startled as she felt as the man strode away. Where was the arrogant, overbearing Adam Stewart she had disliked for so long? The man that she couldn't remain in the same room with for more than ten minutes without angry sparks flying between them? For the rest of the trip, her guardian couldn't have been more thoughtful or considerate, making sure that Kimiko's and Lani's every comfort was attended to, regaling the two young ladies with amusing stories of his days before the mast, so that Lani was almost sorry when the ship docked before dawn at Honolulu.

A surrey was waiting at the wharf to take the two women to the Tucker house on Beretania Street. Adam stood a moment beside the carriage after the Hawaiian driver had stored the women's luggage under the seats. "I have to go to my office, but I'll stop by this evening," he said. Then clearing his throat, he said, stiffly, "Just to see that you're settling in properly."

"I'm sure we'll be fine," Lani assured him, adding politely, "I'm not sure what state the house is in, but perhaps you'll come by for dinner."

As it turned out she needn't have worried about the state of the house. Mr. Stewart must have sent a message on ahead from Maui, for a full staff was waiting when the surrey rolled up the circular driveway before the house. There were even some familiar faces, Lani saw, delighted, servants who had worked for her Uncle Daniel. The house was sparkling clean, as if it had been closed for only a day instead of almost two years, while the garden, with the golden shower, scarlet poinciana, and jacaranda trees in full bloom, was a seething mass of color.

As she passed the door of her uncle's study, Lani saw that the flowered rug was gone, replaced by a pale, lime-green rug. The gun cases had disappeared, too, and with the room filled with the fragrance of vases of ginger and plumeria, it seemed an extension of the garden. Adam Stewart's doing? Lani wondered, surprised that the man should have realized how she had dreaded seeing the study again, the terrible memories it would always evoke for her. It was impossible, though, to feel anything but pleasure in this sunny, fragrance-filled room.

She ran her hand lightly, caressingly over her uncle's polished desk. "Good-bye, Uncle Daniel," she said softly, for the first time able to think about him without pain.

In the kitchen, Ah Sing was once again in complete control, assuring Lani, with an air of injured dignity, that of course he could prepare a dinner for a guest that evening. Did she want six courses or eight? Lani assured him that a simple dinner would be all that was needed. Then she hurried upstairs to help Kimiko with the unpacking and to decide what to wear that evening.

She finally settled upon a gray-and-white satin striped cotton, with a high, starched collar and tight-fitting, long sleeves, one of the few gowns she owned that was not a *holoku*. To achieve the popular S-shaped effect, she hung on to her four-poster bed gasping for breath, while Kimiko, muttering disapprovingly to herself in Japanese, tugged at the laces of the corset girdling her mistress's already tiny waist. When Kimiko had finished, Lani gazed approvingly at the finished product in her mirror. With her hair pulled back into a chignon and the modish, grown-up gown, she was sure she looked several years older than her almost seventeen years.

Adam Stewart arrived promptly at eight o'clock. Unlike the man on the ship who had been such a delightful companion, her guardian spoke hardly at all during dinner, gazing at his hostess with that look of brooding intensity that always disconcerted Lani. After dinner, when she served him brandy in the front parlor, she was startled when he drank it quickly, then went to stand before the fireplace.

"Won't you sit down, Mr. Stewart?" she asked, taking a seat herself. If it weren't for the fact that she couldn't imagine her guardian being unsure of himself about anything, she could have sworn he was nervous as a cat.

"If you don't mind, I'll stand," he replied gruffly. He gazed absently around the room, then turned his gaze back to Lani. "It won't do, you know, your living here alone."

Oh, dear, Lani thought, sighing to herself. So that was the reason for this visit. Her guardian was evidently determined that she should have another chaperone.

"I'm too old for a governess," she pointed out tartly.

The black brows darted together in a scowl. "I wasn't thinking of a governess," he replied. The broad shoulders stiffened, and Adam's feet braced as if he were once more back aboard the ship, the deck dipping perilously beneath him. "I was thinking, Miss Tucker, that I should move into the house with you."

Lani's startled eyebrows shot upward. Somehow she managed to speak, though her voice sounded strangled. "You don't think, Mr. Stewart, that your living here might not cause gossip?"

The scowl darkened Adam's face. "I've decided that we should be married," he said bluntly, then watched, an alien feeling of helplessness sweeping over him, as he saw shock freeze Lani's face, the blue lavender eyes widening incredulously.

Silently, Adam cursed his own ineptitude. He was going about it all wrong, he knew, but then he had never asked a woman to marry him before. He supposed he should have brought flowers, gone on his knees with a romantic proposal, but somehow he had thought all that foolishness wouldn't be necessary. He had been absurdly confident that Lani felt as he did, that she had been possessed by the same startling but wonderful sensations as he had when he had held her in his arms and they had ridden out the storm together. The truth

was he had been amazed at the sudden depth of his feelings
for the girl. Why hadn't he seen it sooner? Marriage was the
perfect solution to his problem. As her husband, he could see
that Lani was protected and cherished.

He shifted his feet uneasily, wishing the girl would say
something, not just stare at him with those wide, stunned
eyes, even as he thought how very lovely those eyes were,
the color of jacaranda blossoms, beneath the pale graceful
sweep of eyelid. He discovered he had an irresistible desire to
kiss those silken eyelids, to feel that soft body close in his
arms again.

For her own part, Lani didn't know whether to laugh or be
angry at her guardian's outrageous proposal. *He* had decided
they should marry. If she had had any thought at all of
entertaining the proposal—which she certainly hadn't, she
thought furiously— the insufferable arrogance of the man
would have dissuaded her.

She rose to her feet in one swift motion as Adam walked
toward her, his hand reaching out to her, his voice all at once
holding an edge of uncertainty. "I know I'm older than
you. . . ."

"Age has nothing to do with it," Lani said brutally, stepping back, away from that outstretched hand. "I don't love
you, so of course I can't marry you."

Lani watched the hardening of the gray eyes, the lines of
the strong jaw growing taut. She could not know that it
wasn't her refusal of his proposal that had put that look on
Adam's face, but her drawing away from his hand.

As if she couldn't stand for him to touch her, Adam
thought, a fury surging through him such as he had never felt
before in his life. A frightening desire possessed him to take
the girl in his arms, to tear away the prim gown she wore and
inflict upon the soft body his own pain and passion, until she
responded to him with the same overpowering hunger that he
felt, her mouth open and eager, moaning softly beneath his,
her skin on fire at his touch.

Lani saw the anger flaring in the narrowed eyes, the grim
determination in the cold set of the mouth, and stood para-
lyzed, unable to move, even as she told herself that this was
1891. There was no way the man could force her to marry

him. Yet, because beyond the anger she thought she glimpsed a flash of pain deep in the flint-gray eyes, she heard herself stammering, unhappily, "I'm sorry, I didn't mean to hurt you."

Then both the anger and pain were gone, and Adam Stewart's face was once again hard and closed to her. "Please don't concern yourself with my feelings, Miss Tucker," he said with a slight, mocking bow. "I won't pine away because you've refused me. What I had in mind with my offer was more in the way of a business proposition." His glance passed almost indifferently over her young, slim figure. "I assure you that when I make love to a woman. I prefer . . . shall we say . . . a more seasoned companion."

Lani took a sharp, indrawn breath of rage. With a self-control that would have made Rebecca proud, she swept with a dignified hauteur to the front door and held it open. "Then we have nothing more to discuss, do we?" she said coldly. "Good night, Mr. Stewart."

Chapter 13

The clerk in the outer office of Stewart and Sons gazed a little nervously at the determined young woman standing before his desk, demanding to see Adam Stewart.

"I'm sorry, but Mr. Stewart is very busy preparing for a business trip to the United States. Perhaps if you give me your name, I could set up an appointment for tomorrow."

"Miss Tucker," Lani said, smiling pleasantly, but with a touch of steel beneath the velvet soft voice. "And I want to see Mr. Stewart today."

The clerk's manner changed, the nervousness turning to surprise. He was, of course, aware that his employer was Lani Tucker's guardian. He remembered being among the curious onlookers at Mr. Daniel Tucker's funeral and from a distance glimpsing the niece, her shoulders hunched, her thin face streaked with tears. Certainly that unprepossessing child had little in common with this lovely, self-assured young woman standing ramrod straight before him. The jaunty, small-brimmed straw hat and the fashionably tailored skirt and jacket were only a shade darker than the amethyst eyes gazing haughtily at him.

The clerk scrambled to his feet. "I'm sorry, Miss Tucker, perhaps if I tell Mr. Stewart that you're here . . ."

"Never mind, I'll tell him myself."

Lani swept by the desk, pushing open the door of the inner office, with the clerk scurrying, protesting after her.

Adam had risen to his feet at Lani's abrupt entrance. Now he gestured the clerk out of the room and, coming around the desk, held out a chair for his visitor as he asked, "To what do I owe the unexpected pleasure of this visit, Miss Tucker?"

Adam Stewart's voice held a mocking politeness, but Lani felt the forbidding darkness of that chill gray gaze upon her face as her guardian returned to his own chair behind the desk.

"I want you to dismiss Miss Palmer," Lani announced.

One dark, straight eyebrow slanted upward. "Why? Miss Abigail Palmer came with the highest recommendations when I hired her as your companion. Isn't her work satisfactory?"

"I don't need a companion." Lani's voice trembled with irritation. "And I can't stand the woman!"

Adam smiled thinly. "I seem to recall that you didn't care for Miss Kalia, either, in the beginning."

"It's not the same," Lani protested. "Miss Palmer is always telling me what to do, and who to see, what time I should go to bed, and when I should get up in the morning. She even insisted that I have smallpox shots when I remember clearly having the shots years ago. Then she went with me to the doctor! What's worse, she watches me every minute. I feel like a prisoner in my own home!"

"The visit to Dr. Carruthers was my idea, not Miss Palmer's," Adam said calmly. "When we returned from Maui, there was an outbreak of smallpox in Honolulu. Since you haven't had any shots or a medical examination in some years, it seemed a sensible precaution to take. As for Miss

Palmer watching you every minute, I'm sure you're exaggerating. In any case, you must be aware that any impropriety on the part of a young woman, living alone, is bound to cause tongues to wag. Miss Palmer is simply following my orders. She hasn't interfered with your social life, has she?''

"Oh, no. I can attend all the sewing circles, croquet parties, and musical societies that I want!'' And at none of those activities, Lani thought bitterly, did she have the least chance of running into Keith Stewart again.

Adam surveyed Lani's expensive gown and modish hat and said dryly, "From the bills I've been receiving, I gather Miss Palmer hasn't interfered with your visits to the local dressmakers either.''

Lani flushed, annoyed. Her new wardrobe had been outrageously expensive, but it was her money, wasn't it? Anyway, what was the good of all the beautiful gowns she had hanging in her closet, if she had nowhere to wear them? And with gimlet-eyed Miss Palmer sticking beside her like a leech, the possibility was remote that she would meet Keith Stewart, or any young, eligible men to escort her to the court parties at Iolani Palace. Although, to be fair, Lani had to admit she couldn't blame Miss Palmer for not being invited to court. With the prince consort's death in August, the widowed Queen Liliuokalani had gone into mourning for several months, along with her court. There were still diplomatic parties to be invited to, though, and the much-sought-after invitations to "hops'' aboard the British and American naval ships stationed in the harbor. At this rate, Lani thought, aggrieved, she would be old and gray before she met any eligible men.

Lani gazed speculatively at her guardian. Was it possible? she wondered suddenly. Was that why Adam Stewart had hired a dragon like Miss Palmer as her companion in the first place? She remembered uncomfortably that astonishing proposal of marriage she had received from Adam Stewart. Since she had turned down his marriage proposal, was he making sure that his ward met no other suitable men? Oh, not because he loved her, she decided angrily. He had made his true feelings toward her only too abundantly clear, but because she had wounded his male pride by refusing him.

Adam rose to his feet. "I'm sorry to have to rush you off, Miss Tucker, but as my clerk said, I am rather busy."

"Then you won't get rid of Miss Palmer?"

Adam shrugged, his voice impatient. "I'll speak to her when I return, but from what you've told me, I see no reason to change my mind about the woman."

"Then I'll fire her!"

Adam shrugged again, his face guarded, but she could see a glint of anger flashing for a moment in the narrowed eyes. "That's your prerogative, of course. But I should remind you that your allowance, as small as you seem to think it is, could be cut even further. And I don't think the Honolulu dressmakers will be as happy to see you if I pass the word that I will no longer be honoring your bills. The household staff, which is certainly more than you need, could also be reduced. Your maid, Kimiko, for example . . ."

"You wouldn't dare!"

"Wouldn't I?" Adam asked, his voice ominously quiet.

Lani felt a helpless anger pounding in her temples as she stared into the man's face, the ruthless set to the long mouth, the chill gray eyes, and knew he meant exactly what he said. She felt her hard-fought composure slipping away from her, and before a furious retort could rise to her lips, she got to her feet, and without a backward glance she stalked from the room with as much dignity as she could muster. In the outer office, the clerk was on the telephone, explaining to a caller that Mr. Stewart was departing the islands in the morning and not making any business appointments for at least two months.

Once out on the street, Lani walked slowly away from the business center. Although it was January, the early afternoon sun was hot, reflecting from the shop windows, beating against her eyelids. The air, redolent from the tuberose and plumeria leis being sold by the Hawaiian street vendors, and the less attractive odors from the nearby fish market, seemed to shimmer dizzily around her. Usually she enjoyed strolling along, looking in the shop windows, listening to the colorful hawkers along the street touting their wares, but she was still too angry to think of anything but Adam Stewart.

How could she have liked the man, even a little, she wondered, annoyed. That arrogant, overbearing creature she had just left had nothing at all in common with the thoughtful, amusing companion who had shared the excitement of the storm with her aboard the ship from Maui. It was as if her guardian were like the character in the new book by Robert Louis Stevenson that Rebecca had had her read, a Dr. Jekyll and Mr. Hyde, two completely different men in one body. Well, somehow, someway she had to get out from under the man's thumb, she decided, as well as away from the ever-vigilant eye of his proxy, Abigail Palmer. But how?

Although she had recklessly threatened her guardian with going to an attorney if he tried to sell Palekaiko out from under her, she knew no lawyers in Honolulu. In any case, she suspected that most attorneys would side with Adam Stewart. What she saw as a high-handed, exasperating officiousness in running her life, they would no doubt consider necessary measures her guardian was taking to protect his young charge.

As for friends that she could turn to for help, the only young women she knew were those she had met at sewing and musical circles, and none of them could be considered close friends. There was, of course, Kimiko, who was much more of a friend than a servant, but although the young Japanese girl might sympathize with her mistress, there was little she could do to change things.

Intent upon her thoughts, Lani did not notice at once that she had left the business center of town behind and was at the edge of the Chinese quarter. Now she stopped and gazed around her with curiosity and dismay, as the sights and smells assailed her. She knew, of course, it wasn't only Chinese who lived in these hovels. It was Hawaiians, too, who had lost their tiny plots of land to the large sugar plantations and drifted into the city, families living in one room but, with typical native hospitality, always willing to welcome one more relative or friend to stay with them.

How was it possible for people to live under such crowded, miserable conditions? Lani wondered, gazing, appalled, at the laundry flapping on balconies, the filth that littered streets, and the dark narrow passageways between the buildings. Then several men came stumbling out of an alleyway, their faces blank, drugged. The sweetish odor of opium that clung to their clothes as they passed her mingled with the smell of open sewage coming from within the buildings. Lani felt her stomach contract, and she turned and fled.

When she finally found a hack stand and was driven home, she still felt faintly ill. As she entered the house, Miss Palmer came hurrying down the steps. Although only in her late twenties, the tall, thin woman seemed at least ten years older, with her rust-colored hair pulled severely back from a narrow, bony face, and her brusque, efficient manner.

Her mouth folded into a thin line of disapproval as she said reproachfully, "Oh, there you are, Miss Tucker. I've been quite concerned, wondering where you were." Noticing the girl's paleness, she stepped swiftly forward. "Are you feeling ill?"

"I'm fine," Lani said quickly, not sure which annoyed her the most, her companion's constantly hovering around her, or Abigail's old-maidish fussing about her health.

"You might at least have told me you were going out. Where were you?"

"I wasn't aware that I had to keep you informed of my every movement." Lani gazed coldly at the woman. "But I'm sure the next time you report to Mr. Stewart, he'll tell you that I was at his office."

Twin scarlet blotches of color bloomed in Abigail Palmer's sallow face. "You misunderstand, Miss Tucker," she said tartly. "Since no one knew your whereabouts, the servants were unable to tell your caller when you would be returning."

Lani had brushed by the woman and started up the stairs. Now she stopped and swung around, startled. "I had a caller?"

Miss Palmer nodded. "A man. He wouldn't leave his name. He said he wanted to surprise you."

"What did he look like?" Lani asked eagerly.

"I didn't see him." Abigail's mouth pursed in disapproval at a young lady receiving male callers who refused to leave their names.

Lani hurried up to her room, her heart beating faster with hope and disappointment. Could it have been Keith? But why wouldn't he leave his name? And why had he waited so long to come and see her?

Then two days later, reading in the garden in the shade of the hau lanai, she saw a man on horseback coming up the front drive of the house. With the sun behind him, Lani could not distinguish his features until he slid off the handsome bay mare, dropped the reins over the pommel, and strode toward her.

Her book fell to the ground as she sprang to her feet with a cry of pleasure. "Tom! I don't believe it. I thought you were still away at college."

Her childhood friend had changed, she saw at once: his chest and shoulders had filled out, and his face, too, so that the Stewart nose and jaw no longer seemed too large for the rest of the face. The lanky, loose-limbed boy she remembered was gone. In his place stood a man, full grown. Only the fine, light brown hair and the sherry-colored eyes were the same, as Tom smiled down at her, grasping both her hands warmly in his. "I arrived two days ago on the *Claudine*. I came to see you, but you weren't home. I would have come back sooner, but with Adam away on a business trip I've been busy at the office."

"Your brother didn't say a word to me about your graduating and coming home," Lani protested.

Tom laughed. "I didn't graduate. I just left. I wasn't learning anything I wanted to know, and I felt I could be more useful here in Hawaii." He smiled sheepishly. "I guess the truth is I was homesick. There wasn't a day went by that I didn't miss the islands." His hands tightened on Lani's, his eyes warm on her face. "Especially certain people."

How beautiful she was, Tom thought, his breath harsh in his throat, even more beautiful than he remembered, with the new womanly curves to her body. He had had the company of enough women in the last two years to realize that what he felt toward Lani Tucker wasn't simply a boyish crush. He wanted her this moment with the same sharp intensity that he'd felt that night years ago on the beach, only more so, because now he knew it wasn't a casual tumble he wanted, or a desire to prove himself as a man. He wanted to wake up every morning for the rest of his life and find Lani beside him in bed. It was a man's longing he felt now, not a boy's, a man's need and desire for the woman he loved.

Lani was aware of the eager warmth in the pale brown eyes gazing down at her so intently. She remembered the last night that she had been with Tom here in this garden, when he had tried to kiss her and she had pushed him away so unceremoniously that he had tripped and fallen over a lawn chair. She had the feeling that this Tom Stewart standing before her now would not be so easily discouraged.

She smiled reproachfully, pulling her hand free. "I seem to recall you wrote me all of a half-dozen letters while you were away."

"Oh, I'm not any good at writing letters," Tom said easily. "But I've kept in touch. That's one of the reasons I wanted to come home, because of what I've been hearing from Lot Lane and some of my other friends."

"About me?" Lani said teasingly. "My life's deadly dull. What could anyone write you about me?"

Tom shook his head. "No, not you," he said. "It's what's been happening here in Hawaii, the plots against the queen's life."

"You surely don't believe the queen is in any danger?" Lani asked, startled. "She's very popular with the people."

Tom scowled down at her impatiently. "She's not popular with Lorrin Thurston and his friends in the Reform party. They've never given up wanting to get rid of the monarchy. That's what Thurston's doing in Washington right now, drumming up support from President Harrison and Congress to force Hawaii to become a part of the United States." Tom's voice was bitter. "With Thurston and his *haole* friends running the country, of course."

Lani vaguely remembered Lorrin Thurston from the times when the man had visited her uncle. A short, stocky man with a round face and a self-righteous air, he hardly fit her image of a murderer. "I can't believe Mr. Thurston would harm the queen," she protested.

"Not Thurston himself," Tom said darkly. "But I wouldn't put it past some of his friends. The queen's already received several anonymous threatening letters. Thurston and his crowd have found out that Liliuokalani isn't a puppet whose strings they can pull as they wish. She'll never consent to handing over Hawaii and its people to foreigners whose only interest is how much money they can squeeze from these islands."

Lani saw the light of battle glowing in Tom's face, heard

the outrage in his voice at the thought of his beloved islands being threatened, and she smiled to herself. That hadn't changed, she thought, amused. Tom might not have Hawaiian blood in his veins, but he was still Hawaiian to the core.

To change to a less volatile subject, she asked, "What did your brothers say about your leaving college? Were they very angry?"

"Adam was *huhu loa*. He raked me over the coals for a while, but in spite of the bad economy, Stewart and Sons is growing fast. I guess he decided that, rather than ship me back to college, I might as well start learning the business. As for Keith . . ." Tom's voice fell away. As long as he could remember, he had idolized his handsome, charming half brother, but as hard as he had tried, he had always sensed that his efforts to please his brother always fell short. And Adam's taking over the family business, leaving Tom in the firm but buying Keith out, had driven an even deeper wedge between Tom and his half brother. "Keith's too busy courting Nellie Samuels to worry about me," he said with a forced cheerfulness.

Lani bent down quickly to pick up her book, so that Tom didn't see the flicker of pain in the violet eyes. When she lifted her head again, she smiled and gestured toward Kimiko, coming from the house with a tray. "I was just about to have coffee and some of those little spice cookies of Ah Sing's that you always liked. Won't you join me?"

Tom stiffened, then made himself turn slowly. As much as he dreaded the moment, he had known, of course, that he would be seeing Kimiko again at the Tucker home. Better to get it over with, he thought. To his relief, there was not even a flicker of recognition on Kimiko's face as she bowed and placed the tray on the table beside her mistress. It was Tom himself who felt an uncomfortable rush of emotion as he gazed at the delicate beauty of the young Japanese woman in the pale blue kimono.

How could he have forgotten how lovely she was? he wondered, his throat all at once dry. And he was filled with a sudden, inexplicable anger that she could look at him so calmly with no hint of memory in those faintly angled, almond-shaped eyes, when he recalled only too clearly that slim, golden body arching with such passionate joy beneath him.

Glancing curiously from her maid to her visitor, Lani apologized. "I forgot. Of course, you two know each other, don't you?"

Kimiko, hands tucked within the sleeves of her robe, bowed gravely toward Tom. "Mr. Stewart showed me a great kindness. I will always be grateful."

Tom tore his gaze away from the maid, smiling stiffly. "I was glad to be of help."

"Well, I'll always be grateful to you, too," Lani said, leaping to fill the oddly strained silence. "I don't know how I would have managed these last years without Kimiko." She gazed fondly at the Japanese girl. "First losing Uncle Daniel and . . ." She was about to say, "and having Adam Stewart as my guardian," but cut off the words abruptly. After all, Tom was Adam's brother. It wouldn't be fair to ask him to take sides in what was her own personal battle with her guardian. ". . . and having to leave Palekaiko," she finished instead.

Tom's warm eyes filled with sympathy. "I was sorry that I wasn't able to stay for your uncle's funeral, Lani. His death must have been a terrible blow. Adam wrote me that you were living at the ranch on Maui. How did you happen to return to Honolulu?"

Lani explained about her tutor and the circumstances of her returning to Honolulu, carefully refraining from placing any of the blame on Adam for her forced departure from Palekaiko. Neither she nor Tom noticed Kimiko's quiet departure.

The maid went quickly through the downstairs hall to her small bedroom off from the kitchen. It was only when she was safely inside the room, with the door shut, that she sank to the floor on her knees. Naturally she had always known that even if Tom Stewart should return to Honolulu she would have no place in his life. But what she hadn't known was the agony she would feel, seeing her lover again. This is how it must feel, at the moment of hara-kiri, she thought numbly, a knife stabbing into the softness of her abdomen, the terrible pains cramping her. She buried her face in her hands, crying without a sound as the tears poured down her face.

For ten minutes Kimiko allowed herself the self-indulgent luxury of her tears. Then she got stiffly to her feet and splashed cold water on her face before she once again went about her chores.

Chapter 14

"I'm not at all sure that Mr. Stewart would approve of this." Miss Palmer stood in the doorway of the bedroom, her narrow lips tightening disapprovingly as Lani adjusted a satin rosette at the shoulder of her ballgown. The rosettes were of the same pale blue satin as the gown, which draped softly across the bodice then fell in long, graceful lines to a heavier satin train.

Lani had no doubt that her guardian wouldn't approve of her attending a diplomatic ball at the palace, but Adam Stewart, thank heaven, was still away from Honolulu. And since she was attending the ball with Tom Stewart, her guardian's brother, there was little that Miss Palmer could do except fuss and fume and make dire predictions about the unhealthiness of the night air causing inflamation of the lungs.

Abigail studied the bodice of Lani's gown uneasily. It wasn't that the satin neckline wasn't modestly cut, but somehow the artful draping seemed to draw one's eye deliberately to the bountiful swell of curves beneath. Then, she gave a sharp gasp of surprise as she saw the rope of pearls that Lani was attaching around her slim neck. She recognized the perfectly matched pearls at once as the necklace Jasmine Tucker wore in her portrait hanging in the stairwell.

"Where did you get that necklace?" she demanded.

"From the safe deposit vault at the bank," Lani replied.

"Mr. Trumbull allowed you to remove such valuable jewelry?" Abigail's voice grew shrill with indignation at what she obviously considered the bank manager's dereliction in duty in allowing the pearls to be taken from the safety of the bank.

"Why not?" Lani asked blandly. "The necklace belonged to my grandmother, and now it belongs to me. Why shouldn't I wear it if I want?" She fastened pearl pendants of the same lustrous ivory color as the necklace to her ears, and pulled several strands of her dark hair, piled in soft curls on top of her head, to fall gracefully across her forehead. Then she stepped back from her mirror and, laughing, dropped a curtsy to Miss Palmer. "Do I look presentable enough to attend a court ball?"

Abigail sniffed. She didn't think highly of kings and queens and monarchies of any sort, much less a court ruled by a Hawaiian royal family that had been little more than pagans when her missionary ancestors had come to these islands. Not that Queen Liliuokalani hadn't been raised a missionary Christian, and was a member in good standing of Kawaiahao Church, but Abigail had heard disturbing stories that the new queen had also given money and support to the Catholic, Mormon, and Episcopalian denominations that were regrettably growing stronger in the islands.

"You look very nice," she said starchily, but as she studied Lani Tucker she knew that the girl did not just look nice. She was alarmingly beautiful in the blue satin gown that concealed even as it revealed the ripe curves of the slim, sensuous body. Despite the blue-lavender eyes behind thick black lashes, Abigail was suddenly very aware of the girl's part-Polynesian ancestry. There was a soft glow to the creamy skin and a warm, inviting softness in the eyes, an unconscious fluid grace in the way the girl moved that Abigail had noticed in Hawaiian women.

Abigail felt a frisson of fear. Surely if she had noticed the disturbing beauty of the girl, others would see it, too. Men, of course. Hadn't that been one of the recurring problems of the early missionaries, Hawaiian women, scandalously and blatantly *moe kolohe,* sleeping mischievously, luring men into sin as easily and casually as the fruit of a fig tree attracted bees.

An unexpected stab of resentment pierced Abigail's virginal body. It was as if the Polynesian woman possessed some forbidden, secret knowledge about the male sex. Hastily she thrust aside such an unseemly thought, returning her attention to the problem at hand. Lani Tucker was, after all, her responsibility, but what could she do to protect the girl from her own inherited nature, short of locking her in her room?

Abigail sighed to herself, clasping her hands together. If only Mr. Adam Stewart would return soon, she prayed, before it was too late.

Tom was waiting for Lani in the hallway as she descended the staircase, and the flattering look of admiration that leaped into his face when he saw her made any uncertainty on Lani's part disappear. She cast a quick, pleased smile toward her grandmother's portrait, then swept confidently down the stairs.

"I wish we didn't have to go to the palace," Tom said softly as he placed her short satin cape over her shoulder. "I wish we could go somewhere and be alone."

"But I'm looking forward to my first court ball." Lani smiled, tucking her hand into his arm and pushing aside a vague feeling of guilt at the almost too open adoration she saw in the sherry eyes. "How did you ever manage to get an invitation? The girls at the sewing circle say that since it's the first big ball that the queen's given since coming out of mourning, everyone's been pulling all sorts of strings, trying to be invited."

Tom grinned as he escorted her to the waiting carriage. "Actually, it's all very mysterious, my getting an invitation to the ball. And there was a note with it, unsigned, suggesting that if I had no other young lady in mind, that Miss Lani Tucker might be willing to accompany me."

Lani gave him a teasing smile. "And did you have any other young lady in mind?"

Tom's hand tightened on hers. In the darkness of the carriage she could not see his face, only the golden light in his eyes warm upon her own face. "You know there's no one else," he said huskily.

Once again a feeling of guilt stung Lani, and although she didn't remove her hand from Tom's grasp, she was relieved when the carriage quickly reached the palace, only a short distance from the Tucker home. A line of carriages was discharging passengers in front of the palace veranda, the steps lined with a row of Hawaiians resplendent in blue velvet jackets and knee trousers and white silk stockings.

Once inside the palace, Lani gazed around her, for a moment speechless, then blurted, "Oh, how beautiful!" Although electricity was no longer uncommon in Honolulu, many homeowners, like her uncle, still preferred gaslight. The palace, however, was completely lit by electricity, and the glittering crystal chandeliers in the throne room, that tonight had been turned into a ballroom, were reflected over and over again in the full-length, gold-framed mirrors set into the wall.

After their names were announced by the chamberlain, Lani advanced on Tom's arm down the length of the ballroom, at the end of which Queen Liliuokalani stood with her ladies in waiting to receive her guests. For a moment, Lani felt as nervous as she had been at the queen's luau at Palekaiko, when she had waited with Rebecca to meet the queen for the first time. Once again, though, Liliuokalani put her quickly at ease, smiling warmly as she greeted her guest, who curtsied deeply before her. "I'm so pleased you could join us this evening, Miss Tucker." She turned graciously to Tom. "And my gratitude to you, Mr. Stewart, for bringing Miss Tucker."

The queen's gaze turned back questioningly to Lani. "Our friend, Rebecca, she's well?"

For a moment, a sharp sense of loss swept over Lani so that she could only stammer, unhappily, "Rebecca . . . Rebecca's no longer with me, Your Majesty."

Sensing the girl's unhappiness, Liliuokalani tactfully changed the subject, although her gaze was thoughtful as she turned at last to greet her other guests. Her warm smile, her soft, musical voice never altered, but when John Stevens passed through the receiving line, the dark expressive eyes hardened for a moment as she gazed at the minister of the United States.

What a detestable man, she thought, even here, at a social occasion, gazing contemptuously down his long nose at her, the same way he had at her first meeting with him after she had become queen. He had behaved toward her then as no gentleman would to any woman, much less a queen. His manner had been rudely insulting, his voice threatening. She must strictly obey the supreme authority of the constitution of 1887, he had lectured, and place herself wholly in the hands of the conservative and respectable men of the country if she wished to retain her throne.

In other words, Liliuokalani had realized bitterly, she must be queen in name only. She must accept a cabinet not of her choosing, a cabinet of men she could not trust, whose loyalty lay elsewhere. She must accept the humiliation of the shameful bayonet constitution that deprived her people of the right to a voice in their own government and turned the making of their laws over to men whose first allegiance was to some faraway foreign government.

John Stevens wasn't her only enemy, though. Her dark gaze moved down the receiving line. There were others here in this very room, men who smiled to her face and conspired against her behind her back, members of Lorrin Thurston's secret annexation club, pledged to destroy the monarchy. Lili's mouth twisted scornfully. Did they really think they could keep their club a secret, that her marshal wasn't aware of their treasonous activities?

The receiving line was finally drawing to an end, she saw with relief, and it was time for the dancing to begin. Ordinarily, she would have opened the ball by dancing the royal quadrille. She was, however, still in mourning, and she allowed herself to be escorted to a scarlet, velvet-covered chair at one end of the ballroom. Then, at a signal from her, Henry Berger led the Royal Hawaiian Band through one of her favorites, a Hawaiian melody that the German band leader had set to the lively tempo of a polka.

As she sat watching the dancers—women in their colorful ball gowns, naval officers in white uniforms with gold braid, black-frocked gentlemen with diplomatic decorations glittering across their chests—the queen's own feet, discreetly hidden by the folds of her black velvet gown, unconsciously tapped in rhythm with the music. It was times like these, she thought sadly, that she missed her husband the most. Oh, not that John had ever enjoyed music and dancing as much as she did. It was his physical presence beside her that she missed.

Well, at least she had the comfort of knowing that after she had become queen, John and she had drawn closer together. Liliuokalani's face darkened, remembering the nasty gossip that had circulated after John's death that it was his mistress that had been with him at his deathbed. Naturally, when she had realized her husband was dying, she had sent for the woman who had loved John enough to bear his child. It was the way of old Hawaii. Possessiveness, sexual jealousy between men and women, had never been part of the culture of the Hawaiians.

Liliuokalani sighed to herself. Of course, the missionaries had never understood that. Just as they had understood little else about the natives they had come to civilize. The Hawaiians' taking the time to enjoy life and the beauty around them, their refusal to pile up possessions, was seen as laziness. Sharing a friend's food and goods, without having to ask permission, was a simple act of hospitality, but to the *haoles* it was thievery. Even the custom among the Hawaiian chiefs of giving up one's child in *hanai,* or adoption, was considered shocking, but to the Hawaiians a child was not a possession but a gift of love to be shared.

Liliuokalani herself had been adopted into the Paki family, and since she could not have children of her own, she had happily adopted several *hanai* children who were her joy and delight, including John Aimoku, John's handsome young son. And that, no doubt, had caused more whispers and gossip, Liliuokalani thought, sighing to herself. Then she pushed such mean-spirited thoughts from her mind and, settling back in her chair, gave herself up to the pleasure of Herr Berger's music.

Lani was watching the dancers whirling around the floor, too, but with trepidation as well as delight. She had been secretly relieved when Tom had apologized for not asking her to dance, grinning regretfully. "I'm not very good at polkas. I fall all over my own feet."

Lani would never have admitted it to Tom, but her own knowledge of ballroom dancing was limited to those evenings in the front parlor at Palekaiko, with Rebecca laughing and humming along, attempting to instruct her pupil in the latest dance steps. Watching the dancers hop and slide and whirl around so effortlessly, Lani suspected uneasily that dancing with Rebecca was not at all the same as whirling around this crowded dance floor in the arms of a man.

"I believe this dance is promised to me, Miss Tucker."

Lani turned, startled, to look into the laughing eyes of Keith Stewart. He reached for the *carte de danse* that hung from her wrist. Not knowing anyone who would ask her to dance except Tom, she had not bothered to look at the dance card that had been handed to her by the chamberlain when she entered the ballroom.

"Yes, there's my name," Keith said, gravely studying the card, which was decorated with a crown resting upon a tasseled cushion and listed the dances for the evening. "You'll excuse us, Tom?"

Before her escort could answer, Lani felt herself being led onto the floor. A few minutes later, she realized that dancing with a man was, indeed, different than dancing with Rebecca. It was much, much better!

As Keith led her expertly through the polka, her body felt light as thistledown in his arms, her feet seeming to move of their own volition in time with the music.

"Enjoying yourself?"

"Oh, yes." She leaned back in his arms, smiling up at him. "But I'm dying to know. How did you manage to get your name on my dance card?"

"I've always found it pays to have friends at court," he said lightly. "I happen to know the gentleman who hands out the dance cards to the ladies." He gave her a conspiratorial wink. "And I also happen to be friends with the queen's chancellor who sends out the invitations to the balls."

"You were the one who had the invitation sent to Tom," Lani said, all at once understanding.

He nodded, laughing. "I promised you, didn't I, that I'd see that you got to a court ball? And that we'd have the first dance? Since I wasn't able to escort you myself, I arranged for what I hope was a satisfactory substitute."

Of course, Lani thought, her happiness for a moment dimmed. She had forgotten about Nellie Samuels. Her glance swiftly searched the room and found the young woman dancing with an elderly, portly man, who was obviously her

father. Nellie hadn't changed much since she had known her
as a student, she decided. The most attractive feature in her
overly plump, wide-jawed face was still her eyes, a pale,
luminous blue, with a look of appealing helplessness about
them. At the moment, Nellie's eyes were fastened upon
Lani's partner. The look of unhappiness on the girl's face
made Lani feel vaguely uncomfortable, and she looked hastily
away.

Keith was aware, too, of Nellie's eyes upon him, and
thought, indifferently, it would do Nellie good to worry a
little about him. Oh, she was willing enough for him to dance
attendance on her, but when the subject turned to marriage,
she always managed to turn coy and evasive, without the
spine to stand up to her father, who wasn't too pleased about
his daughter's new suitor.

Deliberately now, knowing that Nellie was watching, Keith
smiled at the young woman in his arms as he murmured
softly, "You didn't think I'd forget my promise to you?"

He was pleased to see the pink that feathered out along
Lani's cheekbones, a shimmering quicksilver light in the
blue-lavender eyes. "I was hoping you wouldn't forget,"
Lani said. "I was afraid I'd never see you again."

Keith felt a jolt of surprise and pleasure at the girl's
boldness, her lack of coquettishness. His interest piqued, he
allowed his glance to roam appreciatively over the skillfully
draped lines of the blue satin gown, imagining only too easily
the soft, young body beneath, a body, he wagered shrewdly,
that for all the girl's boldness had never known a man's
touch.

When he had first seen the grown-up Lani Tucker at
Palekaiko, he had been sure, with an unerring sense about
women that had never failed him, that the girl would be a
passionate bed partner. It might be pleasureable, he thought
now, to be the one to awaken and instruct that young, ardent
body, to hear her first cries of rapture and see those astonishing amethyst eyes blur with desire.

Even as he thought this, Keith was wondering absently
where the girl had found the money to buy the undoubtedly
expensive gown she wore. He was well aware that Daniel
Tucker had gone through most of the Tucker estate before he

died. Was it possible, he wondered suddenly, that his brother, Adam, had purchased the gown for his ward?

The thought brought a gleam to Keith's eyes. He knew Adam well enough to know that his brother was seldom given to such quixotic impulses, especially not where women were concerned. Could it be that Adam had developed more than a guardian's fatherly interest in Lani Tucker? If so, Keith decided gleefully, bedding the young woman could be even more of a pleasure, since it meant not only bringing Nellie to heel, but revenging himself against his brother at the same time.

When her companion remained silent. The pink, staining Lani's cheekbones, flared out across her face. Had she been too daring, she wondered, embarrassed, in admitting to Mr. Stewart that she had been hoping to meet him again. All the books of etiquette and manners that Rebecca had had her read had stressed that men didn't like forward females.

Then, almost casually, she felt her partner's arm tighten around her waist, the sunny blue eyes laughing down at her as Keith said, "A mare of mine is entered at Kapiolani Park Saturday. I seem to recall that you're an excellent horsewoman. How would you like to ride her in the ladies' race?"

In her excitement, Lani almost missed a step. "Could I?" And then, uncertainly, "I've never ridden in a horse race before."

"Neither have most of the other ladies," Keith assured her. "It's all in fun. Of course, if you're afraid to ride Sunbeam . . ." His voice trailed off regretfully.

"I'm not afraid!" Lani protested at once. There had never been a horse at Palekaiko that she had been afraid to ride. "It's my companion, Miss Palmer," she admitted with a sigh. "I think she'd tie me to the bedpost rather than let me ride in a horse race!"

"Let me worry about Miss Palmer," Keith said, grinning roguishly, as the dance came to an end. "Now I'd better get you back to Tom. He looks like he's ready to come charging out on the dance floor after you."

Tom did have a sulky look on his young face when Lani rejoined him. He was staring, annoyed, after his brother's broad back as Keith strode away. "I didn't know you knew

Keith,'' he said accusingly, as the orchestra played a slower piece and he led Lani back onto the dance floor.

"You certainly don't mind my dancing with your brother?" Lani asked, her eyes widening innocently while she maneuvered adeptly to keep her feet out from under Tom's as the tempo of the schottische picked up.

Tom scowled darkly. Naturally, he couldn't speak against his own brother, but he knew all about Keith's reputation with women. And Lani, of course, was much too young and naive to cope with a man as experienced as Keith. His arm tightened protectively around his partner's tiny waist. Well, he would look after her, he thought proudly, possessively. He would make sure that he had all the rest of the dances with her.

It turned out, however, that it wasn't his brother that Tom had to share Lani with for the remainder of the evening. Friends he had forgotten he had descended upon him, all wanting to dance with his partner. Boys that at school, Lani thought, amused, hadn't given her a second glance now clustered around her, pleading for a place on her dance card.

At midnight, when an elaborate champagne buffet supper was served in the adjoining dining room, the competition reached a red-hot pitch over who was to fetch Miss Tucker a second helping of food or another glass of sparkling fruit punch.

"I hardly had a chance to speak two words to you alone all evening,'' Tom complained when the ball finally ended near dawn. At Lani's insistence, the carriage had been sent away, and they walked the few blocks to the Tucker home. Her feet pleasantly aching from all the dancing, Lani stopped and impulsively removed her shoes and stockings, walking barefoot beside Tom on the soft dirt road.

"We're alone now,'' she pointed out, smiling up at her companion. Her pale, lovely face, lifted to his, caught the moonlight, her eyes shimmering, reflecting its radiance.

Tom gave a stifled groan. They had reached the garden of the Tucker home, and he pulled Lani into the darkness cast by the high branches of an African tulip tree. His arms closed hungrily around her.

It was not the fumbling embrace of the ungainly boy Lani

remembered from years before. The mouth on hers was gentle but firm, the strong arms holding her tightly so that she could not have escaped even if she had wanted to. And after the first instinctive stiffening of her body against the unfamiliar, searching pressure on her lips, she found, to her own surprise, that she did not want to escape. It was all in all rather pleasant, the warmth of the mouth moving against hers stirring delicious sensations inside of her that she had never felt before. Her body felt delightfully relaxed within that embrace, so that she was startled when Tom's arms suddenly fell away. She could hear his harsh breathing, and the almost angry tension in his voice as he demanded, "You do love me, don't you, Lani?"

She gazed up at him, bewildered. "Of course, Tom. You're my very best friend."

"I don't want to be your friend!" Tom fought to regain his self-control, reminding himself of Lani's youth and inexperience, even as he ached to reach out and crush the girl again in his arms. He mustn't frighten her by trying to rush her. If only, he thought despairingly, she weren't so beautiful, or he couldn't still feel the warmth and shape of her body fitting against his. "That is," he finished unhappily, "of course, I want to be your friend, but . . ."

Lani stifled a yawn politely behind her hand. She was all at once exhausted. All she wanted to do was crawl into her bed and sleep for a week. Reaching up, she kissed Tom lightly on the mouth, murmuring, "I had a wonderful time. Thank you so much for asking me."

Then, before Tom could pull her back into his arms, she had slipped quickly away into the tree-shrouded darkness of the garden, and he heard the front door closing behind her.

Chapter 15

Lani was waiting on the front steps of the veranda Saturday morning when Keith arrived on horseback, leading a golden sorrel.

"Oh, she's beautiful," Lani breathed, running her hand over the mare's silken flank, the coat rippling like polished gold.

"Sunbeam's small, but she's powerful," Keith said, pride filling his voice. "Island-bred, but her dam had English racing blood in her." Then, cocking an amused eyebrow at Lani, he asked, "You weren't planning on wearing those clothes, were you?"

Lani had dug out a pair of dungarees and a shirt that she had brought with her from the ranch. What else would she wear riding in a horse race, she thought. A formal riding habit would just get in her way.

Behind her, Miss Palmer had come out of the house, the woman's voice shrilly triumphant. "I told you, Miss Tucker. A lady doesn't wear breeches in public."

Keith swung off his horse, gracefully doffing his white hat, which was wrapped with a lei of jasmine like carved ivory, toward Miss Palmer. "You're right, of course." He smiled disarmingly. "How fortunate Miss Tucker has someone like you to look after her best interests."

Then he removed a package from the saddle of his horse and handed it to Lani. His back was toward the woman standing on the steps so that she couldn't hear him whisper to Lani, "I think you look charming. But why don't you put on this riding *pa'u*? It's what the rest of the young ladies in the race will be wearing."

When Lani returned fifteen minutes later, a short cape floated from the shoulders of a black velvet jacket. From the

142

waist down she wore a brilliant green bifurcated skirt, and she held in her hand a long, flowing silk train. Keith Stewart was still standing, hat in hand, talking to Abigail, and Lani couldn't help noticing, amused, that her companion's usually sallow face was flushed like a school girl's.

"You musn't concern yourself, Miss Palmer," Keith was saying gravely. "I promise to take very good care of my brother's ward. And horseback riding is such a healthy activity for a young woman, don't you agree?"

The warmth of the man's gaze upon her face made Abigail Palmer feel an odd, but not unpleasant, breathlessness. She had naturally heard the stories whispered about Keith Stewart— not that she listened to gossip. Now, having met Mr. Stewart, she realized how cruelly false such rumors were. No man with such perfect manners and proud bearing could be anything but a gentleman. And hadn't his grandfather, after all, been one of Hawaii's first and most respected missionaries?

Keith and Lani led their horses out to the street, where Lani stopped beside the stone mounting block and faced her companion, curious. "What did you tell Miss Palmer?"

"That I was taking you for a horseback ride."

"And the horse race?"

"How forgetful of me," Keith said, his expression of feigned chagrin making Lani giggle. "I'm afraid I completely forgot to mention the horse race."

Lani glanced regretfully down at the long skirt and train and shook her head. "The *pa'u* is beautiful, but I can't imagine riding a horse in it, much less winning a race."

"Let me show you." Before she could step up onto the mounting block, Keith had lifted her easily onto the golden sorrel, his hands lingering a moment around her waist before he drew the split silken train through the stirrups so that it floated gracefully above the ground on each side of the horse.

"Don't worry," he said, as Sunbeam sidestepped a little nervously. "For the past several days I've had one of the stable boys ride her with a tablecloth flung across the saddle, so that she's accustomed to the feel of a skirt on her back."

Lani spoke soothingly to the mare, discovering at once that the long, parted skirt didn't interfere with her handling of Sunbeam. What a gorgeous animal, she thought happily,

admiring the horse's glossy, golden mane, its smooth, even
gait as, with Keith beside her, they cantered away from town
toward Kapiolani Park. And how wonderful to have a fine
horse beneath her again, reminding her suddenly of the way
she had felt when Tom and she had gone for that late night
swim at Waikiki.

Thinking of Tom, though, made her vaguely guilt stricken,
although, of course, she told herself firmly, there was no
reason for her to feel that way. Tom couldn't have taken her
to the racetrack in any case because he had gone to work at
the Stewart sugar plantation for several days.

When they reached the racetrack at Kapiolani Park, the private
booths had already been set up, decorated with the colors of
the stables that had entered horses in the race. The booths
took the place of a grandstand, and the area around the track
was already crowded with people. Women in white, wasp-
waisted dresses, with banners of their favorite jockey's color
streaming from their white hats, strolled arm in arm with
mustachioed men in crisp white linen suits.

Families were gathered around picnic tables already groaning with food, but most of the Hawaiians present bought their
poi and pop from vendors, while listening to Mr. Berger's
Royal Hawaiian Band playing rousing marches. Keith's booth
had his gold-and-green racing colors flying above it, and his
servants had laid out a lunch of stuffed turkey, watermelon,
and ice cream, as well as glasses of wine and fruit punch, for
his guests.

Lani was surprised to see that Nellie Samuels and her
brother, Paul, whom Lani remembered dancing with at the
palace, were among Keith's guests, which included wealthy
haole merchants, planters, and bankers and their wives. Nellie, in a white, lacy dress, greeted Lani coolly, then turned to
Keith with a possessive smile and said, "You are going to
accept my wager on the first race, aren't you?"

Lani knew that betting was not allowed at the racetrack,
but that a great deal of private betting took place among the
men, especially at Cunha's tavern not far from the track. A
woman, however, attending the races, laid wagers on a race
with her escort and, if she won, received a gift of candy or a
crystal bowl the next day.

"You should save your wager until the ladies' race," Keith said genially. "Miss Tucker is going to ride Sunbeam for me, and I'm sure she'll win."

Just for a second, an expression of anger touched the helpless blue eyes, then Nellie turned to Lani, her voice lightly malicious. "How exciting. And what a charmingly authentic Hawaiian *pa'u*. Did you inherit it from your great-aunt Lani? I've heard she was a great believer in Hawaiian traditions."

So Nellie had heard the scandalous story about her great-aunt, Lani thought, that she had married her half brother, Kale, following an ancient Hawaiian custom. Her hand tightened around the pearl-handled riding whip she held, the explosive anger she hadn't felt in a long time beating in her temple so that her head throbbed. How she would love to wipe that knowing smirk off Nellie's face!

And then, almost as if she were standing beside her, she heard Rebecca's calm voice. "When you lose your temper, Lani, you've lost the argument."

Lani smiled sweetly at Nellie. "Why, no, Mr. Stewart was kind enough to lend me the *pa'u*." She turned to Keith, resting her hand on his arm in a proprietorial way that caused a dull surge of color to stain Nellie's face. "The fruit punch looks delicious. Do you suppose I could have a glass?"

Paul Samuels stepped hastily forward. "Let me get you a glass of punch, Miss Tucker," he said eagerly.

"Why, thank you." Lani gave the young man a ravishing smile that sent him happily stumbling off to the punch bowl. Other young men she had danced with at the court ball quickly surrounded her, vying for her attention, while Keith excused himself and slipped away. "I've just time to place a few bets myself," he told Lani, grinning.

From the expression on his handsome face, though, when the races were run, she decided that his selections had not done well. There was the same strained look about his eyes that she had noticed on her Uncle Daniel's face when he returned from an unsuccessful day at Kapiolani Park.

The ladies' race was the last race of the day. Keith escorted Lani to the paddock where a stable boy had Sunbeam saddled and already warmed up.

"Worried?" Keith asked, smiling down at her. The sunlight touched the glints of red in his thick, dark-brown hair, and slanted off the strong cheekbones. The look of strain was gone from his face, and he looked young and carefree, his blue eyes dancing with excitement.

"A little," Lani admitted, looking around her at the other young women in brilliantly colored *pa'us*. They were all amateurs like herself, but, judging from their relaxed airs, they had all probably ridden in other ladies' races. And all riding horses that were much larger than Sunbeam, she saw uneasily.

"Don't be," Keith said confidently. "But remember, Sunbeam's trained to break. She'll take off like a bolt of lightning when the flag goes down, so hang on and don't land behind the saddle. Then just give her her head, and she'll do the rest."

He reached down and brushed her lips with a kiss. "For luck," he said softly. Then he gave her a leg up onto her horse, adjusting the long train again through the stirrups, and stepped back out of her way.

Lani could still feel the soft, warm pressure of those lips against hers as she rode Sunbeam to the starting post. As the horses for the ladies' race jockeyed for position, though, she was too busy trying to handle a nervously impatient Sunbeam to think of anything else. Finally, all the horses were lined up, and the flag fell.

She forgot Keith's warning about the sorrel's breaking fast, and almost did land behind the saddle as the horse shot forward. At the last moment, she managed to grab the reins tightly and hold on to her seat. Her balance had been thrown off, however, hampering Sunbeam's stride. She had been out in front from the starting post, but several other horses were passing her now, dirt flown up from a damp track, splattering Sunbeam and her with mud.

Lani's mouth tightened determinedly. She had to win. It wasn't only that she had always hated losing, but what would Keith think of her if she lost the race? He was depending upon her. She mustn't let him down. Shifting her weight slightly in the saddle, she was only dimly aware of the thundering roar of the crowd of onlookers as she felt Sunbeam find her stride, her legs stretching out beneath her.

She was passing one horse, then another, pelted by stinging clumps of mud that were flung back at her by flying hoofs. Her hair pinned on top of her head slipped free and streamed behind her. She made up one length, then two, and she was in the home stretch, neck and neck with the lead horse, a lean black stallion. She remembered her whip that she hadn't thought to use and brought it down across Sunbeam's flank. Sunbeam surged forward, her legs hardly seeming to touch the ground, and she was past the finish line a length ahead of the black stallion, while the crowd roared its approval.

Hands were pulling her from the horse, Keith's arms enfolding her in a quick, tight hug. Someone was piling leis of gardenias, jasmine, and glistening silvery ginger blossoms over her shoulders and around Sunbeam's neck. A glass of champagne was pressed into her hand, more champagne was poured over Sunbeam's head.

Keith's eyes were a bright, glossy blue with excitement. "I knew Sunbeam could do it," he said triumphantly, hugging Lani again. "All Honolulu will be talking about this race before the day is over."

It wasn't only the race, though, that became the main topic of conversation in Honolulu. It was the young woman who had ridden Sunbeam to victory. If the appearance of the beautiful and virtually unknown Tucker granddaughter at the court ball, cutting a swath through Honolulu's eligible young bachelors, hadn't caused a sensation, her riding the golden sorrel in the ladies' race would have ensured her successful launch into Honolulu society.

And for all the still-strong missionary influence, it was a gay, fun-loving society. The old, aristocratic missionary set still left a party when the dancing began, but the sons and daughters of the nouveau riche merchants and sugar planters, often the descendants of missionaries themselves, danced till dawn, then went for a quick swim at Waikiki before heading home. Lani was soon swept up in the social whirl by her new friends. She was asked to champagne picnics in Palolo Valley, midnight sails to Ford Island, and croquet parties that lasted all night, with the participants holding a torch in one hand and a mallet in the other.

"I don't ever see you anymore," Tom complained one

afternoon when he stopped by the Tucker home. He had
found Lani in the garden, a bowl heaped with flowers before
her, as she wove a half-finished lei of pale yellow plumerias.

"That's not true. I went with you to the hop last week
aboard the USS *Pensacola*, didn't I?"

Tom scowled, remembering how he had had to share Lani
with a dozen eager young naval officers who monopolized her
dances all evening. Anyway, he was darkly suspicious of the
reason for the *Pensacola*'s extended visit to Honolulu in the
first place. The American minister had said grandly, when
questioned, that the *Pensacola* was in Hawaii to "guard
American interests in the islands." Guard them against what?
Tom wondered, annoyed. And what right did the United
States have to post one of its warships permanently in the
harbor of a friendly country?

Lani giggled. "You know when you scowl at me like that
it's almost like your brother, Adam, were here."

If only Adam *were* here, Tom thought, mentally continuing
his list of grievances. Before his brother had left, Adam had
said something about investigating a new, more disease-resistant
strain of sugar cane that had been developed in Louisiana, but
surely he should have returned long before this. At first, Tom
had thought it would be easy, even fun, managing Stewart
and Sons with his brother away. Instead, he had found running the many business interests in which Stewart and Sons
were involved occupied almost his every waking moment.
And the possibility that any wrong decision on his part could
affect the company disastrously, as well as the lives of the
hundreds of men who worked for Stewart and Sons, had
given Tom many a sleepless night.

"I wish Adam were here," he said, gazing, exasperated,
down at Lani. "I'd bet he'd have something to say about your
behavior at the Cummins party last weekend."

Lani had been concentrating on her task, her tapering
fingers skillfully weaving the garland of plumerias. Now she
let the lei fall to her lap and looked up abruptly, her voice
suddenly cool. "I can't imagine why you'd think I'd have
any interest in what your brother has to say!" And then,
uneasily, "What did you hear?"

The party at the Cummins's home on Windward Oahu had

been the social event of the season. Guests had been brought
from Honolulu in the Cummins's private steamship and entertained on the way by musicians and hula dancers. At the
Cummins's luxurious home, an elaborate dinner had been
served on an open lanai from flower-bedecked tables, and the
dancing and entertainment continued by the light of torches
and Chinese lanterns until late at night.

"That you got out on the floor and danced with the hula
girls," Tom said accusingly. "Paul Samuels was telling everyone about it this morning at the bank."

"You don't consider the hula gross and lascivious, the way
the missionaries do?" Lani asked innocently. "I remember
your telling me that the hula was an ancient, sacred Hawaiian
dance, and that it was narrow-minded bigotry that made the
early missionaries ban the dance." Her lovely smile was
gently taunting. "Or have you joined the missionary crowd?"

"Of course not," Tom said, affronted. He had studied the
history of the hula and knew that the dance had served as part
of the Hawaiian religious ritual, honoring their gods and
passing along stories and legends. The more sexually explicit
hulas, which had particularly shocked the early missionaries,
had been used to bring together childless couples in the hope
of increasing their fertility.

Yet knowing all this calmly and intellectually, Tom discovered that the thought of Lani dancing the hula in public, her
lovely, swaying body being ogled by men like Paul Samuels
and his friends, made him rage inside. "It's not the same,"
he said tersely. "Hula dancers who are paid to entertain at
parties like the Cummins's don't know the first thing about
performing the hula properly."

"I wasn't very good at it either," Lani said, laughing. She
tossed back an armful of black, gleaming hair and rose gracefully to her feet. "But your brother dared me, and you know I
never could turn down a dare."

And that was something else, Tom thought gloomily. Didn't
Lani realize that all Honolulu was buzzing about his brother,
supposedly practically engaged to Nellie Samuels, being seen
so often in the company of Lani Tucker? Not only was Nellie
Samuel's nose out of joint, but Tom had even heard, in-

censed, that wagers were being laid between certain gentle-men as to which young lady Keith would bed first.

With Adam away, Tom had decided that it was his respon-sibility to speak to Keith. If Keith was serious about Lani, that was one thing, but when he had approached his brother to discover his intentions toward Lani, his brother had grinned wickedly and said, "My intentions? What they've always been when women are involved. To have a good time, of course, the best that money can buy."

"There are things that money can't buy," Tom had replied pompously.

Keith shrugged. "I agree with Sam Parker. The only thing that money can't buy is poverty."

"You can't buy a woman like Lani Tucker," Tom pro-tested hotly.

Keith's blue eyes glittered with amusement. "Do I detect a note of jealousy?" He clapped Tom on the back, his smile mocking. "Don't worry, little brother. You'll find as you get older that women are like easily opened calabashes. If you lose one, there's always plenty more in the market stall."

"Lani's not like . . . like that," Tom stammered, wishing miserably that he didn't feel so boyishly awkward around Keith. He stiffened his shoulders, his chin sticking out pugna-ciously. "And I won't let you take advantage of her!"

"No?" Keith's handsome face hardened. For a split sec-ond, as he gazed at his half brother, Tom glimpsed an open hostility behind the sunny, transparent blue eyes, a hostility, Tom remembered suddenly, that even as a child his brother would turn upon anyone who tried to thwart or frustrate him.

"Just how will you stop me, *kanake*?" Keith asked, his voice jeering. "Shall I show you just how easy it would be to get your little Lani into my bed? All I'd have to do is crook my finger and . . ."

A blind rage swept over Tom then, or he would never have been foolish enough to strike out at his brother. The fight, if it could be called that, was finished in a matter of minutes. Tom wasn't even sure what happened, except that his fist had never once touched Keith's face. Nor was his own face marked. With a lightning swiftness, Keith had sidestepped, caught Tom's arm, thrown him off balance, and sent him crashing heavily to the floor. Still holding the arm, twisting it ever so slightly so that pain ran agonizingly down into Tom's shoulder, Keith had smiled down at his brother lazily and drawled, "It's a little something I picked up from my Japanese friends. Jujitsu, I think they call it."

Remembering that humiliating incident now, Tom felt a queasiness in his stomach. Oh, not because he had so easily lost the fight, but the nasty shock of realizing that his own brother hated him.

He had been so wrapped up in his own thoughts that at first he didn't hear Lani as she slipped the lei she had made over her head and asked, "Do you like it? I'm wearing it with my *holoku* this afternoon to the charity luau the queen is giving at Washington Place. I know Miss Palmer says it isn't dignified for a woman to wear *holokus* in public, but it's so much more comfortable, wearing a *holoku* to a luau. Anyway, the queen wears *holokus*, and I think she looks very dignified, don't you?"

When Tom didn't answer immediately, she placed a hand on his arm and asked coaxingly, "You're not still angry with me, are you?"

It was very difficult, Tom discovered, to stay angry with anyone who looked as lovely as Lani did at that moment. The lei of fragrant, pale yellow blossoms framed a face that was like a flower itself. The creamy skin had a soft, moist bloom to it, while the pink, sensuously curved lips had the softness of rose petals. She was wearing a flowered cotton *holoku* which fell loosely around the slim body and moved gracefully when she moved. To Tom's mind, there was no question. The *holoku* was a much more becoming garment for a woman than the pinch-waisted, corseted gowns that were the fashion.

He shook his head, grinning. "I'm not angry. I'm just sorry I didn't get to see you dance the hula."

"Well, then I'll dance the hula, especially for you, at my birthday party next week at Palekaiko," Lani promised, her eyes sparkling.

"You're having your birthday party at the ranch?" he asked, surprised.

"It was Keith's idea," Lani said happily. "For my birthday present, he's taking all our friends on his own ship to

Maui. I've already written Loki, and she's having a luau
prepared for us. Oh, nothing so grand as the one we had for
Queen Liliuokalani, of course, but it will be great fun, with
the guests staying on in the guest cottages overnight, just as
they did when my father entertained at Palekaiko.''

"What does Miss Palmer say about all this?"

Lani shrugged her shoulders. "Oh, you know Miss Palmer.
She's been following me around like a prophet of gloom and
doom ever since I won the race at Kapiolani. I'm sure she's
written your brother that I'm headed straight for perdition.''
She suddenly giggled. "That's what's so perfect about having
my party at the ranch. Keith found out that Miss Palmer is
terrified of water, and she won't step foot on a boat. So I
won't have to worry about her looking constantly over my
shoulder at my birthday party.''

And Keith won't have to worry about an inconvenient
chaperone, Tom realized at once, frowning to himself.

"You will come to my birthday luau, won't you?"

Tom wasn't sure what he could do to protect his beloved
from being seduced by his brother, but he was sure as hell
going to try, he thought grimly.

He forced a cheerful smile to his face as he assured Lani,
"Wild horses couldn't keep me away."

Chapter 16

This had to be the night that Keith would propose to her. The
thought ran happily through Lani's mind as she dressed for
her birthday luau in her bedroom at Palekaiko. Oh, not that
he had said anything about marriage in so many words these
last weeks, but the warmth in his eyes when he looked at her,
the way he constantly sought out her company, and the many
times his hand lingered on her arm for no reason, even the
fact that he had gone to so much trouble for her birthday,

using his own ship to bring her guests from Honolulu, all spoke more loudly than words.

Thinking of her guests brought a small frown to Lani's face. It had been an unpleasant shock to discover that Nellie Samuels had been one of the guests Keith had brought aboard at Honolulu. However, when she had managed a few minutes alone with Keith aboard the ship, he had assured her that the girl had practically invited herself, and, naturally, he couldn't be rude and turn her away.

All at once guiltily remembering her duty as hostess, Lani turned to Kimiko, who was helping her dress, and asked, "Were there enough beds for everybody?"

"Plenty enough," Kimiko assured her. "Every cottage, every bed in house, full."

"And a room set aside for the ladies to change?"

The changing room would be used by the guests she had invited from the neighboring ranches. Some of the women guests would arrive on horseback with their evening gowns wrapped in oilskin and tied to their saddles.

"All ready, Lani-san."

The maid finished adjusting the garland of pikakes on Lani's dark hair, then stepped back, a pleased smile hovering on her lips. There would be no other woman at the party as beautiful as her mistress, Kimiko thought proudly, hastily pushing aside the painful thought that Lani Tucker's loveliness would only make Tom Stewart look at her mistress with an even more abject longing on his young face.

Lani turned to look at herself in the mirror and gave a startled laugh of pleasure. The white, heavy silk *holoku* was all the success she had hoped it would be. The bodice fit tightly, the neckline cut daringly low in front and wired higher in the back, with modified mutton-leg sleeves ending in a ruffle of lace. The skirt hung straight to the floor, while in the back, the shimmering silk burst into a tier of bustle poufs cascading down onto the long train. Her dressmaker was worth every penny she had charged to make the *holoku*, Lani thought happily, shrugging aside the unpleasant thought that her guardian undoubtedly wouldn't agree when he received the enormous bill for the gown.

Well, after tonight she needn't concern herself anymore

with Adam Stewart and his parsimonious ways. Once she was married, she wouldn't be bothered with a guardian at all. She would have a husband to look after her. Keith Stewart would be sharing this house with her, this room . . . her glance flew to the virginal, white ruffled bed . . . and a rosy flush of color swept from the creamy swell of skin just above the deep neckline up to the smooth forehead.

Lani had grown up among Hawaiians, for whom lovemaking between a man and woman was a natural, enjoyable part of life, not something to be ashamed of and hidden, so it wasn't embarrassment or fear she felt now at the thought of sharing her bed with Keith Stewart. It was instead a delicious anticipation, spreading its warmth through her body. She could hardly wait for the moment when her lover held her in his strong arms and brought her that mysterious, special pleasure she could only imagine but she was sure would be wonderful. Lani hugged her arms around her, her violet eyes softly shining, filled with dreams of desire.

"Will you wear the pearl necklace?"

"What?" She forced her mind back to the present, to Kimiko waiting patiently for an answer. "Oh, the pearls, no. Pili gave me this to wear for my birthday luau."

Carefully she lifted the lei from the damp towel. She remembered the love that had shone deep in Pili's dark eyes when he had given her the half-dozen strands of white jasmine, and the sadness in his voice as he said, "My *keiki* doesn't need me anymore. My Paakiki now fine, grown up *vahine.*"

She had flung her arms around him. "You mustn't say that, Pili. I'll always need you. And you don't have to worry any longer about the ranch," she assured him. "We'll have all the money we want soon."

Quickly then, she had told him about Keith Stewart, how once they were married, there would be no more worries about the ranch being sold. She was sure that Keith loved Palekaiko as much as she did, and although naturally one didn't talk about such things with a future husband, from the extravagant way Keith spent money he was obviously wealthy and could afford to put the ranch back on a paying basis again.

"So you see, Pili," she finished eagerly, "it's only a matter of time and Palekaiko will be the way it used to be, with the finest stock and pastures, just the way it was when father was alive."

Pili's wise gaze searched the girl's face. "You sure, big happiness in your heart for this man?"

"Of course I'm sure," Lani said, a little hurt that the *luna* should question her feeling for Keith.

Pili nodded gravely. "Then I have happiness in my heart for you, too."

As Lani slipped the jasmine leis over her head, the blossoms as fragile and beautifully carved as a priceless necklace of ivory and pearls, she remembered the sober, questioning look on Pili's face and felt a nervous quiver in her stomach. Oh, not about her love for Keith Stewart. Of that she was as certain as of her love for Palekaiko. But suppose, just suppose, Keith Stewart didn't feel the same?

Of course he did, she told herself firmly. Studying her radiant reflection in the mirror, the white *holoku* a perfect foil for her pale skin and black hair, her dark lashes swept demurely downward over violet eyes that shone with determination. It was just that sometimes a man had to be reminded of what was within his grasp, what he might lose to another man if he didn't act quickly. This evening, she decided, it was time that Keith was reminded!

When she joined her guests who had already started gathering in the garden, the pig had been removed from the *imu* and the fragrance of succulent pork mingled with the scent of the flowers and *palapalai* fern with which Loki and Kimiko had decorated the tables. Japanese lanterns hung from the trees, and torches, like golden flowers, lit the lanai where the food was served. In the background, *paniolo* musicians played Hawaiian waltzes and, as the evening progressed, more rollicking, bawdy tunes.

Too excited to eat, Lani, with a glass of champagne in her hand, moved among her guests. Although she made sure that the female as well as the male guests were having a good time, it was the men upon whom she bestowed her closest attention and flashed her most entrancing smiles. When the dancing began, she was quickly surrounded by a coterie of unattached males, all eager to have the next dance with their hostess. Passing from one pair of arms to another, Lani made a point of outrageously flirting with each and every one of her partners.

Gradually, of course, she became aware of the irritated glances being cast her way by some of the women present whose male friends she was confiscating. But it was her birthday, wasn't it? Lani thought, smiling up into the eyes of her partner, whose name at the moment she wasn't sure she remembered. Why shouldn't she enjoy herself at her own party? Especially when Keith Stewart danced with Nellie Samuels in his arms, and she saw that his handsome face—his blue eyes fastened upon Lani and not his partner—had a most satisfactory look of annoyance in it.

It was at that point that she heard the sound of quarreling voices coming from a group of men standing near the punch bowl. Her partner groaned, "Oh, Lord, no. It's Tom Stewart on his soap box again, all that tripe he's always spouting about Hawaii for the Hawaiians. You'd think he'd be proud of the white blood in his veins instead of spouting off like a *hapa haole.*" Suddenly remembering that his hostess was part Hawaiian, he stammered. "Not . . . not that some of my best friends aren't Hawaiian."

Lani smiled coldly at the man, murmuring "Excuse me" as she stepped from his arms. Walking toward the quarreling men, she could hear Tom shout angrily at Paul Samuels, "She's the queen, damn it. I won't have her name insulted in my presence."

"Liliuokalani's more perverted than her brother," Samuels replied contemptuously. "Everyone knows she listens to *kahunas* and mediums."

"That's a lie!" Lani was close enough now so that she could see Tom's big hands ball into fists, an expression on his face she remembered from their years at school together, the wild look Tom always had just before he started swinging those powerful fists.

Hastily she stepped between the two men. "I refuse to have anyone fighting at my party." She cast a mischievous smile at both men. "Unless it's over me, of course." She placed a hand on Tom's arm, her voice gently coaxing. "The entertainment's about to begin, and you haven't forgotten you promised to sit with me?''

With a last dark look toward Paul Samuels, Tom allowed himself to be led into the garden where an area had been cleared for a display of fireworks, exploding in a shower of gold-and-silver stars against the night sky. Then as the last string of firecrackers finished their thunderous crackling, hidden drums began to beat, and the dancers came from behind the screen of trees, swaying to the drumbeats and the rhythm of gourds and bamboo flutes.

The young hula dancers that Keith had imported, Lani saw at once, were not skilled performers. Although they were graceful and seductive, rotating their hips so their legs glinted in the moonlight, flashing their eyes at the men, all their movements were too pronounced, too obvious. And when they danced, seated on their heels, swinging their upper bodies to the beat of the split bamboo they held in their right hands, they made mistakes and giggled like school girls.

All at once, Lani felt herself being pulled to her feet and propelled toward the dancers. Tom was laughing down at her, his face so darkly flushed she wondered uneasily how much he'd had to drink. ''You said you'd dance the hula for me,'' he said.

''Not now,'' Lani protested, embarrassed.

''You promised,'' Tom insisted stubbornly. ''You danced for the *haoles* at Cummins's party, now you can dance for me.''

Rather than cause a scene, Lani kicked off her shoes and joined the dancers who made way for her, laughing, pulling her into their midst. At first, she concentrated on remembering what Loki had taught her, to keep her knees flexed, the movement of her shoulders to the minimum, while her hands, arms, feet, knees, and hips all moved in harmony. Slowly, her awkwardness slipped away as her young, supple body found the rhythm of the drum beat, and her arms and hands gracefully told the story of the hula.

Around her, the dancers laughed and threw into the music a phrase, the rattling noise of their feathered gourds like the swish of retreating waves on sand. Their hip movements became faster, more lewdly suggestive. The drums beat louder.

The sound of the drums, their commanding, incessant beat, pulsed in Lani's blood, her body obeying, almost atavistically, a primitive command that was older than time. As the drum beat deepened, on and on, faster and louder, she became aware of Keith Stewart standing among the guests, watching her. The torch light flickered across the slanted bones of his face. The clear blue eyes beneath the dark, straight brows, fastened upon her, shining with a burning intensity that made her heart pound even faster.

The rest of the onlookers might not have been. It was for one man, alone, she danced now, her hips swaying slowly, tantalizingly, beneath the weight of the white silk *holoku*. The shimmering *holoku*, as it clung to the lush curves of her body and moved with the undulating movements of her hips, was somehow more revealing than the ti-leaf skirts and scanty tops of the hula dancers. Deliberately, she danced closer to Keith. Her tapered fingers outlined her breasts, her slim waist, the voluptuous swell of her hips, then she held her hands out to the man, offering her body to him for his delectation. She was so close to him now, she could see the flecks of moonlight in the pale blue eyes watching her.

The drums became louder, faster. The hula dancers, surrounding her in a half circle, called out lilting phrases of encouragement as her hips began to rotate more quickly in obedience to the drum beat, became the rolling, sensual movements of a woman in the throes of lovemaking. With one part of her mind, Lani knew she was behaving scandalously, but she no longer cared. All the love for Keith Stewart she had kept bottled up inside herself for so long, all the unspent passion of her young, passionate body, was revealed in her seductive, swaying movements as she danced closer and closer to Keith.

When her tapered fingers touched her lips, then floated, open-palmed, toward the man, in the symbolic gesture of a woman giving herself to her lover, she was oblivious of the shocked expressions on the faces of her other guests. Nothing existed for her now but the drum beat pounding savagely in her blood, the soft, fragrant night wrapping around her, and her lover, waiting in the darkness, to take her in his arms.

The drums swelled to a crescendo, ending so abruptly that

for a moment Lani, as if pulled back from a dream, gazed around her, dazed. Then she saw, appalled, the white, shocked faces staring at her, and she turned and fled into the darkness of the trees. Her face was burning, but her hands were ice cold. Keith was waiting for her. He pulled her into the darker shadows of a monkeypod tree, his arms crushing her so hard against him that she felt the breath leave her body.

"What a tempting little passion flower you are," he murmured hoarsely. "Christ, how I want you. . . ."

For a moment, the hoarse, strained voice, the cruel tightness of the arms around her, frightened Lani, as if it were a stranger holding her. Until Keith's mouth found hers in the darkness, as warm as the night around her, his tongue probing at the softness of her lips, evoking sensations within her that were not at all the same as when Tom Stewart had kissed her. These lips were not gently seeking, but hard, insistent, boldy demanding entrance. She felt her lips parting, responding instinctively in the same atavistic way something deep inside of her had responded to the drumbeats when she danced.

Then the arms released their cruel hold, one hand stroking the silken softness of the *holoku*, slipping down the slender back, while the other hand slid beneath the plunging neckline of the silk gown and caressed the even silkier swell of flesh beneath. A trembling excitement began inside of Lani at the touch of Keith's hand against her breast, so that it was almost painful to twist away, murmuring against his mouth, "No, don't. . . ."

But the hand did not stop its practiced seduction until the satin peak was teased to tautness, and Keith laughed softly, triumphantly at Lani's startled gasp of pleasure. "This is what you want, isn't it? Why pretend? This is what you've wanted all along."

The fingers continued, teasing at the taut peak, as Keith's voice whispered urgently, his breath warm against her face. "Come to my cottage tonight, and I'll show you how much I love you." Then, when she didn't reply at once, he added harshly, "Or is it that you don't love me?"

"You know I do."

"Well, then, why should we wait? If you really love me, what else matters?" His lips found the smooth column of her throat, caressed the soft hollow at its base. "Say you'll come, my love," he whispered. "Prove that you love me. . . ."

"Yes." The word seemed wrenched from deep inside of Lani.

Abruptly, she felt the hand withdraw from her breast, her gown being pulled back over her shoulder. Keith sighed regretfully. "I hate leaving you, my sweet, even for a little while. But you'd better make yourself presentable and return to your guests. You've caused enough of a sensation for one night."

He kissed her again, a deep, possessive kiss that left Lani shaken when he finally pulled away and disappeared into the darkness. She hurried to the back of the house and slipped in through the kitchen, making her way to her bedroom. In her mirror she saw, dismayed, that the jasmine garlands were crushed beyond repair. Her hair fell disheveled around her shoulders, and her face was noticeably flushed. She removed the lei and splashed cold water on her face. There was no time to look for Kimiko, so she did what she could to repair her damaged hairdo herself. When she had finished, she couldn't help wishing cravenly that she could stay hidden here in her room, rather than face her guests again. But, of course, Keith was right. She was the hostess, and she must return to her party, as uncomfortable as it might be for her.

Well, after tonight it wouldn't matter, she told herself, smiling dreamily. Once she and Keith were married, the gossip about her shocking behavior tonight wouldn't make any difference. Absently, she realized that Keith hadn't mentioned marriage, but, naturally, he was too much of a gentleman to have asked her to his room if he didn't plan to marry her.

She was still smiling as she hurried down the front stairs, then stopped, her smile fading as she saw Adam Stewart waiting at the foot of the staircase.

"What are you doing here?" she demanded, startled.

"I'm delighted to see you, too," he drawled.

Realizing how inhospitable she must have sounded, she said, quickly, "I'm sorry. It's only I thought you were still in the United States."

"I returned on the *Mariposa* yesterday morning. Miss Palmer informed me that you had left for Palekaiko an hour before I arrived to celebrate your birthday here at the ranch. I decided to join the festivities.''

No doubt, Abigail Palmer had informed her guardian of a great many other things, Lani thought bitterly, which had brought her guardian rushing to Maui. She advanced slowly down the staircase, wondering if her guardian had seen her dance the hula earlier, and discovered that she was oddly flustered at the thought that he might have.

''Have you been here long?''

''I've only just arrived.'' Adam's voice flattened. ''Naturally, if you'd prefer I leave . . .''

It suddenly occurred to Lani that the presence of Adam Stewart on her arm when she returned to the party could be a great help in facing down the scandalized glances that were sure to be coming her way.

''Of course I don't want you to go. I'm delighted you could come to my party.'' She gave the man a brilliant smile, tucking her hand into his arm. ''In fact, I insist that you must dance with me. After all, it is my birthday.''

There was a quizzical look in the dark gray eyes, but obediently Mr. Stewart led the way out onto the lanai, where a quick glance around told Lani that Keith had discreetly disappeared. The hula dancers had disappeared also, but the musicians were playing a romantic waltz for the guests who had not already drifted off to bed, the moon so low in the sky that the garden was filled with tangled shadows.

Lani discovered that Adam Stewart's presence beside her, his hand resting lightly, protectively on her arm, was daunting enough to deflect the outraged glances of some of the women guests. And not just outrage, she noticed, amused. As she walked beside Mr. Stewart to the area that had been cleared in the garden for dancing, she heard one young lady whisper enviously to her friend, ''Will you look at that! Now she has all three of the Stewart brothers wrapped around her finger.''

Lani had to repress a giggle, trying to imagine Adam Stewart wrapped around any woman's finger. Yet, as her guardian swung her easily into a waltz step, she was very aware of his hands resting firmly around her. All at once, she was reminded of the night of the queen's luau when some vital force from the man had seemed to be flowing into her through those hands.

Wanting to forget that disturbing memory, she said, hastily, "You dance very well, Mr. Stewart."

"You sound surprised," he said, amused. "And do you suppose you could manage to call me Adam? After all, I am a rejected suitor."

The gray eyes laughed down at her, but for a moment Lani thought she saw something else behind the laughter, a look in her guardian's eyes that made her wonder, stunned. Was it possible? Had Adam Stewart's marriage proposal not been just a business proposition, pure and simple? Could it be that it wasn't wounded male pride he had felt when she rejected him, but something deeper?

Lani could not resist a thrill of triumph at the thought. After all these years of having to live under Adam Stewart's thumb, of being forced to do his bidding, from his threats of selling Palekaiko to enduring the impossible Miss Palmer, how gratifying to know her guardian was as vulnerable, as open to a woman's wiles as the next man.

She smiled provocatively up at the man and murmured, "Perhaps you gave up too quickly, Adam."

She felt his arms tighten around her, a wintry smile in the gray eyes that made her feel suddenly distinctly wary. "What makes you think I've given up?" he asked, almost casually.

Well, really, Lani thought, her triumph changing to annoyance. What an impossible man. She would have walked off and left him standing alone on the dance floor, but she remembered belatedly that she had already caused one scene at her party tonight. She didn't dare create another.

She forced herself to smile at her partner, reminding herself that she only had to endure his company for another hour or two, until the party was over and she could go to Keith's cottage. It might even teach Adam Stewart a much-needed lesson in humility, she decided sternly, letting him believe she was interested in him, and then rejecting him again.

For what remained of the evening, she stayed by Adam's side, flirting with him charmingly, as if she were unable to tear herself away from him, succeeding so well that finally

she began to wonder, worried, how she would ever manage to
gracefully break free of the man. Then as she and Adam were
strolling through the garden, they came across Tom, peacefully passed out beneath an algaroba tree.

Shrugging ruefully, Adam knelt down beside his brother,
then, looking up at Lani, said, "I'd better see that he gets to
bed." His intent gaze searched Lani's face. "Will you wait?
There's something I want to talk to you about."

She gave him a melting, intimate smile. "There's something I want to tell you, too, but I'm afraid it'll have to wait
till morning." She pretended to stifle a yawn. "It's much too
late for serious conversation."

Before he could insist, she hurried back to the lanai, where
the few drunken revelers who were left didn't even notice as
she slipped into the house and up the stairs. She would have
something to tell Adam Stewart, she thought, relishing the
pleasure she would feel tomorrow when she told her guardian
that she was marrying his brother.

Kimiko was waiting in her bedroom to help her mistress
undress. The maid slowly and painstakingly checked each
piece of clothing before putting it aside for washing or hanging it carefully in the wardrobe, while Lani waited in an
agony of impatience for the girl to leave. Even after Kimiko
finally left, though, Lani could still hear voices on the lanai
and in the garden, the servants clearing up the remnants of the
luau. It wasn't until all the torches had been extinguished and
the only sound from the garden was the sleepy chirping of
birds that Lani pulled on her sheer cotton robe and crept down
the back stairs.

When she stepped out of the house, the moon was hidden
behind a bank of clouds, and the darkness closed around her
so thick she couldn't see her hand before her face. She knew
the garden too well, however, to have any trouble finding her
way in the dark. The cottage where Keith was staying was
only a short walk from the main house, but when she reached
the small lanai her heart was pounding, as if she'd run all the
way. There was a nervous fluttering in her throat, and her
mouth felt dry as a bone. Without giving herself time to
think, afraid if she did she would turn and flee back to the

house and the familiar safety of her bedroom, she pushed open the door.

The inside of the cottage was as dark as the garden. For a moment she stood, disoriented, until her eyes grew accustomed to the blackness and she was able to make out darker shapes that were pieces of furniture. As she approached the bed, her slippered feet making a whispering sound over the mat-covered floor, she saw a dark, shadowy figure rise from the bed. And she knew with a rush of joy it was Keith, waiting for her to come to him.

With a soft cry, she ran into his arms.

Chapter 17

Lani had expected Keith's arms to immediately close around her as they had in the garden earlier. Instead, unexpectedly, they hung at his side. Was he expecting her to make the first move? she wondered. Hesitantly, she rose on tiptoe and placed her lips softly against his. The mouth was quiet, cool beneath her own. Bewildered, she stepped closer, her mouth moving slowly, longingly across those unresponsive lips. Her arms lifted, her hands crept behind his neck and tightened, pulling his mouth closer to hers.

She felt a tremor pass through the taut body she held in her arms, and suddenly the mouth was no longer unresponsive. The arms moved and tightened, almost convulsively, around her, her pliant curves molded so close to Keith's muscular body that she realized at once that he was wearing no night clothes at all. The feel of that warm flesh penetrated the sheer gown and robe she wore, and something else, something alien and hard pressing intimately against her.

Momentarily dismayed, she tried to pull away, but the arms around her, oddly gentle for all the strength of their grasp, would not release her. The mouth on hers moved almost lazily, teasing and caressing, not just her lips but across her cheeks to her closed eyelids, though always returning to taste again her mouth, each time seeking deeper within its softness. All at once, she no longer wanted to leave the circle of those hard arms, or for the mouth to stop its tender assault, sending waves of pleasure through her body. She could not bear to have him leave her, so that when he suddenly stopped, she cried out in soft protest and pulled him close to her again.

He muttered something beneath his breath. Her robe fell away to the floor, and she was being lifted and lowered gently onto the bed. She felt his mouth at her breast, his tongue teasing, caressing, until the peak stood taut and proud, while his hand slid downward. Thrusting aside the filmy gown, the hand slid along her satin thighs and upward. She shivered as raw pleasure raced along her nerve ends when he touched her, the sensations mounting unbearably.

She was aware that he had swung himself above her. She wished she could see his face, but it was shrouded in darkness. Reaching up, she traced from memory with her fingers the familiar face, the straight nose and long mouth, running her hands lightly over his hair, delighting in the crisp feel of it beneath her fingers. Then her hand moved downward, gliding over the broad, muscular shoulders, across the taut chest, feeling the muscles in that chest jerk beneath her touch.

He gave a muffled groan as his own hands caught and held hers, imprisoned, away from him, his voice low. "You'll marry me, tomorrow, as soon as possible?"

"Of course," she said impatiently, wishing that like him she was wearing nothing at all, so that there would not be even a sheer cloth between her flesh and his. She arched her body upward, to bring herself closer to him, to that alien hardness that was not alien anymore as her thighs parted eagerly to receive him. He entered her slowly, carefully, so that the pain she felt was transient, quickly forgotten, as he thrust deeper. Finally, there was no longer any memory of pain, only an explosion of joy, and she lay spent, drowsy with love, in his arms.

When her body had ceased its pleasant throbbing and she could almost think clearly again, she thought how foolish she had been to worry for a moment that it wasn't marriage Keith had in mind. "Mrs. Stewart," she murmured happily. "Mrs. Keith Stewart. I've waited so long for you, darling. Do you really think we can be married tomorrow?"

At first she thought it was her imagination, the stiffening of his body in her arms, but she knew she didn't imagine the sudden, bewildering coldness in his low voice. "It's almost dawn. You'd better leave."

Slowly, reluctantly, she got to her feet, found her robe in the darkness, and wrapped it around her. Then she stood uncertainly beside the bed. "Is something wrong?" she asked. Had she somehow disappointed him in their lovemaking, she wondered unhappily. Was that why he was sending her away so abruptly?

As if he sensed what she was thinking, he swung out of bed and pulled her roughly into his arms. Any doubts that she had about having failed him were dispelled by a kiss that spoke louder than any words and left her limp and breathless in his arms. Gently he urged her to the door. "It'll be light soon. You mustn't be seen leaving here," he said softly.

He was right, of course, she thought, relieved. It would be disastrous if she were seen leaving a man's cottage in her nightgown and robe.

She brushed his lips with one last, lingering kiss, then slipped out the door. Although it was still dark, the clouds had scattered and she could make out the shape of Haleakala, a darker indigo blue than the sky around it, an early morning star shining faintly above it. In a few more moments she knew the silvery ghost dawn would blaze up above the summit, and if she didn't hurry, Charlie would be rattling his pots and pans in the kitchen, preparing breakfast for the *paniolos*.

She made it to her room without being seen and fell exhausted into bed. She thought she would be too excited to sleep, but the minute her head hit the pillow she plunged ocean-deep into sleep.

When she awoke again, the room was filled with sunlight and Kimiko was padding around softly, laying out her mistress's clothes for the day. Memory rushed back, and Lani stretched luxuriously. Except for certain pleasantly aching muscles, she had never felt happier or more vibrantly alive.

Then she realized how late it was, and remembered there was a lunch planned for her guests before they boarded the ship and returned to Honolulu. She swung out of bed. "You should have awakened me sooner, Kim."

The maid shrugged, her face impassive. "No hurry. Loki say okay you sleep. Everyone sleep late."

Lani heard the hint of disapproval in Kimiko's voice and wondered if Kim had heard about the hula she had danced at the party. No doubt she had, as well as all the other servants. Loki, she was sure, wouldn't be at all disturbed by Lani's behaving in what Loki would consider a perfectly natural fashion. Evidently, though, Kimiko didn't feel the same. Lani even wondered, a little uncomfortably, if Kim somehow knew about her late night visit to Keith's cottage.

Well, there wasn't time to soothe Kim's ruffled feathers, she decided as she bathed and slipped into a blue muslin ruffled gown, with a demure high-boned collar, hoping that the prim gown would offset the rather immodest picture she had presented the night before, performing the hula in her silk *holoku*.

As she hurried down the stairs, she found that her guests were already gathered on the lanai, where tables had been set with pink damask cloths, heavy silver, sparkling crystal, and Crown Derby china. A fluffy pink carnation lei hung on each chair.

She saw Keith at once at the far side of the lanai, but since he was talking to Nellie Samuels, his handsome face bent attentively to the young woman, she decided not to join them. Had he already told Nellie that he had proposed marriage to another woman last night? If so, the girl was taking it well. Nellie, in a white foaming gown, looked prettier, her plain features softer, than Lani had ever seen her.

Adam and Tom were standing together, too, Tom rather the worse for wear, his eyes red rimmed, a hangdog look on his young face. Looking at Tom, Lani felt a faint stirring of guilt. She must tell him as soon as possible about Keith and her, she thought, if he hadn't already guessed.

Then as Charlie came in to tell her the food was ready, Nellie Samuels stepped shyly forward.

"May I make an announcement, Lani?" she asked. She

smiled sweetly, but there was a gleam of smug triumph in the look she gave her hostess. She reached for Keith's hand, holding it tightly. "Mr. Stewart . . . Keith and I, are to be married." She gave a soft, nervous giggle. "Actually, you're all the first to know. We haven't even told Papa yet."

Lani felt as if she had been hit a blow just below her heart. She stood rigid, unable to breath, unable to move, all her senses frozen. Dimly, as if her vision were clouded, she saw a fleeting look of anger touch Keith's face, before he turned, smiling, to Nellie, who smiled shyly back at him, her eyes shining softly. All at once, Lani recognized that new softness in Nellie's face. It was the same look she had seen on her own face when she had looked in the mirror that morning, the look of a girl no longer but a woman fulfilled.

She tasted a sudden, sour nausea in her throat as she realized that Keith must already have proposed marriage to Nellie, even before she had gone to his room last night. Waves of embarrassment scorching her skin, mixed with the beginnings of anger, melted the odd frozen stillness that had imprisoned her. She discovered that she could breathe again, that she was humiliatingly aware of the covert glances her guests were casting her way, some sympathetic, some curious to see her reaction to Nellie's announcement after the way she had thrown herself at Keith Stewart the night before.

And she became aware of something else. Adam had moved quietly to stand beside her. His arm rested lightly around her waist, but she was acutely conscious of the strength of that arm supporting her as he cleared his throat and announced with a wry smile, "It seems that Miss Samuels and my brother have stolen our thunder. Last evening Miss Tucker did me the great honor of accepting my proposal of marriage. The ceremony will take place tomorrow afternoon, here at Palekaiko."

Lani hardly felt the second shock to hit her, as if her mind and senses were still reeling, unable to cope with two blows within the space of five minutes. She gave Adam a sideways, startled glance. He couldn't be serious, and yet he was smiling down at her, for all the world like a doting groom to be, and his arm, tight around her waist, made it impossible for her to pull away.

She could feel her own lips curving automatically into a set smile as she accepted the best wishes of her guests crowding around her, but it was like some other woman standing there, a stranger, smiling, giving the proper responses.

Tom came up to her, touched her cheek lightly with lips that felt dry and cold, and she saw in his sherry eyes a pain that reflected her own, before he turned quickly away.

Tom slipped quietly from the lanai and entered the house. His head ached from too much to drink the night before and the thought of food turned his stomach, even if he could have endured sitting across the table from Lani, knowing now that she could never be his. He found the liquor cabinet in the parlor, poured himself a stiff drink, and downed it quickly, without tasting it.

He stared broodingly at his empty glass. Well, at least if he had to lose Lani to someone else, he thought glumly, he was glad it was Adam and not Keith. Strange, but it had never once occurred to him that Adam might be his competition. Somehow he had the impression that Lani had never cared much for his older brother. Which just proved how little he knew about women, he decided morosely. Shoving the cork back into the bottle, he decided to take the liquor back to his cottage and finish it there.

The blinds in his cottage had been pulled against the early morning sun. When he stepped into the room, it took several seconds for his eyes to adjust to the cool gray dimness. At first he didn't see Kimiko. She was standing in the shadows, her hands tucked into the sleeves of her white cotton kimono, her eyes cast downward, reminding him of that other time, when he had first met her at the brothel. He caught her scent, the faint tea and citrus fragrance suddenly triggering other memories: the delicate, Dresden beauty of that small body beneath the kimono, the sweet softness of her mouth beneath his, and the way she had given herself to him with unstinting, unquestioning warmth.

She stepped out of the shadows into a path of sunlight, and lifted her gaze to his. Her dark eyes were filled with sorrow and compassion. "If you wish, I go," she said softly.

So she knew, Tom thought, his face flushed with misery. She knew that her mistress had chosen his brother. Was that why she was here, to console him? But all at once it didn't matter why she was here. In two strides he had crossed the room, and all that mattered was her soft, slim arms holding him close with unbelievable strength. The kimono parted, and his overheated face was pressed against her cool breasts, her hands gently caressing the nape of his neck while she crooned to him tenderly, as if he were a child needing comforting. Her hands deftly undressed him, then pulled him to the bed, her arms holding him close, until he finally found blessed oblivion, burying himself in the softness of her body.

Lani thought the lunch would never end. Afterward, she didn't remember what she ate, or what she said, or even bidding farewell to her guests as they departed for the ship that would return them to Honolulu. Voices, faces, were all blurred. Her first clear memory was finding herself seated in the front parlor of the house, and Adam pressing a glass into her hand. "Drink it," he ordered.

Obediently she lifted the glass and swallowed the liquid. The fire of the liquor scalding her throat, bringing tears to her eyes, jolted her out of her numbness.

"That's better," Adam said approvingly, studying her face, then took the large, overstuffed chair across from her. "Now we can talk."

Lani put down the glass, her voice stiff. "There's nothing to talk about."

"Our marriage? Will tomorrow be too soon for the ceremony? I hate to rush you, but I do have to return to Honolulu as soon as possible."

She stared at him, speechless, then blurted, "You can't . . . you can't mean . . . you certainly don't intend to hold me to what you said. . . ."

"I meant every word of it," he said flatly. "And I don't recall hearing you object to our impending marriage." He shrugged indifferently. "Of course, if you prefer, I can publicly withdraw my marriage proposal."

Lani winced. It was bad enough, being rejected by Keith after she had so obviously thrown herself at him. If a second Stewart brother should withdraw his offer of marriage, she would never live it down. And it was true, she realized, she hadn't protested when Adam Stewart had made his surprising announcement. She had been secretly relieved, grasping eagerly at his words to save face and salvage her damaged pride after Nellie's announcement.

She flared angrily. "A gentleman would allow a lady to break an engagement." Suddenly remembering his other offer of marriage, she asked, suspiciously, "Or is this just another business proposition?"

"Call it what you want," he said coldly, his face with that obdurate, stony look that she remembered so well. "The offer stands."

So it was a business merger, not a real marriage, he had in mind. And she was surprised to find herself thinking, well, why not? She could never feel toward another man the way she had felt toward Keith. She didn't even want to. Why should any sane woman want to open herself to such pain again? A marriage of convenience, with no possibility of being hurt or betrayed, was much more sensible.

Outside the open window, she could hear the *paniolos* lining up at the ranch office built on one end of the house. It was Saturday afternoon, payday. She heard their big bell spurs, their rich Polynesian laughter as they planned their Saturday night's fun, how they would spend their wages. Except, she thought, without her marriage to Keith, without the money he would have brought to the ranch, there would be no more wages, no more jobs. Some of the men had been born at Palekaiko, had never worked anywhere else. What would happen to them if the ranch ceased to exist?

She sat up straighter, forcing her voice to a coldness to match the man's sitting across from her. "If the marriage is a business proposition, then what is there in it for me?" she asked.

There was a flicker of anger, quickly stilled, in the narrowed eyes watching her. Suddenly, unexpectedly, Adam laughed. "What did you have in mind?"

Lani took a deep breath and spoke quickly. "I want enough money to put the ranch on a solid financial footing again."

Adam frowned. "That would take a small fortune."

Lani felt her hands trembling in her lap and hid them in the fold of her skirt. She wasn't sure whether she was fearful

because Adam Stewart might refuse her offer or panic stricken
that he might accept. The silence between them seemed to
stretch out interminably. She could hear a guitar being strummed
softly as the *paniolos* waited patiently outside the office for
Pili to pay them, heard the ticking of the huge grandfather
clock in a corner of the room that had come to her father from
his New England grandmother.

Then she heard Adam Stewart's chair being pushed back
with a grating sound over the hardwood floor as he rose to his
feet. "Since we're negotiating on the terms of our contract,"
he said dryly, "I have several conditions of my own."

She glanced up, warily. "Yes?"

"First, I want to be a full partner with you in owning the
ranch."

She hesitated a moment, then nodded. Since Adam would
be providing the money, it was only fair that he should be a
half owner of Palekaiko.

"Second . . ." He paused, his glance traveling slowly,
deliberately over her tense body. "Upon entering into this
contract, you will fulfill all the duties and responsibilities that
a wife usually performs."

Her violet eyes flared wide, a dull flush spreading beneath
the creamy skin of her face. He couldn't mean . . . but, of
course, she realized that that was exactly what he did mean.
And, grudgingly, she had to admit that as her husband he
would have the right to expect her to share his bed. Had she
really expected they would live together as brother and sister?
Perhaps if she hadn't made love last night with Keith, if she
hadn't discovered how it felt, giving herself freely, joyfully to
the man she loved, the thought of lying with any other man
might not have made her feel almost physically ill. Her hands
clenched in her lap, her fingernails jabbing painfully into the
softness of her palms. She mustn't think of Keith! After all,
what had that rapture brought her but pain?

She got slowly to her feet. "Very well," she said, so softly
that Adam had to strain to hear her.

"Ordinarily, I seal a contract with a handshake," Adam
said gravely. Behind his sober voice she had the feeling that
he was laughing at her. "But in this case, a kiss might be
more in order."

"If you wish," she said coolly, closing her eyes and lifting her face primly to him. At first, his mouth on hers was lightly caressing, but when she stood unresponsive, stiff as a board within his embrace, the mouth became more insistent, slanting back and forth across her lips so that all at once she was reminded of Keith's kissing her the night before. And the only way she could endure the agony that slashed through her then was to hold herself rigid, her arms held across her breast, braced against the pain.

Abruptly the arms around her fell away. She opened her eyes to find Adam staring down at her, his gray eyes thoughtful. "I might as well have settled for the handshake," he said.

She lifted her chin haughtily at his implied disappointment in her kiss. "I agreed to fulfill my marital obligations. I didn't promise to enjoy them," she said tartly.

So that was how it was to be, Adam thought, studying the willful set of the girl's lips, the defiance in the brilliant amethyst eyes. He smiled to himself wryly but not without anticipation. It promised to be a stormy wedding night.

Chapter 18

The very small, very informal wedding of Lani Tucker to Adam Stewart took place the following day in the garden of Palekaika. The bride wore a simple pink-sprigged muslin gown with a pink rosebud garland in her hair and an open lei of maile over her shoulders. She had chosen Kimiko and Loki as her attendants and Pili, wearing his best *paniolo* outfit and a proud smile, to give her away. Adam had persuaded Tom to stay on as his best man, and the only guests were the employees of the ranch, the house servants, and the ranch hands.

Lani never discovered where Adam had found the Hawaiian preacher who performed the ceremony. A large, handsome man with dark, flashing eyes, he held the religious ardor of the early missionaries in the deep rolling cadences of his booming voice. However, the red carnation lei he wore, the beaming smile he bestowed upon the bride and groom, the spirit of aloha that seemed to pour from him, was pure Hawaiian.

Up to the last minute, she had not been sure that she could go through with the marriage ceremony. As Pili escorted her to the makeshift altar under a banyan tree where Adam and the minister waited, she had to fight back an almost overwhelming impulse to turn and run. When Adam had turned and watched her approach, his hair looking more red than brown in the sunlight, his deeply tanned, sharply angled face was that of a stranger. But a stranger who looked heartbreakingly like Keith. If only it had been Keith standing there, waiting for her, how she would have flown to his side, as if her feet had wings. The thought sent waves of desolation through her. She saw Adam's eyes, watching her, narrow in that familiar, piercing gaze, as if he knew exactly what she was thinking. When she reached the altar, he stepped quickly to her side. His hand reaching for hers might have seemed a lover's gesture, but the grip was too strong for her to pull free.

The marriage ceremony was over with more quickly than she had thought possible. As she turned away from the altar, after Adam had dropped, this time, a very chaste kiss on her lips, she caught an expression on Kimiko's face that surprised her. It was a fleeting look, but one of such love and adoration that the girl's delicately shaped face seemed lit, for a moment, from within. Curious, her mistress turned to see to whom the look was directed.

And she wondered, shocked, how long had Kimiko and Tom been lovers? Yet she knew it wasn't shock alone she felt, but jealousy. Oh, not because Tom had once been her suitor, but because Kim so obviously felt the way Lani had felt about Keith. And Kimiko did not have to deny herself the embraces of the man she adored.

Beside her, Adam's hand tightened on her arm, his voice low. "Don't look so unhappy, Paakiki." Amusement crept into his voice. "Remember, in gaining a husband, you lose Abigail Palmer."

She smiled in spite of herself, then asked, "How did you know I was called Paakiki?"

"I heard Pili call you that." He grinned teasingly down at her. "It means stubborn, doesn't it? Somehow it suits you."

Before she could reply, her guests had swept forward and surrounded her, demanding her attention. The *paniolos* heaped garlands of flowers around her; the Japanese and Chinese servants presented hastily gathered gifts, exquisitely wrapped, many of them from their own small store of treasures. Loki wept happily.

There wasn't time for a wedding party. The newly married couple had to leave immediately after the ceremony to catch the afternoon steamer to Honolulu. The crossing was even rougher than usual, so that even Lani, who was a good sailor, felt squeamish, and Kimiko, her face frozen with misery, was unable to rise from her bed. Tom, who was returning to Honolulu on the same ship with his brother and sister-in-law, also turned out to be a bad sailor. While Lani did what she could to make Kimiko comfortable through the night, Adam was kept busy looking after his brother.

It wasn't exactly the way he had planned to spend his wedding night, Adam thought as he and his new bride drove away from the wharf in Honolulu the next day, Kimiko following in another carriage with the luggage. He studied Lani's face, noticing the marks of weariness there, for all that she sat stiffly erect beside him. But weariness was all he saw there, he thought, relieved, his eyes moving swiftly over her face.

She must have felt his gaze upon her, for she suddenly turned, her voice snappish. "I wish you wouldn't do that."

"Do what?"

"Look at me, like a shopkeeper taking inventory."

"You're tired," he said soothingly. "Not that I blame you for being irritable." He reached for her hand, stroking it gently. "Last night was hardly the perfect wedding night. But don't worry, Paakiki. I promise you, we'll make up for it tonight."

He felt her hand stiffen, but she did not draw it away, only turning her face away from him to stare out the carriage window.

Did he really think she didn't prefer the seasickness, she thought bleakly, to sharing his bed? Then she took a closer look out the window. The carriage wasn't driving up into the Nuuanu Valley where the Stewart family home was located, but heading up Beretania Street, stopping finally before the pillared veranda of the Tucker home.

She gave Adam a startled glance, as he came around and helped her from the carriage. "Why are we stopping here?"

"This is where we'll be living," he replied. "There didn't seem to be any sense in letting this house stand vacant."

And Keith, no doubt, would want to bring his bride to the Stewart family home, Lani realized, and wondered wearily how long it would be before she could think of Keith and Nellie Samuels without a fresh stab of pain, as if each time were the first time.

Once again she was aware of her husband's sharp, penetrating stare, but Adam's voice, when he spoke, was carefully noncommittal. "If you prefer, I can find us somewhere else to live."

"No," Lani said hastily. At least living in her own home, with her familiar things around her, made being married somehow more palatable.

She started up the stairs, then stopped when she realized Adam wasn't following her. "I'll be busy at the office the rest of the day," he said when she glanced back over her shoulder. "Oh, and I'll have my clothes and some personal items sent over sometime today," he added casually. "Would you have someone unpack them? I think, perhaps, your uncle's room would be best for me."

Did that mean they would have separate bedrooms? she thought, relieved. Except, of course, separate bedrooms didn't necessarily mean separate beds. It was, after all, only a short walk from her uncle's bedroom to hers.

Pushing that unnerving thought from her mind, she threw herself into her unpacking as soon as Kim arrived with her luggage, then went over the menu for dinner that evening with Ah Sing before he left for the market.

The cook's eyes crinkled at the corners with knowing

laughter. "Don't worry, missy. I make fine number one wedding dinner for you and your *kane*. You see."

Lani had already become aware of the giggles hidden behind hands, the sidelong glances that had been cast her way by the servants since she had arrived home. No doubt Honolulu was gossiping, too, about Lani Tucker's sudden marriage to Adam Stewart, especially since it had been so obvious she had set her cap for his brother. Well, let the old biddies gossip, she thought. What did she care what they said?

Returning to her bedroom, she found Kimiko struggling with several satchels spread out on the bed. "Mr. Stewart's clothes," Kim said. "They just arrived." She glanced helplessly at the wardrobes and chests of drawers already filled with Lani's belongings. "No more room."

"They don't belong here anyway," Lani said sharply. "Take them to my Uncle Daniel's bedroom."

Her maid gave her a bewildered glance and looked as if she were about to protest, but a second glance at her mistress's face made her change her mind. After Kimiko had gone, taking the bags with her, Lani went to the window, staring, without seeing, out over the garden. How was she ever going to get through this evening? And not just this evening, she thought, but the months and years stretching endlessly before her. Her head was already beginning to pound, and the heavy, cloying scent from the Lady of the Night vine that grew outside her window, which she usually enjoyed, all at once turned her stomach.

She turned away from the window and began to pace around the room. She had the feeling that walls were closing in on her, as if she were in a prison. A prison of her own making, she reminded herself bitterly. No one had forced her to marry Adam Stewart. She had made the choice freely. She suddenly stopped her pacing, frowning at her reflection in the mirror. She knew why she had married Adam, to save face and to save Palekaiko, but for the first time she wondered: why had Adam married her? Certainly she had no illusions that he loved her, any more than she loved him. A business arrangement, he had called it. Or was it much more simple than that? A man like Adam Stewart, who was fast becoming one of the wealthiest and most influential men in Hawaii, needed a wife to take care of his home, to help entertain his friends, to bear his children to carry on the family name.

At this last thought, a sick feeling suddenly lurched through Lani. For there was something else she was sure a *haole* like Adam Stewart wanted in a wife. To a Hawaiian it wouldn't matter if a woman had taken a lover before she married. But to a man like Adam Stewart who came from stern, missionary stock? And hadn't she read somewhere that a man could always tell when he made love to a woman whether or not she was still a virgin?

Lani sank down on the edge of the bed. The pounding of her head was reaching a crescendo. Finally, wearily, she rose to her feet. First, she must somehow get through facing her husband across the dining room table. She would worry about the nerve-wracking, revealing intimacy of the marriage bed later.

Facing her new husband across the dinner table, however, proved no problem. Adam did not show up for dinner. Lani waited as long as she could, but when it became embarrassingly clear that her husband was not coming home for dinner, Lani ate alone, forcing herself to swallow the food that Ah Sing had so proudly prepared.

Ignoring the sympathetic glances of the servants, and carefully not allowing herself to show her own irritation, Lani finished the dinner then took a stroll through the garden, pruning shears in hand. As she snapped viciously with the shears, beheading roses, it was Adam Stewart's face she saw in her mind's eye. How dare he not bother to show up for dinner? Snap, snap, clip, clip. Wilted roses fell decapitated around her. How dare he humiliate her before the servants?

Finally, it grew too dark to see the flowers. She returned to the front parlor, where the gas lamps had been lit, and picked up a book to read. When it was almost ten o'clock and Adam still hadn't returned, she got to her feet, not sure whether she was more relieved or annoyed at his absence. In any case, she refused to wait around half the night for her husband to return, she thought, taking a lamp in her hand and ascending the staircase to her bedroom.

Kimiko had already laid out her night things, not her usual simple cotton nightgown but a special gown made of white silk, Valenciennes lace, and satin ribbon that Lani had ordered from Paris months before. She remembered when the gown had arrived how carefully and happily she had packed it away for her trousseau, imaging the ardent warmth in Keith's blue eyes when he saw her in the gown on their wedding night.

Her face stiff with misery, she picked up the gown to pack it away again. Then she hesitated. Well, it wouldn't do any harm just to try the gown on, she decided. Of course, she had no intention of wearing it for Adam, but it seemed a shame not at least to see what she looked like in it. She undressed quickly then slipped the gown over her head. The gown fell in a silken cloud around her, the material so fine spun she felt as if she were wrapped in gossamer. It was sheer as gossamer, too, she saw as she gazed at herself in the mirror. She could glimpse the curve of breasts that might have been carved from ivory, but for the soft, rosy peaks.

The knock at the door came so unexpectedly that she barely had time to whirl, startled, when the door opened and Adam stepped into the room.

For just one second the gray eyes swept over her, the lamplight behind her displaying to full advantage the body beneath the diaphanous gown. Her heart thudding in her chest, Lani realized that she might just as well have been wearing nothing at all. Then, as if it were an everyday occurrence to find her, half-clothed, waiting for him, Adam advanced into the room, removing his jacket and tossing it onto a chair. "I'm glad you're still awake," he said, his voice matter of fact. "I was afraid you might be asleep."

Why wasn't she asleep, Lani raged inwardly. In another few minutes she would have been. If she hadn't been so vain and wanted to try on the gown, if she had gone straight to bed . . .

Ignoring her frozen silence, Adam continued to undress, his voice politely apologetic. "I'm sorry I couldn't let you know that I wouldn't be here for dinner. There were a great many matters that needed my immediate attention." He frowned absently. "I know Daniel didn't approve of modern conveniences, but I've made arrangements to have a telephone installed in the house. That way, when I'm going to be late, I can call you and let you know.''

As he talked, he removed his shoes, his shirt, and trousers. When Lani realized he had no intention of stopping there, she flushed and averted her eyes quickly, but not before she glimpsed broad shoulders and a chest that narrowed down in a thrust of hard muscles and black hair to lean hips, one hip with a jagged scar across it.

After a moment she heard the bed sag with his weight and his voice ask mildly, ''You do plan to come to bed, don't you?''

She hesitated a moment longer, then turned to put out the lamp.

''No, leave the lamp lit.'' His voice was still mild, but there was a note of command beneath so that her hand fell away.

Adam watched her walk slowly, reluctantly, toward the bed and remembered how she had flown across the room that night at the guest cottage when she thought he was Keith. The same shock and anger ripped savagely through him now as it had that night after they had made love and she had called him by his brother's name. He had had no idea that it was Keith's cottage the sleepy servant had shown him to after he had put Tom to bed. Only that the bed was empty and he had fallen into it, exhausted. But even half-asleep as he had been when he had suddenly awakened to find Lani in his room, how could he have deluded himself into believing it was his bed she was seeking?

Or perhaps, he thought ruefully, remembering the feel of that soft, yielding body against his, driving all thought of sleep from his mind, he hadn't wanted to question the miracle of her being in his arms, warm and eager for his caresses, the way he had imagined for so long. For at some point in those months he had spent in Louisiana, missing Lani more than he had ever thought possible, he had discovered it was not guilt or compassion he felt for Daniel's niece, but love. Stubborn, proud, willful—difficult as Lani might be, he could not imagine a life without her.

He had returned from his trip determined that they would marry. When she had seemed happy to see him at her birthday party and clung with flattering attention to his side all evening, he had foolishly allowed himself to believe she felt the same.

Well, there was no fool as blind as a man in love, he thought now, his mouth setting grimly. If it weren't for the fact that it was his own self-respect involved, he supposed he might have even found a certain irony in the situation. Letting Lani continue to believe that it was Keith who had made love to her, he would be competing with himself when they made love. Yet if he told her the truth, he would expose himself as a lovesick fool and, damn it, a man had his pride! More than likely, she would end up hating him anyway for having deceived her.

There would come a time in their relationship, he rationalized, when their marriage was on a sounder footing, that he would tell her the truth. But not now. Not tonight when he could feel the tension in her body as she slipped into bed beside him and started to tug the cover hastily over her.

Gently he reached out a hand and pulled the coverlet away from her, so that she was exposed to his view. And saw the anger flash in her eyes, her body rigid no longer with apprehension but with rage. Well, anger was better than the self-sacrificing look of martyrdom that had been on her face, he thought grimly. Better a furious hellion in his bed than a body as cold as gruel. And at least he had the advantage of knowing the fires of passion banked in that slim body, a passion that once having been awakened would not be as difficult to arouse to fever pitch again.

His narrowed gaze traveled with deliberate appraisal over the stiffly held body, his smile cold. "I forwarded a sizable sum to the ranch today. If this is how you plan to fulfill your part of our agreement, I'd say I was getting very little value for my money."

The black fury that shot through Lani at his words was like a wind roaring in her ears. Her mind seemed to explode. As if she were a harlot to be bought and sold, she thought, outraged, as she flung herself at him, wildly clawing and kicking at any part of his anatomy she could reach. It was a one-sided encounter. Her opponent made no move to retaliate. He simply held her away from him as much as possible, until, exhausted, she lay motionless, vaguely aware of his hands removing the filmy gown. Then, an arm clamped around her so that she could not move, she felt a hand move gently, exploring the length of her body with butterfly-soft caresses.

She was not aware of the exact moment when her anger became something else, a sensation entirely different and yet deliciously familiar, a warm throbbing that started wherever the hand touched and spread in slowly widening circles through her body. Oh, it was not the wild, pulsating excitement she had felt the night of her birthday party when Keith's caresses had blotted out everything else from her mind. Adam's knowing caresses sent rivulets of pleasure through her, but she was always aware of what was happening around her, the night fragrance from the garden, the sleepy, chirping sound of a bird, the rustling sound the wind made through the curtains.

When Adam swung himself above her and gently entered her, her passionate young body responded instinctively as if to an unspoken command, her arms reaching up to enfold him, pulling him ever closer. Only all at once it was no longer Adam's arms holding her. She closed her eyes, and it was Keith's face she saw in her mind's eyes. Her lips parted, smiling with an unconscious tenderness as she saw brilliant blue eyes looking down at her, filled with a melting love and desire, and felt her beloved's hands and mouth and body bringing her an almost unendurable, mounting ecstasy. Then, so quickly she could have cried aloud with disappointment, the pleasure peaked and ended, leaving her feeling oddly bereft and empty.

When she opened her eyes again, it was no longer Keith's face above her, but Adam staring down at her. She swallowed hard against the sharp misery of loss surging through her. Adam's face was very still in the dim gaslight; only for a moment she thought she saw something move in the gray, icy depths of his eyes. Then she felt him pull away from her. Without a word, he left the bed and padded across the carpeted floor to the door.

"Where are you going?" she asked, surprised and hurt. In some odd, uncomprehending way, she wanted Adam to stay with her, to comfort her.

Her only answer was the door closing quietly behind him.

Chapter 19

"Lani-san, one moment, please."

Lani, in her riding clothes, was on her way to the stable when Kimiko waylaid her in the hallway. The maid made a gentle, apologetic gesture with her hands. "It's Ah Sing. He wants to know if Mr. Adam will be home for dinner tonight."

Although Kimiko's voice was as deferential as always, her mistress saw the flash of sympathy in the dark almond-shaped eyes. Lani's hands tightened on the leather crop of her riding whip. She would not be pitied, she thought furiously. Not by her own maid. But she knew it wasn't just Kimiko, but all the servants who were curious about the many missed dinners and late nights when the master of the house arrived home long after his wife had already retired for the evening. One evening when Adam had called at the last minute to announce that he wouldn't be home for dinner, Lani had even caught a look of disapproval directed toward her by Ah Sing. As if, she thought, annoyed, it was somehow her fault that a bride of six months wasn't able to keep her husband home more often.

"Tell Ah Sing there'll just be myself for dinner this evening," she said coldly. "And he's not to bother preparing a large meal. I'll have something light on the veranda."

As she left the house and strode across the garden toward the stable, she couldn't help wondering wryly what the servants thought about her husband having his own bedroom. Not that Adam didn't visit his wife's bedroom occasionally on the nights when he wasn't working late, but she could hardly complain that her husband's conjugal demands were excessive. Or that he was an inconsiderate lover. Adam's lovemaking was much like Adam himself, competent, disciplined. He carefully made sure that this wife was thoroughly aroused by his caresses before possessing her, and that she found her satisfaction before he took his own. All the while they made love, though, Lani always sensed that there was a part of her husband that held back, that never lost control. And always afterward, without a word, he would leave her bed and return to his own room.

Well, what had she expected? Lani slashed irritably at a flower head with her whip. She should be grateful that her husband hadn't questioned her about what he must have realized was her lack of virginity, and that he wasn't perceptive enough to sense that when they made love, it was another man his wife was imagining holding her, embracing her.

And, thank goodness, Adam wasn't a jealous husband, she thought now as she entered the stable and saw, her eyes glowing with pleasure, the golden sorrel that Mikala had saddled and waiting for her. She remembered the morning, a week after her marriage, that Sunbeam had been brought to the house by Keith's stableman.

"A wedding present from Mr. Keith Stewart," the Hawaiian had said, grinning proudly, as he presented the reins to Lani. Lani had gazed, numb with shock, at the horse she had ridden to victory at Kapiolani Park racetrack. Her first outraged impulse had been to return the gift immediately. How dare Keith think she would accept a wedding present from him after the humiliating way he had treated her, much less such a valuable thoroughbred as Sunbeam.

Then the stableman handed her an envelope. The note inside in Keith's scrawling handwriting was brief, making Lani's heart squeeze painfully in her breast. "I can never forgive myself for hurting you. But if you will accept Sunbeam as a wedding gift, I can at least live in the hope that someday you will forgive me."

Lani had crumpled the note in her hand. Sunbeam, as if remembering her, gave a soft neigh, blowing out of coral-lined nostrils. Almost automatically, Lani's hand reached out to caress the silken mane, remembering the exciting feel of those rippling muscles beneath her when she had ridden the mare last. Then she had heard Adam coming down the front steps behind her.

At Adam's questioning glance from the horse to her, she said, "It's a wedding gift, from Keith." Although Adam had never mentioned the incident, she was sure that he had heard of the ladies' race she had won, riding Keith's golden sorrel. And the other stories about Keith and her? she wondered uneasily. Had he heard those stories, too? When her husband said nothing, she continued quickly. "I'll return her, of course."

Adam shrugged indifferently. "Do what you want, but I see no reason why you shouldn't keep the horse."

Lani was surprised to feel a sharp jab of anger at his words. She was his wife, she thought. Didn't he care at all that another man, whose name had been romantically linked to hers, was giving her such a valuable present? But her anger quickly vanished as Sunbeam nuzzled at her hand with a velvet soft mouth, and she knew that she had made her decision. She would keep the mare.

She told herself it was because she missed Jubal and the joy of riding a fine horse, but guiltily she knew, without putting it into words, that the truth was that every time she saw Sunbeam she was reminded of Keith. There was still pain in the memory of Keith's betrayal, but oddly the pain had become almost pleasureable, a hurt she hugged to herself, as if unable or unwilling to give it up.

Now as she swung onto Sunbeam's back and cantered down the driveway, she couldn't help wondering if that wasn't why Keith had given her the horse. He must have known that every time she rode Sunbeam she would think of him. Had he wanted her to know he hadn't forgotten her any more than she had forgotten him?

Because of the estrangement between her husband and his brother, there had been no need to invite her brother-in-law to their home after her marriage, but in a town the size of Honolulu, and moving in the same social circle, it was inevitable that she would one day run into Keith. The first time it had happened, at a musicale the queen had given at her country home to which Lani and Adam had been invited, her brother-in-law had been graciously polite toward her, nothing more. And after the initial awkward shock, Lani had discovered that she was able to talk casually to her former lover without betraying anything of the turmoil she was feeling.

Whenever Keith did appear at any social occasion, Nellie
Samuels was always with him. There had been no date set for
a wedding, although a formal engagement party had been
given at the Samuels home in June. Of course, Lani knew
that meant nothing. Her own abrupt marriage was out of the
ordinary. Yearlong engagements were the usual custom between affianced couples. No doubt plans for Keith's and
Nellie's wedding would be announced in a few months.

The thought sent a queer, breathless pain through Lani, her
hands loosening on the reins so that Sunbeam turned around
and gave her an inquiring look. The mare was too intelligent
not to know that she wasn't allowed to gallop until they
reached the outskirts of the town.

And they were still inside the city, riding past the Iolani
Palace where the guards stood self-consciously at attention,
because the legislature was in session in the government
building across the street from the palace. The Stewarts had
been among the invited guests attending the glittering pomp
and ceremony of the opening of the legislature in May. The
queen, with a coronet of diamonds on her head, had been
driven from the palace in a coach drawn by a span of black
horses, while a booming salute had sounded from the battery
on Punchbowl and the Queen's Household Guards in battle
dress presented arms. Indoors, the traditional feathered plumes
of *kahilis* were held high around a throne covered by a
magnificent scarlet and gold feather cloak.

Everyone had applauded, Lani as proudly as the rest, as the
queen delivered her address, pledging firmly "to preserve the
independence of the kingdom." But the conciliatory mood of
the opening legislative ceremony was short-lived, as one
stormy, disruptive legislative session followed another. No
sooner would the queen appoint a cabinet when the legislature, controlled by *haoles* or disgruntled *hapa-haoles* who had
never forgiven the queen for not being given positions in the
government, voted its dismissal. Four cabinets came and
went, one only in existence for a few hours.

"Why shouldn't the queen be allowed to appoint a cabinet
of her choosing?" Lani had protested indignantly to her
husband one evening when Tom had come by for dinner and

the subject of conversation, as always when Tom was present, turned to politics.

"Because she's a constitutional monarch," Adam said. "And the constitution gives the legislature the right to approve or disapprove any cabinet the queen appoints." His long mouth twisted in a wry smile. "Obviously, Liliuokalani would prefer a new constitution that would give the monarch more power."

"It isn't only the queen who wants to get rid of the bayonet constitution," Tom pointed out. "She's received petitions signed by over two-thirds of the Hawaiian people asking for a new constitution. Why shouldn't she listen to her people?"

"Aren't those the same people who've foolishly persuaded the queen to pass a lottery bill?" Adam asked, lifting a skeptical eyebrow.

"What's wrong with Hawaii having a national lottery?" Tom demanded. "The money will be used for the good of all Hawaiians, not just the favored few, and will help build railroads and roads around the islands."

"Who actually will get the money from the lottery is open to question," Adam said dryly. "And you know as well as I that the Hawaiians and the Oriental laborers will wager their own lives at the drop of a hat. It's the poor who will be fleeced by a lottery."

"How touching you should be concerned for the poor," Tom sneered. "Aren't the *haoles* more concerned that the profits from the lottery won't go into their own pockets? I don't recall your *haole* friends worrying about the poor when they tricked the Hawaiians out of their land, or when they brought in the Chinese and Japanese as little better than slave laborers to work the sugar plantations."

Lani saw her husband's face darken at Tom's words. She was aware that the relationship between the two brothers, which had once been so close, had become more and more strained these last months. When Adam finally spoke, his voice was icy. "If you spent more time at work and less time playing at politics, you'd know that Stewart and Sons did away with contract labor at our plantation several months ago. But then you haven't put in an honest day's work at the office for some months now, have you?"

Tom's young face flushed with anger. He sprang to his feet, glaring at his brother. "If you don't think I'm pulling my weight just tell me, and I'll be glad to quit."

Lani gave her husband a stricken look. He mustn't let his brother go, not like this, with a permanent rift between them that they would both regret. She was trying desperately to think of something to say to ease the tension when behind her Kimiko, who was helping serve the dinner, suddenly dropped a tray of glasses. The sound of smashing glassware, and Kimiko's cry of dismay, brought Tom immediately to her side.

"Are you all right?" he asked anxiously. "You're not hurt?"

Kimiko hastily knelt down to retrieve the tray as she murmured softly, "I am ashamed I am so clumsy."

"Don't be silly," Tom said. "Everyone has accidents. Here, let me help you."

As he assisted Kimiko in removing the tray and broken glassware from the dining room, Lani realized, relieved, that in the confusion of the dropped tray, the furious words between Tom and Adam had been forgotten.

She glanced over at her husband to see an amused look in the gray eyes watching the departing couple. "She's a clever girl, Kimiko. I hope Tom realizes how fortunate he is."

Lani's eyes widened, startled. "You know . . . about Tom and Kim?"

The gray eyes turned to his wife were no longer amused. For a moment they seemed to pierce right through Lani. Then Adam said mildly, "I'm not blind, you know."

Remembering those words now, Lani wondered with a sudden uneasiness, was it possible that Adam saw more than she realized? The idea was disquieting, as if for the first time it occurred to her how little she actually knew about her husband. By now she had reached the busy intersection of Beretania and Nuuanu streets, where cumbersome drays and rushing carriages made Sunbeam skittish, and she was too busy concentrating on controlling her mount, as she threaded her way through the traffic *mauka* toward the Pali, to think of anything else.

*   *   *

It was much later that evening that Adam made his way to a small house on Judd Street. With all its shades drawn, the house seemed deserted except that every few minutes a man would walk swiftly and quietly through the night, down the path to the back porch, knock twice, then slip inside the door. Soon more than a dozen men were gathered in the Thurston's large front parlor, talking softly among themselves. They immediately fell silent, though, when Lorrin Thurston got up to take charge of the meeting.

The stocky man with the bristling mustache glanced slowly around the room, then announced gravely, "Gentlemen, I must have your word that what is said here this evening will never reach outside these walls. No written record will be kept. Our meetings must be completely secret, or our very lives may be at stake. For what we are discussing here this evening is treason."

Sitting in the back of the room, Adam Stewart thought, amused, that for a practical, hard-headed lawyer, Lorrin Thurston had a definite flair for the dramatic. Everyone in the room knew that Charles Wilson, the queen's marshal, had his men watching Thurston's home and office day and night, and that these secret meetings, plotting the overthrow of the Hawaiian monarchy and the annexation of the Hawaiian Islands to the United States, were hardly a secret to the queen or her supporters. Probably the only reason Wilson hadn't moved to squash the conspiracy against the crown was the lack of physical evidence, and the fact that the queen was reluctant to bring to a public trial for treason some of the wealthiest and most influential men in Honolulu.

Adam shifted uncomfortably on the hardback chair. Reluctantly, he had come to the pragmatic conclusion that Lorrin Thurston was right. Hawaii's future lay with the United States. Not only was Hawaii's economic prosperity bound to America, but whoever held the islands would control the whole Pacific. And it was obvious to Adam that if America didn't take over the small kingdom, these valuable islands inevitably would be swallowed up by some other world power, England or Japan.

Nevertheless, the furtive manner in which the annexationists were going about seeking their goal, sneaking around to

meetings in the dark, plotting the queen's destruction behind
her back, left a bad taste in Adam's mouth. Of course, he
realized dourly that Liliuokalani would probably plot the
destruction of the *haoles* in this room if she could get her new
constitution approved.

Adam's gaze wandered around the room, noticing not for
the first time that there were only white men at the meeting.
Surprisingly, many were not wealthy men of property but
young professionals and lawyers like Thurston, men who
believed fervently that the Hawaiian monarchy was corrupt
and incompetent and must be changed for a more stable form
of government run by white men. The sugar planters present,
although Adam had no doubt they would side with annexation, if necessary, didn't look so confident as their leader told
of his recent secret mission to Washington to discuss the
annexation of the islands to the United States.

"Unfortunately, I wasn't able to speak to the president
personally," Thurston said regretfully, "but I did speak with
several important members of Congress and the secretary of
the navy. The secretary of state indicated if we come to
Washington with an annexation proposition, we will find an
exceedingly sympathetic administration."

One of the planters rose and asked, his voice agitated,
"What about our contract labor laws, Lorrin? Such laws are
illegal in the United States. What good will it do if annexation gets us a higher price for our sugar, but we have to pay a
higher wage to our workers to produce the sugar? What we
need are ten thousand more contract laborers, so that our
Chinese and Japanese workers have to work or go hungry."

Across the room, a man, not a planter, shouted angrily,
"We've imported too damn many Japs and coolies as it is. A
few more years and they'll be taking over these islands. What
we need to do is ship them back where they came from. What
if in her new constitution the queen gives the vote to the
Orientals as well as the natives? We *haoles* will be outvoted
easily."

"Gentlemen! Gentlemen!" Thurston lifted his hands for
silence. "I can assure you there's no cause for alarm about
our losing our contract laborers when annexation takes place.
I've been told, unofficially, that some loophole in the Ameri-

can law can be arranged. As for the queen's new constitution, even though she's surrounded herself with some of the worst elements in the country, she hasn't sunk so low as to plan to give the vote to the Orientals.''

A low murmur of surprise ran through the assembly. One man asked, startled, ''You've seen the queen's proposed constitution, Lorrin? I thought no one had seen it except the queen and her immediate advisers.''

Lorrin smiled smugly. ''The queen's private secretary happens to be unofficially on the payroll of one of our strongest supporters in the judicial department. We've only managed to see the preliminary draft, but at this point the new constitution will give the vote to all Hawaiians, men of property or not, and take away the vote from all foreigners who are not naturalized or married to an Hawaiian.'' Thurston's glance moved sternly around the room. ''Such a constitution would disenfranchise a great many *haoles* who have businesses and have lived in Hawaii for many years.''

''That's crazy!'' a man in the first row, with a slight German accent, complained. ''The common natives have no idea what is good for them. The Hawaiians owe everything, their institutions, their government, their judiciary system, to men like us who've worked hard all our lives, while the *kanakas* lie around in the sun, doing nothing.''

''I agree,'' Thurston said. ''I've lived among the natives all my life. There are some among them who have managed to lift themselves out of the indolent rut of their friends, but the majority are unfit to exercise authority. Unhappily, despite the hard, unselfish work of the early missionaries, the Hawaiians are more incapable now of governing themselves than they were twenty years ago. That is why it is so important that the monarchy be abolished before it can do more damage than it's already done.''

A white-bearded gentleman spoke up, his face troubled. ''Surely, Lorrin, some other, less drastic way can be found to get the queen to step down? Perhaps if we offered her money to abdicate?''

Lorrin shook his head. ''We can bribe some of the Hawaiian legislators in the Liberal party to vote our way without any trouble, but the queen is much more stubborn in character than her brother. She will never abdicate of her own accord. She is determined to gain personal control of the government.'' He smiled grimly. ''Let me remind you, gentlemen, you can't fight the devil with rose water instead of a club. The day will come when we must all face the decision to overthrow the queen, by force, if necessary. In the meantime, we can continue to gain support for our cause by placing stories in the American newspaper about the queen's incompetence.''

''Those new laws she's supporting—the lottery and legalizing the sale of opium—surely we can use them as a club against her.'' The man with the German accent spoke up again, glancing around with a knowing smile. ''We all know the missionary crowd will never sit still for either of those bills.''

Adam saw a frown touch Lorrin's face briefly at the faintly condescending tone in the man's voice. Thurston, he knew, was very proud of his missionary forebears. It wouldn't only be the missionaries, though, who would be upset at the legalizing of opium, he thought. He knew several prominent businessmen, including his brother, Keith, who had made a good business of smuggling opium into the islands. They wouldn't be happy about a law that would wipe out their profits overnight.

Thinking of his brother, though, brought back other memories, and a blackness settled over Adam's features. Sending the golden sorrel to Lani as a wedding present had, of course, been Keith's none too subtle way of infuriating his brother, while maintaining a hold, however tenuous, on Adam's wife. Adam's first impulse had been to send the horse back, but he knew the gossip would quickly spread through Honolulu that he had returned his brother's wedding gift, reigniting the rumors and questions about Lani's sudden marriage. And, more important, he had seen his wife's face, the longing there, when she had looked at the sorrel. He knew how much she enjoyed her daily horseback rides, and that there wasn't a mount in the Tucker stables that could compare to Sunbeam.

However, it wasn't his brother's wedding gift that Adam brooded about later, when the meeting finally ended and he made his way home through the quiet, darkened side streets.

It was remembering the way his wife looked when he made love to her, her black hair fanning out over the pillow, her sculptured eyelids closed so that her eyelashes lay dark shadows over her cheeks, a softly tremulous, dreamlike smile on her pale pink lips, so that he knew, intuitively, like a knife turning in his gut, that it was Keith she was imagining holding her in his arms. That was why he couldn't bear to lay with her afterward, why always, after the travesty of their lovemaking was finished, he returned quickly to his own room.

The house was dark when he let himself into the front door, except for a small night light the servants had left for him in the hallway. Though he ascended the stairs quietly, Lani, pillows piled behind her in bed, heard Adam's footsteps on the stairs. Quickly, she put aside the book she was reading. She had ridden longer than usual that day and, tired, had gone to bed early, but had been unable to sleep. Nor had she been able to keep her mind on the book she was reading.

A restlessness possessed her, as disturbing to her senses as the moonlight drifting through the open window, an odd ache in her thighs that had nothing to do with her strenuous horseback ride. Perhaps it was the restlessness that had caused her to put on one of her filmiest nightgowns, to leave her bedroom door standing open so that Adam would be sure to see her, still awake, when he returned home. After all, it had been almost two weeks since her husband had made love to her. Of course, she had no way of knowing whether that was unusual between a husband and wife, but it seemed a long time to her!

She could not see her husband's face, only his elongated shadow as he stood in her doorway and said, "I thought you'd be asleep."

She stretched slowly, luxuriously. "It's a warm night. I thought I'd read for a while."

It was a warm night. Adam saw that Lani had thrown off her bedcovers, and her creamy skin gleamed with a faint glow of perspiration. Her arms stretched languorously above her, pulling her rose-peaked breasts taut beneath the filmy nightgown she wore, and her soft lips were curved into an inviting smile.

Studying his wife, a hard, driving anger possessed Adam. He had no illusions why she had waited up for him, why she was enticing him to her bed. So that she could lie in his arms while he made love to her, pretending he was Keith. Well, not tonight, he thought savagely.

He shut the door behind him, his voice harshly mocking as he advanced toward the bed. "Not too warm a night, I hope, for what I have in mind."

Quickly he extinguished the lamp, discarded his clothing, and, slipping into bed beside Lani, drew her into his arms. When the hands thrust aside her gown and moved in gentle, practiced caresses over her body, Lani sighed softly and felt the ache in her thighs slipping away, a by-now familiar contentment taking hold of her. Her body offered itself passively to the pleasure those hands were bringing her, while her mind drifted away of its own accord to focus upon another man, another face, smiling down at her.

Then suddenly, shockingly, the hands caressing her were no longer gentle but hard and bruising on her body. Startled, her eyes flew open. It wasn't Keith's but Adam's face she saw above hers in the pale moonlight, his gray eyes blazing down at her with a terrifying anger. Panic-stricken, without even knowing of what she was afraid, she tried to pull away, but it was too late. And this time when Adam possessed her, it was not as before, slowly, with infinite care, followed almost immediately by a sweet release. The deep, punishing thrusts, the movements of his body within her, made her gasp with a pleasure that supplanted any other memories she had of lovemaking. She felt herself being lifted to higher and higher plateaus of passion until there was nothing left in the world but a desperate need to reach the fulfillment always tormentingly beyond her reach.

Her body arched upward in a frenzy to hold him close, but he deliberately pulled himself away from her, lifting himself above her, his mouth at her lips and breasts, teasing, nibbling, adding to the exquisite sensations engulfing her as he commanded hoarsely. "Touch me. Hold me."

At first timidly, then more boldly, she allowed her hands to move over his muscular body, to caress and hold that warm hardness in her hands, and somehow sensing the pleasure she was bringing him only served to increase her own pleasure.

"Say my name," he ordered, his tongue, lightly as a feather, caressing the outline of her mouth.

"Adam," she moaned softly.

"Again."

"Adam!" She thought she screamed his name, but she would never know because immediately his mouth covered hers, and the hardness was inside of her again, only this time she was vaguely aware that, unlike the other times they had made love, Adam was no more in command of his emotions, of controlling what was happening between them, than she was. Their bodies moved in unison, as if they were one, and she was aware of nothing else around her but the two of them, their passion carrying them swiftly, inexorably to a final shattering height of rapture. She felt a long shudder pass through his body, and she thought she heard him murmur against her lips, "My love," as they clung together, their bodies entangled in the sweet aftermath of passion.

It was several moments before she felt him leave her, and almost involuntarily she reached out for his hand. "Don't go," she pleaded. How could he leave her now?

She could barely make out his face in the mistlike moonlight that bathed the room, and for a moment she thought she had only imagined the appraising, searching look in the narrowed eyes gazing down at her, as if he were seeking for something in her face.

Then he swung out of bed and said, his voice cold, "My room is just down the hall. If you want me, you know where to find me."

And once again, the door closed quietly behind him.

Chapter 20

In the Blue Room of the palace, Queen Liliuokalani, wearing the lavender silk gown and diamond tiara she had worn for the adjournment of the legislature that morning, gazed at her ministers gathered around the table with mounting disbelief and rage. How could they now, at the last minute, refuse to sign the new constitution she had placed on the table before them?

"You know that my people have petitioned for this constitution for months," she protested, trying to control her anger. "Crowds have been waiting for hours in the palace grounds to hear my announcement that a new constitution has been promulgated. What am I to tell them?"

The minister of finance said nervously, "Perhaps we should postpone any decision until later, when we've had more time to study the document."

The queen glanced at him coldly. "You've had a draft of the constitution in your possession for several weeks now. You all agreed that a new constitution was needed. You encouraged me in this undertaking. By refusing now to sign, you've led me to the edge of a precipice and left me to leap alone."

The minister of the interior glanced around the table, as if for moral support, before returning his gaze to the queen. "A constitution cannot be changed legally except by a constitutional amendment, Your Majesty, ratified by the voters."

The queen's mouth tightened bitterly. "No such procedure was followed when my brother was forced to accept the present constitution. And the right to grant a constitution to the nation has been, since the very first one was granted, a prerogative of the Hawaiian sovereigns."

The attorney general shifted uneasily in his chair. "There are prominent people who will consider this new constitution a revolutionary act, depriving them of their suffrage. There could be an uprising if we went ahead with it."

Lilioukalani glanced contemptuously at the man. He was afraid, she thought, afraid of Lorrin Thurston and his downtown party of *haoles* whose only goal was to take her throne away from her and hand her beloved country over to foreigners.

"The only men who will be deprived of the right to vote are those foreigners who owe their allegiance to other countries, not Hawaii," she pointed out. "What other civilized country allows a man to vote and seek office without ever becoming naturalized? Those are the same men who rush to seek protection under the guns of a foreign man-of-war when they quarrel with the government under which they live."

"If you'd wait, just a little longer," the attorney general urged. "Perhaps at some future time . . ."

The temper that her missionary teachers had warned Liliuokalani about suddenly broke free. She slammed a regal fist down on the table, her dark eyes flashing. "You are traitors, all of you! I will listen to no more advice from you. My people have waited long enough for justice. We will wait no longer. Get out. All of you!"

Three of her ministers hurried from the room. The fourth man, Samuel Parker, the minister of foreign affairs, rose quietly to his feet. He glanced disdainfully toward the door. "They'll go running straight to Thurston and his crowd downtown to tell them what's happened here."

"I know," Liliuokalani said, her voice suddenly weary but her back held rigidly straight. She glanced at her minister of foreign affairs, a tall, handsome, ducal-looking man. Sam Parker's American great-great-grandfather, John Young, had jumped ship and become an adviser to Kamehameha I. He had married a Hawaiian *alii* wife, and his descendants had accumulated a fortune, living more royally and flamboyantly than the royal family itself, on the famous million-acre Parker ranch on Hawaii. Although respected by the *haole* community, Sam Parker had always been loyal to the monarchy.

"You said very little at our meeting. Do you think I was wrong, too, to try to promulgate the new constitution?"

Parker shrugged, but his gaze, studying the queen, was sympathetic. "I think the constitution will be just the excuse Thurston needs to try and pull the government down. You've stirred up a hornet's nest, Your Majesty."

Outside the open window, Liliuokalani could hear the Royal Hawaiian Band and, when they stopped playing, the murmur of many voices, the people eagerly waiting for her to make the announcement that they had a new constitution that would give the right to vote to all the Hawaiian people.

"What will I tell them?" she whispered, half to herself.

"If you'd like, I'll speak to them," Sam Parker offered. "Or your marshal can send them away."

Liliuokalani got stiffly to her feet, ignoring an overwhelming feeling of humiliation and defeat. "No, I'll speak to them.'' She was the queen; it was her duty. She had promised her people a more just constitution, and she had failed them. But she would not give up her dream of a new constitution, she thought, straightening her shoulders proudly and walking with regal grace to the veranda overlooking the palace grounds.

Lani Stewart was among the crowd waiting for the queen to appear. She had been returning in her carriage from an errand in town when she had seen the people gathered before the palace, and had told her driver to stop.

"Better you stay here," her Hawaiian driver had said. He had heard rumors in town of trouble brewing, and he was sure Mr. Stewart wouldn't approve of his wife's being anywhere near the *pilikia*.

"I want to know what's going on," Lani insisted. "Wait here for me."

She left the carriage before the driver could assist her, joining the natives in their Sunday-best attire, waiting before the palace. When the queen came out on the veranda, she spoke quietly to the people, but Lani could hear the sorrow and repressed anger in the woman's voice. Liliuokalani addressed her people in Hawaiian, and although it had been years since Lani had spoken Hawaiian, she had no trouble following the queen's words.

Liliuokalani told the people that she had prepared a constitution in which the rights of all had been regarded. "I was ready and expected to proclaim a new constitution today, but with regret I say I have met with obstacles that prevented it." Lani heard a murmur of anger rustle through the people standing around her, a few men lifting clenched fists. The queen must have seen the anger, too, for she commanded, firmly, "Return to your homes peaceably and quietly. The time will come when I will proclaim a new constitution. Go with good hope, and do not be disturbed or troubled in your minds. Your welfare is dear to me. I shall not cease trying to help you and preserve the kingdom. Keep me in your love as you have mine. With sorrow I now dismiss you."

What had happened? Lani wondered. The last time she had spoken to the queen, Liliuokalani had seemed so confident that she would be able to proclaim a new constitution. It had been at a small dinner party the queen had given at her country home. After dinner, she had taken Lani into an adjoining room to show her the grand piano she had been given by Hawaiians, who knew the queen's love of music.

"How Rebecca would love this piano," Lilioukalani said, and then added, with a questioning glance, "You have not heard from our friend?"

Lani shook her head and thought suddenly: If Rebecca had remained with her, perhaps none of it would have happened— Keith's betrayal, her own hasty marriage to a man who spent most of his time away from her. "I miss her," she said unhappily.

The queen nodded, her face sympathetic. "It is hard to lose a good friend." Then, softly, as if speaking to herself, "And harder to be betrayed by those you thought were your friends."

"You have many friends, Your Majesty," Lani said loyally. "The Hawaiian people are devoted to you."

The queen's face brightened, her dark eyes sparkling, so that for a moment she looked young and happy. "Once I proclaim my new constitution, there will be so much I can do for my people," she said eagerly. "I have a plan to set aside sections of the crown lands in small homesteads, with provisions preventing the land from passing into the hands of the large sugar plantations. The lottery will bring in money so that we can build more schools, hospitals, roads, and railroads. And every Hawaiian will be allowed to vote, not just those with money and property."

Remembering the queen's words now, it was hard for Lani to realize that the unhappy woman on the balcony was the same woman who had spoken so happily to Lani only a few months before. For a short time after the queen retired from the balcony, her audience milled around uncertainly, one old man wailing softly in despair, tears streaming down his face. Then gradually the people began to push quietly toward the palace gates. Lani found herself being pulled along, as if caught up in an undertow. Suddenly the bright sun overhead darkened, and the ground dipped alarmingly beneath Lani's feet.

The next thing she knew she was seated on the steps of the octagonal pavilion. One Hawaiian woman was holding her in her arms while another one was fanning her with a palm frond. The woman gave a small cry of relief when the girl opened her eyes and struggled to sit erect.

The women had sensibly opened the high, tight collar of Lani's bodice, and a third woman brought a glass of water, which Lani drank gratefully. "It is too warm a day to wear tight, hot clothes," the woman bringing the water scolded gently.

Lani saw Tom pushing his way through the people gathered in a curious circle around her. "What happened?" He bent anxiously over Lani. "Are you all right?"

"Of course I'm all right." She was annoyed with herself for fainting. She had never fainted in her life. And she suspected it wasn't the heat or her tight clothes that had caused her dizziness but something to do with what the doctor had told her when she visited him that morning.

She got to her feet, and Tom said quickly, "I'll take you home."

"That's not necessary. My carriage is right outside the Kinau Gate."

Tom insisted, however, so after thanking the women she allowed him to escort her to her carriage. He climbed in beside her, giving her a worried glance. "What are you doing in that crush anyway?"

"Why shouldn't I be there?" she asked. Then shook her head, bewildered. "I don't understand. Why didn't the queen proclaim her constitution as she had planned?"

"Because her ministers are a bunch of lily-livered cowards," Tom said, his face filled with scorn. "Except Sam Parker, and I suppose he was out voted. No doubt Thurston and his crowd have already heard what happened. I'd lay odds that they're already making plans to get rid of the queen and take over the government."

"How can they?" Lani asked. "There's only a few of them, and they have no military force."

"They have John Stevens, the American minister to Hawaii, in their back pocket," Tom said, scowling. "And he has the USS *Boston* in the harbor, with fully armed marines aboard just waiting for orders to be sent ashore."

"President Harrison would never allow that," Lani protested, "using American troops to interfere in the sovereignty of another country."

Tom slanted an amused eyebrow at her, reminding her suddenly and disconcertingly of her husband. "What a little innocent you are, Lani. Do you really believe the president doesn't know what Stevens is doing here in Hawaii? Stevens has been against the monarchy, and for the annexationists, ever since he arrived in the islands."

They had arrived at the Tucker home, and Tom helped Lani from the carriage. He studied the girl's pale face. "You're sure you're all right? Perhaps I should stop by the office and ask Adam to come home."

"No, don't!" Lani shook her head quickly. As far as she was concerned, her husband was much too obsessed with her health as it was. She rested her hand coaxingly on Tom's arm. "I'm fine, really I am. Promise me you won't say anything to Adam."

Reluctantly, Tom agreed. Not that Adam and he were doing much talking these days, he thought. His sherry-colored eyes fastened soberly on his companion's face. "It will be a difficult weekend for a lot of families in Honolulu. They'll have to choose finally, between the queen and the annexationists. Which side will you be on, Lani?"

Lani's eyes darkened to a deep amethyst with indignation. "I'm on the queen's side, of course. How can you ask?" Had Tom forgotten that Hawaiian as well as *haole* blood flowed in her veins? She smiled proudly at Tom, remembering that night on the beach so long ago now. "Hawaii for the Hawaiians. Isn't that what you once told me?"

Tom did not smile back. "It won't be easy," he warned soberly. "The annexationists have a great many powerful men in their camp."

As she watched Tom stride away, Lani decided to wait up for Adam, who had telephoned earlier that he would not be home for dinner. Not that that was unusual, Lani thought, frowning to herself. Adam spent more time at the office than at home. And he had not been to her room for more than two months, not since . . . a warmth swept over her, remembering the last time she and her husband had made love. Hastily she blocked the memory from her mind, concentrating on the news she had to tell her husband when he returned home.

But she was more tired than she thought, and when Adam returned home at midnight, he found his wife curled up, fast asleep, in a chair in the front parlor. She didn't waken when he carried her upstairs to her bed, undressed her, and tucked the covers gently around her. Then he stood for a long moment beside the bed, hungrily studying his sleeping wife, a look of tenderness on his face that Lani wouldn't have recognized.

It was certainly not on his face the next morning when Lani stormed into the dining room where her husband was eating breakfast and waved a copy of the *Advertiser* angrily in his face. "Did you see the editorial?" she demanded. "They're saying the queen is fomenting revolution with her constitution, that she's out to destroy life and liberty in the islands." She threw the paper on the floor. "As if it weren't the annexationists who are fomenting revolution, trying to depose the queen!" she said bitterly.

"The *Advertiser* is owned by the Reform party," Adam pointed out mildly. "What would you expect them to say? I'm sure the queen's newspaper, the *Bulletin*, is making equally wild accusations."

Adam had hoped that Lani wouldn't be upset by yesterday's political turmoil, but he should have known that was impossible. He thought, wryly, how much more upset his wife would be if she had attended the various meetings that he had yesterday, in which furious businessmen had threatened to kill the queen, or at the least have her shipped off to some distant Samoan Island where she could no longer be a threat to them. Saner heads had fortunately prevailed. Thurston, however, had immediately seized the opportunity to form a Committee of Safety, composed of thirteen men, to protect American lives and take whatever action was necessary against the queen and her new constitution. Adam, along with several others, had asked that the committee take no immediate action. The ministers should be given time, they argued, to convince the queen to withdraw her constitution.

Now Adam shoved aside his coffee cup and rose to his feet. "It's all a tempest over nothing," he said, with more confidence than he felt. "Her ministers will persuade the queen to issue a statement that she won't try to proclaim a new constitution, and that will be the end of the matter." He cast a stern glance at his wife. "In the meantime, I want you to stay at home today. There shouldn't be any trouble in town, but there's always a few hotheads, looking for excitement."

When his wife didn't reply at once, her face taking on a mutinous air, he said, with an ominous quiet in his voice, "I can always lock you in your room."

"You wouldn't!" she said indignantly.

"Oh, but I would," he said coldly. "And you know I would."

She lifted her chin defiantly. "I'm not a child that you can lock away in her room."

"Then stop acting like a child." He walked around the table and stood, gazing down at her. "I want your word that you won't leave the grounds today."

Lani remembered how her uncle had forbidden her to go into town when Wilcox had attacked the palace and how she had disobeyed him. She glanced up into her husband's eyes, as cold as the gray morning mist over Haleakala. Adam wasn't her uncle, she realized. She would disobey him at her peril. "Oh, very well," she agreed sulkily. Probably Adam was right anyway. The queen would withdraw her constitution, and the whole affair would blow over.

Adam's misgivings, however, proved only too true. The queen issued a signed statement on Monday morning that she would make no changes in the constitution, except by lawful amendment, but Monday afternoon, the Committee of Safety called a mass meeting of the foreign residents of Hawaii at the armory.

The hall grew hot and steamy, the buzz of voices like a swarm of angry bees, as more and more men pushed their way into the armory to denounce the queen. But it was when Lorrin Thurston rose to his feet to address the assembly that the hall fell into a breathless silence.

Fists clenched, Thurston swiftly dismissed the queen's offer to withdraw her constitution, saying contemptuously, "Her word is worth nothing. Royal promises are made to be broken." His arms gesturing dramatically, he continued with self-righteous fervor. "We have not sought this situation. Last Saturday, the sun rose on a peaceful and smiling city; today it is otherwise. Whose fault is it?—Queen Liliuokalani's! It is not her fault that the streets have not run red with blood. She wants us to sleep on a slumbering volcano, which will one morning spew out blood and destroy us all."

He had his audience now hanging raptly to his every word, nodding, murmuring agreement, so that when he finished his speech—with the rousing words, "Has the tropic sun cooled and thinned our blood, or have we flowing in our veins the warm, rich blood that loves liberty and dies for it?"—the whole audience jumped to their feet, and the room rang with tumultuous applause.

As it turned out, the businessmen revolutionaries did not have to shed any of their own blood after all. That same afternoon, the American minister ordered four boatloads of fully armed marines and sailors from the USS *Boston* to march ashore "to protect American life and property." However, it was obvious to Liliuokalani as she stood on the palace balcony and watched the American military march by, a coldness gathering inside of her, that the troops were not being dispatched to the other side of Honolulu where most of the Americans lived. Their guns were directed at the palace.

Tuesday afternoon, once again in the Blue Room, Liliuokalani listened quietly to her ministers urging her to resign to avert violence and bloodshed.

"Marshal Wilson still holds the police station," Sam Parker objected. "He'll fight to the last man if the queen gives him permission to do so."

Yes, Liliuokalani thought. All along, her marshal had wanted to use force to quell the *haole* rebellion, but she had resisted, fearing the bloodshed that was sure to follow. How could her few badly armed soldiers stand up to the might of the United States?

"If you resist further," Samuel Damon, the representative from the newly designated provisional government, warned, "a great many people will be killed. And what will be the use? The provisional government has taken over the government building, the treasury, and the archives. The American minister has already recognized the new government, and Sanford Dole has accepted the presidency."

The queen flinched inwardly. Judge Sanford Dole was another good friend she thought she could trust who had betrayed her and gone over to the enemy.

As if guessing her bitter thoughts, Parker leaned forward, speaking quietly. "At least Dole will be a better man for the job than Thurston. And to give Dole credit, he did try to convince Thurston to have the Princess Kaiulani appointed as regent until she came of age. But Thurston and his committee refused."

So there was no way out, Liliuokalani thought wearily. One of the largest, most powerful nations in the world, professing to be a just and Christian country, had crushed her little island kingdom as carelessly as one steps on an insect. No, she thought furiously. It wasn't America or the American people who had committed this crime. It was only a few men like John Stevens and Lorrin Thurston.

She suddenly remembered as a child of five when the British, in the person of Lord George Paulet, had taken over the Hawaiian kingdom by force. When the British government in London had learned what had happened, they had immediately repudiated Paulet's actions. Why couldn't the same thing be true of the American government? she thought hopefully. Surely, once the president learned the true facts about what had happened here these last few days, she would be reinstated.

She turned to Samuel Damon with regal dignity, refusing to allow him to see the pain tearing her apart inside. "I will surrender," she said, her voice steady, "but under protest, and I surrender not to the revolutionaries but to the superior force of the United States of America."

It was not much of a victory, refusing to surrender to the provisional government, but if the *haoles* thought she had meekly given up, they would find out differently, Liliuokalani thought, her face more resolute than ever. Somehow, she would continue to fight for her kingdom. She would never give up.

Chapter 21

By Tuesday evening, all Honolulu knew that the monarchy had fallen. The new government immediately put the city under martial law in fear of a counterrevolution by royalist supporters. A volunteer army was hurriedly recruited to supplement the American marines and sailors, and the port of Honolulu was closed, to discourage royalist opposition from spreading to the other islands. The Government Office Building, across from the palace, was sandbagged and garrisoned for use by the handful of white men who now comprised the provisional government of Hawaii.

"Stevens wasted no time raising the American flag over the palace," Tom said bitterly, several days later when he stopped by and visited Lani. "And the soldiers of the PG vandalized the palace from top to bottom. They carried off the furniture, the mirrors, and chandeliers. One of the soldiers even bragged that he and some other men had gambled over the jewels from Kalakaua's crown."

Tom's face was haggard. He looked as if he hadn't slept in days. After Kimiko had ushered him into the garden where Lani was writing letters under the shade of the hau arbor, she went at once to fetch a tray of food and a pitcher of chilled fruit juice. Instead of withdrawing as she usually did when Tom was with her mistress, the Japanese girl stood to one side, watching, to make sure the young man ate every morsel.

"Is Liliuokalani safe?" Lani asked anxiously after her guest had absentmindedly finished the tray of food.

"The queen's staying at Washington Place. Since she's received death threats and the PGs have dismissed her household guards, the Lane brothers, myself, and others have been taking turns guarding the house." Tom's eyes darkened with frustrated fury and humiliation. "If only she had allowed the marshal and his men to fight. . . ."

But Lani had been among those who had watched the U.S. marines and sailors parade in front of Iolani Palace on Monday. How could Marshal Wilson and his small group of poorly armed men stand up to the artillery and Gatling guns the troops from the *Boston* carried with them? She understood Tom's rage, though. She remembered her own feeling of helpless fury, as she watched the American troops march by. And for the first time, she had felt ashamed of her *haole* blood.

"What will happen now?" she asked Tom.

"The PGs have already sent a delegation to Washington, requesting annexation. Naturally, they wouldn't allow any of the queen's representatives aboard the *Claudine* so that she could present her case to the American government. And all government workers are required to sign an oath of allegiance to the PGs or lose their jobs." Tom grinned proudly. "When they tried to get the Royal Hawaiian Band to sign the oath, all the band members quit. They said they'd rather eat stones than be disloyal to their queen."

"There will be those who sign the oath, no matter how they feel," Kim said quietly. "A man must feed his family."

"If I were a man, I'd never sign the oath," Lani said fiercely. "I'd die first."

Tom got to his feet. "The queen is still confident that when she is able to send her own delegation to Washington and the American people hear the true story of how her government was overthrown, she'll be returned to the throne."

"Do you think so?" Lani asked hopefully.

Tom shook his head, his face grim. "I think the only way the queen will get her country back is if enough Royalists are armed and seize the country back from the PGs by force."

Kim sent her lover a frightened look, then crossed to his side swiftly. "You mustn't speak so," she warned softly. "You don't know who might hear. Promise me you'll be careful."

Tom saw the fear gathering in the almond-shaped eyes, and reached out and held Kim's hand gently in his own. "Don't worry, I'll be careful."

For a moment, watching the two of them, Lani felt her throat ache with tenderness. She wondered what it would be like to have a man love her so intensely, that just the touch of her lover's hand could place that look of adoration on Kimiko's face. Then she looked away quickly, as if she were intruding where she did not belong. When she looked back, Tom and Kimiko were once again standing carefully apart, Kim's hands tucked demurely into her kimono sleeves, and Tom was reaching for his hat.

"I have to get back to Washington Place," Tom said. "It's my shift for guard duty."

Lani walked with him to the front gate, casting a worried look at her companion. "Kimiko's right. You won't do anything foolish, will you?"

Tom shrugged unhappily. "The queen has asked all her supporters to be patient and keep the peace until she can send delegates to Washington to plead her case. The PGs have filled the American newspapers with lies about rioting in the streets here in Honolulu. I suppose Liliuokalani feels any actual unrest would only work against her in the eyes of the American public."

"I've read the nasty lies they've written about Liliuokalani in the Honolulu newspapers," Lani said indignantly. "Isn't there something we can do to stop them? Perhaps if I talk to Adam. He knows the editors of most of the newspapers."

Tom turned to stare at her, an expression on his face that sent a quiver of unease through Lani. "What is it? What's wrong?" she asked.

"Don't you know, Lani?" Tom asked quietly. "Adam's one of them. He's been in on the plot to overthrow the queen from the beginning. I thought you knew."

Lani's hand tightened on the gatepost. "No," she said. "No, I didn't know."

Or was the real truth, she thought, she hadn't wanted to know. It was a much more comfortable marriage, not inquiring too deeply into what her husband felt or thought.

Tom looked unhappy. "I'm sorry, Lani. Perhaps I shouldn't have said anything. I love my brother, but," he gestured helplessly, "you know Adam."

No, Lani decided later that evening, as she sat on the

veranda, waiting for her husband to return, she didn't know Adam Stewart. She knew the rather stuffy, overbearing man who had been her guardian, the man who had calmly discussed marriage with her as if it were a business merger, nothing more, who had made love to her with the same proficiency he did everything else. But the man who had shared her bed two months ago, who had taken her ruthlessly, without tenderness, who had made her feel as if she had no will of her own, forcing her to say and do things that made her flush to remember, she hadn't known that man at all.

This time when Adam returned home, well after the dinner hour, and found his wife waiting for him on the veranda, she was wide awake. She was wearing a pale blue muslin gown that blended with the deep blue twilight so that at first he didn't see her. Then she rose to her feet and moved into the lamplight, and he saw the tension in her carefully still face, the stiffness of a body that usually moved with such natural grace.

Adam could imagine only too well the creamy softness of that body beneath the moth-fragile gown, the rosy peaks of breasts and satin-soft thighs. And in spite of having schooled himself well, he felt desire inexorably tighten within him, turning his voice harsh as he demanded, "Shouldn't you be inside?" It had rained late that afternoon, and there was still a damp chill in the January evening.

"I was afraid I might miss you. I wanted to talk to you."

"Can't it wait till morning? It's been a long day."

"No, it can't wait." Lani took a deep breath and spoke in a rush. "I've booked passage on the morning steamer for Maui. I'm going back to Palekaiko to live."

"I see." She could read nothing in the opaque gray eyes studying her face. "Our bargain is broken then?" he asked, almost indifferently.

She shook her head. "I don't want a divorce, if that's what you mean. I'll stay married to you. . . ." A flush ran beneath the creamy flesh. "But I can't . . . I won't live with you."

Adam wasn't sure whether it was anger or desire that whipsawed through him then, as he looked into those brilliant violet eyes, the softly curved chin lifted proudly. How easy it would be, he thought, to wipe that haughty disdain from her face, to take his wife in his arms and prove to her once again the depths of passion within her that could so quickly turn that tense body warm and yielding beneath him, to watch those coolly scornful violet eyes become shimmering pools of desire.

Lani saw the indifference in that impassive face stripped away. A muscle beside the hard mouth jerked, the gray eyes narrowed, and she stepped back quickly, struggling to keep her voice calm. "I know you can force me to stay with you. . . ." Then she fell silent, under the raking gaze of those merciless gray eyes, suddenly, embarrassingly, remembering what he had said after they had made love the last time, that she was the one who would have to come to his bed the next time.

Like a wire snapping between them, Adam turned his gaze away, and Lani took a deep ragged breath, trying to recapture her poise as she continued firmly, "I can never forgive or forget how you betrayed the queen and the Hawaiian people."

Adam's startled gaze flew back to his wife. He had assumed she was leaving him because of Keith. "Are you saying you're leaving me because Liliuokalani couldn't hold on to her throne?" he asked, bewildered.

"Because you and *haoles* like you forced her to abdicate," she corrected him sharply. "First, you stole their land from the Hawaiian people, and now you've stolen their country from them."

Adam sighed wearily. "In the first place, before the white men came, the Hawaiian people didn't own any land at all. All the land was owned by the king and his *alii*. The king allowed the people to work the land at his pleasure as long as they paid him tribute, but not one inch of soil belonged to the Hawaiian people.

"In the second place, there was nothing I or anyone else could have done to stop the overthrow. Perhaps fifty years ago, Liliuokalani could have held on to her kingdom, but the monarchy's days have been numbered for years. It was only a matter of time. If it hadn't happened this week, it would have happened next month or next year. These islands are some of the most valuable real estate in the world. If it hadn't been the

Americans, it would have been the French or the British or, more than likely, the Japanese who took over these islands.''

Exasperation crept into Adam's voice. "Don't you read the papers? In the last few years, Japan has become a world power. Their navy is stronger than any other in the Pacific. And there are more than twenty-five thousand Japanese here in Hawaii, whose first loyalty is still to the emperor. How long do you think Hawaii could hold out if Japan attacked these islands?"

"Are you saying that it's all right if America takes these islands from the Hawaiian people, but it's wrong if Japan does?" Lani asked scornfully.

Perhaps because her words cut too close to the bone, Adam's temper exploded. "No one could take these islands if the Hawaiian people were strong and wise enough to hold on to them!"

Lani walked slowly to the front door, at the last moment turning to face her husband, her voice cold. "I hadn't realized you thought Hawaiians were cowards and stupid. What will you think of your own child, I wonder, when it's born? It will be part Hawaiian, too, you know, just as I am."

She had reached the bottom of the staircase, when Adam's hands on her shoulders spun her around to face him. She was startled at the undercurrent of alarm she heard in his voice. "Are you telling me you're pregnant?"

She hadn't planned to tell him at all, Lani thought, annoyed with herself for blurting out the news. She had been afraid that if she told Adam, he would insist upon her staying in Honolulu, where he could keep an eye on her. She pulled herself free from his grasp. "The child will be born in August at Palekaiko," she said firmly.

In the brighter light of the hallway, Adam noticed the lines of fatigue in his wife's face, and felt a by-now familiar icy fear. Was it safe for his wife to bear a child? he wondered, and cursed himself for not having thought of such a situation arising.

"Have you seen the doctor?" he asked curtly. "Are you all right?"

"I've seen the doctor, and I'm fine," she assured him, surprised at his concern, but then, naturally he would be concerned, she realized. Wasn't that an unspoken part of their marriage agreement, that she would bear Adam an heir to carry on the Stewart name? A healthy heir, of course.

"Perhaps it would be best if you did return to the ranch," Adam said thoughtfully. In spite of the PGs' boasts that the majority of the responsible members of Honolulu sided with them, Adam knew, in reality, the overwhelming majority amounted to only a few hundred men. The town was rife with disquieting rumors of insurrection, so much so that President Dole, in fear of assassination, did not feel safe enough to sleep at his home at night. It was hardly an atmosphere conducive to the peace and quiet an expectant mother needed, Adam decided. "I'll drive you to the wharf tomorrow myself and make sure you and Kimiko have proper accommodations aboard the steamer."

"That won't be necessary."

"I insist," Adam said politely.

As if they were strangers who happened to share the same house, Lani thought, inclining her own head in courteous agreement. She was pleased that Adam wasn't standing in the way of her returning to the ranch, yet as she climbed the koa staircase, she felt a pang of irrational annoyance. Her husband might at least have made a token effort to keep her here in Honolulu with him!

Her irritation was quickly forgotten, though, in the excitement of returning to her beloved Palekaiko and seeing the many changes that had been made in the ranch in her absence. With the money from Adam, she had purchased new blooded beef cattle, pure registered Hereford bulls, which had been shipped to the ranch from America. Pili had had new fencing and paddocks built, while a recently completed pipeline brought in much-needed water. Rye grass and clover were growing again in pastures where they hadn't been cultivated since her father's death. Even the ranch house itself had a new coat of paint, and the furniture that Lani had ordered for the house while she was in Honolulu had arrived, replacing old, worn pieces that had seen their best days.

For several weeks Lani did nothing but ride with Pili on inspection tours around the ranch. She arose at daybreak to find Jubal saddled and waiting for her and spent the whole day in the saddle. When she returned to the house at night she was too tired to think of her husband and the role he had played in the betrayal of Liliuokalani, too exhausted to do anything but slip into the warm bath Kimiko always had waiting for her, force down the tray of food that was also waiting, and fall asleep almost before her head hit the pillow.

Then one morning early in May, she awakened to discover she had overslept. The sun was already pouring into her bedroom, and as she dressed hastily she saw that the Cloud Warriors, ready for combat, had already gathered above Haleakala. She hurried down to the kitchen and found Pili seated at the table, having a cup of coffee, while Charlie was making more noise than usual as he cleaned up the kitchen after feeding the *paniolos* who had already eaten and left for their day's work.

"I'm sorry I'm late," Lani apologized, taking the cup of coffee that Charlie handed her and shaking her head at the steaming pork and sweet potatoes, her stomach turning queasy at the smell. "Kimiko must have forgotten to awaken me."

"No damn good, you no eat," Charlie said, glaring at her.

Lani knew he wouldn't budge until she ate something. "Milk and bread then, Charlie. And maybe a slice of papaya." Mollified, but still mumbling beneath his breath, the Chinese cook stalked away, and Lani turned her attention back to her head *luna*. "I thought we'd visit the brood-mare pasture this morning. I think Ginger is ready to *haanau*."

Pili put down his coffee cup. "I told your maid to let you sleep." A smile touched the grooved face as he looked at the young woman seated across from him. "Ginger is not the only one ready to *haanau*."

"It won't be for several months yet," Lani protested. "I can still ride." At first, the thought of having a baby had thrilled her, a child here again at Palekaiko, having all the happy and exciting times she had had growing up on the ranch. But lately, she had become more exasperated than thrilled by the whole tedious process, the early morning sickness, her feeling of wanting to sleep all the time, even the weight of the baby growing inside of her, making her feel awkward and swollen.

"No more horseback rides," Pili said calmly. He had

received a letter from Adam Stewart shortly after Lani had
arrived at the ranch. The letter had made it very clear that Mr.
Stewart was relying on Pili to look after his wife's health and
welfare while she was at the ranch. As if, Pili thought now,
gazing fondly at Lani, he needed to be told. He would lay
down his life for the daughter of Matthew Tucker, as would
any of the other *paniolos* on the ranch.

It wasn't the girl's health that worried the *luna*, though. It
was the unhappiness he saw shadowing the clear blue-lavender
eyes, the same color as the *lani*, the heavens over Haleakala
when the Cloud Warriors turned away. He remembered the
happiness shining in those eyes when she had spoken to him
of Keith Stewart, and yet she had married the other brother.

He spoke gently. "Not good for woman be sad when she is
going to have baby."

"I'm not sad," Lani said, then looked quickly away from
that deeply lined face. She had never been able to lie to Pili.
But as dearly as she loved Pili, she had no intention of telling
him or anyone at the ranch that she had left her husband.

"Sometimes mare scared first time she have colt. Are you
scared, Paakiki?"

She looked back at him, startled. "Why should I be afraid?"
She was not like the *haole* girls at school, who, to her scorn,
hadn't known the first thing about how women had babies.
After all, she had watched the miracle of foals being born
when she had been only a child.

Pili nodded and, finishing his coffee, got to his feet. "I go
look to the mares. You stay and catch-up work in the office."
He shook his head with mock sadness. "All that paperwork
makes my head hurt."

Lani knew there was no point in protesting further. Pili
could be twice as stubborn as she was when he set his mind to
it. She finished her breakfast and walked back to the office.
The office had always been her father's domain, and she
could still sense his presence there. His pipe tray stood on the
desk, the bottles of medicine he had used to treat both men
and animals were in a nearby cabinet, and branding irons
hung on another wall. Lani sat a moment, listening, as if the
next moment she might actually hear her father's voice exploding in anger, or filling the room with laughter.

Then she sighed and reached for the mail that she hadn't bothered to look at in weeks. Most of the letters were ranch business, but there was a letter from Adam, in which he hoped she was well and that if she needed anything, she was to let him know. Except for the fact he had signed the letter, "Obediently, your husband," it might have been one of the many short, formal letters he had written her when he had been her guardian.

Quickly, she put the letter aside and picked up the Honolulu newspapers that came by ship and were always a few days old. When she had first arrived at the ranch, the news had all been bad for the royalist cause. President Harrison had approved the provisional government's request that Hawaii be annexed to the United States and had sent the treaty to the Senate for approval. And then the PGs had run into an unexpected snag. President Harrison, who had lost his bid for reelection in November, left office, and Grover Cleveland took over the presidency in March.

Not only had the new president withdrawn the treaty, but he had sent Special Commissioner James H. Blount to Hawaii to investigate the overthrow of the monarchy. The first thing the commissioner, a close-mouthed ex-Confederate from Georgia, had done was to order that the American flag be lowered and the Hawaiian flag raised in its place. All American sailors and marines were returned to their ship. Then, to the further delight of the royalists, within a month's time Minister Stevens had been abruptly dismissed from office and left the islands.

The newspapers that Lani now read through quickly announced the homecoming of the queen's delegation from Washington. Hawaiians had turned out in cheering crowds to greet their commissioners with leis, the crowd so great that the state carriage could hardly get through to Washington Place where the ex-queen waited for a report from her ambassadors. The queen's commissioners announced that they had talked to President Cleveland, and he had denounced the lawless occupation of Honolulu under false pretexts by U.S. forces and assured the queen's representatives that justice would be done.

Queen Liliuokalani had been right, Lani thought happily.

One had only to be patient and wait. Justice could only mean that it would simply be a matter of time now and the queen would be restored. She had just thought this when she was startled by the baby kicking her hard. She had felt the baby moving inside of her before, but never such a positive announcement of its existence.

A bemused smile on her face, Lani placed her hands gently, lovingly, over her stomach. For the first time, she tried to imagine the child growing inside of her. What would it look like, she wondered. Would it have reddish-brown hair like its father, his gray eyes? But what if it didn't? What if it had dark hair, Polynesian features? Would Adam love it the less? The thought sent a jagged pain through Lani, and for a moment she bent over, as if protectively hugging the child inside her.

"You work too hard. You make yourself sick," Kimiko scolded from the doorway.

Lani got slowly to her feet. "Don't fuss, Kim. I'm fine."

But she allowed the Japanese girl to coax her into eating a light lunch and taking a nap, although she insisted she wasn't tired. The sound of Kimiko moving quietly around the room, her slippers making soft, slapping sounds against the floor matting, the distant faint rumble of a sugar mill, soon lulled her to sleep.

As one drowsy sun-lit day followed another, May slipping almost imperceptibly into June, Lani had the feeling that she was suspended in limbo. She still spent her mornings working in the office, but in the afternoon she took walks in the garden, or simply sat, listening to the drowsy sound of bees in the fig trees, her mind and body content to do nothing but wait in dreamy anticipation.

When she awoke suddenly one night early in June, she thought it was the baby's kicking that had awakened her. And then suddenly, unbelievably, her bed slid across the room and crashed into the wall. The house seemed to be dancing beneath her. She had barely scrambled out of the bed when it raced away from her into another wall.

It was like walking uphill on the pitching deck of a ship to make it to the door. Lani could hear voices screaming, and she stumbled in the hallway and fell to her knees. Vaguely she remembered in her long ago babyhood, such a thing as this had happened when the island had been shaken by a volcanic eruption. But it hadn't been Haleakala, had it? she thought, dazed, trying to remember, as she pulled herself to her feet by hanging onto the doorjam. Haleakala was a dead volcano.

Then Kimiko was beside her, her face pasty white and holding a lantern with one hand and slipping the other around Lani's waist, as she helped her down the stairs and out of the house. The ground was a living thing, shuddering and flinging itself back and forth beneath Lani's feet. Through the noise of screaming servants, rushing from their houses, carrying small children and precious possessions, she could hear the cattle stampeding in the pastures, dogs howling, and birds screeching as they flew into the air from swaying trees.

But the most frightening sounds came from deep within the ground, strange rushing sounds, grumblings and groanings as lava and gases pushed to break through the earth's crust.

Kim was still beside her, holding her, and she pushed the maid away. "I'm all right. See to the others."

Then above all the other strange, violent sounds, she was aware of the terrified whinnying of the horses in the stable. She could imagine Jubal rearing, striking out at the wooden stall with his hooves, frantic to be free, and breaking his leg in the process.

She saw that several *paniolos* were already heading for the stable, their lanterns bobbing erratically in the darkness. Jubal would be too terrified to go with any of them, Lani thought. He'd know my voice. He'd come with me.

Several times she fell awkwardly to her knees, trying to reach the stable as the ground twisted and humped beneath her. Always she managed to struggle to her feet again. At the stable, the ranch hands were already leading out the nervous thoroughbreds, the eyes of the horses wild in the lantern light.

The stable was groaning, splintering; a portion of the roof fell away to the ground. She saw Pili leading out one of the horses, but it wasn't Jubal. She never knew how she got inside the stable or located Jubal's stall. She recognized the horse's nervous whinnying, and spoke to him calmly, soothingly. Jubal's hooves had already broken partially through the

stall door. Desperately Lani looked around for a bridle, a
rope, anything to act as a lead, when all at once the stable
floor seemed to lift beneath her feet. She was flung to the
ground just as the terrified horse leaped over what was left of
the stall door.

Lani felt something hit her, a crushing blow, the pain like a
whip curling around her body. Then Pili was beside her,
leaning over her, protecting her with his body as the earth
turned over and fell on top of her.

Chapter 22

"Mrs. Stewart! Lani, can you hear me? Your baby is coming.
Do you hear me?"

The world had turned right again, but it was a dark world
filled with excruciating pain. Her body was caught in a vise,
and as the darkness receded the vise twisted and tightened so
that she screamed aloud with the pain. She was dimly aware
that she was back in her bedroom, and that the violent
shudderings of the earth had diminished. Dr. Linsey, who had
tended her aches and pains when she was a child running
around the ranch, was at her bedside, forcing some vile-
tasting concoction down her throat.

"Don't," she muttered thickly, choking and swallowing.
Why didn't he let her alone? She had already sensed that if
she could only drift back to that darkness again, lapping at the
edge of her mind, she would no longer feel the pain.

"Lani, listen to me." The doctor's voice forced its way
into her consciousness. "You have to stay awake. You have
to help me, or your baby will die."

This time his words penetrated through the pain. Lani's
eyes opened, alarmed, her voice weak and groggy. "Too
soon . . . for baby."

It *was* too early for the baby to be born, the doctor thought, but that wasn't his only concern. The girl had been unconscious for almost twenty-four hours, and he had no idea whether the blow she had received in the stable had caused internal injuries or even if the baby was still alive. The contractions he could feel beneath his hand, though, were strong and steady. That was a good sign.

He smiled reassuringly down at Lani. "Babies come when they want to, and yours is definitely on the way."

The vise suddenly closed, pincer sharp, around Lani, and despite the medicine the doctor had given her, a scream ripped again from her throat at the indignity of the pain. She cast a pleading glance to the bottle that sat on a table beside the bed, but he shook his head, his voice gentle. "I can't give you any more medicine, Lani. You have to be conscious. You have to push when I tell you. Do you understand? Remember that time when you were eight and you were thrown from your horse and broke your leg? Pili had to set your leg himself, and he had nothing to give you for the pain. He bragged to everyone how brave his *keike* was. You'll have to be brave like that again, child. For your baby's sake. I promise you, it'll be over soon."

But it wasn't over soon. The labor continued through the long, warm night. To Lani, it seemed as if she had barely time to rest from one agonizing pain when another followed. And the baby still stubbornly refused to be born. The world narrowed down to the bed of agony in which she lay. The pain disappeared for a few moments then returned stronger, more ferocious, tearing at her perspiration-soaked body, so that she twisted helplessly back and forth on the damp sheets.

She was no longer sure whether it was day or night. Once, when the pain had momentarily withdrawn, she saw through the window a dark red glow filling the sky.

The doctor, wiping the perspiration from his face, glanced toward the window and said, "Mauna Loa's blowing its top again."

It wasn't Haleakala then, Lani thought groggily. It was the volcanic eruption of Mauna Loa on the island of Hawaii that had caused the earth to tremble and shake here on Maui.

Then another pain tore through her body and she screamed, forgetting the volcanic eruptions, forgetting everything but the pains that would not let her rest. Toward morning she was too weak even to scream. Her body was reacting blindly, instinctively to the pain now, pushing down when the doctor told her to, until finally, exhausted, she could no longer fight off the blackness surrounding her, and she sank into the darkness as if into a bottomless sea. When she surfaced again, she was aware of someone with soothing hands bathing her face and body with cool water. Forcing her eyes open, she glimpsed Kimiko leaning over her. The expression on the girl's face sent a chill racing through Lani.

"My baby's dead?" she whispered.

"No, no, Lani-san," Kimiko said quickly. "You have a small, beautiful daughter."

"I want to see her." Lani struggled to sit up, but was startled at how weak she was, like a newly born kitten. Her arms didn't have the strength to hold her daughter when Kimiko brought her and held her so that Lani could see that the child was indeed alive and beautiful.

Then the doctor came into the room and she noticed that his face had the same worried expression as Kimiko's, and fear gripped her again. "My baby's all right?" she asked.

"Your daughter's fine," the doctor assured her, lifting her wrist and holding it to feel her pulse. "But you need to rest."

Then it's me, Lani thought calmly. There's something wrong with me. But somehow it didn't matter now that her baby was safe. She drifted off to sleep, a restless sleep filled with nightmarish dreams. In her dreams, she was attempting to chase after something or someone, but whatever it was always remained just ahead of her, outside of her vision. And gradually, little by little, she was running slower and slower, as if iron weights were attached to her feet. It was a grueling, impossible effort just to lift them, to place one foot before the other. She gasped for breath, but each breath she took was a knife stabbing into her lungs. Every muscle in her body throbbed and ached. And yet she knew, in the manner of dreams, that she had to keep running. If she stopped, something dreadful, dark, and formless following close behind would overtake her.

Once she thought she glimpsed what was ahead of her, a man's figure, in the distance, walking slowly away from her.

But even as far away as he was, she recognized that swift, arrogant stride. She called his name, but when he stopped and turned, it wasn't Keith looking back at her. It was Adam. How angry he looked, she thought, his mouth set in that familiar uncompromising line she knew so well. He was beckoning to her. She even thought she heard his voice, brusque, commanding, "You can't give up, Lani."

What did he care how tired she was, she thought irritably. Why should she keep on running? Whatever was behind her, overtaking her, no longer mattered. All she wanted was to sink into the soft deep darkness at her feet and rest. But Adam's voice would not let her stop; cajoling, tender, scolding, it urged her on. When she felt herself falling, Adam's hands reached out and caught hers in an iron grip. "You mustn't give up, Lani. I won't let you give up." The voice pounded inexorably in her head, and she clung to those hands as if to life itself.

She was still clutching Adam's hand when she awoke. At least she thought she awoke and saw Adam sitting beside her bed. His face was ashen and gaunt, the sharp, slanting bone structure looked as if it would cut through the skin. She was too tired, though, to be sure it was really Adam sitting there, or if she was still dreaming. This time, though, when she drifted off to sleep, there were no more nightmarish dreams. And when she awoke again, she knew she was not imagining the mynah bird screeching outside her window or Dr. Linsey, standing beside the bed, his pockmarked face smiling down at her. "So you've decided to return to the land of the living. How do you feel?"

She thought a moment. "Hungry," she said.

The doctor nodded, pleased, as his hands ran lightly, skillfully over her legs. "No problem moving your legs?"

"Of course not," she said, wincing a little when he touched her upper leg, where an ugly black and blue bruise had formed. She pushed herself to a seated position in the bed, then, remembering, asked quickly, "Where's my baby?"

"We found a wet nurse in the village to feed her. You can see her in a short while," he assured her.

"Why can't I nurse my baby?" Lani asked, worried.

"Perhaps in a few days, when you're stronger. You had a

difficult labor, and after you had the baby you started hemorrhaging. It's a miracle you're alive.''

John Linsey was a believer in miracles, but he couldn't help wondering if this time it wasn't Adam Stewart who had kept his wife alive. The man had refused to leave his wife's bedside, as if by his own stubborn strength of will he was determined to keep her alive. He had refused to give up hope, even when the doctor had been sure that there was none, that his patient, lying so terribly still, hardly breathing, had lost too much blood to survive. Only once had Lani Stewart spoken, and then it was to call out the name of a man, not her husband. The doctor couldn't help wondering how Adam Stewart must have felt to hear his wife, in what could have been her last moments, call out to another man.

Still, the private relationship between a man and his wife was none of his concern, the doctor reminded himself, and turned his full attention again to his patient. After he had completed his examination, he smiled cheerfully. ''You're doing very well for a woman who had her baby during an earthquake.''

''Was there much damage?'' Lani asked, remembering the terror of those hours when the earth had gone wild.

''Not here on Maui, a few houses knocked down, that's all. We haven't heard yet the damage that Pele caused on Hawaii.'' The doctor shrugged and grinned. ''That's what some of my Hawaiian friends are saying, that the goddess Pele caused the volcano to erupt as a sign of her anger, because the *haoles* forced the queen to give up her throne.''

''You don't believe that?''

Maui was largely royalist in sympathy, and she remembered that Dr. Linsey, whose missionary parents had died nursing Hawaiians during a cholera epidemic at Lahaina, was an outspoken opponent of the annexationists. ''No,'' he said grimly, ''although I like to believe that a just God is not fooled by the self-righteous pretensions of the men in the provisional government. They can say what they will, but in the end it's greed and a lust for power that rule them.'' He shook his head sadly. ''To think that the sons and grandsons of missionaries who came to these islands to save the Hawaiian people, have made a mockery of . . .''

He broke off abruptly, shrugging sheepishly. "Sorry. What you need is rest, not a lecture. And I have to look in on my other patient. . . ."

"What other patient?" Suddenly, Lani remembered the stable, the roof crumbling as the floor leaped and twisted beneath her, and Pili. . . . "It's Pili, isn't it?" she said alarmed, half rising from the bed.

The doctor pushed her gently back against her pillows. Then filled a glass with a liquid that he insisted she swallow. "You don't have to worry about Pili," he assured her. "He's a tough old *kanaka*. He has a broken leg and a dislocated shoulder, but he was hurt a lot worse a few years back, when that wild bull tossed him. He'll be up and around before you are."

"How soon will that be?"

"Oh, you'll have to stay in bed for several weeks before you get your strength back."

"I can't," Lani fretted. With Pili and her both unable to work, who would run the ranch? They had a contract to deliver beeves in Honolulu, and there was a valuable registered bull arriving at Lahaina from a ranch in Texas within a few days. But whatever the doctor had given her was taking effect quickly, so that it was an effort to ask sleepily, "My husband? Has he been told about the baby?"

The doctor gazed down at her, surprised. "I thought you knew. Mr. Stewart's here at the ranch. He arrived after the baby was born. He never left your bedside until he was sure you were out of danger."

So it hadn't been a dream, Lani thought drowsily, Adam sitting beside her bed. And the rest, she wondered, had that been a dream? Adam's voice like a lifeline to which she had clung desperately. But there was another part to the dream, if she could only remember . . . but the next moment the drug took effect, and she was asleep again.

The next week all she did was sleep and eat. Twice, a beaming Kimiko brought in her daughter. The second time, when the child was placed against Lani's breast, the mouth and tiny hands working at the breast brought the milk flowing. Lani felt like laughing and crying at the same time. "Isn't she beautiful, Kim?" she asked proudly, examining

the pink, starfish hands, the black silken fuzz that was beginning to appear on the perfectly shaped head.

"Beautiful," Kimiko agreed. "And see how long her fingers are. She will be tall like her father."

Lani wondered what Adam thought about the baby. Was he
disappointed? Even as small as she was, the faint Polynesian
cast to his daughter's features was plain to see. Probably he
didn't think about the baby at all, she decided. Any more than
he thought about its mother. After all, he hadn't been by to
see her, even though she had been told he was still staying at
the ranch. But then what had she expected? she thought,
remembering how they had parted in Honolulu. It had been
only Adam's sense of duty, she was sure, that had brought
him to Maui after his child's birth.

She was surprised at the sharp sense of hurt she felt at
Adam's indifference to his daughter, and forced herself to
think of other things, of the ranch and all the work no doubt
piling up while she laid around in bed.

"Dr. Linsey might at least let me work in the office," she
fussed. "If those beeves aren't sent to Honolulu by tomorrow,
we'll lose the contract, and if the bull isn't picked up at the
dock . . ."

"The bull's been picked up, ornery as hell, and the beeves
are already delivered," Adam said from the doorway.

For a moment, Lani hardly recognized her husband. Instead of his usual conservative businessman's clothing, Adam
was wearing a *paniolo*'s trousers, a colorful kerchief around
his neck, and a shirt that looked as if it hadn't been off his
back in days. His shock of reddish-brown hair needed comb-
ing and his unshaven face was tired, Lani saw, but it wasn't
the frightening gauntness of the man who had sat beside her
bed. It was the weariness of a man who is physically exhausted.

He sank down into a chair, stretching his booted feet out
before him, rubbing almost absently at his bad hip as he
groaned softly and said, "I never knew a boatload of cattle
could smell so bad." He sniffed thoughtfully at his shirt.
"Though I don't suppose I smell much better."

"You brought the beeves to Honolulu?" Lani asked, amazed.

"With the help of the ranch hands. A day to get the cattle
down from Haleakala, two days to market, and two days

back. And then Pili reminded me that the bull was waiting to be picked up at Lahaina. And, oh, yes, there were a few dozen other jobs he mentioned that had to be done."

"You don't know anything about running a ranch," Lani said uneasily.

"Pili said much the same thing, in stronger terms," Adam agreed, yawning. "But I suppose I can learn."

"What about your business in Honolulu?"

"Tom can look after things for a month or two, until Pili's up and about again. It's about time that young man settled down and earned his keep."

Kimiko, who had been standing quietly by the door, said softly, "I will draw a hot bath for Mr. Adam," and quickly withdrew.

Adam got to his feet and came over to the bed, gazing curiously down at his daughter nuzzling eagerly at her mother's breast. "Young Jasmine has a hearty appetite," he said, a flicker of amusement in his gray eyes.

Although his glance had skimmed over Lani, she was suddenly, unaccountably pleased that Kim had brushed her hair that morning until it fell in soft, lustrous waves over her shoulders and that she was wearing one of her prettier, lacy nightgowns. Then Adam's words sank in, and she gave him a startled glance. "Jasmine?"

He shrugged. "The child had to be named, and I thought you might like naming her after your grandmother."

"Yes," Lani said, smiling down at her daughter, who for the moment was no longer hungry, her eyes closing sleepily. "I think my grandmother would like it, too." She shifted the sleeping child to her shoulder, turning the radiant smile she had given the child to her husband. "Would you like to hold her?"

Adam stepped back hastily, an alarmed look on his face. The first and only time he had picked up his tiny daughter she had screamed to high heaven, startling him so that he had almost dropped her. "I'm much too dirty," he said lamely.

How could he not want to hold his precious daughter, Lani thought indignantly, but none of her feeling showed in her face, as she said stiffly, "Thank you for helping out with the ranch work, Adam. You shouldn't be inconvenienced for too

long. Dr. Linsey tells me I'm regaining my health very
quickly.''

Adam gazed down into the cool, remote face of his wife,
remembering she had the same expression on her face the day
she announced she was leaving him. And it didn't help
matters any that, in spite of the pallor left over from her
illness, his wife had never been more beautiful. Motherhood
agreed with her, he decided, his gaze, almost against his will,
lingering on the tempting fullness of breasts that brought back
other delightful memories.

As if aware of his thoughts, a flush rose beneath the pallor,
and Lani hurriedly pulled the frothy bodice of her gown over
her breasts.

Anger pulled at Adam, in spite of his bone weariness.
Well, even if his wife were anxious to get rid of him, he
thought grimly, he had no intention of leaving until he was
sure she was completely recovered and Pili back on his feet.
"It's not an inconvenience at all," he assured her, smiling
tightly. "I'm simply looking after my own interests, or have
you forgotten that I'm half owner of Palekaiko? Now, if
you'll excuse me, I think I'll use that bath that Kimiko
mentioned."

After he left the room, Lani buried her face against the
sweet-smelling softness of Jasmine, surprised to discover that
tears were rolling down her cheeks. Annoyed, she brushed
them away with the back of her hand. Dr. Linsey had warned
her that it was normal for a new mother to sometimes cry for
no reason. It had nothing to do with Adam's indifference to
his Hawaiian daughter or the fact that little, after all, had
changed between them. If only Dr. Linsey would let her get
out of bed, she thought restlessly. She was sure her odd fits
of the blues would disappear once she was busy with ranch
chores again.

Then one morning three weeks later, she did leave her bed,
abruptly, without waiting for the doctor's permission. Instead
of bringing Jasmine in for her usual early morning feeding,
Kimiko darted into Lani's bedroom, her porcelain-textured
face that seldom showed emotion frantic. "The baby! She's
not in the nursery!"

Lani was out of bed, even before Kimiko stopped speaking, racing into the nursery next door to her bedroom. The lovingly carved crib that had held several generations of Tucker children was empty.

Then from the lanai downstairs she heard a horse's nervous whinnying, the sound of her husband's deep laughter. She was down the stairs and out the door with Kimiko close behind. Both women stopped short, staring at Adam on horseback, controlling his horse easily with one hand, while the other arm was wrapped around his daughter, seated on a pillow before him. Jasmine was gurgling happily, one small hand wrapped securely around her father's thumb.

At the accusing glances being flung his way, Adam said hastily, "I just took her for a short ride. I thought it was time my daughter and I got better acquainted." He gazed proudly down at Jasmine's dark head. "She didn't cry once."

Muttering furiously in Japanese, Kimiko stepped forward and took the baby into her arms, giving Adam one last outraged glance before disappearing into the house.

Lani felt her knees give way under her. She sank down on the step. Adam dismounted quickly, throwing the reins to a *paniolo* who had come running up to see what all the hubbub was about. Adam bent anxiously over his wife. "Are you all right? You shouldn't be out of bed."

Lani lifted her face to his, and he saw that she was laughing even as her blue-lavender eyes were bright with tears. She shook her head. "I'm fine. I thought . . ." the words came in a hiccuping rush. "I thought you didn't like Jasmine."

Adam looked nonplussed. "Not like my own daughter? Why should you think that?" Worried, he slipped an arm around his wife's waist, lifting her to her feet. "You're not making sense. Let me help you back to your room."

Lani looked longingly around her, taking deep breaths of the fresh morning air coming down from Haleakala, bringing the scent of eucalyptus trees, along with the sweetness of wild ginger and ripe guavas. "Please, Adam, can't I have breakfast downstairs?" she begged. "I'm so tired of being shut up in that bedroom."

"Well, I suppose just this once shouldn't hurt," Adam said reluctantly.

But after that morning, Lani took all her meals downstairs,

and it wasn't long before she had coaxed Adam into letting her work in the office. Then, as the weeks passed and Pili still wasn't able to sit a horse—"old bones heal slowly," Dr. Linsey explained cheerfully—she occasionally rode with Adam when he left the house early in the morning with the *paniolos* for the day's work. If she was going to be gone for more than a few hours, she would take Jasmine along in a soft leather pouch that Pili had made, which hung on the side of her saddle. Jasmine, swaddled in a cotton blanket with only her head showing, like an Indian papoose, seemed to enjoy the horseback rides as much as her mother.

The first morning Adam and Lani rode together, one *paniolo* after another found an excuse to ride back and join them. They enthusiastically welcomed Lani back, while greeting Adam with the same mixture of affection and respect that Lani realized, a little jealously, they had given her father.

One August morning, as Adam and she were inspecting the brood pastures, a young *paniolo* watched Adam ride on ahead to check on a mare that was about to foal. "That one rides like hell and brave like any-kind," the boy said proudly. "The day we swam the beeves to the whaleboats to take them to market, we saw a shark. Beeves all stampeded to shore. We all thought *pau,* new *luna,* not go in ocean again." The boy chuckled. "Damn my eyes, if he didn't help us turn the beeves and ride steers out to the boat like a real *paniolo.*"

The young ranch hand gazed uneasily at the young woman beside him, who suddenly had lost all color in her face. It wasn't as if she didn't know about the sharks that sometimes appeared in the ocean at Makena when a shipment of Palekaiko's beeves was herded out to a steamer, he thought, puzzled.

When Adam returned, and the young *paniolo* rode away, he took one look at his wife's face and asked, "What's wrong?"

"Johnny was telling me about the shark at Makena." She was suddenly, unaccountably, furious with Adam. She had seen what a shark could do to a steer, much less a man. "You could have been killed!"

Adam reached down and gently tweaked his daughter's nose. "I've seen sharks before, you know," he said quietly.

"Any seaman has. If it had been a school of sharks in the water, or a tiger shark, I wouldn't have taken the chance. But a snout-nose shark, alone, is a coward." An almost boyish grin of satisfaction slipped across Adam's face. "And we didn't lose one steer."

Lani studied her husband. The hard, slanted lines to his face, the narrowed gray eyes, had not changed, but there was something different about Adam, she realized. The man sitting relaxed and at ease on his horse, his face darkly bronzed by the sun, was not the same hard-driven businessman who had left the house in Honolulu early in the morning and not returned till late at night. Adam seemed to be actually thriving on the hard work of managing the ranch, the element of danger that went along with so many of the jobs the *paniolos* did each day.

Although he still favored his bad hip, the limp was no longer so noticeable, and, feeling more at ease with her husband, Lani had even found the nerve to ask how the accident causing his injury had happened. "A drunken seaman came at me with a harpoon when I ordered him below. Luckily, he was too drunk to take good aim, and the harpoon grazed my hip." Adam's voice was matter of fact as he related the incident, and it occurred to Lani that after serving as the captain of a whaler, perhaps Adam didn't find ranch life so dangerous after all.

Later in the morning, when she and Adam stopped for their midday meal near a clump of tall koa trees, it also occurred to her that she had spent more time alone with her husband these last months than she had in all the rest of their married life. In Honolulu, the only time they'd had to talk was across the dinner table with the servants around, or at parties or social occasions when there were always other people present.

Now, as she unpacked the lunch that Charlie had prepared for them and Adam slacked the girths and shook the saddles to cool their horses' heated backs, she thought, amused, she and Adam never seemed to stop talking! Of course, it was almost always ranch talk, but occasionally Adam had let slip some incident from his own youth, and she had caught a glimpse of the joyless household in which he and his brothers had been raised by a cold, martinet father, so different from her own happy childhood.

Before she sat down and ate with Adam, she took off her shirt and washed herself in a nearby water trough. At first, she had felt ill at ease, washing herself with Adam watching, now she unself-consciously splashed the clear, cool water on her face and breasts, before she took Jasmine into her arms and fed her.

Adam flung himself down on the blanket beside her. She eyed him contentedly as her daughter kneaded at her breast. She couldn't help thinking how the *paniolo*'s clothes suited her husband's long, muscular frame, his body made even harder by the physical labor of the last months. Then a squirming Jasmine, frustrated at not immediately finding her food source, began to wail, and Adam, who had been catnapping, came immediately awake. He smiled lazily at his daughter as he slipped an arm around Lani so that her head rested comfortably on his chest.

"Our daughter's going to have a temper, just like her mother," he said teasingly.

"You mean just like her father, don't you?" Lani retorted in mock indignation.

But she felt too peaceful and drowsy to even pretend to fight. A family of doves cooed in the branches of a smoke-blue tree, a flight of white butterflies drifted by, and the fragrance from maile creepers filled the sun-lit air around her. Both she and Jasmine fell asleep.

When she awoke again, she was still cradled in Adam's arms. She could feel that narrowed gray gaze on her face even before she opened her eyes. But it was not that intense, appraising gaze that had somehow always frightened her. There was a softness, a warmth in the gray eyes gazing down at her that stirred an answering warmth and need within her.

Adam knew at once by the faint quickening of his wife's breath, the widening of the lilac eyes as if against a too bright light, that Lani would not deny him if he wanted to make love to her. Only what would that prove, he thought harshly. It wouldn't erase from his memory his wife's calling out to Keith with almost her last breath. Oh, he could take her as he had that night in Honolulu, deliberately and violently forcing from her mind and body all thought of another man for a short while. But he could never reach deep enough into her heart to demolish the memories of Keith that lay buried there. Not until she came to him of her own free will, offering him proudly and joyously her soft, eager body as well as her stubborn, loyal heart, would he know that his brother no longer possessed any part of his wife.

Lani lay quietly in Adam's arms, her eyes searching her husband's face uncertainly, the hardness that was suddenly there that had not been there before. "What are you thinking?" she asked.

Then, dismayed, she felt her husband pulling her abruptly to her feet, his voice carefully emotionless as he said, "I'm thinking we'd better get moving, or we'll never get the corrals in the south pasture checked before it gets dark."

Chapter 23

The next morning the Stewarts had their first argument since Adam had arrived at the ranch. The summer roundup was about to begin—gathering up the cattle spread all over the flanks of Haleakala, herding them into paddocks, earmarking the new calves, and branding the steers. Lani was up and dressed before daybreak in her oldest riding togs, but when she came downstairs with Jasmine sound asleep in her arms, Adam stopped her in the hallway.

"You can take Jasmine back upstairs. You won't be riding with us today."

"I've always helped with the roundups," Lani protested.

"Not this time. You'll only be in the way."

She stiffened indignantly. "You're letting Pili ride with you, and he can barely hobble around."

"I can't stop Pili," Adam said harshly. "But I can stop you." A familiar impatient hardness tightened the long mouth, the gray eyes gazing coldly at Lani.

Then slowly the gray eyes lost their frostlike chill, as Adam studied his wife's beautiful, rebellious face, the sleeping child in her arms. When he spoke again, his voice was still firm, but softer. "Look, Paakiki, you know better than I what roundups are like, working from sun-up to dark in the dust and heat. Even if you were strong enough, a cattle drive's no place for a baby."

Reluctantly, Lani knew he was right. She had worried herself about having Jasmine with her. Adam shrugged ruefully. "Anyway, I'm going to have enough trouble keeping up with the *paniolos* today, without making a fool of myself by taking a spill in front of you and Jasmine."

Fear all at once pinched at Lani's heart. She knew that danger rode with every ranch hand on a roundup. Adam was a good rider, but she had seen experienced *paniolos* gored, even killed, chasing down and lassoing the wild steers that roamed the upper heights of Haleakala. And a man with a bad leg . . . Lani lowered her eyelids quickly, afraid that her husband would sense what she was thinking. She knew Adam's pride, how he hated to be reminded of his injury.

She dragged back the words of warning that sprang at her lips, and said instead, trying to make her voice casual, "Well, since I won't be riding with you, why don't you take Jubal? He's well trained at running cattle. "

She thought Adam was going to refuse, but after a moment he nodded, his voice as casual as hers. "Thanks, I will." Then he turned and went out to the kitchen to join the ranch hands, who were already heading for their mounts. Lani could hear the *paniolos* laughing and joking with one another, as if they could hardly wait to challenge the wild old bulls up on the mountainside, some of whom, like outlaws, had defied capture for years.

She stood in the kitchen doorway, Jasmine stirring sleepily in her arms, and listened to the sounds of creaking leather and the eager thud of hooves as the ranch hands rode away, the vast dome of Haleakala looming blackly against the stars in the distance. At the last moment, Pili wheeled his horse around and rode back. Leaning from his saddle, he looked down at Lani. "Shame-my-eyes if any-kind happen to bossman," he said quietly. Then he turned and joined the others.

For the rest of the day, while working in the office, Lani's gaze kept drifting back to the slopes of Haleakala. She knew every trail threading the volcano's flanks. She had even traveled on horseback inside the immense, dead crater with her father, explored the lakes of congealed lava, the gray-and-black cinder cones, the masses of rocks twisted as if some giant had tossed them playfully around, and had glimpsed the dazzling beauty of the silver swords that grew within the mysterious, silent bowl of the cavern.

Always before, Haleakala had been her friend. Today, though, when she looked at the volcano, all she could think of was Adam up there, chasing a wild steer across the mountain slopes, Jubal stumbling and falling in one of the lava pits hidden by brush. Or a rogue bull, escaping Adam's lasso, turning and charging his attacker, ripping the man and horse open with his wicked horns. Just working with the frantic beeves within a corral, a man could be crushed. . . .

Hastily Lani removed her gaze from the slopes of the volcano and tried to concentrate on the papers spread out on the desk before her. The figures blurred before her eyes. If anything happened to Adam . . . she was shocked at the pain that ripped through her at the thought, as if she had been the one swiped by a bull's vicious horns. She stared down at her hands, clutching tightly at each other, in her lap. When had it happened? she wondered, bewildered. When had her feelings toward her husband changed so that she could feel pain like this at the thought of losing him? Was it possible to fall in love slowly, imperceptibly, day by day, so that you didn't even know the exact moment when it happened?

It was Keith she loved, she reminded herself, and was startled to discover that she had to remind herself of that fact, and even more surprised to realize that she hadn't thought of Adam's brother in months. Even the pain she had always felt when she thought of Keith was gone, as if scar tissue had grown over the wound.

She got to her feet and began to pace restlessly, her thoughts in a turmoil. For even if her feelings toward Adam had changed, how did she know what Adam felt toward her? Dr. Linsey had let her know, discreetly, that she was well enough for her husband to join her in her bed. No doubt, he had told

Adam the same thing. Yet her husband had made no attempt to come to her room at night. And yesterday, when she had awakened from sleeping in Adam's arms, he must have known that she wanted him, but the way he had acted had made it very plain that he had no interest in making love to her.

Lani glanced down at herself, at the worn dungarees and faded *palaka* shirt she wore constantly these days. She frowned thoughtfully. It was no wonder her husband wasn't interested in making love to her! She looked like a boy, and a pretty scruffy one at that. A mischiveous smile pulling at the corners of her mouth replaced the frown. Well, that could be changed, Lani decided, hurrying from the office. What she had to do was remind her husband that she was not only a woman, but a desirable woman.

It was dark before Adam and the *paniolos* returned. Lani had waited dinner, and after washing and changing his clothes, her husband joined her at the dinner table on the lanai. She had had Charlie prepare Adam's favorite dishes, delicately broiled mullet, golden sweet potatoes, hot biscuits, and fresh mangoes and guavas in a wine sauce. The lanai was lit by candles, flickering softly in a faint trade wind. Pink and white plumerias filled a Chinese porcelain bowl in the center of the table.

As Adam ate, Lani studied his face covertly across the table, as if in some odd way she expected him to look different. Aside from lines of weariness in his face, though, he looked much the same, his gaze friendly, interested in what she had to say. He told her of the roundup, how many steers they had branded, how many calves, the old brindle bull John had roped after it had evaded him for three years.

"Once they're fattened up in the paddocks, we should have some prime steers to ship to market in the fall," Adam said. He frowned thoughtfully. "It's too bad we have to rely on the inter-island steamers to get our beeves to market. They're always late in arriving, or they don't show up at all. The ranches on Maui and Hawaii should have their own steamer, one fitted out especially for transporting cattle."

As if I were his business partner, nothing more, Lani found herself thinking, struggling to hide her irritation. She had taken several hours to dress for dinner that evening, trying on and discarding one gown after another, finally settling on a gauzy *holoku* of a mist-like blue shade that matched her eyes and showed to best advantage the soft curves of her shoulders and arms. She had tucked a peach-shaded plumeria into her hair, which she had brushed until her arms ached, then let the hair hang loose, curling up slightly at the ends, as it spilled loosely over her shoulders.

Studying herself at last in her mirror, she had decided, pleased, that there was no way this evening that Adam could confuse her with a boy. The *holoku* fit tightly around her breasts and hips, then flared out gracefully around her ankles, making it abundantly clear that she had regained the softly voluptuous figure she had had before she had become pregnant. Her face no longer held an unattractive pallor but glowed, as if brushed by the sun.

And all evening long Adam hadn't said a word about how well she looked, she thought, infuriated, his gaze as impersonal as if she were still dressed in pants and a shirt.

When he finished eating, Adam got to his feet, stretching, then winced a little at the protest of muscles that had been overused. "I think I'll turn in early," he said. "It's going to be another long day tomorrow."

Lani walked up the stairs with him, pausing hopefully at her bedroom door. "Would you like to look in on Jasmine?"

"I already did, before I came down to dinner." He reached down and dropped a chaste kiss onto her uplifted face. "Good night, Paakiki."

Lani walked into her room, restraining the almost overwhelming impulse to slam the door shut behind her. Adam had the bedroom next to hers, but there was no connecting door between. She could hear him moving around his room as she undressed, slipped into her nightgown, and took one last look in the nursery to make sure Jasmine was sleeping soundly. After she got into bed, she could still hear Adam. He was whistling softly. The careless tune grated on her nerves so that she sat straight up in bed, glaring at the wall. It was perfectly obvious that her husband was not coming to her bed again tonight.

She remembered, a little belatedly, that she was the one who had told her husband in Honolulu that she no longer wanted to live with him as husband and wife. But she was sure her words, spoken in the heat of anger, wouldn't keep Adam from her bed if he wanted to be there.

Lani threw aside the coverlet and got abruptly to her feet. Her skin suddenly felt too warm, too tight. Even the wisp of a nightgown she wore felt too heavy against her skin, reminding her of that night in Honolulu, so long ago now, when she had waited restlessly for Adam to come to her room. A flush raced from her breasts to her hairline as she remembered exactly what had happened when Adam *had* come to her bed that evening.

And afterward . . . Lani frowned, trying to remember what Adam had said as he left her that night. Something about if she wanted him, she knew where she could find him. Of course, he hadn't meant it, she decided hastily. He couldn't possibly expect her to go to his room, seek him out in his bed. She couldn't humiliate herself that way, she thought proudly. Then unexpectedly she found herself remembering all those nights Adam had come to her bed and she had lain in his arms, imagining it was another man making love to her. A dull flush of shame burned her face. Did she really believe that Adam, who always seemed to sense what she as thinking, hadn't known what she was doing?

Almost absently now, she thought of Keith, but it was like trying to recapture a dream after awakening in the morning. The harder she tried to remember, the more dreamlike Keith's features became. It was Adam lying in the next room who was the reality, who had been there all the times she had needed his strength—when her uncle had died and when Rebecca had left her, when Keith had betrayed her and held her up to ridicule before her friends, and when she had almost died, after Jasmine was born.

Hesitantly, she stepped toward her bedroom door. Perhaps it was already too late, she thought uneasily. Perhaps she had waited too long to put aside her childish dreams, and Adam had grown tired of waiting for her to grow up. Yet she knew she had to try. If he rejected her, her humiliation would be no worse than what Adam had suffered at her hands. Her heart slamming in her chest, she left her room and knocked softly at Adam's door, then opened it slowly. Adam was still awake, she saw in the light from his bedside lamp.

"Is something wrong with Jasmine?" he asked, sitting up quickly.

She shook her head, her throat closing convulsively so that she wasn't sure she could speak. The cool, gray gaze turned to her, gave her no help.

"What is it?" he asked.

She could hear the pounding of her heart in her ears as she slowly crossed the room to his bed, her knees threatening to give way beneath her. Suppose she *was* too late. Suppose Adam no longer wanted her. She stared helplessly down into his face, as she tried to find the right words. All at once, close-up, she saw the flicker of amusement in the gray eyes, the muscle beside the long, firm mouth twitch, as if he were trying very hard not to smile. She had steeled herself for anything, but not for this.

She gave a gasp of anger. "Damn it, Adam Stewart. You're laughing at me!"

She turned to flee, but his arms caught her, and in one motion she was on the bed and he was beside her. His hands pinned her shoulders to the mattress, one leg flung over hers, as she struggled to break free.

When, at last, exhausted, she lay still, Adam smiled down at her, laugh lines radiating from eyes that were no longer chill but filled with warmth. "I'm sorry, darling," he said, choking back a laugh. "I couldn't help myself. You looked like a vestal virgin offering herself up as a human sacrifice." His mouth reached down and closed over hers, at first lazily caressing the corners of her lips with the tip of his tongue. Then as her mouth parted beneath that gentle, insistent pressure, and allowed him entry, her own tongue moved shyly, then more boldly, against his, until his mouth took complete, fierce possession, and he pulled her body against the length of his so that every part of her touched him. When his mouth finally, breathlessly left hers, but remained not more than an inch away, he whispered teasingly against her lips, "Was it so difficult, my love, the walk to my bed?"

"You knew!" She drew back accusingly. "You knew all along. You were waiting for me!"

He lifted his head, his voice warm with hidden laughter. "After that romantic dinner, it wasn't hard to guess, not to mention that fetching gown you wore, which left very little to the imagination." He slanted an amused eyebrow. "I'm surprised you didn't have one of the *paniolos* strumming a guitar in the garden to complete the seduction scene."

"I thought of it," Lani admitted, breaking into sheepish laughter. "But I knew they'd all be tired after the roundup." She ran her fingers lightly over the deep lines of weariness in her husband's face, her voice, concerned, "You must be tired, too."

"Never that tired," he said, grinning, as he slipped off the filmy nightgown and tossed it to the floor. Then he turned down the lamp and slid his hands tantalizingly, slowly over her body, his mouth teasing and capturing the rose-soft peak of each breast. This time she did not have to be told what to do. Her hands moved almost of their own volition to pull him closer, stroking the crisp hair at the nape of his neck. She could feel the hard muscles bunched in his back, relaxing at her touch. But they both had denied themselves too long and neither wanted to delay that moment when they became part of each other, their pleasure spiraling upward swiftly to a shattering explosion of joy that left them tangled, exhausted, in each other's arms.

After a few moments, when he started to pull away from her, Lani remembered the other times when he had left her alone afterward, and clung to him desperately. "No," she whispered. "Don't leave me."

He kissed her eyelids, smoothing the damp hair back from her face. "I have no intention of leaving you, ever," he said quietly. Reaching across her, he lit the lamp beside the bed, then gently took her chin and turned her face to the light, so that he could look deeply into her eyes. In the lamplight, he could see the faint sheen of tears, like violets after a rain, caught between the dark lashes.

"Say it," he commanded softly, urgently, his searching eyes never leaving her face.

Lani's mouth curved in a blissful smile. "I love you, Adam Stewart," she said. Then when those gray piercing eyes still probed, still searched her face, she blurted uneasily, "Adam? You do believe me, don't you?"

He didn't answer, turning off the lamp and pulling her once

again into his arms in the darkness. It had begun to rain. She could smell the rich, damp fragrance from the garden, hear a kona wind begin to lash across the sky, the distant crash of thunder, sounding like the sea roaring against the coast. By his steady breathing, she realized that Adam had fallen asleep, and she snuggled into the sheltering curve of his arms. He murmured her name in his sleep and pulled her closer.

Just before sleep claimed her, too, Lani realized that Adam had never answered her question. Didn't he believe she loved him? And, for the first time, she wondered uneasily: Was it possible, perhaps, that trust, like love, took time to grow?

Chapter 24

On the morning of Friday, December 22, 1893, almost a year after the provisional government had overthrown the Hawaiian monarchy, a strangely quiet crowd of *haoles*, Hawaiians, and Orientals waited on the waterfront of Honolulu for the arrival of the *Alameda*. Not that it was unusual to have almost all of Honolulu at the waterfront when a ship arrived from America. Ships, after all, were Hawaii's only link to news of the outside world. The crowds at the waterfront, though, were usually noisy and boisterous, with a band playing loudly, and the lei sellers busy distributing their wares. Those people expecting letters would mill around the post office until mail sacks from the ship had arrived and letters hastily distributed, opened, and read. Newspapers from America were quickly passed around, with someone always leaping onto the veranda and eagerly shouting headlines aloud to the waiting crowd.

This morning, though, everyone at the wharf knew that the news the *Alameda* was bringing would decide the fate of Hawaii and the monarchy. Royalists crowding together, bolstered their confidence by reminding themselves that Commissioner James Blount's report, submitted to President

Cleveland, had placed the blame for the overthrow of Queen
Liliuokalani squarely on the *haole* businessmen, and stated
that without the support of the former American minister,
John Stevens, and American troops, the revolution could
never have succeeded.

The royalists had been further encouraged in November
when a new American minister to Hawaii had arrived. Albert
S. Willis had assured the queen that President Cleveland
would do all in his power to undo the wrong that had been
done her. Then, as a condition for Cleveland's support, Willis
had spent several weeks trying to persuade Liliuokalani to
grant full amnesty to all those who were instrumental in the
overthrow of her government. Finally, reluctantly, the queen
had agreed. So what could possibly stand in the way now of
the monarchy being restored? the royalists thought hopefully.

On the other hand, the supporters of the provisional government nervously eyed the two American warships in the
harbor, their decks bristling with stacked weapons, this time,
they knew, for possible use against them. The PG leaders,
however, had assured their followers at a mass meeting that
American troops would never fire on fellow Americans to
prop up a foreign throne. If, however, the impossible should
happen, the executive building had been heavily fortified.
The number of government troops had been increased, and
guns and ammunition had been issued to the Citizens' Guard
who would fight to the death, they had loftily proclaimed,
to preserve their way of life against ignorant, *haole*-hating
natives.

Then a murmur like a rustling wind ran through the tense
crowd. One man after another heard the fateful words and
passed them along to his neighbor. Word had been flashed
ashore from the *Alameda* that Lorrin Thurston was aboard,
coming home with the triumphant news that America was in
an uproar of protest against President Cleveland's support of
Queen Liliuokalani, and that the Congress of the United
States would not support a restoration of the monarchy.

Armed PG policemen moved uneasily through the crowd
after the news from the *Alameda* had been received, worried
that a wrong word could set off a wave of violence, like a
match at a tinder box. But there was no violence. The Royal-

ists were too stunned at the sudden, unexpected death of their cherished dreams, and the PG supporters were too anxious to hurry off and tell their friends the good news.

Tom Stewart was not stunned as he strode swiftly away from the waterfront. Fury, like red-hot, molten lava, flowed inside of him. In his narrowed, icy gaze, the rigid set to the long mouth, he bore an astonishing resemblance to his older brother, Adam. The royalists had been fools, he thought grimly, to rely on the good will of Americans to win back their country for them. Now they would do what they should have done in the beginning. They would fight back against the PGs in the only language the *haoles* understood, with guns.

In her bedroom at Washington Place, the queen stood at the window, staring bleakly at Kawaiahao Church across the street from her home. So it had all been for nothing, Liliuokalani thought wearily. She had wanted the *haole* traitors banished from Hawaii, their property confiscated, so that they could never menace her people again. Instead, when Mr. Willis had insisted, she had put aside her desire for vengeance and had promised President Cleveland that she would grant amnesty to all those who had conspired against her. And now she knew it would have made no difference what she had promised. The result would have been the same, another heartbreaking betrayal by those she had trusted.

Even the conversations she had had with Mr. Willis, supposedly confidential, had been twisted by her enemies, given out to the newspapers and a shocked world, that "the savage Hawaiian queen planned to behead all the whites who had driven her from her palace." Liliuokalani's full lips tightened in anger. Why should she have made such a ridiculous threat? Not that there hadn't been times when she had forgotten her Christian upbringing and wished her enemies dead, but it was not in the Hawaiian tradition to behead enemies. But then, why should one more lie about her in the newspapers bother her? Hadn't she read stories in the newspapers that called her "heathenish," "immoral," and "a dirty squaw."

Her gaze focused unhappily on the graceful steeple of the Kawaiahao Church. And it was not only her enemies who had maligned her. Even the ministers in the church she had attended and loved from childhood had turned against her, spreading vicious lies about her lack of morals, calling her a polluted woman. It was a small source of satisfaction to her that those ministers who had tried to preach such lies about her to their native Hawaiian congregations had been turned out of their pulpits.

A flash of sunlight against metal on the roof of the church made her draw back instinctively from the window. Her friends had warned her that there were men stationed on Kawaiahao Church's roof with guns aimed on Washington Place, with orders to shoot the queen on sight.

She withdrew to her desk, trying to calm herself, searching for a ray of light in the darkness surrounding her. The American Congress had turned against her, but at least they had not agreed with the PG's request to annex the Hawaiian Islands to the United States. And President Cleveland was still her friend. As long as her country was not taken over by America, there was always the possibility that the provisional government could be overturned. She mustn't give up hope, she thought fiercely. She mustn't give up hope.

The news, when it reached Maui, that America would not support the restoration of the queen, hit Lani like a thunderclap. At first, she could not believe it. Hadn't the Blount Report made it very clear that the provisional government had usurped the rightful government of Hawaii, against the will of a majority of the Hawaiian people? How was it possible for the American Congress to support such an illegal action?

She read and reread the newspapers that had arrived by boat from Honolulu that morning. There must be some mistake. Gradually, though, as she realized there was no mistake, her emotions changed from bewilderment to sadness and finally anger.

Adam had spent the day on ranch business in Wailuku. When he returned that evening, he knew at once that his wife had heard the news from Honolulu. He recognized the danger signals, the flush of pink along the cheekbones, the amethyst eyes polished to a high gloss, the way Lani's hands were clasped tightly in her lap. Not that she said anything to him about the news from Honolulu over the dinner table. Although they talked easily on almost every other subject, the deposing of Queen Liliuokalani was a topic that was always carefully avoided between them, as if skirting dangerous waters. Lani spoke very little at all at dinner and retired early.

Adam wasn't too surprised when he went up to his bedroom later and discovered that his wife was not in his bed, although ever since that night Lani had come to his room she had shared his bed every night with unabashed eagerness. Now he scowled at the empty bed and then at the door he had had constructed between Lani's bedroom and his. The door was closed. Well, if his wife thought he was going back to leading the life of a celibate, she was badly mistaken, he thought, annoyed.

Without bothering to knock, he stalked into her bedroom. Lani was sitting up in bed, the newspapers scattered on the coverlet around her. At his abrupt entrance, she glanced at him, then gestured helplessly to the newspapers. "How could they? Rebecca taught me how much Americans value their freedom. How could they deny the Hawaiians the same freedoms they enjoy?"

Adam felt his temper dissipate when he saw his wife's woebegone face, the almost childish brightness to her eyes as if she were holding back tears. He sat down on the edge of the bed and took one of his wife's hands in his, his voice rueful. "The Americans are people like any other, not saints. And if you remember your history, they fought a revolution to get rid of being ruled by a king. I doubt if they're very fond of monarchies."

"It's not the same at all," Lani protested hotly. "Liliuokalani is a good queen. The Hawaiian people love her."

Adam sighed. "The monarchy is ended, Lani. Why can't you accept it? There's nothing you or I or Liliuokalani can do to restore her throne."

"No!" Lani snatched her hand free from her husband's grasp. "Liliuokalani would still be queen if it weren't for *haoles* like you and your friends who don't care who or what you destroy," she said bitterly. "All you care about is money and power."

Adam got to his feet, his gray eyes narrowing coldly. "You seem to have forgotten it was *haole* money that built your beloved ranch. And it was for my *haole* money that you married me, wasn't it?''

He saw Lani flinch, her face going pale, and cursed himself silently for losing his temper, even as he could still feel the anger building inside of him. "Look," he said, gruffly, "I didn't come in here to argue politics with you. . . ."

In one graceful movement, Lani was out of bed and standing before him. "Oh, I know why you're here," she said with cool disdain. In another graceful motion, she had stepped out of the slip of a nightgown she wore and kicked it to one side. The moonlight drifting in through the window lined the curves and hollows of her slender, nude body with silver, but a faint pink flush of anger ran beneath the creamy skin. "This is what your *haole* money paid for, isn't it?" she asked, her violet eyes mocking.

She heard the sound of the slap across her face before she felt the impact of the blow. But strangely it wasn't the pain of the blow she felt. It was the tortured anguish she saw twisting Adam's face, the gray eyes staring at her disbelievingly, charged with such pain that she could not bear to look into them. She hid her face in her hands, not even knowing she was sobbing until she felt the warm tears between her fingers.

She heard Adam say brokenly, "Darling . . . don't, please don't cry." She felt his hands gently pry her hands free so he could see her face, and heard his sharp, indrawn breath when he saw the imprint of his hand, white against her pale skin. He left her for a moment and came back with a cold, wet cloth that he placed against her face. Then he picked her up and carried her to the bed, sliding in beside her and pulling her into his arms.

She could not stop crying, her body racked with sobs, and wasn't sure if she was crying for Liliuokalani and her lost throne, or for Adam and herself, the love and trust that had slowly, tenuously, been growing between them, destroyed in just a few reckless moments. At last, spent, drained of all emotion, she lay quietly in Adam's arms, his hand stroking her hair tenderly until she fell into an exhausted sleep.

When she awoke again, still half asleep, she reached over drowsily, as she did every morning, to where Adam should have been sleeping beside her. There was no one there. Her

eyelids flew open as she discovered that she was not in
Adam's bed, but her own. At the same moment, memory of
the night before rushed back, and she sat up in bed, her
thoughts in a guilty turmoil. Even as upset as she had been by
the news from Honolulu, how could she have said the hurtful
things she did to Adam—a flush burned her face—and behaved the way she had? She would have to apologize to him,
she thought, scrambling out of bed, somehow find a way to
make it right again between them.

In the mirror she saw the faint purplish bruise on her
cheek, and realized she had forgotten all about Adam's slapping her. Then, remembering the look of anguish on her
husband's face afterward, she was sure Adam hadn't forgotten. She glanced thoughtfully toward the closed door between
the two bedrooms. Perhaps she wouldn't have to apologize at
all, she realized. No doubt Adam felt even more guilty than
she did and was eager to apologize to her. As she slipped into
a flowered cotton *holoku* and ran a brush quickly through her
hair, she smiled in anticipation. Naturally, she would accept
his apology, she decided magnanimously; well, maybe not
immediately. In fact, it might be better if she took her time
and let him come to her, seeking forgiveness.

Then she heard Adam moving around in his bedroom, and
forgot all about waiting for him to come to her. After all,
what did it matter who apologized first? Impatiently, she
pulled open the connecting door.

"Adam, I'm sorry . . ." Then she fell silent. Adam wasn't
in the room. It was Kimiko, straightening the room. "Mr.
Adam not here," the young woman said, glancing at the
bruise on her mistress's face, then quickly turning away. She
reached into the sleeve of her kimono and pulled out an
envelope, her downcast eyes not meeting Lani's, her voice
unhappy. "Mr. Adam left early this morning to catch steamer
to Honolulu. He said, give you this when you wake."

Lani took the envelope back into her bedroom, pulling out
the sheet of paper with hands that felt suddenly nerveless.
The letter was brief.

"My dear wife: Urgent business matters require my immediate return to Honolulu. I have spoken to Pili. He assures
he is strong enough to return to full-time management of the

ranch. If there is anything you or Jasmine need, he is to let me know at once. With the present unsettled conditions in Honolulu, it is safer and more sensible for you and Jasmine to remain at Palekaiko. Please believe me when I say I am sorry for any unhappiness I have caused you, but perhaps this separation is best for both of us."

Lani read and reread the letter, crumpled it up and threw it away, then retrieved it and read it again, as if trying to find some hidden meaning behind the carefully chosen, emotion-less words. Her first shocked disbelief changed to a misery too deep for tears, like a great, cold stone in her chest, and then, gradually as she read and reread the terse words, into a searing rage. How dare he leave Jasmine and her this way, as if his wife and daughter were unimportant encumbrances to be put aside when it suited his fancy?

When she picked up the letter again, she did not crumple it but tore it into a dozen pieces, her face frozen with anger. No doubt Adam thought she would be crushed by their separa-tion, that she couldn't manage without him. Well, she would show him that she could manage quite well. She tore off the *holoku* and slipped into her dungarees and shirt, crushed a hat over her head, and stalked from the room. She had run the ranch with only Pili's help before, and she could do it again.

She discovered Kimiko hovering unhappily in the hall out-side her bedroom door. Although she did not look at her mistress's bruised face, Lani could guess what the young woman was thinking, what no doubt everyone on the ranch now knew; that Adam Stewart had not only left his wife and child, but had struck his wife in the bargain.

Raw anger pulled at Lani's nerves, and she snapped, "Haven't you anything better to do? Why aren't you taking care of Jasmine?"

Then ruthlessly pushing aside the guilt she felt at the hurt look on Kimiko's face, she stalked by the maid and down the stairs. It was a guilt that became harder and harder to ignore as the weeks passed, and almost everyone at Palekaiko felt the sting of Lani's wrath, from the lowliest yard boy to Pili himself. Charlie would face the wall and mutter Chinese curses beneath his breath when she came into his kitchen, and the *paniolos* who used to tease and joke with her now had a way of disappearing when they saw her coming.

"Well, I don't ask anymore of the hands than I ask of myself," Lani said irritably to Pili one day in March, after upbraiding Johnny for not mending a paddock fence so that several steers being fattened for market had wandered off. Except for the short times she spent with Jasmine during the day, she worked from sun-up to sunset, either in the office or overseeing the ranch hands. But no matter how exhausted she was when she fell into bed at night, she didn't sleep well. She often woke up in the morning as tired as when she went to bed, which didn't improve her disposition.

Now she frowned at Pili, who had said nothing while she scolded Johnny; she could see the disapproval in the dark, wrinkled face. "It's time Johnny learned, a ranch job is work, not play," she said, annoyed.

"I am sorry you have big sad in your heart, Paakiki," Pili said quietly.

"I'm not sad!"

A faint smile crinkled the lines. "I think *punipuni*."

Lani sighed to herself. It was foolish to try and lie to Pili, who knew her almost as well as she knew herself. "I'll get over it," she said fiercely.

Pili shook his head. "I see what kind look Adam have in eyes. He got big aloha for you."

"Then why did he leave?"

Pili shrugged. Who could explain the way of the *haoles?* "Go to Honolulu. Ask Adam. More better than carry this sad kind-thing in heart."

"I can't," Lani blurted unhappily. Suppose when she got to Honolulu Adam didn't want her there? Oh, she knew he wouldn't turn her and Jasmine away from the house. But she couldn't bear going back to their previous existence, when Adam and she had barely tolerated each other's company in the house.

Pili studied her face gravely. "My Paakiki never a coward," he said.

His words struck home. That evening Lani began making plans to return to Honolulu with Jasmine and Kimiko. She decided not to tell Adam that they were coming. At least then he couldn't write and tell her not to come. Whatever he had to say to her, however painful, he would have to say to her face, she decided firmly.

And tried not to think of what she would do if Adam told her he wanted to make their separation permanent.

Chapter 25

When the inter-island steamer from Maui arrived at Honolulu, Lani was surprised to find Tom waiting on the dock.

"How did you know we were coming?" she asked, as her brother-in-law pushed his way to her side through the crowd of people waiting to greet the arriving passengers.

"I didn't," he admitted. "I'm here to pick up mail from Maui." He looked over her shoulder to where Kimiko was standing quietly behind Lani, Jasmine in her arms, and he smiled broadly. "But I'm glad I am here," he said, his eyes filling with warmth as his gaze lingered on the Japanese girl. Then his glance returned, puzzled, to Lani. "Adam didn't say anything about your arriving today."

"He . . . he doesn't know," Lani replied, then added lamely, "It's to be a surprise."

If Tom was curious about his sister-in-law's absence from her husband's side for several months, and now this unexpected arrival, he asked no questions, saying cheerfully, "Well, I certainly hope your being in Honolulu improves Adam's disposition. He's been cross as a bear these last months. I stay away from the office as much as possible."

The stewards were carrying off the luggage, and Tom said, "I'll see about hiring a hack to take you home."

"You needn't bother. We can manage."

Once more Tom's glance returned to Kimiko, as he said firmly, "It's no bother at all. I insist."

After the luggage had been strapped on top and shoved

under the seats of the hired carriage, Tom joined Lani, Kimiko, and Jasmine inside the coach. As the carriage drove by what used to be Iolani Palace, Lani noticed, surprised, that the Hawaiian flag was flying over the building.

She gave Tom a questioning glance, and he said, scornfully, "Oh, the PGs have adopted the Hawaiian flag as their own. Now the Hawaiians no longer consider it their flag. And the provisional government these days calls itself the Republic of Hawaii. Of course, it's not really a republic. Eighteen men have appointed themselves to run the country and make the laws, but I supposed they think a republic sounds better to the American people, the same way they're talking about a constitutional convention and trying to get the Hawaiians to register to vote."

He laughed grimly. "Naturally, their new constitution will make sure that the PGs don't lose control of the government by allowing the majority of the Hawaiians, or the Orientals, to vote. And no one can register who doesn't take an oath of allegiance to the so-called Republic of Hawaii, so, of course, the Hawaiians who are allowed to vote are refusing to register." He suddenly chuckled. "The word is that the Hawaiian women refuse to be wives to those men who do register!"

The hack was turning from Richards Street onto Beretania, and Lani caught a glimpse of Washington Place. The queen's home had a shuttered, closed look behind its garden of tamarind, ironwood, royal palms, and monkeypod trees.

"Is Queen Liliuokalani still living at Washington Place?"

Tom had taken Jasmine from Kimiko and was playing patty cake with his godchild, who was gurgling happily in his lap. "Yes, and the Hawaiians still come to her, petitioning for assistance, as if they can't believe that she's no longer their queen. It infuriates the PGs. They've even offered money to Liliuokalani to abdicate. It's not that she doesn't need the money, since her property was confiscated by the new government," Tom said, his face darkening, "but she's refused to take a cent and sacrifice the rights of her people." He added glumly, "I think she still believes that the United States will undo the harm they've done her."

"You don't agree with the queen?" Lani asked, gazing curiously at her companion.

Tom grimaced. "I don't believe thieves give up their loot without a fight." And then, warningly, "And you'd better not call Liliuokalani the queen in public. The PGs insist that she be called Mrs. Dominis, or you'll end up being trailed around by someone like that."

He gestured to a man on horseback following a short distance behind the hack.

"Who is it?" Lani asked, following his gaze.

"One of the PG spies," Tom said indifferently. "They're all over Honolulu, keeping an eye on anyone they suspect has royalist sympathies. The other night they raided a luau held at Mr. Cummins's home, claiming it was a royalist meeting."

Surely Tom was exaggerating, Lani thought uneasily, but when the hack turned up the driveway to her home, she noticed that the man on horseback, who had been following the carriage, stopped outside the gate.

Tom handed Jasmine to her mother, as the servants came hurrying out of the house to greet Lani and to get their first eager view of Jasmine. As the men servants carried in the luggage and the women passed the baby with many expressions of admiration from one pair of arms to another, Tom drew Kimiko into the garden.

In the shade of the hau arbor, effectively hidden from the house, he immediately took her into his arms. When he finally released her, she still nestled within his arms, her dark eyes shining softly with happiness. "Do you know how much I've missed you?" he demanded huskily.

She smiled faintly. "As much as I've missed you, perhaps?"

Although Tom had come to Maui several times, bringing papers from the office for Adam to sign and to see his godchild, his time with Kimiko had been brief, hastily snatched meetings in one of the small guest cottages when everyone else had retired for the night.

Tom sat down on the bench in the arbor, pulling Kimiko down beside him. "I've made up my mind," he announced firmly. "I'm tired of these hole-in-the-wall meetings. We're going to be married."

He wasn't sure what reaction he had expected from his intended, tears of happiness, cries of joy. He had never expected Kimiko to lift her delicately beautiful face to his and softly say, "No."

"What do you mean, no?" Tom asked, startled. "You do love me, don't you?"

"Oh, yes, so much. It hurts . . . here." Kimiko pressed her hands against her middle.

"Then why won't you marry me?"

Kimiko cast her gaze downward so that her beloved could not see the pain in her eyes, as she murmured, "I am not worthy to marry you."

"That's ridiculous!" Tom exploded.

Kimiko shook her head. "You know where you found me," she said quietly. "Others could know, too. I think your brother, Mr. Keith, already suspects that I worked for Wo Tai." Her gaze flew proudly to Tom's face. "You are a respected, important man in Honolulu. Your wife must be respected, too."

"I don't give a damn what Keith or anyone else knows about you," Tom said angrily.

Kimiko's hands crept into her kimono sleeves, misery eating away inside of her. How could she expect her lover to understand? He was not Japanese. He couldn't know that she could never return to her family. By becoming a whore, she had dishonored them and was dead as far as they were concerned. Nor would any decent Japanese man marry her. And without family, a Japanese woman was nothing. How could she bring such dishonor to Tom, for whom she would gladly lay down her life?

She got slowly to her feet. "I can never marry you," she said slowly, and there was no mistaking the finality in her voice.

She watched anger turn her beloved's face a beet red. What she couldn't know was that Tom was remembering another marriage proposal he had made in this same garden. The humiliation of that rejection by Lani, and now Kimiko's refusal to marry him, pulled his pride to a breaking point. His voice grated roughly. "You don't love me. Isn't that it? Isn't that why you won't marry me?"

Kimiko said nothing, and his anger was fueled by the calm, exquisite beauty of her face, as emotionless as if it were carved from smooth ivory. While he was being cut up inside, he thought, furious, she felt nothing. For the second time in his life, he had made a fool of himself over a woman. Well, it wouldn't happen again.

"Don't expect me to beg you," he said coldly. "And don't expect to see me again."

Then he turned and stalked away from the hau arbor, and out of the garden.

Ah Sing stuck his head in the dining room door, frowning at the uneaten food on Lani's plate, then at the empty chair across the table from her. "Cook swell food. No one eat," he said crossly. "Food always spoil. Better I go work in restaurant."

It was an old threat that Lani knew better than to take seriously. "I'm sorry," she said soothingly. "The meal was delicious. I must have eaten too much at lunch."

Mollified, the cook departed, grumbling beneath his breath. Lani got slowly to her feet, carefully averting her eyes from Adam's empty chair. Had Tom told his brother that his wife and daughter had arrived from Maui? Is that why Adam hadn't come home for dinner? No, she decided, she had asked Tom not to tell Adam, and Tom wouldn't break a promise. No doubt, Adam, as usual, was simply working late. From what she could gather from the servants, her husband was at the office these days more often than he was home.

She went upstairs to check on Jasmine and found her daughter sleeping soundly in a crib that the servants had found in the attic. The small room, which had been a guest room, was rapidly taking on the appearance of a nursery, she thought, amused. Jasmine's toys were already scattered about, and there was a rocking chair in one corner, perfect for rocking a baby to sleep, that had not been in the room before.

For several minutes she hung over the crib, studying her sleeping daughter, the black hair, soft as down, the surprisingly long eyelashes, the rosebud of a mouth, and her heart turned over with love. At least, no matter how Adam felt about her, she was sure he loved his daughter. Except, an iciness crept over her. She had been sure Adam loved her, too, hadn't she?

She left the nursery and started down the stairs, pausing beside the portrait of her grandparents. Sometimes, when she stood like this, studying the portrait, she had the feeling that her grandmother Jasmine was standing beside her, as if she could almost reach out and touch her if she tried hard enough. Her gaze moved to her grandfather Morgan, with his hand resting so possessively on his wife's shoulder. Suddenly she found herself remembering something her Uncle Daniel had told her, one night when he'd had too much to drink.

He had been at his mother's bedside when she died, he had told Lani, his voice slurred. "She was lying so still, I thought we'd already lost her. Then she opened her eyes and smiled. She had such a beautiful smile. But she wasn't looking at me. She was looking at someone standing behind me. Then she said my father's name. And she was gone." Lani remembered the misery in her uncle's voice. "I always knew that she loved my father more than anyone else. It was as if she couldn't wait to join him."

How much in love they must have been, Lani thought wistfully, wondering how it would be to have a marriage as happy as her grandparents' had been. Yet she remembered another story she had heard whispered about her grandparents, that her grandfather had been forced to marry Jasmine Babcock, and when his wife had refused to sail with him, had had his wife brought, drugged, aboard his whaling ship.

Lani had always refused to believe the outrageous story, but now all at once she knew it was true. And if her grandparents' marriage had started off so badly, and yet succeeded so well, wasn't it possible that there was hope for her own marriage?

She clung to that hope as she strolled through the garden and admired the geraniums and roses her uncle had imported from America, now in full, blowsy bloom, their scent overshadowed by the heavy fragrance of ginger, lilies and gardenias planted nearby. How hard her uncle had worked, she thought, transplanting foreign flowers and shrubs into his Hawaiian garden, just as the *haoles*, from the moment of their arrival in these islands, had tried to transplant a foreign culture onto the easy-going Hawaiian people.

The alien flowers and shrubs had taken root and flourished

in Hawaiian soil. Would the foreign culture someday flourish, too, she wondered unhappily. Was Adam right, that it was impossible to stop the changes that the white men had brought to these islands? But she didn't want to think about politics, not tonight, when her ears were attuned, listening for the sound of Adam's surrey returning. In her mind she was shaping and reshaping words that she would say to him when he did arrive.

She thought she heard the telephone ringing and rushed back into the house, but central had dialed the wrong number, and Lani scowled as she replaced the receiver to the ugly black box attached to the hallway wall. She supposed the telephone had its uses, but there was something so coldly impersonal in talking to people through a machine, without seeing their faces. And she was sure central listened in to all the conversations that were held over the instrument!

When she heard the front door opening behind her, she swung around, startled, but not as startled, she saw at once, as Adam was. All the words she had so carefully planned to say flew out of her head. She had expected he might be furious with her, or coldly indifferent. She hadn't expected that he would simply stare at her, without speaking. Or that his face would look gray and exhausted, as if for weeks he hadn't slept any better than she had.

Without knowing how it happened, whether she took the first step or Adam did, the next moment she was in his arms, their mouths meeting feverishly as their bodies strained together, her hands clasped behind his head, pulling him closer, his hands pressed against her back, molding her soft body to his hardness.

She didn't remember who suggested they go upstairs, only that once in Adam's bedroom, she was discarding her clothes as rapidly as Adam, racing to the bed, and once more into his arms. Their lovemaking was like the first night they had made love at Palekaiko, their hands and mouths seeking each other hungrily, their passion flaring in a frenzy of impatience, as if neither could bear to wait. Lani gave herself with the same quick, wild abandonment that was driving Adam, so that in their pell-mell, almost immediate merging, a boundary was crossed, and it was impossible to distinguish if he possessed her, or she possessed him.

This time, afterward, it was Lani who fell asleep, exhausted by the two-day boat trip from Maui, the early morning arrival at Honolulu, and the strain of waiting for Adam to show up at the house. When she jerked awake again, she was alone in bed, and dawn was spreading its pearl-gray light through the room. She thought at once of Jasmine, awaking, frightened, in a strange room, a strange house.

But before she could pull on her robe, Adam came back into the bedroom from the nursery, closing the door softly behind him. As if guessing what Lani was thinking, he said quickly, ''Jasmine's fine. She woke up for a few moments, but I picked her up and she fell back asleep.''

He came over to the bed, pushing Lani gently back against the pillows. ''You should go back to sleep, too,'' he said, worried by the faint shadows he saw beneath the violet eyes.

''I'm not tired.'' She had to find out, she thought. There was no question about how she and Adam felt about each other when they made love. What she had to learn was how he felt about her when they weren't wrapped in each other's arms. ''I have to know, Adam,'' she asked, even as she wasn't sure she really wanted to know. ''Why did you leave Palekaiko?''

He went to stand at the window, his back to her. ''I told you in the note I left. I had to return to Honolulu for business reasons. I'd been away for almost six months. Stewart and Sons can't run indefinitely without someone at the helm.''

''But I thought Tom . . .''

Adam turned to face her, shaking his head. ''Tom means well, but he'll never make a businessman. He has his mind on too many other things, and a company like ours, with so many irons in the fire, requires your full attention.''

Lani slipped on her robe and joined Adam at the window. ''That's not the only reason you left, is it?'' she asked, her gaze holding her husband's with a disconcerting directness.

''No.'' He reached out and gently touched her cheek, without a blemish now, the mark from his blow long since faded. But the tortured look she had seen on his face that night, after he had struck her, was back in his eyes. ''When I wasn't more than ten, I saw my father lose his temper and strike my stepmother. I saw the look on her face. I always swore I would never do that to any woman. That night, when I hit you, I realized I was exactly like my father. I couldn't face the thought that I might hurt you again. I had to get away.''

''You're not like your father,'' Lani protested, flinging herself into Adam's arms. ''And nothing will ever separate us again!''

For a moment, she felt herself being clasped tightly in Adam's arms, and then, to her dismay, she was being pushed gently away. ''I wish that were true,'' Adam said, his voice sober. ''But as soon as you and Jasmine have had some time to rest, I'm sending you both back to Maui, where you'll be safe.''

''Why?'' Lani asked. ''Because of what happened? You can't believe that I'm afraid to stay with you?''

''No, not that,'' Adam said quickly. ''It's what's happening here in the city. Honolulu's a volcano, ready to explode. Everyone knows that the royalists are arming themselves, and the government has increased its forces and declared martial law. I don't want you and Jasmine to be caught in the middle of a bloody revolution. I'll have Tom pick up some steamer tickets. . . .''

''Jasmine and I are not going back to the ranch. We're staying right here with you.''

Although his wife's voice was placid, Adam recognized the willful look in the determined amethyst eyes, the stubborn set to the chin. He suddenly found himself remembering a similar conversation he'd had with a young, equally defiant Lani here in this house, when he planned to ship her off to Maui and had to threaten to have her dragged, kicking and screaming, aboard the boat before she'd agree to go.

''Damn it, Paakiki,'' he groaned. ''Do you always have to argue with me? Can't you for once just agree with me?''

And did she have to look so beautiful, he thought, vaguely annoyed, her black, lustrous hair falling in a dark cloud over her shoulders, her pale-blue satin robe only partially closed so he could glimpse the tempting swell of gleaming breasts, the dark shadowy valley between them, knowing very well that she was wearing nothing beneath the robe. He had only to reach out and undo the sash, to run his hand over those silken thighs, and she would be as eager as he was. . . . He took a painful, ragged breath and tore his gaze away from his wife. "You're going back to Palekaiko, and I don't want to hear another word about it," he said harshly.

Lani's deep eyelids lowered over the shimmering violet eyes, her voice meek. "Well, of course, darling, if you feel so strongly about it, Jasmine and I will do whatever you want."

She stepped closer to him. Somehow her robe had opened completely, and as she rose on tiptoe, her arms lifting to encircle him, he felt the silken loveliness of her body sliding upward against his naked flesh, sending a hot, searing need knifing through him. Her pink tongue teased at the corners of the hard, uncompromising mouth, as she murmured, "But I don't have to leave this very minute, do I?"

Making an inarticulate sound, Adam scooped her up in his arms and carried her to the bed. And this time when they made love, it was not in a frenzy of impatience but slowly, as if they had all the time in the world to explore every pathway of passion, deliberately prolonging each exquisite pleasure to the fullest. The violet eyes never once closed, growing steadily darker, blurring with a passion that brought tears sparkling in the tangled eyelashes. Adam tasted the saltiness of the tears with his tongue, buried his face in the musky fragrance of her hair while his hand slid between her thighs, moving inside of her until he heard her gasp and murmur his name, a soft, sweet moan deep in her throat. Her body arched upward, reaching for him at the same moment he entered her, and neither could then delay or hold back the rushing tide of their passion, carrying them, finally, breathless, hearts pounding, to a safe, quiet harbor.

Lani lay content within the circle of his arms, and when finally he gently pulled away, he thought she was asleep. But the moment he left her side, her eyes opened, a murmur of protest on her lips.

The pearl-gray dawn had left, and a bright golden sunlight filled the room. Adam brushed the softly curved lips with a kiss. "I have to go, Paakiki," he said regretfully. "I'm

already late. . . ." He gazed down at his wife, obscurely
troubled by something he saw in her face. "Nothing's changed,
you know," he said, trying to make his voice firm. "I'm still
sending you and Jasmine back to Maui."

"Of course, darling," Lani agreed, smiling sweetly up at
him, her violet eyes luminous, laughter caught in their depths.
"Whenever you say."

Which only made Adam wonder uneasily as he left the
room: since his wife was so graceful in defeat, why should he
feel that he had somehow lost the battle.

Chapter 26

On the fourth of July, the provisional government officially
proclaimed itself the Republic of Hawaii in a ceremony on the
front steps of the palace. The sea of white faces attending the
early morning ceremony were protected by armed citizen
guards and sharpshooters on the palace veranda to make sure
that an uprising by citizens of the republic didn't mar the
festivities.

Lani refused to attend the ceremony with Adam. "How do
they dare call Hawaii a republic?" she asked Adam contemptuously as they rose from the breakfast table. "Who elected
Dole and the rest of those traitors to office? Not the people of
Hawaii."

"It's the losers of a revolution who are the traitors, the
winners are patriots," Adam pointed out mildly. "And the
entire diplomatic corps, including the United States minister,
has recognized the republic. The monarchy is gone forever,
no matter what the royalists delude themselves into believing
when they're plotting revolution at Cunha's saloon."

At the startled look that for a moment touched his wife's
blue-violet eyes, Adam frowned, exasperated. "Marshal Hitchcock is a sly old fox. He undoubtedly knows all about those

secret meetings at Cunha's, as well as the guns and ammunition that the royalists have hidden around the island. Hitchcock and his spies probably know where every cache of arms is buried.''

''Not every cache,'' Lani almost blurted, then bit back the words and looked quickly away from her husband.

Adam studied his wife's face, the guilty flush spreading beneath the creamy skin, with a growing sense of alarm. He had long suspected that Tom was involved with the royalists in their plotting to restore Liliuokalani to the throne. Now he took Lani's chin in his hand and forced her to look at him, his gray eyes steel-bright with anger. ''If I thought for one minute that Tom has recklessly dragged you into his dangerous conspiracies . . .''

The sculptured eyelids lowered swiftly over Lani's too-revealing eyes. When the heavy black lashes lifted again, the violet eyes shone guilelessly up at her husband, her mouth curving in a sweetly inviting smile as she stepped closer to Adam so that he could feel the tempting pressure of her breasts against him, her hands resting lightly on his shoulders. ''I can't imagine what you're talking about, darling,'' she murmured.

Abruptly Adam took her upper arms in his hands, grasping the soft flesh so tightly as he pushed her away from him that she gasped. ''It won't work, Paakiki,'' he said, his eyes like flint, hard as his voice. ''As much as I'd miss you and Jasmine, if I find out that you're mixed up with any crazy royalist schemes, I'll send you both back to Maui so fast, your head will spin!''

Lani pulled free of the punishing grip on her arms. ''I'm sure you would,'' she said coldly, trying to ignore the flutter of uneasiness in her stomach. ''Now, if you'll excuse me, I must tend to Jasmine. . . .'' And she turned and flounced out of the dining room.

The uneasiness stayed with her, however, when she met Tom several weeks later at an evening band concert on the grounds of the Hawaiian Hotel. Since Tom was still being followed by government spies, he had decided it would be safer not to appear too often at the house on Beretania Street, in order to keep suspicion away from Lani. When Lani wanted to see him, she sent him a note by one of the servants, and they would meet at a social gathering where, in the crush of people, no one would suspect they were having a private meeting.

The outdoor band concerts at the hotel under the baton of Henry Berger were always well attended, and Lani deliberately chose a seat in the dark last row. As she listened to the former Royal Hawaiian Band, she decided loyally that the Portuguese musicians didn't play nearly as well as the Hawaiians who had quit the band rather than swear allegiance to the new government. Nevertheless, it was pleasant, listening to the music, the darkness broken occasionally by colored lanterns hung among the trees, the fragrance of tuberoses drifting from the hotel garden, and the sky studded with glittering stars that even the full moon could not quench.

Then when the band was in the middle of the second half of the concert, she got quietly to her feet. Slipping away into the darkness, she made her way to the dimly lit back veranda of the hotel, which overlooked the mountains rather than the hotel park. With the hotel guests crowding the front veranda to watch the band concert, the back veranda was deserted.

Tom was waiting for her, his voice concerned as he pulled her away from the light into a corner of sheltering darkness. "I got your note. What is it? What's wrong?"

"It's Adam," Lani blurted. "I think he suspects."

She heard Tom draw in his breath sharply. "You mean he knows about the guns buried in the garden?"

"Oh, no," Lani said quickly. "I don't see how he could know about that. He seldom goes into the garden, so he wouldn't notice the newly dug soil. And all the yardmen are Orientals. They hate the new government too much to say anything."

She repeated Adam's conversation with her in the dining room, word for word. When she had finished, she asked, "Is it true? Do the government spies know about the royalist meetings at Cunha's, and where the guns are hidden?"

Tom shrugged indifferently. "Oh, we've always suspected that Hitchcock had his spies within our groups. Most of them we know, and we feed them just enough information to keep them happy. And Cunha's is only one of many places we meet. You don't suppose we'd be foolish enough to discuss plans we want to keep secret in a public saloon? As for the guns, I suppose it's possible they know where some of the caches are buried, but not all of them.'' He laughed softly. "I'm sure they don't know about the guns hidden in the garden of a strong supporter of the government like Adam."

Lani didn't join in his laughter, biting unhappily at her lower lip. After a moment, Tom said quietly, "If you're afraid, Lani, we'll move the guns. Adam's right. It's too dangerous. I should never have involved you in the first place."

"I'm not afraid, Tom Stewart!" she retorted indignantly. "And it wasn't your idea that I get involved. It was my own. You know I'd do anything in my power to help restore Liliuokalani to her throne. It's just . . ." she stared at Tom, her face troubled. "It's just that I hate lying to Adam!" Even coming here alone tonight to the band concert, she had lied to Adam, telling him she was attending the concert with a friend.

"You can stop anytime you want," Tom assured her. "Nobody will think the less of you."

I'll think the less of me, Lani thought sadly. If only, when she lay in Adam's arms, she didn't feel as if she were holding back a part of herself from him. Since their reconciliation, she had given herself to him completely, opening her mind and her heart as well as her body to him. Now she sensed that keeping the truth from Adam had built an invisible barrier between them.

"No," she said slowly. "I won't stop." Then, impatiently, "But how much longer will it be, Tom? How much longer do we have to wait?"

"I don't know," he admitted. "There are those close to the queen who are still counseling patience. They've persuaded her to send an emissary to Europe to try and get support for the monarchy from England, France, and Germany." From the tone of Tom's voice, it was clear that he thought such a royal request was a waste of time.

"What about help from President Cleveland?" All Hawaii was buzzing over the latest rumor that the *Alameda* had arrived with a private letter from the president to the queen, promising aid to the royalists.

"Sam Parker returned from Washington on the *Alameda*. He told me that the president said he could do nothing. Unofficially, though, Secretary of State Gresham promised that no American forces would be used against the royalists if the royalists were prepared to 'chew those PG fellows up.' "

Tom stared glumly away from his companion into the darkness. "That's just it," he said bitterly. "We're not prepared. We don't have near enough men. And not enough money to buy the guns and ammunition we need in California, much less ship it back here without the government finding out what we're doing. The only men who are offering to bring in guns for us are drug smugglers, who know how to put cargo ashore without being discovered. And how can we trust men like that? I'm not even sure I can trust my own . . ."

Tom fell abruptly silent, as several Japanese navy officers appeared upon the veranda, resplendent in white duck trousers, blue caps, and blouses trimmed with gold braid. Small swords like carving knives in sheaths were attached to their belts. They glanced curiously at Lani and Tom as they passed by, then smiled knowledgeably, as if deciding the young man and woman were lovers seeking darkness for their amorous meeting.

The band was playing "Hawaii Ponoi," which Lani knew was always their last number, and she said quickly, "The hotel guests will be coming back this way soon. I'd better go. But I want you to take this. It should help buy a lot of guns."

Tom opened the handkerchief Lani had thrust into his hands. The rope of opalescent pearls gleamed in the moonlight. He gave his companion a shocked glance. "I can't take these. Isn't this the necklace that your grandmother Jasmine is wearing in her portrait?"

Lani nodded. "I was looking at her portrait when the thought came to me to give you the pearls." She smiled faintly. "I suppose it sounds strange, but it's almost as if my grandmother gave me the idea. Somehow I know she'd approve." She added, firmly, "And if there's anything else I can do, let me know."

"You've already done enough."

Lani's chin lifted stubbornly, and it occurred to Tom, in the tilt of her chin, the pride in her eyes, how much Lani looked like the portrait of her grandmother Jasmine. "No," she said softly. "None of us have done enough. Not until these islands are free again."

"I still don't understand why you want to attend this party at Ainahau," Adam said, slanting a quizzical look at his wife, who was doing some last-minute rearranging of her hair in her dressing table mirror. "Archibald Cleghorn may be Liliuokalani's brother-in-law, but he's no friend of hers. He's never stopped blaming her for losing his daughter the chance to inherit the throne."

"That's just gossip," Lani protested. "The Princess Kaiulani writes her aunt regularly from her school in England. Anyway, when the queen was deposed, Mr. Cleghorn sent the princess to Washington to plead that her aunt be restored to the throne, didn't he?"

"I rather thought that was the idea of the girl's English guardian," Adam said dryly. "Cleghorn is too canny an old Scotsman to believe that the Congress would listen to the pleas of a young woman, no matter how beautiful. Cleghorn's certainly clever enough to have made a great many friends in the new government, many of whom will be at his party," he added warningly.

"There'll be royalists there, too," Lani pointed out.

That was true enough, Adam knew. Ironically, in spite of the fact that Honolulu was politically divided between the royalists and those who supported the republic, one side undoubtedly plotting revolution against the other, at social occasions, royalists and members of the republic intermingled, friends and enemies at the same time.

"You don't mind going to the Cleghorn party, do you?" his wife asked, getting to her feet and coming to stand before him. She was wearing a silken gown of off-white, almost the same creamy color of her skin. Although full sleeves demurely covered her arms from her shoulders to her elbows, the draped bodice dipped daringly low so that the amethyst-and-diamond necklace Adam had given her for Christmas was beautifully displayed against the pale, smoothly textured skin. Also beautifully, but perhaps more discreetly displayed, was the enticing curve of the soft, full breasts beneath the bodice, sending a thrust of pure lust through Adam as he gathered his wife into his arms.

"I'd much rather stay home and spend the evening the way we spent Christmas Eve," he whispered.

The Stewart family had spent the Christmas holidays at the ranch, where a traditional Palekaiko Christmas luau was given for all the Hawaiian ranch hands and their families, as well as the house and yard servants. Two days before Christmas a *kona* gale, sounding like surf beating against the walls of the house, had brought black clouds and a raging rainstorm, but within forty-eight-hours the storm had passed. The summit of Haleakala had been covered with a glittering robe of snow, while brilliant sunlight had welcomed the guests to the luau.

Later that evening, after all the guests had gone, Jasmine had been tucked into her bed, and the servants had retired, Adam and Lani had made love on pillows spread before the fireplace in the front parlor. The reflection of the firelight, Adam remembered now, had made his wife's body seem even more incandescent, her lovely face glowing, warm with love, as she had eagerly given herself to him. That night there had been not even the shadow of a constraint between them, the odd, disturbing barrier that he had uneasily sensed between them when they had made love lately.

Now he murmured as his lips moved from her throat to the corner of her mouth, "Jasmine is asleep, the servants are either away or in bed for the night. I could start a fire in the fireplace. . . ." His tongue teased at the tightly closed lips, coaxing them open, feeling under his hands the melting softness of his wife's body beneath the boned and draped silk material.

Lani could feel her desire rising insistently to meet Adam's. Then she forced herself to remember the note from Tom that had been waiting for her when she returned to Honolulu, urging her to attend the Cleghorn party, which meant Tom must have something important to ask of her. She sighed and stepped out of her husband's embrace.

"We can't, darling. We've already sent our acceptance to Mr. Cleghorn." She smiled proudly, her hand caressing the amethyst necklace. "Anyway, I want to show off your beautiful Christmas present." She adjusted the amethyst pin that held the plumed aigrette in her dark hair, pulling absently at the flirtatious fringe of bangs across the smooth forehead. Then she picked up her wrap. "Come along, darling. We don't want to be late."

It was only a short distance to the Cleghorn estate, called Ainahau. The house and grounds had already become legendary, not just because it was where the Princess Kaiulani had been born, but because Archibald Cleghorn, widowed husband of the Princess Likelike, had taken acres of barren land and old taro patches and turned them into one of the most exotic and loveliest gardens in Honolulu.

A tall, strong wall ran completely around the estate, with a tangle of trees and shrubs preventing passersby from looking into the grounds. As the iron gate was unlocked so that the Stewart carriage could pass through, Lani looked curiously around her. It was still light enough so that she could see the jungle of spreading banyan, haus, and feathery coconut trees. Then, unexpectedly, the jungle would disappear and there would be gardens of bamboo, oleanders, and hibiscus, with lily pools filled with starlike pink flowers. The rippling sound of flowing water came to her ears, as well as the more raucous cries of peacocks, strutting arrogantly through the grounds.

They were greeted by Mr. Cleghorn, an erect, Spanish grandee–looking man, with bristling eyebrows, who stood at the entryway to a one story structure separate from the main dwelling. Here, dancing had already begun in the immense room. Gilt chairs and satin hassocks were pushed against the walls to allow more space for the dancers. At one end of the room was a low stage, covered with priceless Chinese rugs, where the flamboyant Princess Likelike and her daughter, Kaiulani, had held court during receptions, but now Hawaiian musicians played a fast-paced schottische.

As Adam swept her out onto the dance floor, Lani looked around in vain for Tom among the dancers, until Adam suddenly chuckled. "Am I that bad of a dancer? If I didn't know better, I'd swear you were looking around for a better partner."

Lani started guiltily, but was saved from having to answer when the dance ended, and another partner immediately claimed her. One dance set led into another, then at midnight a collation of chilled lobster and shrimp, bowls of fruit, and flaky, light-as-a-cloud pastries was served. To Lani's growing alarm, Tom still had not appeared.

Her fears were not helped any when she remembered that early in December a cache of arms had been dug up by a government search party and three royalists had been arrested, charged with conspiracy, and thrown into prison without bail. Tom, like others among the royalists, wondered, worried, who among them had betrayed the cause.

Now Lani couldn't help wondering, terrified. Had Tom been betrayed and arrested, too? Was that why he hadn't shown up at the party? She had to force herself to swallow the delicious food, to laugh and chat with friends, because Adam was sitting with her, and she didn't dare arouse his suspicions that something might be wrong. Finally a business associate of Adam's called him aside for a private discussion, and Lani was able to escape out into the garden.

The night closed softly around her, somehow comforting, as she strolled down a winding, wooded path away from the lights and music. She paused beside a moonlit lily pond in a small glade when a hand touched her shoulder, and in the darkness behind her a man's voice whispered the royalist password, "Missionary."

Lani whirled, relieved. "Tom, where have . . ." Then her voice died away, as she found herself staring, speechless, into Keith Stewart's smiling face.

Chapter 27

"*Aren't you supposed to give me the countersign?*" Keith asked, laughter dancing in the clear blue eyes gazing down at her.

"*Aloha Aina,*" Lani murmured automatically. Then, bewildered, she stammered, "How . . . how did you know?" Her glance searched the darkness behind Keith. "Where is Tom?"

"He couldn't come. Hitchcock's spies are too close on his trail. I've even seen a few here at the party. He asked me at the last minute to come in his place, which explains my fashionably late arrival." Keith smiled down at Lani's stunned face. "I must admit I had a bit of a shock myself when he told me the person I was to meet here tonight."

He shook his head, his voice amused. "I don't suppose my sobersided brother knows that his wife is involved up to her beautiful neck in treason?"

Lani realized uncomfortably that that smile was roaming much too familiar over her, stirring up dangerous memories she would much rather forget. She turned quickly away. "Of course, Adam doesn't know," she said stiffly. Then unable to resist a sideways, curious glace at her companion, she remarked, "I'm just as surprised to see you here. After all, your future father-in-law is practically a member of the government." And Tom had warned her that he suspected Nellie's brother, Paul, was one of Hitchcock's spies.

She broke off, suddenly, awkwardly remembering that she had heard several months ago that the long engagement between Keith Stewart and Nellie Samuels had been broken off. "I'm sorry," she apologized, "about you and Nellie. . . ."

"Don't be. Let's just say Nellie's father and I didn't share the same politics, or much else, for that matter," Keith admitted frankly. "As for Nellie . . ." The lucent blue eyes softened, caressing Lani's face. "You know as well as I that was a mistake from the beginning."

Once again, Lani hastily averted her gaze, but this time Keith reached out and, taking her shoulders, gently turned her around to face him. "Let me say it, Lani, to your face," he begged. "It's something I should have said a long time ago, but I never could find the courage. That evening we parted at your luau, I decided to tell Nellie that it was all over between us, that I was going to marry you, if you'd have me. She became hysterical and told me I had to marry her. She was carrying my child. But I swear to you I didn't know she was going to announce our engagement the next morning at break-

fast. I had hoped I could talk to you first, alone . . . try and
work something out. . . .''

He smiled wearily. "Of course, within a few months I
discovered what Nellie had told me about the child was a lie.
I had been caught by the oldest trick in the book. But by then,
it didn't seem to matter. You had married Adam. And I was
fond of Nellie. I thought perhaps, in time, I could forget you,
I could stop seeing your face in my mind when I was kissing
Nellie. . . .''

Keith felt the slender body jerk beneath his hands, as if he
had struck a raw nerve, and the smile became less diffident,
more confident, as he spread his hands flat across Lani's
back, his thumbs caressing the swell of her breasts as he drew
her close and murmured into her ear, "You haven't forgotten
either, have you? You've never loved Adam, not the way
you love me.''

"Don't!" Lani struggled to break free, but the arms tightened around her, the lips, moving lightly, caressingly, nib-
bled at her earlobe, then, before she could turn her face away,
had captured her mouth, slanting back and forth over its
softness, slowly, deliberately. Frantically, Lani clamped her
lips shut, trying to find enough space between Keith and her
to use her arms to push him away, a little surprised herself
that she felt no response to her former lover's caresses, except
a slight revulsion at the cool, practiced way she was being
kissed. Had it always been that way with Keith? she wondered, peripherally. Had she been too naive, too inexperi-
enced, to realize that Keith's lovemaking, like the man himself,
had always been style without substance, dazzle without
warmth?

Arms, strengthened by cattle roping, shoved hard against
Keith's chest, finally forcing him away from her. She saw a
startled anger stiffen the handsome face, as if her reaction
was not what he had expected, nor her furious words. "I do
love Adam. I always will.''

"Then, perhaps, you don't know your husband very well,"
Keith said after a moment, the look in the clear blue eyes
gazing into her face no longer warm, but one of pure spite. "I
happened to be sitting in on the poker game the night Adam
won a half interest in Palekaiko from your uncle. Of course,

my brother had made sure that Daniel was too drunk to know what cards he was playing." He added cruelly, "Why else do you suppose your uncle put a gun to his head the next morning and blew his brains out when he realized what his good friend, Adam, had done to him."

"I don't believe it," Lani whispered. "Adam wouldn't . . . he's too honorable. . . ."

"Honorable," Keith sneered. "At least I was honorable enough to offer to marry Nellie when I thought she was carrying my child. Adam didn't bother to offer to marry Rebecca when he got her pregnant. Instead he let father hustle him out of the islands on a whaler."

"No! It's not true." Lani had the odd feeling that she could feel the blood draining from her face.

Keith shrugged. "If you don't believe me, drop by the Sisters of the Sacred Word Convent. The child's name is Maile, and you can't miss her resemblance to her father."

Lani shivered, as if the soft night had suddenly turned cold. Stumbling a little, she turned to flee the pretty little glade, when Keith caught her arm.

"Don't you want to hear the message from Tom?" he asked, smiling with icy amusement down at her.

Lani realized she had forgotten all about Tom, the reason she was here at the Cleghorn party in the first place.

"What is it?" she asked, surprised to discover her tongue could still form words, that her voice sounded almost normal.

"You're to move the rifles you have buried in your garden. Tom thinks that Hitchcock's spies might be on to you. Have one of the gardeners that you trust move the rifles by night to Washington Place, where a *kanaka* named Kele will take care of them."

"Washington Place?" Lani asked, startled. "Does the queen know that guns are being buried in her garden?"

"Tom says not. The royalist are trying to protect Liliuokalani from knowing too much, in case the revolution should fail." Keith smiled cynically. "Which is a likely possibility."

"You don't care about the royalist cause at all, do you?" Lani asked, staring into the man's handsome, facile features. For the first time, she noticed that the face was a little bloated, with tiny broken blood vessels in the cheeks, as if from too much drinking, too much of the good life. "Why?" she asked curiously. "Why have you let yourself become involved in it?"

"I don't believe in causes," Keith said indifferently. "But I'm being paid handsomely for smuggling in guns."

Lani remembered then the night of the band concert, Tom's mentioning using drug smugglers to run guns into the island.

"My, what a disapproving look." Keith's voice was softly jeering. "I don't think you approve of my occupation any more than my baby brother does, but as they say, politics makes strange bedfellows. Anyway," he added, his voice almost too casual, "I'm not the only one bringing in guns. I understand there's a big shipment due any day now, that should get the revolution going in fine style. . . ."

He waited, as if expecting his companion to agree, but Lani shook her head absently. "I know very little about dates and plans. Tom always said it was safer if I didn't."

She heard the sound of footsteps coming down the path almost the same moment that Keith did. This time when Keith abruptly reached out, dragged her into his arms, and kissed her, his mouth was deliberately bruising, crushing the softness of her lips against her teeth. When he released her, her mouth throbbed painfully, and she could not speak, only stare, embarrassed, at Paul Samuels, who had appeared between the trees that lined the path.

Paul looked embarrassed, too, but Lani couldn't help observing, also slyly pleased, as he mumbled a hasty apology and turned quickly away back down the path.

Keith's arm still rested intimately around her waist, and she jerked free, glaring at the man in helpless, speechless rage.

"What else could I do?" Keith asked with an injured air. "If Samuels is a spy for the government, at least he won't have anything to report to Old Man Hitchcock about us." He laughed softly, as if he were enjoying Lani's discomfiture. "The kiss was immoral, perhaps, but hardly treasonable."

The sound of his laughter followed Lani as she fled back down the path to the house. When she reached the room where the dancing had begun again, Adam came quickly to her side, his voice concerned. "I've been looking for you." Then he saw his wife's face. "What's wrong?"

Lani put a hand to her forehead. "I have a terrible headache. I wonder if we could leave?"

It certainly wasn't a lie, she thought during the carriage ride home. Her head was pounding, and nausea lay coiled in the pit of her stomach.

When they reached home, and the safety of her own bedroom, Adam said, "I'll get Kimiko to help you undress."

"No, it's late. Don't bother waking her."

"Good." Adam smiled wickedly. "I'd rather undress you myself anyway."

But after he had undone the tiny clasps that ran down the back of her gown, Lani stepped quickly away from him, her voice strained. "I can manage the rest myself." She knew perfectly well where it would lead if she allowed Adam to undress her completely. And she could not bear it, Adam making love to her, not after what she had learned this evening. "I think I'll go straight to bed," she said in a rush. "I can't remember ever being so tired."

She was aware of her husband's gaze searching her face thoughtfully, and she looked quickly away, stiffening a little as he dropped a light kiss on the top of her head. "Have a good night's sleep then," he said, his voice level. "I'll use the guest room, so I won't disturb you when I come to bed."

After she finished undressing and gratefully slipped into bed, she discovered she couldn't sleep after all. She found herself remembering the first time she had seen Adam and Rebecca together at the ranch, how they had drawn guiltily apart when she approached, and the look of unshed tears in Rebecca's eyes. And Adam had never explained to her how he happened to hire Rebecca as her tutor in the first place. It wasn't usual, even in Hawaii where *haoles* and Hawaiians often intermingled, for a white man to hire a Hawaiian woman as a tutor.

Finally, her nerves stretched to the exhaustion point, she got out of bed and found the bottle of laudanum the doctor had given her for a toothache. She took a teaspoonful of the medicine and fell at last into a drugged sleep.

The next morning her headache had quieted into a dull throbbing, but as Kimiko helped her dress, Lani saw that her maid, with lackluster eyes and a look of strain about her mouth, looked more ill than she did. Lani had suspected for some time that Kim and Tom had had a lover's spat, and that it wasn't only because Tom was afraid that the government spies might connect Lani to his activities that he had stopped coming to the house. Several times she had been tempted to question Kimiko, to see if there was anything she could do to heal the breech between Tom and the young Japanese girl, but Kimiko's air of cool reserve had effectively cut her mistress off from any trespassing, however well meant, into Kimiko's private life.

Lani sighed to herself. In any case, she thought, she was hardly the one to be giving advice to others, considering the chaos in her own life! Not that she believed for a minute everything Keith had told her last night about Adam. In the clear light of morning she was sure most of what Keith had said had been a tissue of lies. Even if she could allow herself to believe that Rebecca had been Adam's mistress and had borne his child, she would never believe that her husband had deliberately gotten his best friend drunk to take an unfair advantage in a card game. Her uncle's death had been an accident, just as Adam had told her when she found him coming out of her uncle's study that morning.

Lani frowned at herself in the dressing-table mirror. Now that she thought of it, Adam had never told her what he was doing visiting her uncle so early that morning.

She got quickly to her feet, her head suddenly beginning to pound again. Adam glanced sympathetically across the breakfast table at her when she joined him for a cup of coffee, unable to face the thought of food. "If you're not feeling better tomorrow," he said firmly, "I'm making an appointment for you to see Dr. Carruthers."

"Why are you always sending me off to the doctor every time I so much as sneeze," Lani said irritably. "There's nothing wrong. I just had too much wine last night."

But she was sure he remembered that she had had only one glass of wine at the party. After breakfast, Adam disappeared into the study to work, but when Lani decided to take a ride in the surrey, he immediately appeared on the veranda.

"Why isn't Mikala driving you?" he asked.

"Oh, he had too much *okolehao* to drink last night and he's sleeping it off," she said casually.

"Then I'll drive you," he said.

"No," she said sharply. As her husband's dark brows slanted ominously together, she said, in a conciliatory tone, "I'm in such a foul mood, darling, I'd really prefer to be alone. Maybe the fresh air will make me feel better."

The piercing look was once more back in her husband's narrowed, gray eyes. For a moment, she thought he was going to protest further, then he nodded reluctantly and stepped back. But she was aware that he stayed on the veranda, watching her as she drove away.

She told herself that she was simply going for a drive, that there was no special reason why she turned the surrey toward Fort Street. It was too early in the morning for much traffic, and she was only vaguely aware of the few other riders on the street—several hack drivers and a half-dozen men on horseback. One of the men on horseback was riding a particularly fine gray gelding, she noticed. Was it possible that Tom was right, she wondered nervously, as the gray gelding seemed to stay always a short distance behind her. Could the man be one of Hitchcock's spies, following her?

Then she forgot about the man, as she found herself driving past the Sacred Word Convent, magenta bougainvillea spilling over the high, white brick convent walls. And she no longer could delude herself that the convent had not been the purpose of her outing all along. The sister who came to the iron-grilled gate in answer to Lani's ringing the bell was not at all surprised to have a Honolulu matron inquiring after one of the convent girls. The half-white homeless girls, who were sheltered within the convent walls, where they were taught cooking, sewing, housekeeping, and perfect English by the sisters, were much sought after as servants by wealthy Honolulu matrons when the girls finished their schooling.

She conducted the visitor into a small, cool room with whitewashed walls and a view of the courtyard, where children were playing. "Sister Alicia handles such matters," she said, smiling pleasantly at her visitor. "She'll be in to see you directly."

Sister Alicia wore the same pleasant smile. She had a plump, innocent face, but there was a shrewdness in her glance that took in her visitor's expensive gown and respectable air, a glance that missed very little, Lani suspected.

"I'm Mrs. Adam Stewart," Lani said, watching the face beneath the white, starched coif closely, but if the sister recognized the name, her face betrayed nothing. However, for some reason, perhaps the nun's air of waiting calmly for her visitor to continue speaking, Lani felt as if she were the age of one of the children laughing and romping in the courtyard. "Friends have told me about your . . . your charges they have taken to work in their homes."

The sister nodded. "In the right homes, yes, some of our girls have worked out very well. What sort of position did you have in mind?"

"I have a new baby. I thought perhaps a nursemaid. . . ."

Sister Alicia's face softened. "Our girls make excellent nursemaids. Like most Polynesians, they are very fond of children. Unfortunately, at the moment, we have very few girls of the proper age for such a responsible job." A touch of pride crept into the composed voice. "You can understand, our girls are snapped up very quickly, as soon as we decide they are mature enough to leave the convent."

How old would Maile be? Lani suddenly wondered. The liaison between Rebecca and Adam had taken place before Adam went to sea. That would be fourteen, fifteen years ago, she figured quickly. "None at all?" she asked, disappointed. Had Maile already left the convent for a position in some wealthy Honolulu home? Somehow, she could not imagine Rebecca or Adam allowing their daughter to be hired as a servant. Or had they given up all rights to their daughter when they placed her in the convent?

"I didn't say that," Sister Alicia corrected her at once. "There are two girls who might be of help to you. Elena is sixteen, very pretty, very tractable." She sighed. "Too pretty. Most of our girls marry once they leave the home, but Elena, well, I'm afraid she has a too generous heart when it comes to men. And then there's Maile." Sister Alicia added placidly, "But I assume it's Maile you wish to see, is it not, Mrs. Stewart?"

Lani felt her face flush guiltily. "How . . . how did you know?"

"Your husband has visited Maile on numerous occasions over the last years." Her face saddened. "Particularly after the death of the child's mother."

Anguish ripped through Lani. "Rebecca is dead?"

"We never knew the name of Maile's mother. She brought the baby here shortly after the child was born. Then she disappeared for almost six years. When she returned, she gave money to the convent for the child's support. I think, as soon as she was able to support the child, she planned to remove her from our care. She visited Maile several times here at the convent, then one day, almost two years ago now, Mr. Adam Stewart came and told our mother superior that the girl's mother was dead, and he was taking over the financial care of Maile. He visits the girl, five or six times a year."

"What is she like, Maile?"

"Beautiful, like her mother, and unusually intelligent. I understand Mr. Stewart plans to send her to college in California within a few months."

"I'd like to meet her."

Sister Alicia asked gently, "Is that wise, my child? You surely can't plan to take Maile home with you."

"Why not?" Lani asked, stiffening. "If she's my husband's child, she belongs in her father's home."

The sister shook her head. "We don't know that your husband is Maile's father. Her mother never told us the name of the man."

"I want to see her," Lani repeated stubbornly.

Sister Alicia got to her feet and walked to the window, beckoning to Lani. "You can see her from here, if you wish. She's the girl sitting alone with the book beneath the kiawe tree."

The tree was not far from the window, close enough so that as the girl looked up from her book, Lani could see her face clearly. Maile was beautiful, but not in the voluptuous, Polynesian way her mother had been. The girl's skin was paler, her black hair had bronze highlights, and she was taller and slimmer. It was the slanting bone structure, though, the strong chin and nose, that Lani recognized at once: Adam's features in a girl's face.

There was something else she saw in the girl's face as Maile gazed at the children playing in the courtyard, a look that reminded Lani poignantly of herself as a young girl, after her father's death. A grieving sense of loss, of almost unendureable loneliness, that was covered up by anger and arrogance.

She turned back to the sister, her own chin setting firmly. "I still want to take Maile home with me. At least, she can stay with her . . . her father and me, until she leaves for college." At the sister's helpless shrug, she blurted, "Please. Rebecca was a dear friend. I promise you I'll take very good care of her daughter."

Sister Alicia's wise eyes studied Lani's face then she nodded slowly. "Yes, I believe you, my child, but you understand, it's not possible, not unless your husband informs the convent that he, too, agrees that the girl should come into the household." And with that, Lani had to be satisfied.

When she returned home, she went first to the garden and located Nakamura, the head gardener, who was cleaning out the fish pond. His elderly face impassive, he simply nodded when she told him the rifles must be moved, late at night, to a man named Kele at Washington Place. "The Priory of the Good Sisters backs up to the Washington Place garden. If you could get into the garden through the priory grounds, you'd have a better chance of not being seen." She added, "I'm not sure, but I think a man on a gray horse has been following me. He may be a spy for the government, so be careful."

Nakamura nodded again. "Missy not worry. No one know."

Lani went on into the house. She had intended to go straight up to her room and carefully plan what she would say to Adam. As she crossed the front hallway to the stairs, though, and saw the open study door, she knew she couldn't wait or she would explode.

When she burst into the study, Adam looked up from her uncle's desk, which was strewn with papers, reminding her of how often she had seen the desk cluttered that way when her uncle was alive. Her glance flew involuntarily to the floor where her uncle had lain that morning: she recalled the brief glimpse she had had of his bloody face, the gun beside his outstretched hand, before Adam had put his body between her and the horror.

"Is it true?" she blurted. "Did you win my uncle's half interest in Palekaiko from him in a poker game? Is that why Uncle Daniel killed himself?"

The beginnings of a smile of greeting faded from Adam's mouth. He got to his feet and, walking around his wife, closed the study door behind her. When he turned to face Lani, his cool gray gaze held no hint of what he might be feeling, his voice, quiet. "Yes, I did win Daniel's half interest in the ranch in a poker game. As for your uncle's committing suicide, I don't suppose anyone will ever know the truth about what happened that morning. I prefer to believe it was an accident. Daniel was many things, but he wasn't a quitter. And I'm sure we were close enough friends so that he must have known I never planned to keep what I had won from him, especially when he was . . ." Adam hesitated. . . . "not himself, the evening of the card game."

"You mean, you got him drunk," Lani said bitterly.

Adam sat down on the edge of the desk so that his narrowed gray gaze was level with Lani's furious face. "No, I don't mean that," he said.

"Why didn't you tell me the truth then?" she demanded, "that I couldn't inherit my uncle's share of the ranch because you already owned it."

Adam spoke slowly. "I suppose because I didn't think it was necessary for you to know."

"The same way you didn't think it was necessary that I should know about you and Rebecca, and Maile?" At the flicker of surprise that crossed Adam's face, she said, scornfully, "You needn't bother denying it. I've been to the convent. I've seen your daughter."

"I wasn't planning to deny the fact of Maile," Adam said, and she saw a flash of anger take the place of the surprise, an anger that he quickly controlled as he said, "Perhaps you're right. Perhaps I should have told you about the girl before this, but I gave my word to Rebecca."

"Is that why you hired Rebecca as my tutor, because she was your mistress?"

"I employed Rebecca as your tutor because of my respect for her capabilities as a teacher." The steady gray eyes never left his wife's face as he continued, "But she was never my mistress, and Maile is not my child."

If only she could believe him, Lani thought. She hadn't realized how desperately she wanted to believe him. And yet after all the lies he had told her . . . no, not lies, she realized. Adam had been too clever to lie to her. He simply had never told her about her uncle and the card game, about Maile in the convent and Rebecca. . . .

She burst out unhappily. "You could, at least, have told me that Rebecca was dead." Oddly, his keeping from her the knowledge of Rebecca's death somehow hurt more than any of the other half truths and omissions on her husband's part.

And she was dismayed at the implacability that pulled the muscles in Adam's face, taut, the wary look in the gray eyes, as he got to his feet and said, coldly, "I have no intention of discussing Rebecca with you. Is that understood?"

Had he loved Rebecca so much, then, Lani wondered, feeling a sharp jab of jealousy, so that he could not even bear to talk about her?

"What about Rebecca's daughter?" she asked.

Adam went to sit behind the desk again. "The girl's being well looked after at the convent. And she's leaving for California in the fall to attend college."

Lani remembered the unhappiness she had seen on the girl's face, the sadness and anger she had glimpsed there. "I want Maile to come live with us," she said.

The dark, slanted brows almost met as Adam stared at his wife for a long moment. Then he shrugged and said, "It will cause a great deal of gossip, you know, Maile's coming to live with us, particularly after your little tête-à-tête with Keith last night."

"How did you . . .?" Lani broke off, half-furious, half-embarrassed. Of course, Paul Samuels had always been a gossip. No doubt he had been only too happy to tell his friends about finding Adam Stewart's wife and brother in a passionate embrace at the Cleghorn party. And no doubt those same friends had been telephoning Adam all morning.

"I assume it was my brother who told you about the card game with Daniel, and about Maile," Adam said. And then, his voice turning harsh, "Did you know Keith would be there last night? Is that why you were so anxious to attend the Cleghorn party?"

"No, of course not," Lani protested, but from the fleeting look of anger in her husband's narrowed gaze, she was sure

he didn't believe her, any more than she had believed him, she
realized unhappily. And, of course, she couldn't tell him why
she had met Keith in the garden, not without betraying Tom,
and her own role in the royalist's cause.

She straightened her shoulders. No matter what Adam
thought, or her own feelings, it was Rebecca's child who
must not be forgotten. Maile needed their love. She couldn't
turn her back on the girl.

"I still want Maile to come live with us," she said firmly.

Adam nodded. "If the girl wishes to stay with us, I have
no objection." A wry smile touched the long mouth. "But
you can be sure, we'll be the chief topic of gossip in Honolulu tomorrow."

Adam, however, was mistaken. For that night, at Henry
Bertelmann's beach house off Diamond Head, a small group
of royalist rebels fired upon a patrol sent out by the republic
government to arrest them. And the next morning, all that
everyone in Honolulu was talking about was that the royalist
counterrevolution had begun.

Chapter 28

The news of the skirmish at Diamond Head between the
royalist rebels and government police sent a shockwave of
panic through Honolulu. Evening services at churches were
hastily dismissed, and men left so quickly that they arrived at
their Citizens Guard units still wearing their best go-to-meeting
shoes and suits. Rumors spread that dozens of men had been
killed at Bertelmann's, that the perennial revolutionary, Robert Wilcox, along with Lot Lane, and hundreds of rebels
under their commands, were already marching on the city,
and that *haole* royalists within Honolulu were only waiting
for a signal to join the native uprising.

By Monday, however, the panic subsided somewhat. Gov-

ernment newspapers screamed of "bloodthirsty rebels," but
only one death of a Citizens' Guardsman had occurred during
the brief exchange of gunfire. And instead of marching upon
the city, the royalists had been forced to withdraw their
scattered forces up the cliffs of Diamond Head. The government immediately put Honolulu under martial law, and a
curfew was imposed. No one could move about the city
without a pass, and only official calls were accepted at the
Central Telephone Exchange. Streets leading in and out of the
city were guarded and government buildings barricaded.

Marshal Hitchcock's men immediately fanned out through
Honolulu, arresting Hawaiians and foreigners alike, searching
homes without warrants, and dragging men off to prison if
they were suspected of being remotely friendly to the royalist
cause. The Oahu Prison soon became crowded with hundreds
of political prisoners, four and five prisoners crammed into
damp, tiny cells meant for one. Rations ran short, and the
fortunate inmates were those who received food from the
women waiting outside the prison walls for word of their
fathers, brothers, and sons.

At Kapiolani Park, government troops brought up field
artillery and began pounding the slopes of Diamond Head,
where the royalists were entrenched, while a tug, armed with
cannon, shelled the mountainside from the sea. Caught within
the deadly crossfire, many of the rebels hiding in the gulches
and crevices of Diamond Head were forced to surrender or
retreat into Manoa Valley. Government troops followed them
into the valley, trapping more of the men in the "pen," a
cul-de-sac at the end of the valley enclosed by rocky ridges
and the black sheer face of Konahuanui. Sharpshooters were
posted on spurs and cliffs and raked the triangle with their
murderous fire, killing and wounding more rebels, hiding
amidst the kukui trees and thorny brush. One by one the
leaders of the rebel forces were captured, or surrendered,
until finally only Robert Wilcox and Lot Lane remained at
large.

A week after the counterrevolution began, several of Marshal Hitchcock's men appeared at the Stewart home while
Lani and Adam were having breakfast, with orders to search
the house.

Adam eyed the men coldly. "Are you implying that I am a member of the royalist rebels?"

The young captain in charge of the search party shook his head quickly. He was well aware that Adam Stewart was a member in good standing of the Reform party, with influential friends in the government. "No, sir," he said respectfully. "It's your brother, Tom Stewart, who has been implicated in the insurrection against the government. Several days ago he was spotted by one of our sharpshooters, climbing the west ridge of Palolo Valley with Lot Lane's men. Our man had him in his gun sight. He was sure he couldn't have missed, but your brother hasn't shown up among the rebel wounded we've captured."

Lani saw a white ridge appear on either side of Adam's mouth; she had to bite back her own cry of dismay.

"If my brother's been seen at Palolo, then why are you seeking him here?" Adam asked, scowling.

"Some of the rebels have managed to slip past us over Kealaeli down into the lower valleys and back into Honolulu. And there are trails over the mountains, connecting those back valleys that only the *kanakas* know. We've already searched Mr. Stewart's home in Nuuanu Valley and found nothing. Since we have evidence that your brother is one of the ringleaders in the rebellion, he must, of course, be brought to trial for treason, along with Wilcox, and Nowlein, and the others behind this rebellion."

"Wilcox has been captured?"

"Late yesterday, he gave himself up. He refuses to talk, but Nowlein has given us enough information to convict your brother, and all the others, of treason."

"You have a search warrant, I assume?"

The captain looked pained. "We don't need a search warrant. You must know that, Mr. Stewart. The city is under martial law." The captain glanced, a little uncomfortably, toward Lani. "As a matter of fact, we would also like to question your wife. She has been seen often in your brother's company."

"Since he is her brother-in-law, that is hardly treasonous activity," Adam said dryly. He got slowly to his feet, his icy, narrowed gaze on the captain's face making that officer shift his feet uneasily. "You have my permission to search the house," Adam said. "Under no circumstances do you have my permission to question my wife." Without shifting his gaze from the captain's face, he ordered Lani, "Take Maile and stay in the nursery with Jasmine."

Although Adam's voice was quiet, almost calm, Lani sensed the anger that lay just beneath that surface composure, like the rumblings deep in the ground before Mauna Loa erupted. Perhaps the captain sensed the same explosive fury in Adam Stewart, because he did not try to stop Lani when she got to her feet and, her chin held proudly high, swept from the dining room.

She found Maile already in the nursery, clutching a sleeping Jasmine in her arms. The girl's face was frightened, but her voice was furious. "If those men touch my little sister, I'll kill them!"

In the few short days Maile had lived with the Stewarts, the girl had grown fiercely attached to Jasmine. Lani had thought that the attachment had grown so quickly because Maile in her short life had never had anything of her own to love before.

Now, at the surprise she saw in Mrs. Stewart's face, Maile said, flustered, "I'm sorry. I suppose I shouldn't have said anything, I mean about Jasmine being my sister. But ever since Mr. Stewart started visiting me at the convent, I knew he was my father. We look so much alike. And then when you came and took me home with you, I thought you knew, too." She gazed unhappily at Lani. "Are you very angry with me? Will I have to go back to the convent?"

Lani shook her head quickly. "Of course not. This is your home. "

In any case, the girl's devotion to the baby had been invaluable, especially with Kimiko, who usually looked after Jasmine, sick with worry about Tom ever since the first day of the rebellion. The Japanese girl moved around the house as pale and quiet as a ghost, her usually graceful movements clumsy, her dark eyes charged with fear.

Lani smiled reassuringly at the girl. "No one will hurt Jasmine. Those men are just . . . looking for someone."

"For Mr. Stewart's brother?" Maile grinned sheepishly.

"I was listening at the top of the stairs." She shivered, glancing curiously at Lani. "Is it true what the newspapers say, that the royalist rebels are fiendish murderers?"

"No," Lani said quietly. "They are Hawaiians, fighting for their country."

Maile's young face softened in memory. "I remember my mother told me once that I should always be proud of my Hawaiian blood."

"You remember Rebecca?" Lani asked. So much had happened since Maile had come to live with Adam and her, that she hadn't had time to sit down and talk with the girl about her mother.

"I remember she was very beautiful," Maile said, and then the fierceness back in her voice, she added, "She's not dead, you know. I've seen her."

Lani tried to hide her shock. "Perhaps you only thought you saw her," she said gently. "Sometimes when you want something very much, your mind plays tricks on you."

"No, I saw her," Maile insisted. "At the convent, we're taken several times a year outside, to attend a special mass. The nuns walk along with us, of course," She giggled. "There are always men walking slowly on the other side of the street when we leave the convent. Elena, when the nuns aren't looking, always smiles at the young, handsome ones."

She placed Jasmine carefully back in her crib, and when she turned back to Lani, her face was sober. "The last time we were taken outside the convent, I saw a woman all in black, across the street, watching us as we walked along. It was my mother. I know it was."

Lani heard the heartbreak in the young voice, and she gathered the girl into her arms, her own tears of sorrow for Rebecca mingling with the tears of Rebecca's daughter. The young man from the search party, who knocked and then quickly entered the nursery, stopped short at sight of the weeping women. It was obvious there could be no one hidden in the small room, and he withdrew quickly, but not before Lani drew her skirt disdainfully aside, the contempt in her gaze bringing a heated flush to the young man's face.

After she heard the searching men leave the house, Lani went to find Adam. He was standing at the window in the study, watching the captain's men digging up her Uncle Daniel's rose garden. He turned, when Lani entered, and asked wryly, "Will they find any guns?"

She shook her head, thankfully, and joined him at the window, watching the desecration of her uncle's garden.

"Damn the boy anyway," Adam said in a low, furious monotone. "How could he have been stupid enough to believe a ragtag army of *kanakas* with rifles and revolvers could stand up against cannon?"

But Lani saw the anguish in her husband's face, and she knew it wasn't anger he was feeling toward his young brother, but the same fear that was squeezing painfully at her heart. Was Tom already lying dead in some gully up in the hills?

"Lot Lane's still not captured," she said hopefully. "And he knows the back trails up in the mountains. So does Tom."

"How long can they last, without food or shelter? Not even bananas grow up on those dry hillsides. And if Tom's wounded . . ." Pain jerked beneath Adam's voice. "It's my fault, damn it. Somehow I should have stopped him. . . ."

"Darling, please don't!" Lani could not bear to hear the guilt and raw pain in her husband's voice. "You couldn't have stopped Tom. No one could."

They had not so much as held hands since the morning she had confronted Adam with what Keith had told her at the Cleghorn party. Now she slipped her hand unconsciously into her husband's, and his hand tightened around hers. Then he turned and pulled her into his arms. They clung to each other, each drawing comfort and strength from the other. And Lani could not help thinking how strange it was, that in the darkest moment of their marriage they had never felt so close.

Three days later Lot Lane, barefoot, clothes in tatters, a beard bristling on his face, but with his head held high, strode into police headquarters in Honolulu and gave himself up. When asked, under threat of death, for the names of the white men who had aided the Hawaiians in the uprising, he scornfully refused. Nor would he give any information about the Hawaiians who had escaped into Palolo Valley with him. He was alone at the end, he insisted.

With still no word about whether Tom was alive or dead, Adam managed to get permission from President Dole to question Lane. At first, Lot would not talk to him, but when Adam promised to see that food was brought to the Hawaiians imprisoned with Lane, and their families notified, he relented. He admitted that Tom had been wounded, and that the last he had seen of him was crossing over Kealaeli toward Pauoa Valley. "A *kanaka* named Kale was with him."

"Who is this Kale?" Adam asked.

Lot shrugged. "I never saw him before he joined us, three days before the *pilikia* began." He suddenly grinned in memory. "An old man, but he fought like the devil."

With Lane's imprisonment, the government newspaper put out extras. "The war is over," they announced jubilantly. In the stories themselves, there was no mention of Tom Stewart, perhaps out of deference to Adam's position in the *haole* community, his highly respected missionary grandparents, but more than likely, Lani realized, because everyone was convinced that Adam's revolutionary younger brother lay dead somewhere in the upper reaches of the Palolo Valley.

One newspaper article said cryptically, "With Lane in prison, now there is only one traitor left to be brought to justice."

Lani gazed, puzzled, at Adam. "Who do they mean? I thought the government had captured or arrested everyone involved in the revolution."

"Not everyone," Adam said quietly. "There's still Liliuo-kalani."

When Liliuokalani heard the chime of the doorbell, and heard the male voices in her front parlor at Washington Place, she knew, even before her lady-in-waiting came to fetch her, that they were police officers. Ever since the disastrous end of the attempt to overthrow the *haole* government, she had been expecting that she would be questioned by the police. Not that she would have anything to tell them that they didn't already know, she thought, her heart heavy. Although she had suspected from the first what her supporters were planning, for her own safety she had been told none of the details. And if she had known, she thought proudly, she would never have betrayed her friends.

She expected the men would take her to the police station

for questioning, and since it was a cool, squally day, she took her bonnet, shawl, and handbag with her into the parlor. She was surprised when the two officers refused to show her their warrant, and even more surprised when it was suggested by the men that Mrs. Clark, her lady-in-waiting, should accompany and stay with her.

Stay with her? the ex-queen thought, surprised. But it wasn't until she looked back from the carriage to which she had been escorted, and saw the chief justice of the Republic of Hawaii entering her home, that she felt the first beginnings of fear. All her personal papers, her diaries and letters, were kept in her house. The thought of strangers prying, pawing through her most private thoughts, made her feel for a moment as if she might be ill.

The fear grew stronger as she quickly realized the carriage was not being driven to the police station but to the palace. The once immaculately tended grounds now looked like an armed camp, cluttered with tents and soldiers and brass field-pieces. Liliuokalani did not utter a sound as she was escorted up the wide, curving koa staircase of the palace, trying to ignore the ugly defilement of the rooms around her, which had once been so beautifully furnished.

She was taken to a corner guest room. She remembered the room as being furnished in Japanese decor, but now it was uncarpeted, almost bare, with only a few pieces of bedroom furniture. The colonel who had conducted her to the room informed her stiffly that she was a prisoner of the state, being held for treason, and that "this room was to be her future living quarters."

"My prison," she said, at last realizing the truth.

The colonel avoided looking directly at her. "Mrs. Clark can stay with you. Your meals will be sent in. . . ."

"I prefer to have my meals brought to me from my own home," she said coldly. At least, she thought grimly, she'd have less chance of being poisoned.

"I'll speak to President Dole. I'm sure that can be arranged. Anything else you require, you may ask the guard . . . the officer at the door."

"Thank *Mister* Dole for me," she said deliberately, taking

a childish sense of satisfaction in knowing she was making the *haole* officer feel uncomfortable.

After the man left, Mrs. Clark, whose husband had been arrested several days before, collapsed in tears. In trying to console the woman, Liliuokalani forgot her own fears. That night, though, as she lay sleepless in her narrow bed, listening to the guards tramping outside the door and on the veranda outside the window of the room, was the longest, loneliest night of her life.

She could hear her companion, like herself, unable to sleep, sobbing softly on the couch. She wondered if the woman was thinking, as Liliuokalani was, of the stories they had heard about what was happening to the political prisoners in Oahu Prison, rumors of prisoners having all their clothes stripped away and being thrust into dark cells, without light, food, or water. There were even whispers of men being kept in tanks of ice water until they betrayed the names of others in the insurrection. Liliuokalani had tried not to believe the stories. Surely a Christian people couldn't behave in such a fashion. But now, as she faced the dark night of her soul, she no longer had any faith in the Christianity of the missionaries and their descendants.

The next morning she convinced her captors that Mrs. Clark should be sent home to look after her children, and another friend, Evelyn Wilson, took her place. After that, the days and nights seemed to run endlessly together. She was allowed to receive no visitors or news from outside her prison walls, although Mrs. Wilson had told her that Washington Place had been thoroughly ransacked. Even the songs Liliuokalani had composed over the years had been taken away, because they might contain "hidden messages for her people." The militia were now quartered in the ex-queen's home and had vandalized it and Liliuokalani's possessions as thoroughly as Iolani Palace had been senselessly despoiled. But what particularly grieved Liliuokalani was to learn that all her faithful servants and retainers had been arrested and thrown into Oahu Prison.

When Paul Neumann, who had been appointed by the government as the queen's attorney, finally was allowed to see the queen, his face was grave. He informed her that if convicted of treason, she could be executed. Liliuokalani stared wearily at the man. "Do you really think I care any longer whether I live or die? Now that I have failed my people, it would be easier to die."

"It is not only yourself you must think of," her attorney warned her. "Your supporters in prison will also be executed unless you sign this document of abdication, relinquishing all rights for yourself and your heirs to the throne."

Liliuokalani studied the document, written in such humilating, abject terms that she cringed. The document even stated that she was acting of her own free will in abdicating her throne, without undue influence from the government! Did they think being threatened with execution wasn't an undue influence? she wondered bitterly. Her immediate reaction was to refuse to sign it. For herself, she would have sooner faced death, but Mr. Neumann was right. She must think of those who had been loyal to her. If she could save them from death by signing the document of abdication, what choice did she have?

Her head throbbing from too many sleepless nights, she picked up the pen and asked wearily, when the paper was brought to her again for her signature, "How shall I sign my name?"

"Liliuokalani Dominis."

She stared, puzzled, at her captors. Before she had become Princess and then Queen Liliuokalani, her name had been Lydia Dominis or Mrs. John Dominis. There was no such person as Liliuokalani Dominis.

Then she shrugged and signed the name as she had been told. What did it matter? The important thing was that she was saving the lives of her friends.

Lani and Adam were in the front parlor, with the lamps lit against the gathering darkness, when the soft knock came at their door. Kimiko slipped into the room, tears in her eyes even as she was smiling, so that her face was radiant. "Come quickly. In the kitchen . . . it's your brother."

Adam had already brushed by her and reached the kitchen only a few seconds before Lani. Tom was sitting, slumped at the kitchen table. A crude bandage was wrapped around his chest, blood seeping through the bandage. A tall Hawaiian man stood behind Tom. Although the man's hair was white, his smooth, muscular body made him seem a much younger man.

"My name is Kale," the Hawaiian man said, his gaze fastening, at once, upon Lani. There was, Lani thought, something vaguely familiar about the man, but she could not place where she had seen him before. The man then turned his dark, proud gaze upon Adam. "Your brother's wound needs more care than I can give him, so I have brought him to you."

Kimiko was already kneeling beside Tom. She cast a frightened glance at Lani. Both women had seen the ugly red mortification of the flesh beneath the bandage.

Tom tried to lift his head, his voice thick as he mumbled, "Told him, Adam . . . shouldn't come . . . cause trouble. . . ."

"*Mahalo nui* for bringing him to us," Adam said quietly to the Hawaiian. "If you'll help me carry him upstairs, then I think you should be on your way. You may have been seen coming here."

"There's a small room in the attic," Lani said, thinking quickly. "It was used as a maid's quarters at one time. It still has a bed. If we pile boxes and old furniture in front of the door, perhaps no one will notice it's there."

Adam nodded. With Kale's help, he carried Tom up to the attic, Kimiko and Lani close behind with sheets and towels and bandages and pitchers of warm water. Adam gently removed his brother's clothes, then helped Kimiko remove the blood-soaked bandage and wash the wound. Lani was surprised at her husband's skill, until she remembered that as the captain of a whaler he must have helped tend many a sailor's injuries.

The room was so tiny that there was barely space for Adam and Kimiko, working over Tom, sprawled on the narrow bed. It was also warm since there was no window, only a vent in one wall, and Lani thanked heaven that is was an unusually cool January. Then she suddenly realized that Kale was no longer in the room. Was Tom's rescuer planning on slipping away without giving her a chance to thank him?

She found the Hawaiian man halfway down the staircase, staring at the picture of her grandparents. He turned at Lani's approach. "She was very beautiful, my sister, Jasmine," he said. A smile softened the hard features of his face. "But not as beautiful as her sister, your great-aunt Lani." The dark eyes studied Lani approvingly. "I think my wife would take great pleasure in her namesake."

Lani remembered then why Kale had seemed familiar. She couldn't have been more than a child of five or six, visiting her grandmother Jasmine here in Honolulu, and a tall, handsome Hawaiian man had spent an afternoon with her grandmother. She couldn't remember what her grandmother had told her about the man, or ever having seen him again.

Considering how she had always found the story of her great-aunt's marriage to her half brother, Kale, a source of embarrassment, she was surprised that on meeting her great-uncle she felt no embarrassment at all. "How did you know?" she asked curiously, "about Tom's being my brother-in-law?"

"When you hide out with a man for many days, with bloodhounds and *haoles* with guns chasing you, there is little to do but talk," he said. "Tom told me about his sister-in-law, Lani Stewart, who had given him her grandmother's strand of pearls to help buy guns to fight the *haoles*." He suddenly grinned and gestured toward the pearls that Jasmine Tucker was wearing in the portrait. "Years ago, my sister once sold the same pearls to help me when I got into some *pilikia* with the *haoles*."

Lani followed the man down the stairs to the kitchen door. "Where will you go now?" she asked, worried.

Kale shrugged. "There are small villages high up in the mountains where Hawaiians live in the old ways, and the land is so poor, even the *haoles* have no interest in possessing it."

"It's over, isn't it?" Lani said sadly. "We've lost, haven't we?"

Kale gazed soberly at his great-niece. "Morgan Tucker once told me that the days of the kingdom were numbered from the first day the Hawaiian people welcomed the first foreigner to their shores."

"But you came just the same, you fought with the royalists," Lani protested.

"*Ae*," Kale agreed. "And perhaps someday my great-grandchildren will fight the foreigners again. Or perhaps it will not be the *haole* foreigners,'' he said, his dark face thoughtful. ''The woman nursing your brother-in-law, I've watched more and more like her coming to live in our islands, men and women, even more clever and hardworking than the *haoles*. Who knows, perhaps these new foreigners will some-day sweep the *haoles* away?''

At Lani's woebegone look, he said lovingly, ''Remember, it is only the topsoil the foreigners possess. And the topsoil blows away in time. But the roots of the Hawaiian people go deep into the land that will always belong to them, because it was given to them by Kane and can never be taken away.'' He leaned down and pressed his cheek against Lani's. ''*Aloha nui loa*, my Lani,'' he said softly.

Then he slipped through the partially opened kitchen door and disappeared into the darkness of the garden.

After a minute, Lani returned to the front hall, to reclimb the stairs to the attic, when she saw Maile at the top of the stairs, staring down at her, her eyes wide with fear.

''What is it?'' Lani asked sharply. ''What are you doing out of bed?''

Maile's face was pale, her voice a thin, terrified whisper. ''I heard voices and woke up. Then I looked out the window. There are men with guns at the front gate of the garden. They're coming toward the house!''

Chapter 29

Lani heard the sounds then, too—horses riding up the front driveway, splattering gravel as they came. She ordered swiftly: ''Do exactly as I say, Maile. Go up to the attic and tell Kimiko and Mr. Stewart that a search party is here. They can use the back staircase to the kitchen. Then return to your bedroom, and if anyone comes into your room, pretend to be asleep. Do you understand?''

The young girl nodded and quickly disappeared up the attic stairs. When the loud knocking came at the front door, Lani waited a few seconds, running her hands over her hair and smoothing her dress to make sure she didn't look upset, then walked very slowly to the door.

It was the same captain who had visited the house before, only this time with a large squad of men, she noticed. Most of the men crowded up on the porch, but there was one man on horseback who did not dismount, staying in the shadow of the trees that lined the driveway. She turned her gaze back to the captain, hoping he would attribute her flushed face to female alarm at the appearance of a group of armed men on her veranda. "What is it, captain? Is something wrong?"

"We'd like to talk to your husband, Mrs. Stewart."

Lani looked around her, smiling vaguely. "I'm not sure, at the moment, where he is. He likes to take a stroll before retiring."

"We've had a watch on your house, Mrs. Stewart," the man said bluntly. "We know your husband hasn't left the house this evening. I must insist that you allow me to talk to your husband."

Lani fluttered her eyelashes helplessly. "Of course, captain. I don't see how I can stop you. If you'll wait in the parlor, I'll see if I can find Mr. Stewart. Perhaps you'd care for a cup of coffee while you're waiting?" she asked, as she ushered the man into the parlor, closing the sliding doors behind her.

The man frowned impatiently. "I'm sorry, Mrs. Stewart, but my search cannot be delayed. With or without your husband's permission, we intend to . . ."

The sliding doors suddenly flung open, and Adam stalked into the room. Lani saw, relieved, that he had thought to pull a jacket over his shirt, which was undoubtedly bloodstained. "What the hell is going on here?" he demanded. "Armed men all over my home . . . I want an explanation."

This time, however, the captain was not intimidated, although he did cast a quick look into the hall to make sure that his men were nearby. "The guard watching your house saw one man, perhaps two, skulking in your garden earlier, Mr. Stewart."

"Well, I hope he arrested them," Adam said irascibly. "It's a fine state of affairs when a man's not safe in his own home."

"We've searched the garden. The men can't be found. We believe they entered the house."

"That's impossible. My wife and I have been here all evening. We would have heard something."

"I'm sorry, sir, but I must insist on searching the premises," the captain said stubbornly.

Adam frowned. "And if I refuse to have your men crash through the house, scaring my wife and servants half to death?"

"I'm sorry, sir, but I must. . . ."

The captain's voice broke off as one of his men called from the kitchen, "I've found something, captain."

The captain rushed out of the parlor back to the kitchen. "There, sir." The man pointed excitedly to the kitchen table. "That's blood, isn't it? And Tom Stewart was supposed to be wounded, wasn't he?"

Adam had moved to stand beside Lani, when from the pantry they heard a woman's whimpering cry of pain.

"Kimiko!" Lani was into the pantry before the captain. Blood was welling through the napkin the Japanese maid was trying ineffectually to wrap around her hand.

Kimiko, her face pasty white, gave her mistress an unhappy glance then ducked her head as if embarrassed at the commotion she was causing. "I was cutting mangoes at the table. . . the men with guns frightened me . . . my knife slipped. . . . I am ashamed I am so clumsy." The bandage pulled to one side and the wound could be clearly seen, slashing cruelly across the girl's palm. Blood dripped onto Kimiko's white kimono and the mat-covered floor. Several of the young men in the search party looked away queasily.

Adam rounded upon the captain, his voice stormy. "Now see what you've done. I hope you're satisfied. All right, take your damn men and search the house, but be quick about it. And you can be sure President Dole will hear about this outrage the first thing in the morning!"

The captain gave hasty orders. The two men assigned to checking the attic took one look at the piled-up old furniture, chests, and boxes that crammed the attic untidily from one wall to another, then returned quickly to the second floor to continue their search.

In the kitchen, as the captain and the search party tramped around overhead, Adam rewrapped the napkin more tightly around Kim's hand to staunch the flow of blood. "You shouldn't have made such a good job of it," he said, his voice half-admiring, half-angry. "I'll take you to the doctor. That cut's going to need stitches."

"I saw the blood on the kitchen table," Kimiko said calmly. "I had to make them believe it was mine." She tried to pull her hand free. "There's no need for a doctor," she said impatiently.

"You're going to the doctor," Lani said firmly, feeling a little queasy herself at the thought of Kimiko's taking a knife and deliberately slashing the sharp blade across her palm. "You'll be no good to anyone if you get blood poisoning," she added practically. "Don't worry. I'll stay with Tom until you and Adam get back."

As soon as the search party left, with profuse apologies from the captain, Lani hurried upstairs. She stopped a moment at the nursery, where Jasmine was sleeping peacefully, and at Maile's room. The girl sat up in bed when she entered. "Are they gone?" she asked eagerly, and then added anxiously, "They won't be coming back, will they?"

"I don't know," Lani admitted, deciding it was better not to lie to the girl. She pushed Maile gently back against the pillows, tucking the coverlet around her. "I'm sorry if you were frightened."

"I wasn't frightened—well, not much," Maile admitted sheepishly. She smiled happily up at Lani. "I love living here with you. It's so much more exciting than the convent!"

In the attic, it took Lani several minutes to shove aside the old bedroom dresser that Adam had pushed in front of the door to hide the cubicle. When she stepped inside the room and lit the lamp, she found Tom sitting up in bed. His face was thin and drawn beneath the sunburned skin, and deep scratches from the thorny thickets in which he and Kale had hidden up in the mountains crisscrossed his arms and chest, but he was fully alert and asked at once, "What's happened?"

Lani told him about the search party. When she finished, Tom frowned unhappily. "I'm sorry for all the *pilikia* I've caused you and Adam. Kale shouldn't have brought me here." Then, worried, "Where is Kale?"

"I don't know how he managed it," Lani marveled, pulling a rickety chair up to the bed. "It's like he became part of the night. One minute he was there, the next he was gone."

"I would have died if he hadn't stayed with me after I was shot," Tom said simply. "He found back trails in the mountains that even I didn't know." He studied Lani's face curiously. "He asked a lot of questions about you."

"Kale is my great-uncle," Lani said proudly. "And where else should he have brought you? We've all been half out of our minds with worry about you, not knowing if you were alive or dead."

She was startled when Tom asked abruptly, "Was Keith with the search party?"

"No, no, of course not." Lani's voice faltered, all at once remembering the man on horseback who had kept to the shadow of the trees and had not come into the house. There had been something familiar about the white-clad figure.

"I should never have trusted Keith," Tom said bitterly. "But we needed guns desperately, and he was clever about smuggling them in. I should have known he'd betray us the first chance he got. Ever since the night of the poker game when he got your uncle drunk, I suppose I've known that Keith was no good, but I didn't want to let myself believe it."

"What happened . . . at the poker game?"

"Your uncle lost heavily to Keith. Finally your uncle put into the pot his share of Palekaiko. I think that was what Keith was after all along. He would have won that pot, too, but Adam had sat in on the game, and Adam was always a better card player than Keith. Adam won the hand, and Palekaiko. Keith was furious. I thought he would kill Adam . . . then Adam made me leave. I don't know what happened after that, except I know that Adam went by your house the next morning, to sign the papers transferring the half interest in the ranch back to your uncle."

Tom tossed aside the sheet covering him. "It's warm in here," he said. "Could I have some water?"

It wasn't that warm in the room, Lani thought, pressing her hand, alarmed, against Tom's forehead. She was glad when Adam and Kimiko returned from the doctor. She didn't need to tell them that she was afraid that Tom had a fever. For the next week, either Adam, Lani, or Kimiko sat by Tom's bed, day and night, making sure that he swallowed fluids, keeping cold, wet cloths on his body, changing the perspiration-soaked bed linen. Kimiko would not have slept at all, if Lani hadn't bullied the exhausted girl into taking occasional naps.

By the end of the week, Tom was still weak, but the fever was gone, and he was strong enough to sit up in bed. Within another week, Lani and Kimiko exchanged relieved smiles when their patient irritably insisted upon having some "real food he could sink his teeth into" instead of the broth they had been feeding him.

Tom's returning strength, though, brought a new troubling problem. How long, Lani wondered, could they manage to keep Tom hidden? The weather was getting warmer; the little cubicle would soon be unbearably hot. And although she was sure the servants, who must have suspected that someone was hidden in the attic, were loyal to Adam and her, even an inadvertently dropped remark could bring a more diligent search party back to the house.

Tom's solution to the problem was simple. He would give himself up. "I should have turned myself in right away," he said, early one evening in February. "I haven't any right to be free when those who fought beside me are in prison."

Adam, coming into the room, stooping to get through the low door, overheard his brother. "Don't be a fool," he snapped. "A military court has already tried and condemned to death the *haoles* and *hapa haoles* involved in the insurrection. Do you think you'd get off any easier?"

Tom flinched, then asked, bewildered, "How could they be tried before a military court? There was no declaration of war."

"If they were brought before a civil court, the natives involved in the uprising would have had to be tried by a jury of their peers," Adam explained. "The government knows that a jury composed of natives would never convict any of them."

"And the queen?" Tom asked, staring in dismay at his brother. "Kale and I heard that she'd been arrested, too."

Adam and Lani had attended the queen's trial at the palace. The military court was held in what had once been the throne room, but, now stripped of its beautiful furnishings, was crowded and graceless. The officers of the court sat at a long table on one side of the room; to their right were the prisoners' dock and tables for journalists, and at the other end of the chamber sat the rows of spectators, all white men and women, who filled the room to capacity.

The ex-queen, escorted into the courtroom by guards, was dressed in black, carrying a lauhala fan decorated with violets and maidenhair fern. She walked with firm, deliberate steps, her carriage as haughty as ever, her strong face composed as she pled not guilty. The dark, expressive eyes looking out over the courtroom seemed to know that the trial was a mockery, the decision to convict her long since made, but she would not give her persecutors or the newspaper reporters who watched her avidly the chance to accuse her of behaving in an unqueenly manner.

Liliuokalani retained her composure throughout the trial, even when she listened to former friends and servants, in exchange for being promised reduced sentences, become witnesses against her, and when statements she made to clear herself were not allowed to be entered into the court record. Always, when she was allowed to speak, she spoke in Hawaiian, as if it were her people whose verdict she was seeking, not the military commission, most of whom did not understand the Hawaiian language.

Finally, Lani had been unable to bear it any longer. Her eyes burning with furious tears, she had left the courtroom. Now she looked helplessly at her husband across Tom's bed, unable to speak.

Adam said, his voice flat, "The military court sentenced Liliuokalani to five years at hard labor and a five-thousand-dollar fine." Before his brother could speak, he added quickly, "I'm sure President Dole will commute the hard labor to imprisonment. The goverment's been receiving a lot of pressure lately from the American and British ministers because of the harsh sentencing by the military court.'' He smiled wryly. "It seems that the American newspapers and Congress aren't looking so kindly any longer on the Hawaiian republic.''

"I still think I should give myself up,'' Tom said doggedly. "You can't keep me hidden here forever.''

"What we have to do is get you out of the country, until this hysteria passes,'' Adam said thoughtfully. "If only all ships leaving Honolulu weren't being closely watched. . . .''

He broke off as Kimiko slipped into the room. The girl's porcelain-smooth face had a frightened, shattered look.

"It's your brother, Mr. Stewart.'' Kim moved to stand protectively beside Tom's bed. "He's downstairs. He wants to see you at once.''

Adam turned to Lani. "Stay here with Kimiko and Tom,'' he ordered.

"No.'' Lani got calmly to her feet. "Kimiko can stay with Tom. I'm coming with you.''

Adam looked as if he were about to insist, then, taking a look at his wife's face, he changed his mind.

Keith was standing in the parlor in front of the open French doors that led out onto the side lanai and the garden. As usual, he was dressed nattily in white, carrying a hat with a white jasmine lei wrapped around its brim and sporting the familiar ivory-tipped malacca cane.

Although Lani's face held no warmth of greeting, Keith gave his hostess a dazzling white smile and crossed the room quickly to take her hand. "How good to see you again, Lani, and how beautiful you look, as always.'' Then, glancing toward his brother, he lifted a quizzical eyebrow. "I do hope I'm not interrupting anything . . . important.'' The charming smile was suddenly mocking. "Such as nursing my poor, wounded brother.''

The expression on Adam's face did not alter in the slightest, his eyes as unrevealing as shards of slate. "The house has already been searched several times,'' he said coldly.

"Oh, I know that,'' Keith said airily. "But I'm afraid not very thoroughly. And I gather Tom's little whore managed to throw the searchers off the scent very cleverly.''

"Kimiko is not a whore!" Lani said, furious.

"That's exactly what she is," Keith said, amused. "I didn't remember at first where I'd seen your maid before, but then I remembered Wo Tai's brothel in Chinatown. I'm afraid my young brother has rather deplorable taste in his women." He grinned lazily at Lani. "Present company excepted, of course."

Adam interrupted, his voice sharp. "I'm sure you didn't come here to discuss Tom's morals. Say what you have to say, Keith. I don't have much stomach for a man whose loyalty goes to the highest bidder."

"What a noble sentiment, brother," Keith sneered. "But then you can afford to be noble. While I, unfortunately—" He shrugged whimsically. "—I happen to need a great deal of money very quickly."

"You always need money," Adam said unsympathetically.

Keith sighed. "Let's not play games, Adam. I haven't the time or the patience. I happen to know that a royalist leader wanted by the government for treason is hidden in this house."

He smiled, almost smugly, at Lani, "I'm afraid I can also give evidence in court that your very lovely wife was deeply involved in the recent plot to overthrow the government." He shook his head with feigned sadness. "But as you observed, Adam, my loyalties are negotiable. For a price, I can be persuaded to withhold my information about my brother and your wife from the government police."

Despite her efforts not to show her feelings, Lani felt a shudder run through her as she gazed into Keith's guileless blue eyes. Guileless and completely pitiless, she realized. Then she felt Adam's hand grasp hers, the warmth from his hand traveling through her, warming an icy core of fear forming inside of her.

"Assuming we did agree to your blackmail," Adam asked, "what sum of money do you have in mind?"

"Fifty thousand dollars should get me out of my present difficulties and take care of my future needs."

"Just how am I supposed to raise that much money?" Adam asked dryly.

Keith shrugged impatiently. "I'm not a fool, Adam. Don't you think I know that for months now you've been quietly selling off Stewart and Sons properties on Oahu, the real estate in Chinatown, the sugar plantation. And what you can't raise immediately, I'm sure you can borrow from your business friends downtown." He added almost casually, "Oh, and I'll need the money by tomorrow evening. I've booked passage on the *Alameda* for California, and she's leaving Honolulu the next morning."

Adam's eyes narrowed as he gazed at his brother, his voice deceptively quiet. "And if I decide not to pay?"

"Oh, I suppose you could kill me, here and now," Keith said, laughing softly. "But I don't believe you could do it, Adam. I don't believe you could kill your own brother."

Lani felt Adam's hand crushing hers, so that she bit back a cry of pain. She saw her husband's face, the black, terrible anger there, and felt a stab of fear. Perhaps Keith didn't know his brother as well as he thought.

She stepped between the two men, her voice pleading. "Pay him the money, please, Adam. For my sake." She cast a disdainful glace toward her brother-in-law. "He's not worth killing."

Keith bowed sardonically. "Not very flattering, but well put. Oh, there's one other thing, brother. Until the money is delivered to me aboard the *Alameda* tomorrow night, your wife stays with me."

"Like hell she will!" Adam growled.

Keith's hand slid smoothly into his coat jacket. When he removed it again, a gun was pointed at Adam. There were beads of nervous perspiration on Keith's forehead, but the hand that held the gun, like the voice, was steady. "There's no need for histrionics, Adam. Your wife will be perfectly safe. As soon as the money is delivered to me, I'll tell you where she is and . . ."

Maile suddenly burst through the open French door from the garden, her face radiant. "Lani, you'll never guess . . ."

The girl fell silent abruptly when she saw Lani's face. Maile couldn't have seen the gun in Keith's hand, Lani thought quickly. Keith's back was to the French doors. She moved swiftly toward Maile. "Tell me later," she said, smiling and giving the girl a gentle shove toward the door. "Run along now, child. As you can see, we have company."

Maile cast a startled look at Adam Stewart's glowering face and retreated quickly from the room back onto the lanai.

After the girl had left, Lani went to her husband. "It's all right, darling," she said, "I'll go with him."

"No!"

Keith shrugged. "I would have thought your brother's life, your wife's staying out of prison, would have been more important to you, Adam, but, of course, if that's how you feel, all I have to do is call the guard that's posted outside this house."

He'd do it, Lani thought, chilled. He'd turn Tom over to the hangman without batting an eye. She could see by the frustrated look of fury in Adam's eyes that he knew it, too.

"If you so much as lay a hand upon my wife," Adam said softly, "I don't care where you hide. I'll find you and kill you."

Keith lifted an amused eyebrow. "What do you take me for, Adam? When has it ever been necessary for me to force myself upon a woman? Of course, if you don't feel you can trust your wife with another man, that's your problem, isn't it?" Slipping his cane over his arm, he reached out his hand and jerked Lani to his side. Then frowned, annoyed, at the simple cotton skirt and blouse she wore. "That's hardly suitable riding attire, but it will have to do. There's really no time for you to change your clothes."

He backed slowly toward the French doors, holding tightly to Lani, who perforce followed him. At the doors, he paused a moment. "I'll be waiting aboard the *Alameda* tomorrow night, Adam. Don't be late with the money, and don't try anything foolish, like trying to move Tom. The government police are still watching this house, you know."

Then Lani was being pulled into the darkness of the garden, stumbling after Keith to his horse. He swung her up onto the saddle and mounted behind her, the hand holding the pistol around her waist, the other picking up the reins.

At first, Lani tried to keep track of where they were going. It was a clear, moonlit night, but once they left the back streets of Honolulu and started following dark, winding roads that were little more than hard-packed dirt trails, she lost all sense of time and direction. Every now and then she could hear the soft murmur of waves rushing to shore, and she was sure they were never far from the ocean.

Keith never spoke, and neither did she. His mount was well trained, stumbling only once or twice on the rough road. She didn't know how long they rode; it seemed like hours, although when she did get a glimpse of the ocean, she realized that they had not traveled far beyond town. It could not have been much more than an hour later when Keith turned his horse through a grove of palm trees. The smell of the ocean, the sound of the murmuring waves was much stronger now, and as they came out of the trees into a clearing, she saw a small, dark house sitting at the edge of a cove, the moonlight reflecting against the phosphorescent-coated ocean, making the area almost bright as day.

When Keith dismounted and pulled her off for a moment, Lani's stiffened muscles couldn't move, much less walk, and she felt herself slumping helplessly against him.

Keith laughed lightly, pleased, his hand running caressingly down her spine. "There's no hurry, my sweet. We have the whole night before us."

And all at once, with a strength born of desperation, Lani knew she could not go through with it. She could not force herself to go into that dark house with Keith. She jerked away from him, running back toward the grove, with legs that were stumbling even when Keith easily caught her. She opened her mouth to scream. He clamped his hand tightly over her lips, and she could not breathe, much less scream. For a few seconds she fought against him, against the hand that was smothering her, so that her lungs felt as if they would explode before the moonlight disappeared, and she felt herself spinning away into darkness.

Chapter 30

When Lani came back to consciousness, she found herself in a small beach cottage. The *punee* on which she lay and the mat carpeting on the floor smelled of mildew, and the bamboo shade covering the window was limp and torn. Not that she could see that much of her surroundings. The moonlight barely filtered through the one small window, and although a candle stuck into an empty bottle burned fitfully near her, its feeble light scarcely reached more than a few feet.

She thought at first that she was alone in the cottage, but when she stirred and sat up, Keith came at once to her side. "Are you feeling better?" he asked solicitously, as he sat down beside her on the couch. "I'm sorry if I frightened you, but I couldn't let you scream. Someone might have heard you."

He actually did sound sorry, Lani thought, surprised. And felt a bubble of hysterical laughter rising in her throat.

He pressed a glass into her hand. "I'm afraid it's not very good whiskey, but it's all I could find. It'll make you feel better."

She was going to refuse and then decided she could use something to dispel the hysteria that was once again threatening to choke her. The liquor burned her throat but spread a steadying warmth through her body, so that she was able to look around her and ask, "Where are we?"

Keith got to his feet to refill his glass. "It's just a place I've kept—" He turned, the blue eyes sparkling mischievously. "For those times when I didn't want to be disturbed."

But if he thought her scream would arouse someone, then there must be people in other nearby beach cottages, she thought hopefully.

She cast a quick glance toward the door, and Keith frowned

petulantly. "If you're planning on doing anything else foolish, I can always bind and gag you." The blue eyes were no
longer bright and mischievous but like empty polished glass,
a child's eyes, a child who had never grown up, Lani thought,
shivering.

"I . . . I won't scream," she promised hastily.

"Good." His good humor returned as rapidly as it had
disappeared. He swallowed the contents of his glass quickly,
then refilled it, lifting it toward her, smiling charmingly.
"Here's to a woman who has both good sense and beauty."

Lani watched him nervously, wondering how much he'd
already had to drink.

As if guessing what she was thinking, he lifted an amused
eyebrow. "You don't have to worry." He walked toward the
punee, his glance roaming over the young woman on his
couch, her dark hair falling delightfully disheveled to her
shoulders, a sleeve ripped in her effort to fight him off so that
he could glimpse the soft, creamy flesh beneath. "No woman's ever complained of my lack of performance because of
too much liquor," he said smugly.

When he reached for her, pulling her up from the couch
into his arms, she said, sharply, "Don't!"

He laughed softly, his eyes warm on her face. "There's no
need for you to put up a pretense any longer, my sweet.
You're not some *haole wahine* with ice water in your veins.
Don't you think I know that you want me just as much as I
want you? A man can always tell," he boasted confidently,
his hands skillfully unbuttoning the neck of her blouse as he
stared down into violet eyes, enormous beneath gracefully
arched brows, watching the pink racing beneath the creamy
skin of her face down to the vulnerable-looking hollow of her
throat that he had exposed. "Do you know how often I've
wondered what it would be like, making love to you?" he
asked huskily.

Lani almost blurted, "But you already have," then thrust
back the words. This was not the moment for discussing his
lack of memory, she thought, panic making her heart race,
even as she forced herself to say calmly, "You promised
Adam you wouldn't touch me."

"I promised Adam I wouldn't force myself upon you," he

corrected her, still smiling as he slipped his hand within her blouse to cup her breast, and she jerked beneath his touch.

Feeling that hand move with practiced ease over her flesh, a scream welled again within Lani's throat. Her every instinct was to fight back, to struggle against him, but somehow she sensed that would be a mistake. Instead she forced herself to stand rigid, unresponsive, within his embrace. "I can't stop you from raping me," she said coldly. "That's what it will be. And Adam will kill you when he finds out what you've done."

Keith ran his tongue over suddenly dry lips. He gazed angrily at the girl, sensing the haughty disdain in her *haole* eyes, despite that provocatively ripe Polynesian body. Uneasily, he knew that she was right. Adam would make him pay for laying a hand on his wife. Still, the liquor he had drunk, the feel of that satin-soft flesh sliding beneath his hand, added to the sudden, pressing need he had for a woman. It could be worth the risk, he thought hungrily, and what a sweet revenge to cuckold his brother who had stolen his rightful inheritance from him.

His arms tightened convulsively around Lani, pulling her wooden-stiff body closer, when they both heard the sound of a horse's hooves behind the cottage.

"What the hell . . ." Keith thrust Lani away from him and went to the door. He saw the smile of relief on Lani's face and warned, as he picked up his revolver from a table by the door, "You'd better pray it's *not* your husband, my sweet."

He was gone for only a few short moments. When he returned, Lani felt her heart sink in her chest. Keith was alone and smiling broadly. Without a word, he shoved her into the small second room of the cottage and down upon a narrow bed. Before she could scream, he had tied his handkerchief around her mouth and bound her wrists with a twine so narrow it cut cruelly into her flesh.

There was no lamp or candle in the room, but moonlight fell through the slatted blinds of the one small window next to the bed so that she could see his face clearly, the self-satisfied look there.

Then the door closed behind him, and she was alone in the darkness. The door between the two rooms did not fit tightly, though, and she could easily hear the murmur of voices, the sound of intimate laughter, Keith's and a woman's. She could even hear the clink of glasses. She strained her ears to hear what the two people in the next room were saying, but she could not make out any of the words.

After a short time, to her surprise, the door to her room opened. A woman's figure appeared in the dimly lit doorway, a somehow vaguely familiar figure. The next moment the woman was at her side, leaning over her, quickly loosening the bonds at her wrist, the gag at Lani's mouth, whispering, "There's not much time. I told him I heard someone outside. He's gone to investigate."

"Rebecca! It is you!" In the moonlight, Lani's gaze searched happily the face that was still beautiful, dark hair hanging loosely over the shoulders of a *holoku* that covered Rebecca completely from its high neck to its long, loose sleeves. "Where did you come from? How did you know I was here?" she asked, bewildered.

Rebecca spoke swiftly, her voice low, her head cocked toward the next room. "The sisters at the convent told me where Maile had gone. I wanted to see my daughter. I was at your home this evening, on the lanai, when I overheard what was said in the parlor. I followed you and Keith when you left." As Lani started to rise, she ordered sharply, "No, stay where you are. I had to make sure he hadn't harmed you. Adam will be here soon."

"He mustn't!" Lani grabbed for Rebecca's hand, then realized, startled, the hand must be hurt. It felt oddly clawlike, "Keith will kill him."

A hand brushed her cheek gently. "Don't be frightened, child. It will be all over soon. Now I have to get back, before he returns."

"Wait! I don't understand. Why did you go? Where have you been?"

Rebecca paused a moment at the door, her voice filled with tenderness. "Thank you for looking after Maile. Don't ever let my daughter forget how much I love her."

Then Rebecca closed the door behind her, and she was busily pouring fresh drinks when Keith returned. "There was no one outside," he said, frowning suspiciously.

"I was sure I heard someone," Rebecca said apologetically, as she handed her companion his drink, then stepped back into the shadows crowding the room. She lifted her glass to Keith, her voice softly seductive. "Here's to old friends and lovers."

"Not that old," Keith said, taking a long swallow of his drink, then reaching for Rebecca. "Christ, how I've missed you,"' he mumbled thickly. Then his hand felt the roughness of the thick muslin *holoku* that enveloped Rebecca's body completely, the full sleeves even falling across her hands, and he grumbled, "Why don't you get out of that ridiculous Mother Hubbard?"

When his hand moved to unbutton the high neck of the gown, Rebecca laughed teasingly and stepped back. "Remember the night we made love in the ocean, how the water felt like velvet against our skin. . . ."

"Later," Keith said, still trying to fumble at the tiny buttons. "We'll swim later."

Rebecca pushed him away, still laughing. "But I want to swim now."

Keith made a grab for her, but she gracefully evaded him and was out the door, running toward the beach. She disappeared for a second in the shadow of a clump of kiawe trees leaning toward the water, and when she emerged again, the *holoku* was gone. He caught a brief glimpse of the silver outline of her nude body in the moonlight as she dashed into the water, turning for a moment to beckon to him before she plunged into the surf.

Keith discovered, surprised, that he was having a hard time getting out of his own clothes. His hands seemed all thumbs, his muscles felt oddly uncoordinated. He must have had more to drink than he realized, he thought. Perhaps a swim was what he needed after all, to sober him up. As he raced to the beach and dived into the water, he caught a glimpse of Rebecca, her arms cutting cleanly through the water ahead of him, her black hair seeming to be coated with the silver that floated on the ocean's surface.

He could feel his heart pounding wildly with excitement, like a boy with his first woman, he thought, amused. He could hardly wait to lick the salty water from those silvery

breasts, to feel that silken soft body slip between his legs.
Rebecca was treading water, laughing, waiting for him. She
stretched out her arms to him, pulling him into her embrace.
For the first time, Keith noticed, repelled, that her left hand
was curled like a claw. Then, even more repulsive, he saw
through the clear, pale green water, the ugly, red raised
splotches, like wounds, spread across the still high, proud
breasts. Scarlet lesions like cobwebs disfigured her upper
arms, even covering the soft belly and thighs.

"For God's sake!" The terrifying truth sent shudders of
fear and revulsion through Keith, and he struggled like a mad
man to loose himself from Rebecca's loving embrace. Strangely,
though, he did not seem to have the strength to pull away.
The soft arms held him easily, caressingly. And a new mind-
less terror possessed him; the frightening awareness of his
own terrible weakness, so that he had no strength in his limbs
to fight off that voluptuous, corrupted body. Rebecca held
him effortlessly and lovingly as a babe in her arms.

"My drink," he muttered, the muscles of his throat para-
lyzed, so that the words came out in a rasping whisper. "Damn
you . . . put . . . something . . . in my drink. . . ."

"Now we'll always be together," Rebecca said, smiling
radiantly, her mouth covering his, their bodies entwining,
sinking beneath the surface of the water as if in a lover's
embrace. "My love . . . my love . . ."

As soon as Lani was sure that Keith and Rebecca had gone
from the cottage, she left the tiny room and went to the front
door. She could see Keith swimming out into the ocean after
a laughing Rebecca, the woman turning, her arms outstretched,
pulling him into her embrace. Why hadn't she realized sooner?
she thought. It was Keith who was Rebecca's lover, Keith
who had given Maile the Stewart features. But at the moment
none of that mattered. Only getting away from the cottage
and stopping Adam. She half turned away then stopped, her
gaze returning, centering uncertainly, on the man and the
woman who had disappeared for several minutes beneath the
surface of the ocean. She knew Rebecca was a strong swimmer, but shouldn't she and Keith have come to the surface
again by now?

Then, all at once frightened, she was running toward the

beach, calling Rebecca's name, her gaze searching helplessly for sight of a bobbing head in that silver-spangled sea. Finally, she pulled off her shoes and dress and swam out to the spot where she had last seen Rebecca. She jackknifed time and time again past the crystal greenness, down into the inky-black water beneath, searching frantically and in vain. Her lungs felt as if they would burst, her body a dead weight, and finally the temptation to give up, to let herself sink into that velvetry blackness, was almost overpowering.

When she felt Adam's strong arm around her, pulling her inexorably toward shore, she had no more strength to resist. She would rest, she thought wearily, then try again. Once they reached the beach, though, Adam's arms held her tightly, refusing to let her go.

"Rebecca and Keith," she gasped. "They're out there. We've got to find them."

"It's too late. We can't help them."

Lani was shivering uncontrollably, her voice trembling. "Rebecca . . . I can't just leave her."

"Let her go, darling," Adam said gently. "There's nothing you can do for Rebecca." Then he had picked her up and was carrying her back to the beach cottage, wrapping her in a blanket and rubbing the harsh wool against her body until her skin felt scalded.

"How did you know where to find me?" Lani asked, trying to make her teeth stop shaking.

"As soon as Rebecca realized where Keith was taking you, she stopped a passerby and paid him to bring word back to me."

"I don't understand," Lani said, bewildered. "Keith and Rebecca were strong swimmers. How could it happen? How could they both drown?"

Adam had wondered about that, too. He glanced thoughtfully at the two half-empty glasses of whiskey on the table, smelled one of them, then took both glasses and the bottle to the door and disposed of them. When he returned to Lani's side, he noticed anxiously his wife's shocked, amethyst eyes, the bluish-white pallor to her face.

"Get some rest," he said, lying down on the *punee* beside

her and gathering her into his arms. "We'll start for home as soon as it's light."

Lani awoke as the first rays of the sun fell through the broken bamboo shade. She was alone on the couch, and for a moment, remembering her frantic, futile search for Rebecca in that black water, sorrow gripped her like a cramp, and she had to clench her teeth to keep from crying aloud with the pain. As quiet as she was, Adam came at once back into the cottage. He pulled her to her feet, cradling her in his arms, while the tears fell stormily down her face. Finally, when the sobs had subsided, he held her a little away from him, asking, "Do you feel up to the ride back to town?"

She nodded, ashamed of her own selfishness, remembering that her husband, no matter how deep the differences between Keith and him, had lost a brother, as she had lost a friend. "I'm sorry, darling," she said softly.

For a moment, pain touched the bleak, gray eyes, then Adam smiled tightly and said, "I think Keith would have hated growing old."

Then he helped her dress in her clothes he had picked up off the beach, and she noticed, surprised, as they rode back to town, that Adam was carrying Keith's clothes draped across the saddle, with him the white hat and malacca cane stuck into the saddle bag. She couldn't imagine Adam's wearing or wanting Keith's clothing, and she gave her husband a puzzled glance. "What are you doing with those?"

"You'll find out," Adam said cryptically.

It wasn't until early that evening, though, when she walked into the front parlor after dinner, that she discovered what Adam had in mind. The man standing with his back to her at the French window, in the crisp white jacket and trousers, wearing a white hat with a jasmine garland around the brim and carrying a distinctive malacca cane, made her heart leap to her throat. She told herself it couldn't be Keith, and yet. . .

Tom turned, grinning. "How do I look?" Then his grin faded. "I feel strange, wearing Keith's clothes." He glanced uncertainly at Adam, who had come into the room behind Lani. "Do you actually think I'll fool anyone?"

Adam studied his brother, then nodded. "Why not? You have the family resemblance, and the clothes are the ones that

Keith always wore. And you have Keith's steamship ticket that I found in the pocket of his jacket. If you board the *Alameda* late tonight, and stay in your cabin tomorrow morning when the ship sails, who will know that you're not Keith?''

"But how will you get him out of the grounds?" Lani asked. "I'm sure the house is still being watched."

"They're watching for Tom to try and slip into the house," Adam said. "Keith was working for the government. They'd have no reason to stop him." He gave his brother a warning glance. "I admit it's a gamble. And you'll have to board the ship alone. It would look suspicious if Lani or I went with you.''

"Not alone," Tom said. He glanced toward Kimiko, who was standing quietly in a corner of the room. "I'm not going anywhere unless Kim goes with me." He grinned at Adam. "With Keith's reputation, no one will think twice if he has a woman traveling with him."

He went to stand before the Japanese girl. "Will you go with me, Kim?" he asked, and then said firmly, "I won't go without you." When the girl didn't answer immediately, her glance cast downward, Tom shrugged with boyish bravado. "Well, then I'll just have to turn myself over to the authorities."

"No, you must not!" Kimiko's frightened gaze flew upward and fastened helplessly on Tom's resolute face. What she saw there made her own dark eyes grow softly luminous. She bowed low, murmuring meekly, "I will go with you, *Donna-san.*"

Lani helped Kim pack her few possessions, giving her former maid one last hug after Kimiko had said a tearful good-bye to Maile and Jasmine. Then the Japanese girl sat proudly beside Tom in the carriage that drove them to the wharf where the *Alameda* was docked. Boarding the ship, Kimiko's arm unobtrusively supported her companion when he stumbled in the passageway, his face all at once pale. The cabin steward came hurrying toward them.

"Are you all right, Mr. Stewart?" he asked, gazing curiously at Kimiko.

The Japanese girl giggled, smiling flirtatiously at the steward. "Too much to drink. I take care."

The steward glanced at his well-known passenger. Not that he had ever met Keith Stewart personally, but everyone in Honolulu knew Mr. Stewart's distinctive dress, the white jasmine garland he invariably wore around his hat, the malacca cane he always carried. "I believe you only booked passage for one, Mr. Stewart," he said nervously.

Tom thrust his hand into his jacket pocket and pushed money into the steward's hand. "Passage for two," he said thickly, jerking his chin toward the young woman beside him. "She'll share my cabin." Then glaring arrogantly at the man as he imagined Keith would have done, he said sharply, "It takes a week to get to San Francisco. Damn it, you don't expect a man to do without a woman for a whole week, now do you?" He grinned lewdly at Kimiko, then winked broadly at the steward. "And don't bother waking us in the morning when the ship sails. We'll be occupied. You understand?"

"Yes sir," the steward said, smiling enviously as the door to the Stewart cabin closed.

Once inside the cabin, Kimiko quickly helped Tom to the bed, carefully removing his jacket and shirt. She gave a gasp of dismay when she saw that the wound was bleeding again. Deftly she stopped the bleeding, replaced the bandage, and made her patient swallow some of the laudanum the doctor had given her for her own wounded hand. Tom's eyes were closed when she finished. Thinking the laudanum had already begun to take effect, she began to move quietly away when Tom's good arm reached out and pulled her down on the bed beside him.

His eyes were blurred from pain and the laudanum, but his voice was clear. "As soon as we're outside of Hawaii's territorial waters, I'll have the captain marry us."

If they got out of Honolulu harbor, Kimiko thought, the sharp teeth of fear gnawing at her. Suppose the government police should search the ship in the morning, and discover it wasn't Keith Stewart in his cabin. Or suppose the body of Tom's brother had washed up on the beach, had already been discovered and a hue and cry raised. . . . Kimiko kept her fears to herself and, curling closer within the shelter of her lover's arm, tried to sleep.

The blast of the ship's whistle awoke Kimiko the next

morning. She slipped quietly from the bed and went to look out the porthole. The ship was already pulling free of the dock. From the cabin she could see the wharf, the crowds of people waving and calling their good-byes to passengers aboard the ship, who crowded around the rail. The band on the wharf played loudly as the ship slowly pulled further out to sea, and the leis cast into the ocean by the passengers drifted toward shore.

Tom joined her, his arm tightening around her waist as he gazed at the island he loved slipping slowly away from him. "We're coming back, you know," he said. "They may think they've won, but the battle's not over. . . ."

"Yes," Kimiko said.

He turned her to face him, cocking a stern brow down at her. "And what I said last night about the captain marrying us, I meant every word of it."

Kimiko felt as if she were suffocating. She avoided his gaze, murmuring unhappily, "I cannot be your wife. I am not worthy. . . ."

Tom touched gently the small hand that was still encased in a bandage, the hand that she had mutilated to save him. Then, almost angrily, he pulled her into his arms. "Shut up," he whispered huskily, just before his mouth covered hers. "Just shut up, and let's go back to bed."

Adam waited until he was sure the *Alameda* had sailed with Tom and Kimiko safely aboard before he turned his horse away from the wharf area and rode *mauka*. He was thankful that his young brother was safely away from the islands, but there was a nagging fear that he could not explain beneath the relief he felt. It was the same inexplicable uneasiness that he remembered from his whaling days when a sixth sense had always alerted him to trouble somewhere aboard his ship.

As he rode past what had once been Iolani Palace, he watched absently the government officials with papers in their hands, scurrying efficiently back and forth across the palace plaza, renamed by the government Union Square. The white men who had brought the republic into existence were firmly, competently in control. The leisurely, easygoing days when the Hawaiians had run their government, and there was always time for conversation with a friend, for putting off official duties until tomorrow, were no more.

On the second floor of the left wing of the building, Adam could glimpse the shuttered windows where the ex-queen was imprisoned. Although her quarters were undoubtedly more spacious than a jail cell, Adam couldn't help reflecting on the unconscious cruelty of her jailers, holding Liliuokalani prisoner in her own palace. The government did not encourage stories about the ex-queen's imprisonment, but Adam knew she was allowed no visitors or news of the outside world. She was allowed occasionally to walk under guard on the balcony, and provided with paper and pencil, with which, he had heard, she spent her days composing music.

Adam uncomfortably turned his gaze away from those shuttered windows. For a moment he could imagine only too vividly the living death it must be for a woman like Liliuokalani who, like all Hawaiians, had a special affinity for nature, for the beauty of their island surroundings, to be imprisoned within the drab four walls of a room, no matter how spacious.

Scowling, he forced such unpleasant thoughts from his mind, as the vague, jabbing fear suddenly returned. Adam urged his horse foreward. He wanted to get home to Lani.

Chapter 31

When Lani heard Adam's footsteps in the front hall, she did not immediately rush out of her uncle's study to greet him. Instead she sat quietly on the small, slipper-satin couch by the window, trying to compose her thoughts, desperately reaching inside of herself for a courage she wasn't even sure she possessed. For how did one find the courage to accept the unacceptable?

"Why are you sitting in the dark?" Adam asked, coming

quickly into the room and going to the window, started to pull open the curtains.

"No, don't!" An edge of panic caught Lani's voice. Somehow, it seemed easier to confront Adam when she couldn't' see his face clearly.

When he crossed the room to her side, he saw at once the unnatural stiffness with which Lani held herself, as if she were bracing herself against him.

"What is it?" The nagging fear, like a knife's edge now, dug into him. "It's all right. I've just left the wharf. The *Alameda* sailed with Tom and Kimiko safely aboard."

His wife nodded, and he saw that her hands were clasped tightly in her lap. When she spoke, her voice was low. "I spoke to Maile this morning, after you left." Her gaze was fastened onto her clasped hands. "I . . . I thought she should know that her mother had drowned, that Rebecca wouldn't be coming back."

"That must have been very difficult for both of you," Adam said quietly.

"Yes. Afterward Maile told me that she had spoken to her mother in the garden two nights ago. She said her mother had told her that she wouldn't be returning. Maile said something else. She said that Rebecca looked ill." Lani's hands twisted tortuously together, her voice so soft Adam had to strain to hear her. "And then I remembered that Rebecca had looked, somehow, different . . . to me, too, those moments we spent together in the beach house. Her face was so much paler, and the fingers of her left hand were shriveled. And when she loosened the gag around my mouth, her sleeve fell away for a moment, and I saw the soft underside of her arm. There were thick, ringed patches of red and white on her skin, like the scars of burns."

A shudder passed through Lani. She lifted her face slowly to her husband, her eyes enormous and filled with horror. "Rebecca had leprosy, didn't she? That's why she left Palekaiko so suddenly, wasn't it?" She saw the wariness that narrowed Adam's eyes, turned his face to stone. Before he could speak, she shook her head, her voice despairing. "No! Don't lie to me. Not anymore."

Adam knelt down before the couch, cupping his wife's face

gently in his hands, as if he were trying to draw the splintering pain and shock he saw there into himself.

"No more lies," he promised finally, reluctantly. "Yes,
Rebecca did have leprosy. The night of the queen's luau
when her sleeve caught on fire and burned her arm, she didn't
feel the pain. She knew then. The lack of feeling, the destruction of nerve endings, is how the disease works on the body.
Oh, there'd been other symptoms, but she had ignored them.
Now she couldn't any longer. When I took her to her cottage,
she told me what she suspected. I wanted to take her to a
doctor, but she refused. She knew that he'd have to send her
away to Kalaupapa with the other lepers banished there to
die. She preferred to join the small bands of lepers hiding
out up in the hills of Maui. I gave her all the money I had,
and she made me promise not to tell you or her daughter that
she had the disease."

Adam rose wearily to his feet. "Perhaps I was wrong to
promise, but what else could I do? And it seemed best that
you shouldn't know. . . ."

"That I might have contracted the disease from Rebecca?
After all, we did live together for several years." Lani gazed
down at her body, shivering. "How long will it be, do you
suppose, before I wake up some morning and find that I have
no feeling in my hand or arm, before those red-and-white
splotches, like mildew, cover my body, too?" Her voice was
suddenly no longer flat and toneless, but shrill with a panic
that verged on hysteria. "My God! What of Jasmine and you?
What if I've passed the leprosy along to you?"

Adam jerked his wife to her feet. "No!" he said savagely.
When she could only stare at him, her body trembling beneath the loose cotton *holoku* she wore, her eyes wide and
dilated, her face blank with unimaginable horror, he shook
her roughly until she collapsed like a rag doll in his arms, and
he lowered her to the couch. He took off his jacket and flung
it around her, then sat down on the edge of the couch beside
her. Taking her ice-cold hands in his, he chafed them with his
own, until the gray pallor disappeared from her face and she
was breathing normally again.

He began to speak slowly, carefully. "Listen to me, darling. It's been four years since you were with Rebecca. If you

were going to contract the disease, you would have shown symptoms by now. And despite everything you've heard, leprosy is not that contagious. Many people have a natural immunity and never catch the disease, even after years of living in close personal contact with a leper. And your relationship with Rebecca was never that intimate. You had separate living quarters; you ate together only occasionally.''

"How . . . how do you know so much about . . . leprosy?"

"Remember that trip I took to Louisiana, shortly after Rebecca left and we returned to Honolulu? Well, it wasn't a business trip. Several doctors in Louisiana and California have begun extensive research into the disease. They haven't found any cure, unfortunately, but one doctor I talked to suspects that there are two types of leprosy. One type is tuberculoid and isn't contagious at all. From what you've told me about the way Rebecca's lesions looked, how the muscles of her hand were affected, I'm almost certain that's the type she had. The other type of leprosy . . .'' Adam shrugged grimly. "After four years, Rebecca would have been so disfigured she could never have shown her face in public, or she would have been recognized immediately as a leper.''

Lani winced, but for the first time she felt as if blood instead of ice water was flowing through her veins. She clutched at Adam's hand. "Suppose Rebecca's body washes ashore, and Maile learns . . .''

Adam shook his head. "There's a strong tide at that cove and no reef. It could be days before they find any bodies, if ever. And by then . . .'' He pulled Lani gently against him, so that her sobs were muffled against his shoulder and her tears stained his shirt front.

"Maile must never know about her mother,'' she said, finally lifting her head. She smiled mistily through her tears at her husband. "Or that you're not her father.''

"I never told her I was,'' Adam said ruefully. "I suppose I just let her think what she wanted, because the child was so alone and needed someone so desperately. And I did give my word to Rebecca that I'd look after Maile.''

"We'll both look after her from now on,'' Lani said firmly. "This is Maile's home for as long as she wants to stay with us.''

Adam cleared his throat, looking a little uncomfortable. "Well, as a matter of fact, that's something I wanted to talk to you about, Paakiki. How would you feel if I sold this house?"

"Where will we live?" she asked, startled.

"Well, there's always the ranch," he said, grinning. "How would you feel about our becoming full-time ranchers and living at Palekaiko?"

"Do you mean it?" Lani asked, happiness flooding her face, and then, moving a few inches away from her husband, she gazed suspiciously at him. "Are you doing this to please me? What about your business interests here in town? What about Stewart and Sons?"

Adam shrugged. "As a matter of fact, I've already sold off most of the assets of Stewart and Sons. Tom was always more interested in politics than business, and he was happy to give me his proxy to sell his shares."

He pulled his wife back into his arms so that she was resting comfortably on his lap. "And I'm not moving to Maui just to please you," he assured her, dropping a kiss on her head. "The truth is, those months I spent at Palekaiko I discovered that I enjoy a rancher's life much more than I enjoy sitting behind a desk. At the ranch I had time to spend with you and Jasmine. At Stewart and Sons, my every waking moment is occupied with holding on to the money I have or scheming how to make more."

But that wasn't the whole story, Adam knew. His decision to leave Honolulu also had something to do with the way he had felt driving back from the wharf that morning, past the shuttered windows of what had once been Iolani Palace. Oh, he hadn't changed his mind that the destruction of the Hawaiian monarchy had been inevitable, like a tidal wave that no one could stop. And the white men who controlled the new, efficiently run government were not tyrants. The missionary influence was still too strong in the islands for that. The men in power would take a paternal pride in behaving benevolently toward the native Hawaiians, while, of course, keeping them in their place. Their wives would work hard at their charities to uplift the moral lives of the natives, while their husbands gathered the wealth of the Hawaiian Islands into the hands of fewer and fewer *haole* families.

Only Adam didn't want to stay around and watch it happen.

As she relaxed in her husband's arms, Lani found herself thinking what a dreadful strain it must have been on Adam, all those years he had kept Rebecca's secret. She wondered if her husband hadn't, perhaps, felt guilty, because he was the one who had hired Rebecca, installed her at the ranch, and placed his ward in jeopardy.

Suddenly she understood something that had always puzzled her. "All those doctors you were always sending me to, that was why, wasn't it, because of Rebecca?"

Adam nodded. "And Abigail Palmer had nurse's training," he admitted. "Not that she knew anything about Rebecca, but I wanted someone to keep a close eye on you." He grinned in mock chagrin. "Since I couldn't talk you into marrying me when we got back to Honolulu so that I could look after you myself."

"Is that why you asked me to marry you?" Lani asked, her violet eyes intently searching her husband's face. "Because you felt guilty, because you felt sorry for me?"

Adam remembered he had promised there would be no more lies between them, and he took his time answering. "Perhaps, partly, the first time I asked you," he admitted, remembering the fear that had consumed him, not knowing, at first, whether or not his ward might have contracted the disease from Rebecca, only knowing that whatever happened he was determined to protect and cherish her. She was his responsibility, and if the worst happened, he would make sure that she never ended up on Molokai with the other pitiful walking dead.

"And the second time?"

Adam smiled down into his wife's face, his hand absently smoothing back a wayward lock of hair. Lani's loosely fitted morning *holoku* had fallen off of one shoulder, and he caught a glimpse of the dark shadow between her deep breasts, the gleaming softness distracting him for a second before he said teasingly, "The second time had nothing to do with pity or guilt. It was a business proposition, remember?"

Lani laughed softly. "I don't believe you were thinking of

business at all, the second time you proposed . . . in the guest cottage.'' She smiled demurely up at her husband. "Or do you usually conduct business matters while you're making love?''

Adam straightened so abruptly that his wife almost fell off his lap. "How long have you known it was me, and not Keith, that night?'' he demanded, outraged.

"But, darling, I knew all along,'' Lani said, her eyes wide and innocent. And she thought smugly: Lies between a husband and wife were a mistake, but in this case, considering the provocation, she was sure she could be forgiven a small one!

Adam's eyes narrowed as he searched his wife's face uncertainly, but then Lani snuggled closer to him and somehow the *holoku* fell off her other shoulder, exposing a great deal more of the petal-soft skin, the seductive swell of breasts. For several moments Adam forgot everything else, as his hand slid caressingly over that creamy softness, and his mouth felt the eager warmth of Lani's lips parting beneath his. The sharp thrust of desire they both shared was frustrated by the smallness of the half-moon shaped slippery couch. They tumbled to the deep, lime-green rug, arms and legs still entwined, until, all at once remembering, Lani pulled free and sat up, pulling her *holoku* back over her shoulders, her voice breathless. "We can't darling. Not here. Maile will be returning any minute from taking Jasmine for a walk.''

Adam groaned as he pulled Lani to her feet. She reached up on tiptoe to brush his mouth with a kiss, as she whispered, "Of course, we do have several perfectly good beds upstairs going to waste.''

Their arms around each other's waists, they started up the stairs, Lani, stopping a moment to gaze up at the portrait of her grandparents. The portrait would, of course, go with her to the ranch, she thought, remembering the times she had felt her Grandmother Jasmine's comforting presence here on this staircase. She knew now that probably she would never know the true story of what had happened in her grandparents' marriage, but somehow it was no longer important. All that mattered was that she knew without a doubt Jasmine and

Morgan had loved each other deeply, and in the end they were together, just as she and Adam would always be.

Grandmother and granddaughter seemed to exchange knowing, loving smiles. "I think my grandparents are going to enjoy living at Palekaiko," Lani said happily, just before Adam impatiently picked his wife up in his arms and carried her the rest of the way to his bed.

Epilogue – August 2, 1898

The Honolulu waterfront was crowded this bright moonlit night. Hundreds of Hawaiians had begun gathering in small groups hours earlier when the word had spread through the native communities that Liliuokalani was returning from America this evening aboard the *Gaelic*.

Lani and Adam, holding a wiggling Jasmine in his arms, stood waiting among the strangely quiet crowd, as the ship eased into its berth. After an absence of more than three years, Tom and Kimiko were also returning aboard the *Gaelic*.

Lani, looking very fashionable for a rancher's wife in a mauve bolero jacket and skirt that fit as tightly as wax around her hips then flared to her trim ankles, tucked her arm into her husband's and asked anxiously, "You're sure it's all right, Tom's coming back? He won't be arrested?"

"The government's much too excited about Congress finally approving the annexation of Hawaii to be concerned about an ex-revolutionary returning to the islands," he assured his wife.

The news that President McKinley had signed the bill annexing the Hawaiian Islands had arrived in Honolulu two weeks before. For years, Hawaii's request for annexation had languished in Congress, unable to command the necessary two-thirds vote. Then in April, America had declared war on Spain, and the next month Admiral Dewey defeated the Spanish fleet off the Philippines. "Missionary luck," Lorrin Thurston had said gleefully. For suddenly Congress had realized the strategic importance of the Hawaiian Islands to the United States, as a refueling station and restaging area for its navy in the Pacific.

Glancing around the crowd on the wharf, Adam could see an occasional American sailor, watching curiously the arrival of the *Gaelic*. The navy had been pouring its men into Hawaii for several months now, and their blue uniforms could be seen all over Honolulu. No doubt a foretaste of what was to come, Adam thought. There was already talk of permanent U.S. Army and Navy installations being built in Hawaii, turning the islands into a military outpost for the United States. Thank God, at least, there was no mention of military posts on Maui, he thought, as he gently unfastened his daughter's hand from his ear.

"You don't suppose we could have left Jasmine back at the house?" he asked wryly, swinging the girl down to the ground, then snatching her hand to keep her from racing happily off into the crowd. The family who had bought the Tucker home was off visiting relatives on Kauai and had lent the Stewarts their old home for their visit to Honolulu.

"Of course not," Lani said indignantly. "Jasmine's never seen Queen Liliuokalani."

Adam glanced, amused, at his wife. To Lani, Liliuokalani would always be queen. He had hoped that his wife's opinion of the republic government would soften when President Dole had commuted the death sentences of those *haoles* convicted of treason to hard labor. At last, when convinced that all resistance had been crushed, the government had pardoned all the royalist involved in the uprising, including the ex-queen herself. But to Lani, and many stalwart royalists like her, the men who had engineered the overthrow of the Hawaiian monarchy would always be traitors.

There was a stir among the quiet crowd of people as Prince David, Liliuokalani's nephew, escorted the ex-queen, walking as proudly and gracefully as ever, despite her years, down the gangplank. After she had received her pardon, Liliuokalani had gone to Washington and for months had done all in her power to defeat annexation—and failed. Now she paused a moment to look at the sorrow and devotion in the upturned faces of the Hawaiians who had come to greet their beloved *alii*, even in defeat.

"Aloha," she said, smiling, her rich, musical voice breaking the stillness around her.

As if from one throat, hundreds of voices answered, "Aloha!" And the crowd surged forward as if to carry her to the carriage where the Princess Kaiulani was waiting.

Adam had a wide-eyed Jasmine clutched in one arm while the other circled Lani protectively. They stood to one side, waiting for Tom and Kimiko to debark, as the crowd followed the queen's carriage away from the wharf, *mauka* toward Washington Place.

When Tom and Kimiko hurried down the gang plank, Lani noticed, smiling to herself, that Kimiko did not trail several feet behind her husband like the traditional Japanese wife, but walked beside him, although her eyes still rested adoringly on her husband. And Kimiko's voice was as respectful as always when she bowed and greeted Adam and Lani, only her dark eyes shone with love as she eagerly took Jasmine into her arms.

"A reception is being given this evening at Washington Place for the queen," Tom said after he had enthusiastically hugged Lani, slapped his brother on the back, and planted a kiss on his niece's sleepy face. "I spoke with Liliuokalani aboard the ship, and she said she would like us to be there."

This time, though, Adam insisted that their daughter should remain at home, and Kimiko just as quietly and firmly insisted, over her husband's protests, that she would remain behind with Jasmine.

Since it was such a pleasant evening, the three walked to Washington Place, a Stewart brother on either side of Lani, as Adam asked his brother, "What do you plan to do, now that you have your law degree?"

"Set up practice in Honolulu," Tom said promptly, and then, grinning widely, "and I might just dabble in politics."

Adam sighed. "I was afraid of that." But Lani could hear the affectionate pride in her husband's voice.

Tom's sherry-colored eyes burned with zealous fervor. "The next step after annexation is for Hawaii to become a territory of the United Sates. That way all Hawaiians will have full rights as citizens of the United States. Then, no matter how the *haoles* try, there's no way the government can legally stop all Hawaiians from voting." He frowned. "Of course, it will be more difficult getting the vote for the Orientals, but when we get our own Home Rule party going . . ."

"Don't forget the women," Lani interrupted firmly. "Remember, they're not allowed to vote either."

Adam groaned. "Oh, no! Now I have two politicians in the family."

Then they were at Washington Place, decorated with garlands of maile and ferns, pungent kukui torches lighting the pathways in the garden. They joined the long receiving line that ran through the garden and up to the house—Hawaiians, *haoles*, and Orientals, all waiting to pay their respects to Liliuokalani, who stood in the doorway. Some of the older Hawaiians, who had been the queen's retainers for many years, paid traditional homage by dropping to their knees and inching their way to the feet of their *moi wahine* to kiss her hand.

When it was Lani's turn, she dropped a graceful curtsy. Liliuokalani smiled and held out her hand to her. Lani had written the queen of Rebecca's death, without going into details, except to mention that Rebecca's daughter was living with Adam and her.

"How is Maile?" the queen asked now.

"She's away at college in California, doing very well."

"Rebecca would be pleased," the queen said, nodding, and then added wistfully, "When I was queen, I'd always hoped to establish a college here in Honolulu that all would be able to attend, the poor and the rich." Then she shook her head and said briskly, "It's no good, dwelling on the past." She smiled at Lani, her black eyes that in the past had so often been filled with rage, now serene. "There's an old Hawaiian chant by Kupakee that says it well.

" 'There is no going back, ways now are different. Look forward with love for the season ahead of us! Let pass the season that is gone. . . .' "

Liliuokalani's words echoed in Lani's mind as she and Adam walked back through the garden. The bitterness and hatred she had felt for so long toward those who had betrayed the queen began to drain slowly away. Near her, she could hear muscians playing "Aloha Oe," the poignant love song the queen had finished writing while she was in prison. But there was nothing sad about the happy, laughing guests crowding the garden this evening. Elderly men and women were dancing the hula with the same skill and grace they had when they were young. The fragrance of roses and jasmine filled the night air.

No matter who ran the government, Lani thought, gazing happily around her at the Hawaiian people enjoying, celebrating life as they had for centuries, this would never change.

"Shall we wait for Tom?" Adam asked, gesturing toward his brother who was arguing politics with his friends in a corner of the garden.

Lani shook her head and reached for her husband's hand. Look forward with love, she thought. She smiled up at her husband, and murmured softly, "No, darling, let's go home."

About the Author

Although Marcella Thum is the author of several award-winning nonfiction and juvenile books, she finds particular delight in writing historical romances. She is able to combine her love of historical research and the weaving of suspenseful plots around beautiful, courageous heroines and dashing, handsome heroes.

The author has visited and lived in many fascinating parts of the world, including Hawaii, the setting of her most recent novel, MISTRESS OF PARADISE. Her other books for Fawcett Gold Medal include *Margarite*, *Blazing Star*, *Jasmine*, and *Wild Laurel*.

A touch of romance... from Cordia Byers